Will NoSky

Fragile Delivery

Jennifer must now not only escape detention in order to prove her innocence, but also navigate the relentless pursuit of deranged sociopaths wielding a new weapon that no one has ever seen before.

Unfortunately for the bad guys, Jennifer and her wedding party refuse to back down. Good thing, because the maniacs behind it all intend to take over the entire space station!

If Jennifer stops the killers and proves her innocence, maybe she'll also find a way to get married…

ONE

"Are you going to keep fiddling with that or are you gonna bring me up?" The anxious man asked perched on an outcrop of rock 15 feet below her.

"I've got you on belay. You're not going anywhere."

The tall woman reached around her waist pushing at her bum bag. Once it was swiveled further around in back, it was out of the way of the air traffic controller belay device attached to her harness. Her left guide hand never lost contact with the guide and brake ropes. Of course, she could have just thumbed the auto brake switch on the ATC enabling the small servo, but it was more challenging without it.

"Anytime now dear…" Even though he was not a big man, and had strong forearms, he was starting to tire from the climb. She was much taller than him, so the hand and foot holds she had used didn't necessarily match his on the ascent.

She anchored both feet leaning back to continue bringing him up.

"On belay."

"Climbing," he said.

"Climb."

With both hands on the rope, she used her left guide hand to pull the live rope towards the air traffic controller belay device as her brake hand pulled the brake end out and away from the ATC. He was moving cautious and slow as they had agreed before they started. He was disciplined and she liked that. Actually, she loved that about him. He was a soldier by trade. He still had the short high-and-tight cut of black hair which, when he looked up to reach for another hand hold, was now glistening with sweat. A few drops of sweat started dripping off her nose but it felt really good to her. The sweat made her concentrate all the more on exerting herself dirt-side after being in space for so long. Yeah, doing it manually without the auto servos built into the ATC was much more invigorating.

"Slack," he instructed.

"Thank you," she acknowledged.

With both her hands firmly on the rope, her left guide hand shuffled the rope away from the ATC. He moved sideways when he felt the tension give so he could reach for a better hold off to his right. Once she saw him grab his hold, she locked off the rope with her right brake hand bending the rope across the ATC. It collapsed the ATC onto the locking carabiner and cinched the rope.

"Climbing."

"Climb."

She continued belaying him the last 10 feet until he twisted at the waist and sat down on the wide peak at her feet.

"Belay off," he requested.

"Belay off."

She relaxed her grips on both ends of the rope and shook her hands, balling her fingers into a fist, then extending them to get the tension out.

Jennifer Bane sat down beside Krachalavito Bantor letting her long white legs dangle over the edge. He didn't look over at her; instead he was fixated on the majestic view in front of him. He too spent the vast majority of his life in space, mainly as the Director of Biltmire Space Station, leaving his previous soldier profession behind two years ago.

"First time I came up here with a girl."

She pulled her gaze off the Shavertooth Mountain Range vista turning to face him.

"I'm happy to be the first." She nudged him with her shoulder smiling before her look turned threatening. "Better be the last, too."

Krachy knew she was kidding.

"Come on, I've brought you to my home planet to meet my parents. You think I make a habit of that?"

"Habit of what?"

"Bringing women home to *meet the family.*"

She leaned back unclipping the water bottle from her harness squeezing several gulps into her dry mouth, then handed it to him.

"I don't think they like me all that much."

He finished taking a few swigs. "I'm sorry about that. They're cautious and traditional. They've lived way out here their entire lives. Never been into space. Really don't go many places. I'm not blaming them for that. I think it goes back to when I left to join the Markem Space Orbital Forces when I was young. I didn't even consider joining Beltina's armed services when tensions started to grow between the Beltans and Markems. They live here on Basley which somehow stayed neutral once war broke out between those two. I'm sure they wanted me to stay neutral too. They never talk about it, but I know it's a sense of disappointment for them to have a son that has such a violent nature as they must think I do. Now they see me bring back a girlfriend that used to be a Privateer Space Captain that's spent the vast majority of her adult life in space, and well…" He trailed off studying her face as he came to the decision.

"Well, they know I'm in love with you, and Jennifer, I want you to be my wife."

Leaning over at the waist, Jennifer swung her arms around his neck thrilled to let the flood of emotions she had started learning to release out. Krachy was over seven inches shorter than her 6-foot, thin frame. His crooked smile lit up his face, both arms coming up to embrace her right arm around his neck that was starting to cut the circulation off to his brain. He figured her reaction meant yes because they stayed that way for what seemed like five minutes. He tried to tap out her neck grapple so she'd loosen her grip, but she wouldn't let go. She had no idea he would ask that of her. For that matter, he had not planned it either. The question to marry him just seemed inevitable when he looked into her soft green eyes—today was the day.

The hot sunshine of Basley's class B yellow primary continued to beat down on them causing them to sweat even more with the close body contact. They both had on shorts and a T-shirt, so sun burn would become a real issue if they didn't descend soon. They had started early and it was just past 9 in the morning on Basley's 20-hour day.

They untangled themselves trading smiles but not saying anything. They looked out over the Shavertooth Range which encompassed an area of some 650 square miles. There were over 50 peaks with an elevation over 10,000 feet, all falling between 10,000 and 10,800 feet. Another 80 or so peaks fell below 10,000 feet, with the one they scaled being a mere 2,600 feet high. It was easily accessible on the perimeter of the Shavertooth Wilderness Area. They had hired an air car and driver to bring them to the trailhead where they hiked the mile-and-a-half to Mini Minos peak as it was called. The first almost 2,300 feet of ascent didn't require climbing gear but was a moderate to advanced hike. The remaining 300 plus feet was a strenuous climb they attacked in two sections due to the length of their rope.

Krachy looked over at her admiring her profile. She had a thin, lean face framed nicely by sandy brown hair styled in a tousled lob haircut. For well over a year now he had been the stylist that had been doing her hair. He'd learned how while investigating the fashion industry on Biltmire Space Station. An organic body covering that hid the effects of aging body parts began showing up first within the fashion designers on station. The Synthi-Skin as it was called, was only one of two incredible anti-aging formulas that Jennifer and her team had discovered as part of a plot by planet Markem's former Protectorate Tanner Kory. Kory had found a new race of creatures that concocted the skin and a remarkable serum that reversed the effects of aging that he ultimately intended to use to retake control of the planet. Jennifer and her team had stopped him. She had been a Privateer for 11 years up to that point. After uncovering how the Reverse Aging Serum and Synthi-Skin was formulated by the alien race, she decided to take a leave from Privateering. That was a full year ago. Now 32-years-old, she was for the first time meeting Krachy's parents in the city of Minos on the small planet of Basley. Jennifer and Krachy had met almost two years earlier under very different circumstances. From that first meeting they had stayed friends only becoming close a year ago during the mission to stop Kory from sabotaging democratic elections on Markem, her home planet.

"We taking the lift tube down?" He asked peering down at the hiking trail 300 feet below. They could rappel down.

"We can. We'll have to do it in sections though. Once I double the rope it's only 100 feet long. Let's try to bite off 75 or 80 feet at a time to be safe."

Krachy's eyes stayed fixated on her. He thought it was sexy as hell to see his new fiancé sweating on an exposed rock with the sun beating down on her. Actually, he thought almost anything she did was sexy. He was enamored with his tall, lean warrior woman and made no apologies for it.

Jennifer's eyes lit up. "You gonna be able to concentrate on rappelling off this cliff or are we going to have to service each other to clear our heads?"

Krachy seemed to search for an answer then a half grin teased his lips. "As revved up as I am right now, I might be too tired afterwards to get down safe." He dipped his eyes at her sweat soaked T-shirt front then back at her face.

"You know we could make it just that much easier. We could call the air car driver and have her pick us up right here. I will say that as exposed as we are on this peak if anyone cared to look, they would see the sun reflect off your white ass or mine with ease."

He considered that in a far off stare for a few seconds.

"We are two achingly white individuals aren't we?"

"Not a criticism mind you, just an observation."

"You got any sun gel in that bum bag of yours? You seem to keep quite a few things in there."

"Girl stuff," Jennifer replied shaking her head, but didn't like not telling him the truth. The deception was slight, but she was so used to protecting herself it was habit. Being a Privateer for so many years had burnt self preservation into her DNA. She kept several things in her bum bag that she may or may not ever need. She'd learned a lot from staying alive when it wasn't all that easy to do. She'd also learned a lot from some really smart friends that she still stayed in touch with. They urged her to stay vigilant out of friendship, not to deceive anyone. Jennifer could always count on them to remind her that she'd made enemies in her former profession. That alone convinced her that she'd never allow others to decide she didn't deserve to enjoy her newfound life with this man. That was unacceptable. Therefore, not telling

Krachy everything seemed like a small tradeoff. All she knew was that everything's a mistake until it becomes a lesson.

Krachy pulled out a hand comp from the zippered bladder on his left thigh.

"I'll call the air car driver. She can pick us up here and we can finish exercising in our room." Out of courtesy, they had rented a room in Minos. Krachy didn't want to insult his parents by assuming they could stay at their place.

Jennifer stayed seated while she pulled up the rope. Safest way, no sense standing up having rope near her feet causing a problem. Krachy got a confirm from the air car driver. He let her finish securing the last of the rope. She'd ask for help if she needed it.

It was pretty easy to see the air car as soon as it cleared the tree line near the trailhead a mile-and-a-half away. The grey car contrasted sharply with the trees. The light hum of the grav gen became more audible as it climbed through the sky toward them. When it was hovering 20 feet out from the peak, Jennifer stood up flipping the coil of rope over her shoulder. Krachy watched her plant her feet waiting for her to nod so he could stand up himself. On his feet, he adjusted his stance a few feet back from the edge. Neither of them were now anchored to the cliff, so they didn't make any sudden moves.

As Jennifer was watching Krachy shift position beside her, she saw his eyes suddenly widen in fear but didn't understand why. Then she didn't understand anything at all. Her world went black.

Jennifer wasn't sure how much time had passed. When she blinked her eyes open, the sun was blaring into her skull. Lying on her back, she tried to take stock of her body looking up into the cloudless sky. Well, at least she was alive—check. She didn't fall off the cliff—check. Her heart was pounding in her ears.

When she started to shift position to sit up, that's when it hit her. Her vision blurred, then her stomach lurched, and she knew breakfast was on its way past her taste buds a second time. Not sure how she remembered she was on top of a 300-foot cliff, she turned her head sideways careful not to move. Breakfast tasted terrible a second time. After three final heaves, there was nothing left to do but lay back and try to catch her breath. She was very confused about what had just happened, but it seemed somewhat clear that the air car had slammed into the side of her head earlier. One thing didn't confuse her at all. She was alone.

Krachy wouldn't have left her by his own free will. Some-one had forced him to leave her. It still amounted to the same thing. She was mumbling to herself but her lips weren't mov-ing. Her head really hurt. That meant she was thinking to herself and not making much sense at that. The word concussion moved through her mind. She'd had one before but not this bad. She thought, but didn't quite know. All she wanted to do was rest. However, the heat coming off the rock underneath her was be-coming a force of its own. Even snapping her eyes shut couldn't deaden the bolts of sun piercing her eyelids. Jennifer was in deep trouble. Simple thought—BIG problem.

Hand comp, there had only been one and Krachy had it with him. Bum bag, yes, she could feel it jabbing her back. She was lying on it. Rope, nope. It didn't feel like it was nearby.

Darkness. Darkness, then growing pain. When Jennifer woke up a second time her face felt like it was under an oven coil on broil. She lifted her hands to her face then immediately pulled them back from the pain of touching her sunburnt skin. The sun was much lower in the sky now. She must have been out for a good four or five hours. Struggling up on elbows, her quea-sy stomach allowed her to blink open her eyes to focus. Success. She didn't have very white legs anymore. They were bright red now. Oh well, that wasn't life threatening. The lump under the small of her back felt like a tumor and it hurt like hell. She sat up fighting to keep her balance steadying herself with outstretched hands. Not waisting any time, she tried to ignore the many levels of pain starting with her skull, traveling down her face, her back, then the front of both legs.

How to get down? And, how to get down soon? Jennifer leaned forward peering tentatively over the ledge. The rope was looped over an outcrop of rock dangling 40 feet below. With the pounding in her head, there was no way she trusted her balance enough to climb down to retrieve it. A panic rose in her chest and she arched her back attempting to get the soreness out. It was then she remembered the soreness was caused by her bum bag. The air car driver didn't think to look under her where she'd fallen. The woman didn't know Jennifer was lying on top of it.

The small Anti Grav Harness Jennifer had in the bum bag was a common device. She pulled it out looping the wide, but thin, cordura belt under her butt cheeks securing it below her navel like a seat, more or less. After cinching the AGH in place, she had to rest. While she did, she ran the maneuvers over through her mind at least a dozen times not trusting she was clear headed enough to power it up and go. When she was ready, she focused on the controls on the little palm-sized control unit positioned just right of her lower abs.

The control unit generated the anti gravity wave that extended through the cordura belt like fingers of a radiator. Thin metal bands embedded in the fabric looped in a circle back through the material to the control unit. The AGH was small, lightweight, and foldable.

Before Jennifer powered it up, she fingered the control toggle closing her eyes running through the maneuvers another dozen times to practice with the joy pad. Ready to go, she didn't hesitate, thumbing it on then fingering the small pad lifting her up slowly. Leaning in the direction she wanted to go, she didn't make a straight line down off the cliff toward the trailhead. Instead she floated off to her right aiming for the tree tops well away from the trail below. The lurch moving down almost caused her to retch, but feeling the wind blowing across her burning face and legs felt wonderful. Minor corrections on the joy pad dropped her below an opening in the canopy where she stopped 30 feet above the ground to listen and look. The burning returned to her face and legs but she was finally in some shade that pulled the temp down 10 or more degrees so it was tolerable. She had trouble focusing at first, then the lower light under the canopy came into view. Jennifer waited a full two minutes to see if she was alone. The woman that started this might have left a cleanup team behind to finish the work.

Satisfied, Jennifer eyed a tall tree off to her right. Three limbs arched up from the main trunk. The limbs created a pocket that looked big enough for her to stand in so she could setup. She glided over slowly extending a foot toward the V between the limbs. Inching herself up higher and further into the safety of the billet created by the limbs, she reached out pulling herself in to stand up. Her energy was fading fast. No doubt about it. Otherwise she wouldn't have been breathing so hard, sweating so much, and feeling so terrible. She'd forgotten all about the water bottle not even remembering if it was still back on the ledge. Oh well.

Jennifer leaned back adjusting her feet to get more comfortable in the wedge, then pulled out the Nano Drone from her bum bag. The ND was about five inches long and weighed just over an ounce. She held it between two fingers then pulled out the remote control joy pad that controlled the ND. The RC unit was no larger than a chocolate brownie. When the RC unit powered up, the small vid screen just above the joy pad was dark. Having used it so many times before, all Jennifer did was drop the pencil shaped ND out of her hand and pressed the joy pad activating its grav gen. The ND hovered in place 15 feet below her as the video image kicked in on the RC unit. No time to waste, she looked up spotting a break in the canopy thumbing the joy pad as she watched the ND zoom straight up and through the opening.

Focusing on the small vid screen was a challenge. The concentration it took to do it only made Jennifer's head hurt more. She thumbed the joy pad watching the moving view from the ND gain altitude. She wasn't certain the exact direction of the trailhead air car lot, so climbing up higher was the only way to get a sense which direction the clearing was. Easing back on its speed, she paused to hover and pan. There—20 degrees left was the clearing over a mile away. She aimed the ND up higher urging it forward finally able to do a slow circle of the trailhead air car lot clearing far below. Two air cars were parked, but no one was visible. It was useless to try to remember if those two cars were there when she and Krachy started out earlier that morning. Her pounding head only had so much bandwidth at this point. All she could do was hope the cars belonged to hikers out on the trails. A quick flick of the auto hold on the RC unit hovered the ND in place fixing the view with the exception of the light breeze that swayed the image side to side.

Returning the RC controller to her bum bag, she thumbed the control pad on her AGH stepping out of the crook of the tree letting the unit grab her weight. Jennifer felt much better not having to balance her weight in the tree billet. She started to daydream forgetting where she was for a few moments before remembering she had to make her way to the trailhead. More pressure on the joy pad lifted her higher, but for some reason she felt it would be safer to stay under the canopy. Maybe that was a mistake, maybe not—she just wasn't sure either way. All she knew was that time was running out to do *something* before she passed out altogether.

So up, around, dodging and weaving, she maneuvered herself trying to stay low enough not to get deterred by the spreading canopy limbs above her. After a few minutes she had to break above the canopy to get her bearings. She rose above the tree tops halting to a hover. She grabbed the RC controller and panned the hovering ND in a slow circle twice. On the second pan, she spotted herself in the display zooming in to be certain. Gauging the direction, she pushed the joy pad on her AGH in the direction of the ND seeing herself growing larger in the display. The concentration to manage the AGH, the ND, her direction, and her growing fatigue made her sick.

Out over the trailhead clearing no one was in sight below. It really didn't matter all that much now. If someone wanted to take Jennifer out, there wasn't much she could do to prevent it. Her energy reserves were exhausted. She started dry heaving losing control of the AGH while her sick stomach tried to expel something that wasn't in it. The ground came up fast, and for the third time that day darkness took her.

***

The room Jennifer was in when she opened her eyes was thankfully dim. However, the pressure inside her head was a living demon. She heard a noise from somewhere off to her left that shook her molars making her grit her teeth. A heavy wave of nausea rolled up from her belly making her swallow several times as fast as she could to hold back a dry heave. The swallows worked, but she laid there exhausted from the effort, keeping her eyes closed, gripping cool metal bars with both hands.

The light steps of someone approaching culminated with a fabulous rush that started in her arm, then migrated tranquilly into her chest, then head, providing soothing relief from her nausea. A cool compress was placed over her forehead and eyes as a voice started whispering in her left ear.

"Ms. Bane, I'm the shift nurse assigned to take care of you. You're at Minos Medico Surgical Trauma Intensive Care Unit. Don't open your eyes. Here, let go of the railings and relax. You're safe here and are going to be okay."

With that, Jennifer did as she was told. The soft voice felt like an angel touching her soul. She was clear headed enough to realize she'd been given an IV push of something that took away her intense nausea. She was helpless to do anything but be treated, so she tried to relax and let it happen. All she could think was, *I just want to be treated, I just want to be treated...*

"You were flown in from the Shavertooth Trailhead by EMTs in an air ambulance. The occasional pressure you feel on your legs is an intermittent pneumatic compression device to prevent blood clots. The IPC cuffs around each leg fill with air squeezing your legs. The bed you're in will move and shift too, filling with air at different times to stimulate blood flow and lessen pressure points. The pressure you feel in your nose is a tube that was inserted while you were unconscious. The tube helps decrease abdominal pressure and prevent vomiting. Your skin feels cool because you were tanked for a few hours to repair the severe sunburn you had. You're on a round the clock, 20-hour-a-day watch by people trained like me. All you need to do is rest so you can recover. If you understand squeeze my hand."

The warm physical contact of someone caring for Jennifer made tears leak from both of her eyes. She squeezed the warm hand in her left palm fighting the urge to cry. She mouthed the words, "Thank you," before drifting off into nowhere land where darkness was starting to be her best friend.

***

"I really don't even want to be here, Vana. I mean where the hell is our son? This woman goes mountaineering with him and he never comes back."

Jaymon Bantor, Krachy's father, shifted from one foot to the other looking angrily through the ICU window at Jennifer's limp, resting body. He pulled his leer from her bed locking eyes with his wife. They were both about the same height, no more than five-foot-six. Krachy himself was 5'5".

Vana's eyes burned with anger.

"What, you think I don't want to be out looking for him too, Jay? But where do we start, huh? He's a grown man. He brought this woman back here to meet us because *this is the one*. I mean Krachy's never come home with a woman from off planet before. I don't think it was such a smooth idea to go rock climbing either. All we can do we've done—other than talk to her to ask her what really happened."

"I don't trust her."

Vana wasn't defending Jennifer in the least.

"So, go shake her awake then, Jay. If she can talk, why don't you just beat the truth out of her?"

Her response dripped sarcasm, but it was what she wanted to do all the same. She never trusted Jennifer either, and now that Krachy had disappeared for some unknown reason, it made her all the more suspicious. Her son was a trained soldier capable of taking care of himself. She never liked the fact that Krachy was a soldier, but it was a fact. How could he have been with Jennifer and not seen danger coming his way? He'd been on a mountain peak with a 360-degree view on every side. Jaymon and Vana had already been to Minos City Security HQ. There was even a Detective Agent assigned to the case. It had been two days since Krachy went missing.

"Nurse?" Jaymon stopped the lady as she was going into Jennifer's room.

"Yes?"

"When can we talk to her?"

"Mr. Bantor is it?"

Jaymon nodded.

"Ms. Bane's going to be transferred to the Step Down Trauma Ward in a few hours. The ward's on the eleventh floor. It'd be a good idea to let her continue to rest until the doctor approves the transfer. Her concussion was a Grade 3 Severe. I wouldn't be surprised if she has to spend two or more weeks recovering. You need to understand that she may not remember much at first. She'll have plenty of time to talk to you there."

"I see."

The nurse waved her hand past the scan pad next to Jennifer's door. It glided open on hinges letting her enter.

"This is getting us nowhere, Jay."

"I agree, but I'm coming back later this evening to see if she's been transferred anyway. I want to take a crack at her as soon as I can."

"You want to take a crack at what, sir?"

The authoritative voice startled them both. They swiveled around finding themselves looking up into the eyes of a uniformed security officer. The man was over six-feet tall. That's not what surprised them most. The sturdy looking man was resting his hand on his holstered laser pistol.

Undeterred, and used to looking up at people, Jaymon took a step forward.

"I want to ask her what happened to my son."

The middle-aged man scanned both Jaymon and Vana's face in turn coming to a conclusion.

"I overheard the two of you talking before the nurse went in. You don't seem to have Ms. Bane's best interests in mind. This is a security matter. I'm sympathetic to the fact that your son is missing. My name is Detective Agent Channing Altimer. I was informed that you filed the missing person's report yesterday. I was just at your home out near the Shavertooth Wildlife Management Area. I came here to the hospital next assuming you may want to see how the young lady was doing. With respect Mr. and Mrs. Bantor, I don't like what I heard you say earlier. I'll ask you this once. Do you intend to harm that woman in an effort to find out what she knows about your son's abduction?"

"You think it's an abduction?" The heat in Jaymon's voice evolved into a low growl. He was a man that never backed down. Krachy got that trait from the source.

"I asked you a question, Mr. Bantor." To ease the tension, Altimer pulled his hand off his pistol.

"Stuff it," Jaymon said. Vana crossed her arms with a look on her face that said, *Same goes for me, too!*

Altimer brushed past Vana carelessly pushing her aside to stand in front of Jennifer's door. He turned on a heel pulling a commo off his belt activating it. At the same time his other hand returned to his laser pistol. This time, however, he extracted the LP from the holster letting it fall barrel point down by his hip.

"STICU security, this is Detective Agent Altimer. Code 9, repeat Code 9 in STICU room 3. Code 9, room 3, acknowledge."

"Acknowledge. Room 3 STICU," was clearly audible to all three of them. Just then, the nurse was attempting to leave Jennifer's room. The door had a large window so she could see Altimer's back. She rapped a knuckle a few times on the pane of synth glass then turned her head to listen to something inside the room. The nurse's look didn't change much. She just reached over to the scan pad waving her hand in front of it. The audible deadbolt lock was loud. The nurse took a few steps back having been informed of the Code 9 via an audio feed inside the room. She stood, arms resting at her side, scanning the scene beyond the door.

Just then two uniformed Medico Security Guards came through the double auto doors behind Jaymon and Vana followed by a servo droid vid recording everything in front of it. The waist high servo droid rolled to a stop well away from Jennifer's room. The two guards stopped short seeing Altimer's grip tightening on his LP.

"I'll not ask you both again. Do either of you intend to harm this woman?" The dura steel in Altimer's question was backed up by the two guards stepping forward not just pulling out their laser pistols, but aiming them at Jaymon and Vana.

All Jaymon did was blink. No reaction, nothing.

"Nope, never even crossed my mind. You?" He swiveled his head toward Vana.

"No, of course not. You ready to go, Jay?"

"Yes. DA Altimer, you have a pleasant evening." With that, the couple strode past the two guards toward the double doors. The servo droid panned on its rollers to follow them as they made their way out through the auto doors out of sight.

TWO

"You want to share, Jennifer?" The lead group therapist turned to ask her.

It had been 15 days since she'd been injured. When Jennifer was transferred to the trauma ward, she had started counting the hours of conscious pain. Now she was two weeks clear of the best *and* worst day of her life, so she was counting the weeks. She had requested to sit in on the Temper Control Therapy classes. She started taking them a year ago after almost suffering a full breakdown due to the stress of the mission she was on with her crew. Her temper had been a real problem for a long time. More than one person had died because of it.

"I'm frustrated that I can't find out what happened to my fiancé; his name is Krachy. Five minutes after he asked me to marry him, I was knocked out. When I woke up, he was gone. I need to get on my feet so I can find him. And yes, I'm upset about it. But I can control my anger. I must. If I take another shot in the head anytime soon, I'm going to be in serious trouble. That about sums it up." She sat back in her chair tapping a foot and scanning the faces of the other six people arranged in a circle.

"You mentioned his parents before, Jennifer. They still haven't come to visit you have they?"

"I was told that they saw me while I was in the ICU, but they were asked to leave." She didn't have the strength to elaborate. The episode outside her ICU room upset her to the point of near depression. Krachy's parents hated and blamed her. She had to get past it.

Detective Agent Altimer told her the full story about the episode a few days ago when he determined she was strong enough to hear it. It was just another source of frustration that was weighing her down. To know that Krachy's parents had to be threatened with force to leave her alone was sobering to say the least.

Worse still, there had been no news about Krachy—none. Jennifer leaned over resting her elbows on her knees. This whole thing stunk, but she was not the type of person to feel sorry for herself. She was a person of action. She wanted to get her hands on the air car driver they had hired and *coerce* her to tell the truth. She had played the last few moments before she was knocked unconscious over and over in her head, what she remembered of it anyway. That woman had to be a link to what happened to her man. With how bad her concussion was, she had to think of a new way to strong-arm the truth out of the air car driver when the time came. She couldn't bully her way in if a simple slap to the head was going to take her out. There was help to be enlisted, but she needed to get better first. It was hard to wait, but she did so by giving herself permission to heal. She would be no good to Krachy if she wasn't up to full speed when the time came.

Feeling a ray of hope, Jennifer sat up when she spotted DA Channing Altimer standing behind the door looking at her through the synth glass window. He motioned for her to step outside. Another person in the group had the floor explaining how they felt, so she stood up excusing herself.

Altimer stepped back as Jennifer pushed the door open making her way out into the hallway. She was only an inch shorter than him. Her blue pants and tan T-shirt were loose and comfortable. Since Krachy wasn't around, she didn't have a way to keep her hair styled like she wanted, so it was pulled back in a single braid.

Altimer looked uneasy. His blue uniform was wrinkle free like always, but his brown hair looked like it hadn't been washed. No preamble, no hello.

"The air car driver was found dead this morning, Ms. Bane."

Jennifer let out the breath she'd been holding fearing the first words out of his mouth would include Krachy suffering the same fate.

Altimer didn't understand why she looked relieved.

"Did you hear what I said? The lady was murdered."

Even though that woman was a link to what happened, she knew enough about how the universe worked not to be surprised. Being a privateer for so long hardened her to setbacks like this. Deep down she was just thrilled Krachy may still be alive. And yes, she was secretly satisfied the woman had gotten what she deserved.

She studied Altimer's face realizing that this man was the only person doing anything on her behalf. He was in essence doing the job she couldn't do until she was well enough to do it. But everything had a limit.

"I can't wait any longer, Detective, I want to call in help."

He backed up a pace and put up a hand.

"No, no you are not! You're not going to start bounty hunting."

"I explained what type of work I did. I was always up front with you."

Despite what he knew about her condition, Altimer grabbed her by the arm and pulled her down the hallway. His head swiveled side-to-side looking for a room to go into. There wasn't one, just patient rooms. He let go of her frustrated that he had let his temper get the better of him.

Jennifer waited. She knew how he felt. When her temper began pushing the limits of its cage, it was always difficult for her to control too. This man was a professional, but he was also human. He was at a loss about what to say, or maybe what to do, next in the investigation, she couldn't tell. For some reason, however, she felt he wasn't telling her everything. Time to try on the non-bully approach to see how it fit.

"Let's go get a cup of coffee, Channing. I'll buy."

Her lighthearted tone pulled his head up. Channing was a proud man. She sensed that not being able to find out what happened to Krachy, then having a murder that was linked to his abduction, was an assault on his skills. He wasn't used to that, but was not sure that was even the reason he got mad.

"Okay, Jennifer."

He followed her to the lift tubes.

Once on the third floor, she had to stop and lean against the corridor wall to steady herself for a minute before rounding a few corners to the cafeteria. Not a bad headache today, she was just sluggish and growing tired. Jennifer's recovery was going to take time. After she paid for two coffees, Altimer found a quiet corner away from several groups of Medicos dressed in scrubs. Jennifer and Altimer sat down at a small table against the wall.

Before Altimer took a sip of coffee, he unclipped her bum bag pulling it off his waist and setting it on the table. She had seen it on him but didn't mention anything. She glanced at it and then back at him appreciatively. He took a cautious sip.

"You know what you had in this thing may have saved your life."

Jennifer didn't make a move to pull the bag toward her considering him curiously instead.

"You're a bit of a puzzle, Channing. Mind if I say that?"

He was about to take another drink, then pulled the steaming cup from his lips setting it down. "Not really."

"You're tight lipped too. Plus you're a lot smarter than you let on."

His brown eyes were unreadable. Altimer was quite good at what he did having practiced the look he was using on her many times before. He waited. After a long pause, he said something that caught her off guard.

"The only way you're going to make progress, Jennifer, is if you reconcile with your past."

Just when Jennifer thought he might be vulnerable, or off his game in this investigation, he dove into her past like he knew what was there.

She had to ask.

"Are you from Pinat, Channing?"

There was a very specific reason she asked that. The female philosopher caste of Pinat's social structure had incredible mental powers. While not a female, it seemed like he was reading her mind, which was exactly what females from that planet did. She knew first hand, but almost no one who was not from the planet Pinat understood these abilities. The warrior caste of male Pinatens were the only face most outsiders ever saw. Their society, however, was matriarchal, with the women having developed telepathy. Channing may not be able to read her mind, but if he was Pinaten, he could have asked one of their females to do it for him.

"You afraid I'm going to uncover something about you that you'd rather keep a secret?"

"You keep making this about me, Channing. I understand if you don't want to answer my question. It's obvious you know a great deal about me. But hey, regardless of that, I would be really ungrateful if I didn't thank you for everything you've done for me. I'm not trying to shine you on. You're right about me. I sense you know some of the things I've done. You might even know what I've been through doing those things. You wouldn't be this good at your job if you didn't."

"But you saw me lose my cool upstairs outside the Temper Control class. Maybe I'm not as good as you think."

"It was a puzzle then, upstairs I mean. It's not a puzzle now." Jennifer had him intrigued; she could almost see it.

"Word games, Ms. Bane."

Leaning back in his chair, he took a few sips of his drink eyeing her as if she was just fishing. But she wasn't fishing. Jennifer knew why Channing lost his cool upstairs.

"You were alarmed when I said I'd call in help. Not because you know that two Pinaten vassals have sworn fealty to me as their liege lord. The ferocity in which the warrior caste males on Pinat fight is universal knowledge. Nope. You were alarmed because my two vassals, Dimitri Volodya and Jeffrey Jansen, are already on this planet and have been to see you."

Channing was awesome at being unreadable. She took a sip of her black coffee. The warm liquid relaxed her, clearing her head for some reason. The feeling was most welcome. Maybe she had to exercise her brain, as she was doing now, to feel better.

"Did you lock them up?" She asked. "I mean detain them, quarantine them, whatever Minos Security speak is. There's no way they wouldn't be here right now unless something massive intervened to stop them. You and I both know how they're wired."

"I'm able to hold people for three days, 60 hours from when they broke orbit. That's the extent of my authority to hold off-worlders. Of course, all their entry visas were in perfect order."

"They were quite submissive while all this was going on weren't they?"

"You have two very loyal Pinaten vassals, Jennifer. They said 'yessir' to everything I asked them to do. That's why I'm so alarmed about the help you can deploy. With your background, supported by those two men, I fear for anyone that is stupid enough to get in the way."

He set his coffee down leaning forward.

"However, I am most frightened of *you*."

Jennifer heaved a sigh. She didn't want it to go this way. This is the type of trouble she had been running away from after taking an indefinite leave from privateering. She had very serious doubts about her ability to handle the extreme rigors and stress of that profession. So much so, that she arranged to lease the use of her light cruiser starship, *Viper II,* to her crew members. By doing it that way, she was able to ensure some steady income, and her crew wouldn't be out of their jobs. Leasing *Viper II* to her crew seemed a perfect fix until Krachy disappeared. Now it was all coming back with a vengeance—A vengeance that physically she was in no condition to handle right now.

He leaned back one hand on his cup with a very nondescript and annoying look on his face. Channing was surely a match for her wits, all the more so given the present condition she was in.

"How are you going to play this?" He came right to the point.

She blinked admitting defeat to herself. Dimitri and Jeffrey, her vassals, would show up here soon. It didn't matter when, and she didn't need to know when. Channing had come as a courtesy but also for something more. The *more* was what this whole conversation was all about.

"I want to play it so that no one else gets hurt, and I get to be married to the only man I've ever loved. I didn't tell you that he asked me to marry him not five minutes before that bitch in the air car rammed the side of it into my head. Yeah, that had to be how it was done. I'm a lot taller than Krachy. His eyes lit up like beacons two seconds before I blacked out. The air car caught my head missing his altogether. Whoever was in it wanted him, not me. I was in the way. Why they didn't kill me, I'm not sure. But my past had nothing to do with this one, Channing. Whoever kidnapped Krachy didn't know who I was. They wanted Krachy. For what reasons I can imagine. I will say it's very hard for me to tell you that I want to play this so that no one else gets hurt. I want to hurt people for taking him out of my life. I admit it. But I know you know that. You also know that I can order my vassals to pursue that."

"That is part of the reason I am most afraid of you. The other reason is the littered debris of bodies you've left in your wake in the pursuit of nothing more than a profit."

Jennifer froze unable to respond to the truth behind almost every word he said. Being wrong about part of her motivation allowed her stay seated. He was wrong about his quick over-reaching assumption in one very important way.

Her eyes became icy daggers of pure vindication for all the people she hadn't killed but had saved.

"I'm stopping you right there, Channing. And it's not because if I ordered them to, I could have Dimitri and Jeffrey rip your head off."

She held up a hand signaling for her two vassals, who just seconds before had quietly come to a stop behind Channing, to hold back, which they did just as fast as they had appeared in the cafeteria.

Channing saw her do it, and knew what he'd just avoided. But amazingly he was undeterred. His expression changed to one resembling a look that said, *Okay, there may be some hope for you yet.*

"So why don't you tell me why I'm wrong about you, Jennifer. It does give me a hint of hope that you called off your carrion feeders just now."

Channing was provoking her. Oh no, with her head starting to hurt, she was no match for this man right now. But one thing could not be overlooked. She stood up threateningly.

"Do not ever insult my vassals like that again, Channing! You can think what you want. You, my dear Detective Agent, were not there when I had to make the decisions I did to save my crew and countless lives on Markem and Beltina. Those two fine gentlemen had no say in their lot in life. What they've done for me is genetic. I know you understand that. There's no reason to continue provoking me the way you are. I cannot and will not defend myself like I have in the past. *That* is the only reconciliation I need to prove to you."

She leaned forward placing her outstretched hands on the table leaning right down into his face. For the first time Channing felt very uneasy that he may have overplayed his hand. His torso retreated from her leer.

"The problems I get myself into are always bigger than just me. This one is too, Channing. Are you willing to work alongside us to find out what this is really about? Or does the enormous scale of an off-planet conspiracy frighten you?"

She sat back down, taking a few sips of coffee to calm herself, while she waited for his reply. She had learned in therapy to control her actions and reactions; she was exercising those new skills now.

Channing swallowed.

"You're right, Jennifer."

He sat forward. This was more in line with the conversation he had planned all along.

"I had no right to judge you or your vassals. I apologize. I believe the last thing left to decide is who's going to be in charge of this off-planet conspiracy."

Jennifer almost expected him to smile, maybe at least grin. But no, he was the best she'd ever seen at not being readable. It didn't matter. She knew the answer the same as he did.

"You will, Channing, I'm not up to it."

He reached into his pocket pulling out the power stick for the laser pistol she kept in her bum bag.

"I figured I could take you in a stand-up fight given the condition you're in right now. I wasn't totally sure, so I didn't think it was such a hot idea to let you have access to a loaded LP." He smiled when he handed it to her for the very first time since the conversation began. She looked amused setting the laser pistol down next to the bum bag.

Jennifer's look turned serious.

"It's best that the basis for our new relationship start with nothing but truth, Channing. If you smacked the side of my head right now, I'd puke all over this table. I'm still not ready to chase this thing down yet. You understand?"

Channing sensed it was because she wanted him to wait for her to heal, but also knew that Krachy's time might be running out. She was in a tough spot. He could see that.

"Before you call them over, can I ask you if you'd trust me to use them to help me while you're healing up?"

"I think I'm a different kind of liege lord than what you've read about in your reports. I'm not good at ordering Dimitri and Jeffrey to follow me blindly. I've never had it in me. I care too much for them both. When the time comes, we can ask them and see what they think. I value their input implicitly. If your background data didn't tell you, Jeff is the commander of an impressive operation in his own right. Dimitri almost died 21 months ago saving my life. He's just now back to what I would call near full strength. So you see, Channing, these two men are my family. They're part of me from now on. Just like the fealty implies—until death. The three of us have a long way to go, so I want them to know everything before they get involved. As long as you can keep all that in mind, I think you leading this team will work. In the end though, I won't sacrifice either of them. I would rather die first."

She shrugged. "It's the only way I know how to lead them. Okay?"

Channing saw something in her he didn't understand in the classified file he'd read until just now. It might really be true.

"Did you have a hand in the cease-fire between Markem and Beltina 21 months ago, Jennifer?"

The timing was too coincidental to ignore.

"Yes, but it wasn't something I set out to do. I was, just like you pointed out, trying to finish a mission and get paid. Once I found out the Protectorate of Markem, Tanner Kory, had been the one to actually hire me, everything changed. I helped Markem broker peace to save the lives of my crew and to help Markem down the road to democracy. I was lucky it worked out the way it did. Dimitri saving my life made it possible. He ended up in a coma for seven months because of it. Is that what your file said about me?"

"No, it only mentioned Krachy was close to Ochula Kozlov, the Commander of Markem Space Forces. I put the pieces together. Krachy and Ochula and you, along with the timing—it was just a theory. I'm not certain I believe it though."

Jennifer let that go.

"You're right about many things about me, Channing. But you will keep in mind the motivations won't you? I mean, I'm not a bad person. I try not to be. I have taken lives. I have sleepless sweats about every one of them. You understand?"

"I understand."

"I've been working to control my temper which has been the cause of several deaths that I truly regret. I was in Temper Control Therapy upstairs when you showed up. I've been attending similar sessions for a year."

"Now you see why I held onto the LP power stick?"

Channing wasn't joking. His look was all business.

It hurt to hear that about herself, but it was true. If Jennifer's anger broke it's shackles at the wrong time—well, that was not going to happen. She owned her actions and all of her reactions too. That was a theme she repeated to herself glad she'd learned it in therapy.

"I do. You were honest telling me that you were afraid of me. I can face that. But I won't do just anything to reach the outcome we want on this, Channing. I just can't do that anymore. This injury is already changing me. Once you go through trauma like this, you're never the same. I know that. Every day is a gift. All I want to do is find Krachalavito and let him take care of me."

Her look turned dire just when Channing thought it wouldn't. He could tell her strength was fading.

He chewed on his bottom lip. "What? What is it?"

Jennifer blew her breath out through bulging cheeks. She had to tell him. Channing just wasn't experienced enough to know on his own.

"I'm really tired. But I can tell you this once."

He waited not understanding why she wasn't finishing.

"I've started out on missions like this before. It may have been different circumstances, but the end game always seems to play itself out the same way. I hate that it will, but it just does."

She was confusing him. Before he could ask, she started again.

"There is something bad waiting for us, Channing. The last mission I was a part of, I had to tell Krachy not to tell me the truth about the end game to protect my health. Sure, I had a sense of how awful it was. But, I've never asked him to explain it in detail even though he knew all of it. You're probably not going to understand this unless you've been on my side of the table. Jeff and Dimitri are here because a very good female friend of mine from Pinat reached across space to pitch her mind into my hospital bed. She told them what happened to me so that they would come to help."

His looked turned beyond skeptical. At least he was showing some emotion.

It didn't matter to her that he didn't understand. He would soon enough.

"If my friend from Pinat is already involved, then this is going to get complicated," Jennifer reasoned.

"I know you may not believe me. That's okay. You've not seen what I've seen. Not known the kind of people I've been forced to stop."

She was tiring fast. She wasn't going to be able to complete this conversation explaining the complexities of things this man didn't understand or had not seen. But that wasn't an issue because of her position of standing over Jeffrey and Dimitri.

This gave Channing much more pause than he thought was possible. He was confident in his abilities, but this was something else. Something he didn't fully understand.

"You're saying a lady from Pinat read your mind. That's what you're telling me?"

Just then a six-foot-four, red-haired man placed his large hand on Channing's shoulder. Channing turned looking up into narrow grey eyes.

Jeffrey Jansen was alone, Dimitri nowhere in sight. Jeffrey released his shoulder swiveling around to pull over a chair from a table close by to sit down. His look was serious but not that threatening.

"My Lord is not telling you any of this out of melodrama, Channing. She has seen it all first hand."

Jennifer got up and left the table without another word. She rounded a corner and was gone.

Channing turned back to Jeffrey. "What the hell are you two trying to tell me?"

"It's not something my Lord or I can predict. We only speak from experience. Before you take this on, you want to ask yourself if you really want to see this to the finish. I've seen what trying to finish has done to My Lord Bane. I'm here to protect her. Sure, I want to see Krachy back safe because she loves him. But she's my top priority. There was a reason she left her privateering work behind, Channing. I don't say this lightly when I tell you it almost destroyed her. Now she has what can only be described as a traumatic brain injury. There's a limited amount of strength left inside her to go through another one of these episodes without doing irreparable damage. Dimitri and I are here to make certain that doesn't happen. We're not pawns to move on a board blocking attacks or throwing ourselves in front of laser bolts. We only care what happens to her."

He sat back finished with his speech.

Channing sat and pondered everything he'd just heard. Then his jaw muscles rippled. Jeffrey could almost hear him grind his teeth in defiance. In Channing's line of work, he wasn't used to people hinting that he was weak.

"You're threatening me aren't you? That's what you and her do."

"What you are getting yourself into is threatening you, Channing. You have no idea the kind of work Jennifer, Dimitri and I have done. Were you there when she forced Protectorate Tanner Kory to leave Markem?"

Channing thought: *What? The Protectorate of Markem was deposed when Markem and Beltina agreed to a cease-fire.*

"You're going to sit there and tell me Jennifer deposed him as the head of the entire planet? I listened to her say something to that effect earlier to humor her. She's recovering from an injury and I didn't want to upset her and make her feel worse."

Jeffrey was evaluating this man. If Channing was going to work alongside his liege, he was going to have to understand what that meant. He was going to have to understand the person he was dealing with. It was a lot to absorb. But as usual, time pressures always shrunk Jennifer's ability to plan and prepare. This was just another example of that. The questions in Jeffrey's mind were very clear. *Was this man trustworthy enough to be allowed access to her? Was he going to bare open every detail of his investigation to help? And most importantly, did he have her best interests in mind?*

"That was the first thing Jennifer helped accomplish. The second thing was to capture the former Protecterate Tanner Kory then turn him over to Beltina to avert renewed hostilities with Markem. Channing, you have been here on Basley the last two years while all this took place."

Channing took in a breath swallowing what was he was about to say. He realized that what he'd just been told could be true. He had been dirt-side all that time. If this was a lie, it was well orchestrated. Jansen and Volodya had just been released from custody. He himself had come straight here before they were released to speak with Jennifer first. If they had communicated to set up this rouse with Jennifer, it was done fast.

If what Jansen was saying was true, the woman who just left the table was a part of history.

Channing sensed that Jennifer was dangerous—that she was inimitable in some way. Again, this was something else. Something Channing didn't expect today.

"Jennifer said the last mission she was a part of ended so badly that she asked Krachy not to tell her the truth about how it ended. She said she was worried about what it would do to her. Her health I mean."

"And...your point, Channing?"

"What, you're not going to tell me what that means?"

"Apparently, she just tried to explain it to you. Why don't you believe her? You think Jennifer likes wasting time talking to you when the most important person in her life has been taken from her?"

"I know she's capable, Jansen. Anyone can see that. The background I have on her confirms it. That doesn't make her capable enough to broker the end of a war, then stop the start of another one."

"All the capabilities you're giving her have been supported by committed people that follow her, Channing."

Jeffrey had been there. He had seen it for himself, had watched Jennifer urge, nudge, and guide the Beltan Ambassador into deciding for himself whether to trust her or not. It had happened a year ago after she captured Tanner Kory; all the while he had been operating under an assumed name and identity.

At the time Jennifer was the only one on her team that had figured it out. Once Kory was captured, Jeffrey was with her when she tortured a confession right out of the man's lips—the truth of which was so foul as to make her give up responsibilities as Privateer Captain of her own ship and crew. Her former crew were still family to her, still a part of her life and always would be. Channing didn't know all this. He was an amateur gauged against the standards of Jennifer's profession. Not even a casual participant.

"One of those people is a woman from Pinat that can read minds?" Channing asked.

"Yes."

"You're not from Pinat, Jansen. How is it that you've sworn fealty to her if you're not from there?"

"My genetic kinship tie was given to me by Dimitri."

"Come again?"

"Dimitri has the ability to pass along genetic changes to others using the Right Way."

"The what way?"

"Look, Channing, my Lord does not need me here to educate you on the finer points of Pinaten Kinship Lineage, but, I can tell you this: The Right Way is a genetic mechanism that directs my mind and body. This innate power allows me to honor and serve Jennifer without conscious thought. Dimitri Volodya is from a long line of genetically predetermined oath sworn clans from Pinat. You know enough about their feudal social makeup to understand that they are a different race of people than you or I. The circumstances of how I aligned my kinship tie to My Lord Bane is none of your business, nor will I further attempt to explain it. All you need to know is that I live to serve and bring honor to her. Why is that hard for a smart guy like you to understand?"

"Because you're the Commander of Beltina's *Receiver*, that's why."

"And…once again, what's your point?"

"My point is that one of the reasons my planet, Basley, has been so successful staying out of the war, is that we know everything there is to know about potential enemies. Beltina has a remarkable device that can transport starships instantaneously through hyperspace. That device was the reason Markem had to submit to a ceasefire with them. You're the head of that installation, the commander, and have been since it was being constructed."

"Yes, I am. Are you starting to put any of these connections together, Channing, or are you just regurgitating your intel reports to me? I mean do you actually see any motivations here, Detective Agent?"

Then it hit Channing. This woman *was* who she claimed to be.

"If Jennifer's team includes you, then she could have had a direct pipeline to the leaders of Beltina who are your bosses. And if that's true, then that would mean the leaders of Markem would have listened to her if she tried to act as a go between or broker."

Confirmation was written all over Jeffrey's face. There was no deceit in any of it.

"I see now…" Channing sat back, the cold coffee in front of him a thing of the past. The revelation of it all turned his head toward Jeffrey.

"You're here to interview me aren't you, Jansen?"

"DA Altimer, you have a tiring habit of stating the obvious."

THREE

The two young women sitting on the faded couch in the lobby of the inn flicked a glance at each other. They both nodded—it was him.

The interior of the inn looked shabby; it had probably looked shabby the day it was built. Jeffrey Jansen walked toward the front desk. The desk was covered with an irregular layer of dust everywhere except the center where most of the transactions with guests took place. On either side of the counter, the oil from overlapping never-removed fingerprints made it appear sticky.

The guy behind the counter grunted when Jeffrey asked for his room key card acting as though it was very inconvenient to reach behind him to grab it. Everyone that stayed in the place kept their key card with them except Jeffrey, apparently. He didn't want a trail to lead anyone back to his room if he was searched. That's also why he chose this dump. People staying in this part of Minos City were able to stay anonymous.

The two women waited for Jeffrey to disappear into the lift tube at the back of the lobby. After about five minutes, they sidestepped their way around the other faded couch over to the front desk. The heavyset guy glanced at them.

"What room you need?" He asked, used to giving out room numbers of guests that ordered escorts. He couldn't have cared less who was going up to have fun; he just knew it wasn't him, unfortunately.

"The red-haired guy that came in a few minutes ago," the brunette answered.

The desk clerk's hand dropped behind the counter. When it did, a holo guide materialized next to the two women. The male holo image was transparent light blue, speaking up instantly.

"Follow me," it said, turning in front of them toward the lift tube.

The two women walked behind the man's image. It was a naked body covered with ribbons of dark blue, red, and purple swirls. The body art started at its shoulders then ran around its torso, waist and legs. The holo image was a skinny representation of a man with a tiny dimpled butt that shook as it walked. In to the open lift tube doors it walked turning when the two women stepped in.

The doors on the lift tube closed. The overused tube scratched its way up to the top floor, 11. The holo guide exited ahead of them turning left down the dim hallway. The transparent image approached the third door on the right, turned around fast, extending its left arm in the direction of the door, then disappeared.

The dark-haired woman knocked on the door. After almost a minute, a voice on the other side said, "Come in, it's open."

The brunette pushed open the door. Jeffrey Jansen stood as far back into the room as possible holding a laser pistol at his side. When he saw the two women, he smiled.

"Good to see you, Sami and Adrianna," he said it with something like admiration. "I won't ask how you found me, but Donina and Marco had to have something to do with it."

"Ian thought we could help." Adrianna, the brunette, smiled back at him, leading Sami into the room.

"I recognized you in the lobby but wanted to wait until you felt it was safe to meet," Jeffrey admitted.

Sami was in her mid twenties, Adrianna a few years older. The way they carried themselves made it clear that being in a place like this was not an issue in the least.

Jeffrey studied them both looking them over from head to foot and back again. Adrianna had her hair pulled up in a snood accentuating her high cheek bones. The tight-fitting dark purple dress she wore ended north of her small breasts, the hem just north of her knees and the low spiked heels which she looked used to wearing.

Sami's glistening brown hair was down and parted on one side, so it half fell across one eye. She wore a form-fitting, pale pink V-neck blouse tucked into a grey mid-knee, snug-fitting skirt, cut high on one leg. She also wore mid-height, open toe spiked heels.

Sami smiled brightly. She was standing beside Adrianna, having closed the door behind her.

"Hello, Jeff. How's Jennifer doing?"

"Recovering slowly; she has a severe concussion bordering on a TBI. I just left her with Dimitri."

"Donina hadn't checked on her in over a week-and-a-half when she discovered she'd been hospitalized," Sami said, referring to Jennifer's telepathic friend from the planet Pinat.

"She was pitching her mind every so often just to see how she was doing, at the same time trying not to invade her privacy because she knew Jennifer was spending time with Krachy. As soon as Donina found out Jennifer was injured, I know you and Dimitri got the call to come help. Adrianna and I spent a few days before we left training at Ian's insistence."

She was grateful, not upset, for the training Ian put them through.

"Besides, you know how Ian is when it comes to watching Jennifer's back." Ian McKivey was Jennifer's longest serving officer. He was the first recruit she ever enlisted.

Jennifer began privateering by stowing away on Marco's ship when she was only 19-years-old trying to escape an abusive arranged marriage on Markem. Marco took a liking to her giving her a slot as ship mate, where she learned fast, finally saving enough creds to purchase her first small ship, the *Viper.* Years later, she upgraded to the astra class light cruiser she'd been using ever since, *Viper II.* Jennifer named it after her mentor and friend, Marco Sigretti. Sigretti was known as the Silent Viper due to his ability to always get in and out of trouble undetected. Ian was still First Officer on the now leased V2 following the orders of Captain Kyle Ryan.

The women sat down on the bed facing Jeffrey. He took the only chair in the room near the window placing the LP on the small table next to him with the barrel facing away from his guests.

"Any trouble getting through customs?"

"Routine," Sami replied. "Since this is my home planet, screening was straight forward. Adrianna tagged along as my guest. Neither of us have much of a background that's traceable. No background is always like that for people that get taken into the slave trade, like us. We were easy targets for the slavers because our background is so boring. Our lack of background works the same way getting back on planet. Customs didn't find any red flags, so we were admitted after the health screening. Minos Customs didn't even know I was on *Viper II*'s payroll. Jennifer's Certified Relocation Specialist is thorough."

Jeffrey smiled. From the first days that Jennifer struck out solo as a privateer, she had always enlisted the help of a CRS. The CRS was her bank, investment management company, pension plan, and most importantly, her anonymous means to move and hide funds. She had to pay a substantial fee each month, but it had always proved worth it. Sami and Adrianna's anonymity was just another example of that.

"Last I heard you two were ship mates on Marco's ship."

"I still am," Adrianna said. "But Ian needed more engineering help, so he ask Marco to let Sami join his engineering team on *Viper II*."

She glanced at Sami.

"Before Marco and Jennifer rescued me from being sold a second time to the slavers, I was a mechanic of all things," Sami explained. "My father, his father, my uncles, my family as far back as I remember, all were mechanics. I grew up around the Minos Space Port climbing in and out of every ship imaginable…until I was taken, that is."

Her look grew determined— determined to help Jennifer, or determined never to let that happen to her again, Jeff wasn't sure. No matter.

"I'm glad you're both here; I need some help—"

Adrianna interrupted. "—We owe her Jeff, you know that. Sami and I would be slaves in the sex trade right now if Jennifer hadn't saved us. She gave us a chance to start our lives over, no strings."

Adrianna shot a look at Sami then back at Jeffrey.

"We're here to do whatever it takes…"

"I met the Detective Agent that's assigned to Jennifer's case. He's guarded and, worst of all, inexperienced with missions like this. I'm not saying he's not smart, because he is. You both know there's never enough time to plan, so I need to kickstart things. I need to know what he knows. If he's not going to give us his intel, I intend to take it. I can't wait. Neither can Krachy."

***

"Hey, Altimer!"

One of the detective agents a few cubes away from Channing yelled in his direction. Channing lifted his chin so his eyes would clear the low cube panel.

"What?"

"That air car rental company you had an alert on went active. They've reported a theft."

"When?"

"In progress," The other DA answered.

"Got it, thanks."

Altimer stood up wheeling around as he pulled his hand comp from his pocket. He spoke into it as he jogged toward the lift tubes.

"Hyatt, is Bane in her hospital room with one of her Pinaten vassals?"

After a few moments he heard Sub Agent Hyatt reply. Altimer had instructed the rookie to watch Jennifer's room to let him know if she or Volodya left, and where they were going.

"Yes, both still here," SA Hyatt confirmed.

Already down in the air car port, Altimer darted through the open lift doors starting up his air car with a sub vocal command through his SC. DAs and above were low jacked via a Smart Chip implanted just under the skin behind an ear. The SC had the ability to call for help if another means wasn't available. The chip was also linked to Altimer's hand comp which in turn could start his air car.

He slid behind the controls, urging the security air car's gravity generator to turn toward the takeoff ramp leading up to ground level. Once out into the bright sun, the front windshield auto dimmed adjusting the heads-up-display readout to current lighting.

Altimer snapped a glance at the readout that calculated just over four minutes ETA to the crime scene. By law, only security and emergency vehicles were allowed to fly above building top level. It made for much faster pursuit times, which was by design. Civilian traffic had to stay in one of the four levels close to the ground which meant traffic was routed around obstacles, namely buildings.

***

Adrianna had changed her appearance. She wore a blue Minos security uniform that blended in with all the others on Altimer's floor. Guiding a small anti grav cart, she made her way to the evidence room halting at the door. Two DAs walked by not giving her a glance.

Adrianna spoke up.

"Do you know where Altimer is? He's not in his cube."

She leaned casually against the hall just next to the evidence room door.

The shorter DA turned, shrugging, as the other just then received a call on her hand comp. She continued walking down the hall out of ear shot taking the call. The shorter lady hesitated.

"Not sure, what do you need?"

"I'm only a SA. I can't log in this evidence for Altimer. If he's not around, I have to return it across town to space port HQ."

"What is it?" The lady took a step closer to glance down into the deep bin at the ropes, climbing gear, and a duffel bag.

"Hey, I don't touch anything or otherwise fool with it. I brought it over on orders for DA Altimer to inspect it and then log the items into evidence."

Adrianna lifted her head from the bin refusing to do anything else.

"You're just going to have to take it back then."

The other lady had finished her call and looked back down the hall at the shorter lady.

"I've gotta go." She turned down the hall.

"Yes, ma'am, thanks anyway." Adrianna pushed off the wall nodding. The two women strode down the hall turning a corner.

Adrianna waited, then bent down unzipping the duffel. Inside was an auto card reader and key card compositor. She hit the output key on the compositor. It spit out a scan card that she snatched up then passed over the evidence room scan pad.

The door moved aside; she guided the cart in following behind it. The shorter lady's card was clipped to her belt. When the lady had moved close to the duffel bag, the card reader had auto scanned her card key. Then the key card was reproduced in the compositor. The delay tactic Adrianna used to lure the shorter lady close to the duffel bag had worked.

The evidence room had four isles with shelving units. This evidence room wasn't the main evidence room for the facility. It was only meant as a staging area while cases were worked by DAs on that floor. Once a case was ready for tribunal, the evidence would be transferred to the main evidence room on another floor and prepared.

The lights had auto illuminated. Adrianna scanned the alpha labels on the side of the shelves stepping past the first, then second shelf, cutting left, coming to a stop in front of a data bin about 10 inches wide and seven inches deep. The name on the top edge of the bin glowed dimly:

BANTOR, KRACHALAVITO

In haste, Adrianna grabbed everything in the bin gathering it up in her hands. She turned left starting to make her way back to the anti grav cart to hide what she'd taken, when she noticed the bin to the left of Krachy's:

REF: BANTOR, K

That bin had to be related. She made a trip back to the duffle, pushing the few items from Krachy's bin in, then returned, grabbing the few more items from the REF: BANTOR, K bin.

She didn't want to waste more time, but couldn't shake the feeling that if one bin referenced Krachy, there may be others. After she finished a quick search of the entire room, she identified four more bins that were also labeled REF: BANTOR, K.

The other bins had varying amounts of items in them, but all of them had something, so she took everything, stuffing what didn't fit into the duffel under it and under the ropes.

Adrianna waited for the right time to leave, which was the most critical move she had to make to actually leave the building with her loot.

Jeffrey Jansen was sitting in the row of four chairs just outside Detective Agent Altimer's cube arranged against the wall. He had been escorted there by a female SA whose duty was to not let anyone wander around the building unaccompanied. Jeffrey asked to go to the bathroom. The woman shrugged, turning toward the hall past the row of cubes. She turned right striding down the hall past the evidence room Adrianna was in. Jeffrey tapped the hand comp that was inside his pocket as soon as he stepped past the evidence room hatch.

Adrianna heard the tap on her hand comp already poised to exit the room. Stepping out past the opening door, she dropped her hand in front of the scan pad pivoting off down the hall in the other direction from Jeffrey and his escort.

Jeffrey finished his business while the woman waited. He exited the men's lounge behind her, walking past the evidence room again, then making a left turn down the cube isle to his chair. Before his backside landed, he noticed Detective Agent Altimer rounding the corner off to his left glaring his way and breathing heavily. Channing came up short, sweat glistening on his forehead.

"Why are you here, Jansen?" He asked, winded.

"I came to see you, Channing. Time's wasting, and I'm interested in what we're going to do next." Jeffrey rose to his full height. He was few inches taller than Altimer.

"How long have you been here, no wait—" He turned to the Sub Agent, an ebony young woman watching them both.

Altimer's eyes dipped to her waist trying to read the name on her ID card. He almost focused, then looked back at Jeffrey suspiciously. Frustrated he had been lured away from his desk only to find Jansen here when he returned, he almost yelled at the SA.

"Look at the comp-in log and tell me how long this man has been in the building. Do. It. Now!" His orders evolved into a growl.

The SA blinked but said nothing as she pulled out her hand comp to get the info.

Jeffrey crossed his arms.

"Channing, you look out of sorts. What's going on?" He asked it so deadpan that it thoroughly pissed Altimer off. Altimer knew he had just been set up. However, with the somewhat childish way Altimer was acting, Jeffrey came to the unfortunate conclusion that this man may not be capable of helping his liege much longer.

As if seeing it on Jeffrey's face, Altimer let his legs bend to sit down in one of the chairs. His eyes never left Jeffrey's as he did. Just then, the SA lifted her head from the small HC screen.

"He's been on site 22 minutes, sir."

While the SA informed him, Altimer didn't take his stare away from Jansen. He had only been gone 15 minutes. The fact that the air car had been stolen from the same lot Jennifer Bane had rented her air car was no coincidence. Altimer knew it, and he knew Jeffrey knew it. But that meant very little. He couldn't prove it.

All this time Jeffrey was thinking: *If only this guy would open his thinking; he could have closed down the building exits. He might even have caught Adrianna before she left with her loot. But no, Altimer was not putting it together. A shame, but narrow police minds often behaved that way.*

Then it did hit Altimer. He was sitting now and could read the name on SA Janput's ID.

"Janput, take my ID and see if any evidence is missing from the bin labeled Bantor: B, A, N, T, O, R. Go!" He handed the ID to her.

Looking puzzled, Jeffrey scratched the back of his neck with a finger but said nothing. He took the last seat next to Altimer leaving one chair open between them. He crossed his legs waiting.

Janput returned staring at her superior nervously.

"Bantor's bin is empty. So are several others that reference his name, sir."

Altimer got up without looking at Jeffrey, instead giving the order to SA Janput.

"Take this man into custody. Once you have him secured in the pen, get the Can't Lie team together for interrogation."

Altimer didn't even glance at Jeffrey. He made his way down the aisle heading toward the evidence room.

Fifteen minutes later, Altimer entered the pen, a square little room with a dura steel table that Jeffrey was sitting at. One leg was shackled to the floor. Taking the seat across from him, Jeff watched him enter with a stare that was so relaxed that he looked like he might fall asleep any second.

"Are you going to tell me where my evidence is, or am I going to pump you with a dose of Can't Lie?" Altimer asked.

Jeffrey's eyelids grew heavy. "I don't know..." His head dipped, and he was fast asleep in a blink. Altimer's eyes flew open, his hands coming up to catch Jeff's large shoulders before his head smacked the table.

Jeff started, jerking awake, lifting his head blinking. "...where your evidence is."

Altimer smacked his hands down on the table, pushing himself up to stand with his arms outstretched, the back of his legs scrapping the chair out away from the table. He was losing his cool, not used to being manipulated so deliberately, then having the perp throw it in his face by being bored with the whole stupid mess. He gathered himself turning away from the table, then looking up into the vid cam behind Jeffrey, he signaled with a finger. A few seconds later, two uniformed men came through the door stopping off to Jeff's left. One of them held a medi bag in one fist. They waited.

Altimer glared down at Jeffrey.

"I looked at the vid feed outside the evidence room, Jansen. I saw your female accomplice print up an ID and enter the evidence room. I saw you walk by the door about two seconds before she exited behind you with my evidence. I waited too long to seal the building, but that doesn't matter, because in about five minutes, you're going to tell me who she is and where my evidence is. It'll be a lot easier if you just spill it now. The after effects of that crap in your veins sucks. You know it. I know it. Your liege lord talked about trust. I have a reason for not trusting you with what I know."

"What is it you know, DA Altimer?" Jeff asked.

Channing blew out a long, slow breath.

"Okay, have it your way." He nodded for the two men to proceed. They did.

Jeffrey concluded that Detective Agent Altimer was even less than a casual participant. He was a rank amateur. The enormity of what he *did not know* could very well get his liege lord killed. But he, Sami, and Adrianna had discussed how to get through to this man.

Jeffrey had a suggestion that seemed workable on two fronts. One, it got them the evidence they needed to kickstart saving Krachy. And two, when Altimer witnessed the results of this useless interrogation first hand, maybe then, just then, he would finally understand who he was dealing with.

As the shorter, heavyset man moved to insert the syringe of Can't Lie into Jeff's left forearm, he wasn't all that hopeful. He did know this was the absolute last time he would try. If this didn't work, Altimer was out. If Altimer didn't leave willingly, there were other ways to get him to leave. Dimitri had reminded him of that no more than an hour ago.

Channing watched the med tech administer the drug. He'd sat in on countless sessions like this before. The sessions always started with defiance and always ended with answers—all the answers.

Jeffrey let it happen not pulling his stare from a fixed point on the wall in front of him for over five minutes. His breathing didn't even change. That was the first sign. When he finally looked up at Altimer, what he said was the second.

"Are we through yet, Detective Agent?"

Channing blinked; his forehead creased. Where were the beads of sweat? Where was the nervous twitching? Where was the frantic submission that made subjects spout off at the mouth so fast they couldn't make coherent sentences? Instead, Jeffrey returned his far-off look to the same fixed point on the wall.

Altimer started asking the questions anyway. The only reply he got was a tiring and repetitive, "Are we through here yet?"

After 20 minutes, Altimer nodded for the two other men to leave. He pulled his chair over to sit down in front of Jeffrey trying to insert his eyes into the tunnel vision of Jeff's fixed gaze so that he could study him. He thought he was good at being unreadable. He had never seen a person so utterly indifferent to a dose of this powerful drug before in his life. He started to doubt if the med tech had even given him a real dose.

Jeffrey's face became animated.

"Does any of this convince you who you're dealing with now, Channing? I have run out of patience; this is the very last time I intend to explain it to you."

Channing heaved a ragged sigh of defeat.

"You and Jennifer tried to explain."

"No more time to waste, DA Altimer. None!" The only thing holding Jeffrey back from going ahead and completing this mission without this man was a leg shackle. Unless he heard the right responses, and he heard them soon, he was finished effin' around.

Submitting to the outcome, Altimer looked at Jeffrey but clearly was not liking it. Even though he knew he'd been beat, he still couldn't form the words on his lips. Stubborn habits died hard.

Jeffrey's voice was low and urgent.

"I don't want to have to sift through the evidence, Channing." His next sentence grew in volume until he was yelling. "It's just another waist of my Lord's time!"

Channing was smart enough to know that if Jansen had wanted to kill him he could. His whole body was tense reminding him of what he'd only seen from Pinaten's on vid. However Jeffrey had obtained the blood lust of a Pinaten warrior didn't matter. Even though Jeffrey was not born there, he had it in abundance.

Finally Channing admitted, "Five other people have been abducted. Only one from Basley other than Bantor, the others from off world."

Jeffrey relaxed a bit, but what he'd heard wasn't enough.

Channing could tell. "We don't know if the four off-worlders are alive. The one from Basley has not been discovered dead yet. Bantor included. As far as we know, he's alive too. We can't pinpoint where Bantor is or all the others. If we could, we'd link up with Basley Space Commandos and try to get them all back. We've done joint ops with Basley Space Ops before. That's where we got the intel on the four off-worlders, from our Space Ops team."

Jeffrey relaxed a bit more, still not satisfied. He could say volumes without using his mouth. All this time Channing thought he was good at that, but he wasn't so sure watching the disapproving look on Jansen's face.

"You want to know what all these people have in common? It's easy, Jansen. Every one of them is a highly trained soldier.

Either active or in their past, they're all proven ratings, very good at their fighting profession."

"What don't you trust me to know, DA Altimer? It can't be what you just told me."

"Look I made a mistake…"

Jefferey rolled his eyes.

"…Okay a few mistakes, Jansen. There, I said it. But you and Volodya have come here and, in less than a day, taken over our legal system like it's your own personal playground. You can't run all over me and expect me to let it happen, can you? If I give you something, you have to give me something," Channing demanded.

"Fair enough, what do you want?" Jeffrey actually approved of the way this was going. Altimer would need some backbone if he was going to be any help.

"Let's start with you explaining why the Can't Lie doesn't work on you."

"Before I do, I request that you deactivate the vid cam in the room."

Channing did one better. He stood up, walked over to the vid cam perched up in the corner behind Jeffrey, and pulled the small camera out of the wall dropping it in front of him. He crushed it under his foot, then sat back down.

"Good, now I'd also like to request that you allow my Lord Bane and Dimitri Volodya in the room so that we can stop wasting any more time."

I wasn't expect—Before Channing could finish the thought, he got an alert through his SC. He listened not understanding at first, then he licked his lips looking overwhelmed. A knock came at the door. He hesitated, not believing he'd been played so effectively. He was more ashamed than anything else when he cleared his throat and bellowed, "Enter!"

Scanning the room, Dimitri Volodya brushed past SA Janput. He cleared the threshold, then looked back, nodding for Jennifer Bane to come in.

Annoyed, Channing sat back, his arms dropping to his sides. How SA Hyatt had not seen Bane and Volodya leave the hospital was just another strike to his ego. He tried to gather himself as Jennifer pushed the door closed, then turned to face him. Jansen stood up pulling out the chair so she could sit down. He stayed close to the table, the chain on his shackle preventing him from backing away. Volodya took up position behind Jennifer to the right. His grey casual trousers outlined his short, thick thighs. He crossed his arms stretching the thin fabric on his black quarter-zip pullover, glaring at Channing like he was a danger to everything he touched.

Channing's eyes darted from Volodya, to Jansen, to Bane and back. Then he folded his hands in front of him on the table. He was beat, and had been beaten so fast, and professionally, he was tired just trying to understand how. Jansen and Volodya had only been released five hours ago.

"Ever since Dimitri channeled the Right Way into my genes, I've had a confidence I'd never known up until then," Jeffrey explained to Channing standing to Jennifer's left, legs touching the table, not able to extend the limit of his chained ankle any further.

"The Right Way is best explained as a feeling of vaunted conviction. I'm now able to concentrate and change my identity—my personal self—in a way that makes me safe against any prying attacks on my mind. I've used this Auto Adapt gene mechanism many times. All the attempts have been peaceful, just like today. Because I wasn't born with the Right Way, I get very tired sometimes, like I did earlier when I fell fast asleep. The Right Way is that peaceful. Dimitri was born with that gene mechanism, and he can control it better than me, so he doesn't have that problem. That's the only way to explain what I did, and how the Can't Lie had no effect on me. My Auto Adapt gene mechanism is something I can do without conscious thought. You see, if I did have to think about it, then it would betray my thoughts. In the positions I have to put myself into on my Lord's behalf, that would be very dangerous to me, and ultimately her. That can't be allowed, Channing. This is the type of trust my Lord Bane tried to explain to you. It's not her fault she's weakened. She thought the very best way to show you that she trusts you, was for her to come here without your knowledge and explain all this in person."

Channing looked at Jennifer, a thin smile edging her lips. He liked the picture. She had changed her hair letting it frame her thin face. When she crossed her petite hands on the table, he noticed she'd put on a smart looking tan-topped blue pantsuit. Looking into her eyes made him realize he'd just have to get past his own perceived ineptitude in order to work with these people. One thing he still didn't understand though.

"If you have the ability to do all this, why is it you need me?"

Jennifer swiveled nodding at Jeffrey.

"You told me earlier, Channing," Jeffrey explained. "You've worked on joint ops with your space commandos."

"Channing, I've left my life as a privateer behind," Jennifer said. "A year ago I may have been able to field a sizable force, but I can't do that now."

Channing didn't look convinced.

"But you have these two Pinaten men on your team, Jennifer, and others too. I mean, in less than half a day, you turned me upside down, playing me like a novice."

"You say you're a novice, Channing. You're only a novice at what *I* do, not at what you do."

"What's that mean?"

"Joint Ops and intel with the help of Basley Space Ops." She leaned forward. "We'll need their help if we're going to find out what this is really about."

Channing saw it now. "You need to use me." He didn't like it, but there it was.

"Channing, no one that's worked with me has ever said I've used them. You'll have to stop underestimating yourself if you want to emerge out the back end of this alive."

The gravity of her statement hit home hard.

Jeffrey leaned forward. "Channing?"

Altimer was still focused on Jennifer and didn't seem to hear him.

"Channing?" He asked louder getting his attention. "What is it that you couldn't trust me to know?"

Channing hesitated not because he didn't want to tell him, but because he was still considering how deep he'd got himself into something that he may not live to resolve.

"I thought if you knew the most important thing, you three would team up like bounty hunters and leave a trail of bodies in your wake to find out if it was true."

"What was true?" Jennifer asked.

"An unidentified company is marketing a resort that allows people to hunt for sport."

"Hunt what for sport, Channing?"

"Other people."

FOUR

"Were you able to get it all binned up?" Sami asked Adrianna, as she came up short stopping in front of her.

Sami nodded.

"Yeah, DA Altimer will receive it by restricted courier within an hour."

Adrianna scanned the interior of the Tight Beam Lounge. She slid down next to Sami on the soft, low couch and a line appeared between her brows. "Jennifer not here yet?"

"Dimitri called me an hour ago. He said they needed to do a counter surveillance route. Jennifer wanted to make certain they weren't followed. He mentioned the meeting with Altimer went well, but Jennifer wasn't convinced Altimer was on board yet."

"All the evidence was in the bin I sent. Hopefully once Altimer gets it back, he will be."

Adrianna's hair was swept back away from her face in a way that accentuated her profile. She was back in her purple dress which she pulled down toward her knee as she crossed her legs getting comfortable.

Tight Beam Lounges were upscale. They were dotted all over Minos City but only found in nicer sections of town. The cost of using a booth to communicate via tight beam was steep. Lounges like these were soft lit, low key, and comfortable. You could rent time on secure comp desks and pay for booth time to tight beam trans off world. Lounges like this were a one-stop-shop for techno needs. The few people in the TBL were seated near the back wall of the lounge near the three booths sipping beverages. They were either waiting to use a booth or just had, it wasn't clear.

Sami and Adrianna sat on a low couch against the right-hand wall waiting. Adrianna had met Sami there earlier to catalogue and copy all the evidence she took from Altimer. Adrianna had just returned after leaving to pack it all up and send it back to him.

Sami was in her light pink blouse and grey skirt after ditching the stolen air car she boosted from the rental car lot earlier. The boost was the diversion Adrianna used to snatch the evidence from Altimer. Sami had found a willing chop shop to sterilize the stolen air car in case they needed access to some transport later. She floated the chop owner a few extra thousand creds to have it ready that evening.

A servo droid sensed a new customer had entered and came rolling over toward Adrianna to offer her a beverage. Just then, Adrianna spotted Dimitri holding the synth glass door open for Jennifer to enter the lounge. She waved the servo droid off impatiently. She and Sami stood up.

Jennifer spotted them, her face softening. She looked tired and strained. You could see it in her shoulders. Despite how fatigued she looked, her eyes still had the twinkle of seeing old friends. Sami and Adrianna met her halfway, both their grins lighting up the entire room. The three of them embraced swinging arms around each other. Both women were shorter than Jennifer even in their spiked heels. They untangled, Sami stepping back placing a hand under Jennifer's forearm guiding her over to their low couch. The three of them sat down.

Dimitri pulled a comfortable looking tufted chair over from an unoccupied table and sat down. He smiled.

"Hi ladies, nice to see you."

Sami smiled. "Hi, Dimitri." She looked him over. "You're looking good. When did you get some fashion sense?" She quipped, referring to his handsome pullover and slacks. Aboard *Viper II* where she and Dimitri worked, he wore boring shipboard greys all the time.

"To do one's best, one must blend. Don't you think?" He eyed Sami. She was an attractive young lady, completely at ease with it.

Sami pushed her hair back behind an ear.

"Agreed. Anyway, it's good to see you. Thanks for looking after her."

Dimitri had to think about what she'd just said as a compliment. Caring for his liege lord was genetic. He couldn't stop if he wanted to. He turned toward Adrianna.

"How are you, Adrianna? Marco treating you well?"

"Always." She smiled. "Marco and Donina have become quite the thing. He's really lightened up ever since she got ahold of him."

This piqued Jennifer's interest. Marco was the oldest friend she had. This was still hard for her to accept. She knew they'd been close, but Marco thrived on deceit. The more covert, the more devious, the more gridlocked it got, the more he succeeded for some reason. He always had since the first days she'd known him.

"You don't think Donina is using her..?" Jennifer trailed off looking at Adrianna.

"Using her telepathy on him? Nah." Adrianna reasoned. "He freakin' adores her, Jennifer. We've developed a name for them now. When you see them you'll know why."

"What name?"

"We call them the Cling-Ons." Adrianna snickered.

Jennifer laughed. Sami hadn't heard that one either; she giggled. "Priceless!"

Dimitri curled his lip. "It's nice to see you three ladies laugh. Feeds my soul, it does."

All three of them swiveled to look at him. A sentimental Dimitri Voldoya they had not seen. Sentimental and Dimitri had never belonged in the same thought. For one, Jennifer was thrilled to see it.

"I can always let down my guard when he's around."

The coil of tension in her shoulders seemed to retreat. She leaned back into the soft couch between Sami and Adrianna crossing her arms. Dimitri shifted to one side letting her prop long, crossed legs on the front edge of his seat.

Jennifer was fading fast. They needed to discuss what Sami and Adrianna had discovered from the evidence, but, Jennifer wasn't up to it. She didn't have to say it. They all knew. They also knew that she was handing off the bulk of the decision making to them. It was clear, so Sami waved the servo droid back over and ordered drinks all around.

After handing them out, she sat back next to Jennifer resting her shoulder against hers feeling her warmth. Sami loved this woman. She owed her a debt she could never repay. Jennifer had simply made both she and Adrianna two of her best friends. She never hinted there was even a debt *to* repay. The two of them were family to her, simple as that.

Jennifer took a few sips of her coffee then rested the tall thermo cup in her lap palming it between both hands.

"Jeff's on his way. It took him a little longer after we finished talking to Altimer. Being released from detention required some comp work."

Adrianna leaned back pushing against Jennifer's other arm.

Jennifer realized this was something she needed. Her heart had been pulled from her chest two weeks ago. The one thing that could soften the hurt was being with friends. She wanted to get started finding Krachy, but she was still too weak.

Recovery from a Grade 3 concussion was unpredictable. No two concussions were alike. Healing could take a few weeks or longer, maybe even months. She had to be on the lookout for chronic problems with her cognitive functions. If she needed it, she was going to get a referral to a neuro rehab specialist that could help. Jennifer had a full discharge packet from the hospital that outlined it all.

"We'll handle it when Jeff gets here, Jen. You relax, okay?" Adrianna let her smile linger for a moment, acknowledging she'd make sure the three of them brought Jeff up to speed when he arrived.

The four of them sipped for a moment in silence. After a minute or two, Dimitri lifted his chin eyes pointed at Jennifer. Sami and Adrianna turned to see her fast asleep. Her head had drifted onto Adrianna's shoulder. She pulled the thermo cup from her hands; Jennifer didn't even stir.

Jeffrey came up next to Dimitri placing a hand on his shoulder. The two women stayed where they were. Dimitri stood up, careful not to bump Jennifer's legs. He followed Jeffrey away from the low couch out of earshot.

"Krachy is being hunted. Is that what you heard Altimer say, Dimitri?"

"That's sure as hell what he was implying."

"What about this marketing lead Altimer mentioned? How do we run that down?"

"What Sami and Adrianna has may help, but I was running that through my mind before I got here. If you wanted to find people that liked to hunt other people for sport, where would you look, Jeff? I mean, where do you find someone that wants to target practice on real, live targets?"

Jeffrey shrugged.

"You start by going where they get ammo to do it in the first place," Dimitri reasoned.

Jeff hadn't even considered that. "A firearm merchant? That's what you're saying?"

"That's exactly what I'm saying."

Jeff wasn't dismissing it; he was just considering its scale.

"There are too many to canvas, Dimitri. How can we do that with just us four? No, it's just going to be three of us. We can't leave Jennifer alone. One of us is going to have to stay with her all the time."

"It's less than you think, Jeff." Dimitri was, and always had been, a soldier. He was still the Boarding Team Commander on *Viper II*. He had been a Pinaten warrior before that. He was certain where to start.

"I know how to start narrowing it down. We pick the five largest dealers in the city. We go right to the source at each one."

"What source?" Jeffrey asked.

"The owner. We strong arm him or her and get the information the old fashioned way." This could be expected from Dimitri; he had a different background than Jeff. His dangerous look confirmed it.

"Maybe you're right." Jeff agreed, his voice even. "What's the downside though? There's always a downside."

"The downside is that unless we leave each subsequent owner dead after we finish asking, they're going to alert the hunt organizer. If someone is organizing a hunt like this, it costs a lot to get in. If that's the case, the merchant owner is getting a piece of it to find clients for them."

Jeff's eyes narrowed a fraction. He felt Dimitri was right. He'd competed against people like this with Jennifer before.

"They will think we only have one move. Something that will work for us. But that's not the only move we have is it?"

"No, it's really two moves by approaching it this way. We may get lucky and find out who's organizing the hunt from the owners. Or, we may force the hunt organizer off his game where they come after us and try to stop us. Either way, we have a chance of flushing them out."

"Did Sami and Adrianna tell you what Ian spent a few days training them on before they came here?"

"No," Dimitri answered.

"Ian trained them in hand-to-hand combat."

"It might be best to let Adrianna and Sami handle the interrogations themselves then. They have two advantages we might not."

"How so?" Jeff asked.

"If the firearm store owners are men, they might be susceptible to attractive females. Or, if that's a dead end, they can strong arm it out of them. Either way, it'll be best to send them in together for safety's sake. Only one of us has to watch their back. I can do it."

Jeffrey nodded. "Can you get the locations of the first few merchants off of a comp desk?"

"Of course."

"It's just past six local time," Jeff continued. "There's a good chance most of these places will be open until eight. Taking into account the 20-hour day, that sounds about right. Adrianna and Sami can hit at least one store tonight. The only issue is picking up a good flechette rifle before then so you can cover them from a distance, perform overwatch. I don't know the local laws. There may be a wait period to get a rifle. I don't want to wait."

Dimitri was silent for a moment. "Neither do I. I may just steal it."

Jeff nodded. "Nice, get the address of a few lower end stores as well then. You can scan their net pages and see what they offer, then go by and pick one up."

"I don't intend to go in and ask for what I want. I intend to sneak up from behind and take what I want."

"What about Altimer? If we leave a trail of bodies in our wake, like he said, he's going to pull out of this, or worse, he might have us tracked down. Either way, it's something to consider."

"Yeah, good point. Maybe this—we let the ladies try to work their way in first. Me stealing one lone flechette rifle is not going to point Altimer in our direction, especially if it's in a part of town that's questionable." Dimitri was hesitant to bring up his next fear.

"What is it?"

"What if they have to follow through with trying to seduce the firearm store owners to get what we want, Jeff? I don't want to order them to do anything like that. It's not who I am. You understand?"

"Dimitri, those two ladies are grown ups. They've seen a lot, been through a lot. I hate saying this, but they were sex slaves. We'll just discuss it with them and lay it all out. Besides, unlike when Sami and Adrianna were trafficked by slavers, they have a choice now."

They both glanced over at Jennifer resting peacefully flanked by two ladies that had nothing but her best interests in mind. They turned to face each other.

"I want to get a nice room tonight, a suite," Jeffrey said. "I don't have to worry about Altimer tracking me now. We promised to give him back his evidence and within an hour he's going to get it. The danger from him is lessened, especially for tonight. I want Jennifer to be comfortable. I'll take the three of them there while you get the information and consider how to get the rifle. I'll lay it all out for Sami and Adrianna while Jennifer is resting."

"Okay, Jeff."

They turned making their way back over to the low couch. Without a word, Jeff signaled to Adrianna and Sami that he intended to pick Jennifer up. They leaned out away from her as he bent over scooping her up into his big arms. Jennifer opened her eyes, saw it was him, then looped an arm around his neck grabbing it with the other hand. She closed her eyes, nestling her head into his neck, letting it happen.

Adrianna hustled around Jeff and Jennifer opening the front door for them. Sami followed them out.

Dimitri turned to a comp desk off to his left sitting down to start his scans. He paid the creds for this desk time then sat up considering his approach. He was rethinking it. He pulled out his burner hand comp to sync some data on it from his net scans. Leaning back in his chair, he took a few drinks of water evaluating his plan again. His plan was flawed.

Dimitri concluded that his background lended itself toward a more "direct" approach. A direct approach was his default setting, but he'd worked on missions with his liege lord before that required him to change his tactics to better serve her. He had done that, and it had worked. A few minutes ago he meant what he said to Sami: To do one's best, one has to blend. This was an urban environment, not ship-to-ship or hand-to-hand combat. Jeffrey's comment about how DA Altimer would react if people died was valid. Jennifer was trying to enlist Altimer's help based on where this mission may take her. If the wrong moves were made, early progress may be jeopardized, which meant the search for Krachy would be jeopardized. As her vassal, Dimitri was sworn to prevent that. It was then that he decided to use his

Auto Adapt ability. Enacting its use was going to be far more effective than the old fashioned approach.

Dimitri pecked a few commands into his burner comp and waited. He lifted it to his ear.

"Jeffrey, I have a change in approach that should work better. Can you ask Sami to come back to the TBL once Jennifer's settled? I'll fill you in more later, but I'm going to need Sami's help for what's next. I may need to take a look at the evidence, too. Anyway, it may not be necessary to do a full frontal assault on this after all. Like you said, we have a choice how to approach this. We also may not have to worry about when the firearm stores close. If what I have in mind looks promising, we can do a lot of it whether the stores are open or not."

Dimitri listened to Jeffrey confirm that he understood and that he would send Sami back shortly. He cut the channel then turned his attention back to the net scans. At the same time, he began to alter his conscious thinking using his Auto Adapt. The work on the comp desk began to sharpen in clarity and slow. His body began adapting to the new goal he'd set out in front of it. This genetic change was smooth for Dimitri. He'd had this ability his whole life calling on it out of necessity. He needed it now, and it ringed his vision focusing it on the very specific task at hand. His research went fast. When he had all the data he needed, he synced it on his burner comp so he'd be able to retrieve it when he left the TBL.

Sami came through the front door having changed clothes. She was wearing a black long-sleeved, tight-fitting sheen mock turtleneck and charcoal grey form-fitting slacks. Her slip on black shoes looked comfortable. Dimitri recognized the black bum bag around her waist. It was Jennifer's. She spotted him and smiled. As she approached, she pushed up her sleeves looking like she might be getting ready for a full night's work. Dimitri smiled back at her, pulling over another chair so she could sit down next to him in front of the comp desk.

"Is Jennifer resting, Sami?"

"Out like a light." Sami's features softened. She looked down then back into his eyes warmly. "I've never spent any time close to her, you know, just being a friend, helping her. I regret that, Dimitri. I can't tell you how much it means to me that she can let down her guard enough to submit to the help we're trying to give her. Right after she rescued me off that pleasure base, she found a way to stop the former Markem Protectorate Tanner Kory. After that, she quit privateering. When I realized how tough all that was on her, I wanted to be there for her. This is my chance. You understand, don't you?"

Dimitri nodded back. "More than anyone, except maybe Jeff. I see she let you use her bum bag. You have the download of all the data from the evidence in there?"

"Yes." She reached around unzipping it. She pulled a hand comp out then hesitated.

"All the evidence data is on here. What's not in soft copy was photographed and catalogued under each person it belonged to. There were five other people abducted. Four off-world, one from Basley. All of them were soldiers at some point in their past. Do you think we should cross check any of this data on the comp desk? Won't it be risky?"

"It would, so we won't. I don't want to leave a trail to follow on a public device. We won't sync it with the desk to avoid detection. Check to make sure the sync mate on your hand comp is turned off before we start."

After a few touches to the screen, Sami nodded. "Yeah, it's off."

"I re-thought my plan after you left. I don't want to risk bringing attention to us. Jennifer is trying to get Altimer to help. If deaths are involved early on, that may jeopardize everything."

"So what do you have in mind then?"

"The car you stole for starters."

She didn't understand.

"We're going to use it as an incentive. I'll explain more in a minute." He glanced at the comp desk then back at her. "I've already synced all the data I need from the desk to my burner hand comp. We don't even need to use the desk. I need your help approaching the people I think can help us the most. The places where they work are still open. We still have over an hour to hit a few of the places to see if we can get the help we need."

"You mean the firearm stores, Dimitri?"

For one second, Sami thought he looked angry, and then he looked pleased.

"Oh no, not there. You and I are going to get the help we need at a much easier place to access. Can you call the chop shop that you dropped off the stolen air car at and see if it's ready to pick up?"

"No need," Sami smiled. "I gave the chop owner a huge tip. He sent me a confirmation on my way back here to meet you. It's ready."

"Nice. Then here's what I need you to do. Stop me if you have a better idea."

Sami leaned closer, looping her arm around Dimitri's chair back to listen.

***

The night was warm. Dimitri turned when he heard the dura steel roll-up door start rising. As it rose, light started filling the dark alley around him from the small warehouse within. Then the lights inside dimmed. The door rattled up until it was three-quarters open. Then the headlights on the black air car snapped on, it's grav gen humming lowly. A young black man was leaning over talking in through the driver's window. He smiled as Sami nudged the shiny vehicle forward, patting the open window seal once before it moved out under the open door. As soon as it was out into the alley, the door was already dropping behind it. Sami turned right stopping in front of Dimitri. He moved toward the driver door already opening back out of the way, so he could slide in behind the controls. Sami scooted over the center console landing in the passenger seat as Dimitri got in closing the auto door.

"The guy wanted to go out for drinks. His treat." Sami shrugged.

"He likes generous customers," Dimitri glanced over at her, "and attractive ones." He smiled pulling the air car out of the alley, making a right into light traffic. Speeding up, he changed lanes.

Sami pulled her arms out of the sleeves of her black shirt one after the other, then slipped her hands into the turtle neck lifting the top of it up over her head. She had on a sports bra, which she pulled one, then the other arm out of, sliding it up over her head. Her hand came out from under the shirt dropping the bra in the floor. She pulled the collar down over her head, reaching back to flip her hair out from under it. She grabbed the hem pulling the turtleneck back into place straitening it out around her back and front. She smoothed it over her small breasts, the sheen thin fabric leaving nothing to the imagination.

"How far?" She asked.

Dimitri glided the air car around another corner. "Two minutes."

Sami pulled down the visor mirror; a soft glow flicked on illuminating her young face. Studying herself in the mirror, she pulled some lip gloss from the bum bag in her lap touching up her lips with the faint red, almost brown gloss. She put it back when she was satisfied, reaching back in for an eye pencil. A few careful swipes later, above and below each eye, and she was done. She was just 25-years-old. Less was more at her age. She didn't need much to make herself pretty. She was already that. After brushing her brown, thick hair back into place, re-defining the part to one side, she saw the lights of the store ahead.

Dimitri pulled into the air car lot finding a space well back from the entrance. He wasn't worried about her going in alone. He hadn't been worried about her going into the chop shop either. The chop owner would have been a fool to try anything with her. She carried the bum bag with her just in case anyway; the LP was still inside. Besides, she'd found the place herself. He didn't even ask how she did. He wasn't sure he could have found a chop shop as fast as she did, but that was part of why she was who she was. Sami fell into any role she needed, changing with her environment. He could tell that she didn't even realize she was doing it—second nature, all about survival, all about confidence.

"I'll come out the back entrance if I score. If not, I'll come out front and call you."

"The chop shop guy made you up a duplicate key fob right?"

The key fob was already in her hand along with her burner hand comp. She raised it up showing she had it and smiled.

"Right here. I'm leaving everything in the floor except the fob and hand comp. Snag it all up for me, okay?"

Dimitri nodded. "As soon as you go in, I'll pull around back. Good luck." He smiled.

She nodded, opening the door stepping out. The auto door shut itself closed while she walked toward the entrance.

Dimitri picked the place for a reason. It was a Tech Bazaar. The large store had everything you could imagine in the way of gadgets, toys, joy devices and the like. He'd ask her to go in because guys usually worked there.

Inside the front synth glass doors, Sami squinted her eyes adjusting to the bright interior of the huge store. It was a bit of an assault on the senses going into an emporium like this. She angled out of the way of the entrance to get her bearings. A scan left to right didn't reveal the department she was looking for, so she turned right then left, heading toward the back of the store.

Atop each haphazardly-sized department were xeon signs telling what was available. Sami passed the Pleasure Droids. There were a bunch of different sizes, colors, and shapes for purchase. Carrying cases were available as well so they could be disassembled and stored in a portable carton. She was looking down the aisle past the droids when one off to her right spoke up.

"I'm the type you're looking for, Miss."

A male droid dressed in blue slacks and a white micro fiber T-shirt outlining its physique took a step toward her.

"If you care to find out, you can try me out in the Fit Me Room over there."

The droid swept his arm in the direction of the far wall where private rooms were located. It's mechanical, yet realistic smile widened.

"Gratis of course, sexy lady."

The key to selling one of these was autonomy. If the droid could lure a customer into the act, that was usually enough. It was programmed to sense heart rate, arousal levels, and moisture. There wasn't even a sales person anywhere in site. Not in this department—no need.

Sami heaved an impatient sigh noticing the rising bulge in its groin.

"Go service yourself, Boner Bot."

She spat, turning her attention back down the aisle. She kept moving, but the droid took her suggestion as a command. It reached down, unzipped its pants, and pulled out its unusually long member. She was cutting left past the Cyber Limbs department as it started stroking its tool where it stood.

She glanced at the displays of Cyber Limbs. They had anything you might want, and pretty cheap. Most of them were "fit over your real limb" versions of common body parts. Putting on a cyber hand, for example, would augment your hand and multiply its strength five fold. All the limbs had neural interfaces. The deeper the neural implant, the better the piloting system that ran the joints.

One man was fitted with a power skin trying it out. Sami could hear the servos in the full body exo-skeletal loader as he picked up a heavy syntha crete block by its handles. He raised the block over his head then held it out in front of him before setting it back down. He almost lost his balance until the exo legs auto bent to prevent him from pitching forward on his face.

A lady was seated at a desk near the isle across from a salesman with what looked like a snap on phallus.

"I'm getting it for my husband," she held it up admiring the length. "He needs a little help to get me peaked." Her grin made it clear that she was probably going to add the auto pilot feature whether her husband wore it or not.

Trying to find the department she wanted reminded Sami of why she hated going into these cavernous warehouse bazaars. The way the aisles were laid out didn't give you the chance to walk in a straight line for long. They made you zig-zag past almost every department to find one thing. Targeted foot traffic in the extreme, all by design, of course.

Another right turn and she spotted the department she was looking for on a bright blue xeon sign tucked back in the left corner of the store. Still being herded by the aisle layout, she passed the Mind Massage department. These "step in and recline" booths were the reverse of a real massage. They relaxed the body from the inside out without touch. Said to be twice as relaxing, they even had the happy ending option you could turn on or off. That worked without touch as well, vibrating the person to climax from within.

Making a left, she spotted what she was looking for next to the Bio Furniture department. The lighting was low where the Bio Couches were displayed. Sani droids were parked next to the couches waiting until they heard the familiar sound of orgasm before rolling over to clean and disinfect. From the sound of the lady trying out the Insertion Option on one of the couches, the droid would be on the move soon.

Sami found what she was looking for. The Holo Simulators were curved pods you could walk into and stand up, sit down, or recline in depending on the 3D fantasy you selected to play out. The Holo Sims were designed to be immersive with texture, feeling, temperature, the works. No one seemed to be using the first one she passed, then she stopped in front of the second pod and two salesmen were trying it out. The curved pod door was open. She could hear the young guy inside giving directions to the Virtu Girl leaning over a pool table lining up a shot with her cue. The other salesman was watching the guy inside, nibbling his lower lip waiting his turn.

The young guy inside was bent at the waist perched over the sexy girl that was wearing nothing but a thong, short skirt and lace bra. He was showing her how to hold the pool table cue.

"Use the closed bridge, it's better for long shots, Sweetie. Slide your index finger over your thumb to create a loop."

The Virtu Girl pouted. "But it's so hard. I can't. You're going to have to hold my hips. I'm on tippy toes now and can't reach over that far."

"It's better to get familiar with the open bridge, at least for beginners like her," Sami said loudly.

Both guys turned seeing Sami for the first time. The guy standing to the left of the pod stopped nibbling his lip, his mouth parting in admiration looking Sami over toe to head, openly staring at her pokies. The other guy took a step closer, more or less doing the same thing, but was a bit more subtle, his eyes finally landing on her face. Neither one could have been 20 years old.

"Though certain bridges work better in certain situations, it's best to be familiar with the most common bridge, the open bridge, first," she stated reasonably, smiling at the two guys in turn. "She's a novice, but I can see where it's probably more fun teaching her the *hard* way." She smiled again emphasizing the word.

Nibble Boy blushed, but Cue Boy leered. "The hard way is more fun. That's the whole point isn't it?"

"Point taken, I mean she's gonna get the point sooner or later isn't she?" Sami nodded.

"Pause program," Cue Boy said, "You want to try helping her?"

"I'd rather let you do it. Do it to me I mean." Sami purred.

Cue Boy gulped. Nibble Boy's eyes darted back and forth between the two of them, unsure if he'd actually heard what she just said.

"That means I can help you. Right?" He couldn't help flicking a glance at her breasts. The light shimmering off the sheen black fabric outlined them nicely.

"Sure, you a manager 'round here? I've got a problem I need help with."

"What can I do to you?" He asked.

Sami smiled, realizing that Cue Boy had just propositioned her. She was used to the effect she had on men. The ones that had forced their way into her life were usually much older, and had paid the slaver in advance for the privilege. She didn't feel threatened by this boy in the least. For one, she hadn't been forced to do anything she didn't want to unlike so much of her past. "Who's the best Techie here? If you're a manager, it's probably not you."

Nibble and Cue Boy exchanged glances, willing to let Sami lead them both around by their ear lobes if she asked. At the same time they both said, "Murphy."

"Can we go see him please?" She asked.

"Sure, follow me." Nibble and Cue Boy had on the same blue trousers, black shoes, and white button-down, short-sleeved shirt. Nibble Boy backed up letting Cue Boy brush past him off to Sami's left. He led her to the corner, behind the Holo Sim department, to the Staff Only door. Nibble Boy followed behind, staring at her swinging butt cheeks.

It was darker in the store room with dura steel shelves in two rows that created floor-to- ceiling hallways. Cue Boy took a right turn down the second hall. At the far end was someone sitting in front of a bank of vid screens typing on a key pad.

Cue Boy came to a stop behind the guy in a hoodie.

"Murphy, you got a minute?"

"Piss up a rope, Stevie, I'm busy," the *girl* said. She turned pulling the hoodie down off her head with both hands seeing Sami standing next to Nibble Boy. Murphy snorted. "Jimmy, I have a vid cam you can capture the moment on. You know, if you want to save the profile of her tits in perpetuity."

Nibble Boy, Jimmy, pulled his eyes off the side of Sami's chest blushing hard.

Murphy wheeled all the way around. She tilted her high back office chair looking up at Sami. "What'd you need, Sweetie? You forget the password on your hand comp?"

"My best friend's fiancé was kidnapped so that people can hunt him for sport. I want to find out who did it and kill every last one of the fuckers, and get him back."

"Cool." Murphy grinned.

"I have a few leads. Think you could work your magic and point me in the right direction?"

"You can't afford me."

Sami tossed the key fob to Murphy. She caught it.

"Your newly sterilized black two-door air car is parked out back. I had its ID erased today. The transponder is fresh."

Murphy considered her offer.

"Mind if I run the ID to verify it's clean before I take it?"

"Certainly."

Sami pulled up the scan code for the vehicle on her hand comp. She had synced it earlier before the chop shop erased the transponder. She handed the comp to Murphy. The young woman grabbed it, then placed it on a sync pad. She pecked a few dozen key strokes humming a tune, every so often mumbling *yeah, ah ha, yep*, to herself. She wheeled back around when she was done.

"The leads you have on your comp?"

Glad Murphy seemed satisfied with the payment, Sami smiled.

"Thanks. Can you start with a company named Approach Logic?"

Murphy was about Sami's age. The body art on the back of her hands ran up under the long-sleeved hoodie. The collar of her black T-shirt was loose; more art crept up the back of her neck past it and the hoodie. Her hair was jet black, short on the sides in a buzz cut, longer on top, falling to one side down over her right eye. Sami wondered how she even moved her fingers with two, even three rings, on each one. But her hands moving across the key pad were a blur. After less than a minute, she pointed up to a vid screen on her right.

"You already have something?" Jimmy asked.

"Did you have a mouth fart, Jimmy?" Murphy asked, not turning around.

Jimmy turned back into Nibble Boy, chewing on his lower lip again.

"I found two disbursements from that company's bank to two different people in Minos."

"Can you tell me where they work please?" Sami asked.

"One owns a firearms store called Fire Right and the other one owns Tremble's. Tremble's is a gun shop, too. I'll sync the details to your comp, home addresses, dates, blah blah…" Murphy's hands glided quickly.

"The way Approach Logic is masking their ID is crafty." Murphy turned around looking serious. "If your friend's squeeze was kidnapped, both these firearm store owners got paid the same amount for services rendered. Doesn't look like enough to me to snatch someone. No way, each payment was only 21,000 creds. That amount is not enough to risk the thriving business both these folks are running. Yearly cred flow for each store exceeds 12 million. Tax returns show take home for both owners over 2.9 mil a piece."

Sami wasn't surprised this woman had gotten that far that fast. Nibble Boy was shifting his weight from one foot to the other. He wanted to ask more but held it back. Stevie was getting up the nerve to ask Sami what she was doing later; she could feel it. However, it seemed clear neither of them were going to interrupt Murphy until she was done.

Murphy turned back to her key pad working it hard.

Sami thought of something else. Before she could ask, Murphy spoke up.

"Nope, no more disbursements to either of these people or their businesses from Approach Logic. Just the one time each. However, I can tell you that Approach Logic has only had their bank account active for seven months. I can't find a history of that company having an account with any other bank further back than that."

"Five other people have been abducted," Sami explained.

Murphy spun around waiting.

Sami nodded.

"When was the first person taken?" Murphy asked.

"I only got the data this afternoon. I haven't checked yet…" Sami dipped her head at her hand comp.

It took Murphy less than 10-seconds to pull the data off it. She wheeled back around looking up at Sami.

"First woman was snatched six months, three weeks ago." Then it hit her. "This is a startup. They've only been in business for seven months." Her look turned thoughtful. "Here's my take: The 21k is for a client lead, not for grabbing the prey. Approach Logic is paying the owner of firearm stores to generate client leads. The company must contact them directly, you know, face-to-face, to pitch the hunt idea to the client." She thought of something else pushing herself back around to her key pad.

"Yep, yep, ah ha, oh yeah," she mumbled to herself. Then, "Oh, hell yes!" She turned around smiling. "I would have missed it, but nope, I didn't."

Sami was smart enough to wait. She'd been around all kinds of people, in dozens of places scattered throughout known space and some not known. Being taken by slavers had exposed her to it all. Murphy was unique; she operated on her own wavelength, that was clear. It was also clear she was pleased with herself. Maybe overly so, but there you have it. Geniuses showed emotion the way they wanted to. Murphy's grin lit up the dark warehouse.

"Two days after each commission was paid, a rep from Approach Logic cleared customs after breaking orbit."

Sami looked coy. "The person from Approach Logic came dirt-side to meet their prospective client face-to-face."

"Fuckin' A they did."

"Got a name for me, Mistress Wonder of the Key Pad, Murphy?" Sami smiled.

"Bonisabella Brigham, Lady That Giveth Air Cars to Hackers Extraordinaire," Murphy snickered.

FIVE

Dimitri knew Sami was still excited with what she'd found out inside the Tech Bazaar when she reached over and grabbed his hand. They were seated in the back of an air cab heading toward Minos Space Port on the other side of the city. He'd called for an air cab while he was waiting for her at the back entrance. He figured he could cancel it if she didn't score any information and hop back behind the controls of the stolen air car to pick her up out front, but when she came bounding out the back door of the Bazaar with a huge grin on her face, he knew she'd hit pay dirt. They jumped in the air cab not discussing anything in front of the cabbie.

He shot a smile at her and she squeezed his hand harder smiling back. It felt good. Dimitri dreaded the thought of Sami having to sacrifice her body trying to extract the info they needed from one of the firearm store owners as he'd originally planned. Almost as bad would have been explaining to his liege lord what he'd ask her to do. It was bad enough that he asked her to show off her body to do what she'd just done. But anything, *anything*, that brought dishonor to his liege lord was unacceptable.

As if reading his mind, Sami slid closer to him snugging up beside him, latching her arm around his then interlocking her fingers in his right hand. She sighed leaning into him.

Dimitri looked at her.

"I can't stand the thought of you doing anything you don't want to do."

Sami looked back. Her look was noticeably long, definitely frank.

"For years before I was saved by Jennifer from the slavers, I'd developed the habit of…shutting down my feelings. I've had to look into the eyes of people that treated me so badly; the only way to get past it was to stop feeling anything." She searched his face, finding what she was looking for. "Dimitri, I don't see any of my past in your eyes. I only see truth."

Neither of them spoke. The air cab made several turns finally decelerating down the off ramp to Minos Space Port. The hour was past 9 pm local time. All of the rental air car lots in the city were closed. That was one of the reasons why they'd come out to the space port. The space port was open 20/8. It never closed. It'd be easy to get some transport for what they had to do next. Also, some of the main concourse stores were open, too. This would aid their plan as well.

The two of them got out of the air cab in front of the first launch gate. The night was still warm, a light breeze pulling the day's heat away from the ceramacrete sidewalk leading into the well lit terminal.

"I got what we needed," Sami said as soon as they faced one another on the curb. "Approach Logic is paying firearm store owners for client leads. They float them 21,000 creds then a person named Bonisabella Brigham comes dirt-side to meet with the perspective clients face-to-face. I've got the names and addresses of the two store owners that got their commissions right here." She grinned, holding up her hand comp.

He nodded. "Thank you for doing that, Sami."

Her look turned determined, almost pleading. "No, thank you. Thank you for letting me get us this far." She meant it. The urgency to help Jennifer was pushing her hard.

Dimitri understood all too well. He rummaged in Jennifer's bum bag for a few seconds pushing around the few things Sami had ask him to bring along. He pulled his hand comp out fingering the screen confirming his reservation and transferring the payment creds. He looked at her when he was done.

"I rented us an air car." He glanced back down at the comp screen. "It's in space K 7, behind launch pad one."

"We have a few things to pick up first, right?" Sami was anxious to keep things moving. Dimitri liked that he didn't have to remind her. Besides, they had covered how the whole night might play out when they were back at the Tight Beam Lounge together.

"Right, the shops we need should be out in the main concourse. I'll get my clothes, plus the hardware items if I can find them. You get your—"

The air around them moved, out away, then a coughing vortex pushed at their backs. A rocket was being launched from pad one. Even though the rocket was on the other side of the terminal building, they could feel the engine thrust rumble up through the soles of their feet. The sound came less than a second later. No use trying to talk over the blast wave, so they made their way in through the auto doors into the terminal. People getting ready to leave the terminal off to their left waited until the rocket rumble started to fade before they exited.

Sami and Dimitri turned left heading into the connecting tunnel toward the main concourse. Dimitri reached in the bum bag again pulling out her sports bra handing it to her as they walked. She bunched it in a fist, and said, "—Yeah, I'll get the clothes I need and meet you back next to pad one comp in."

Once they got to the two-story concourse, they split up going in different directions. The synth glass ceiling was curved. Dimitri looked up seeing the rocket from pad one arching away from the space port into the night sky, the bright engine thrust fading with every second.

The shops on the second floor were closed at night, but the ones lining either side of the long, narrow first floor concourse were open. People were heading in different directions to catch a launch. Though the foot traffic was light, all the stores had their auto doors retracted welcoming in the occasional shopper.

Dimitri found the clothes he needed, but the hardware items were harder to find. He finally ducked into a sex shop where he found what he needed. All done, he made his way back to pad one where Sami was already waiting.

She turned falling in beside him as he passed her. They both carried a few plasti shopping bags. Dimitri had thrown Jennifer's bum bag in on top of the stuff from the sex shop. A few minutes later, they were in their rental air car gliding away from the space port accelerating up the ramp that'd take them to the first address.

Sami's face lit up in the dark interior when she fingered her hand comp out of sleep mode. She input the first address but muted the auto voice on the map reader so they wouldn't be interrupted. She studied the screen.

"There's a park a few blocks from his house. We can probably park there and change into the clothes," she reasoned.

"Okay. How far to the exit?"

"About 7 miles; I'll watch for it."

"You remember how we agreed to play this?" Dimitri asked her, flicking a look her way.

"I do. Bad home invader and badder home invader. You're playing the heavy. I put the fear in them, you seal it. Right?"

He nodded.

"This is only going to work fast if we isolate their kids first. I don't want them seeing what we do to their parents, but they have to be able to get to them eventually."

They made it to the park two blocks from the owner of Tremble's firearm store. Dimitri cut the grav gen stopping on a side street next to the small park. It was a nice neighborhood, the modern homes well kept and sizable. With no light inside the air car, they could prepare.

Sami reached into the large shopping bag feeling for her sports bra. Not waisting any time, she simply pulled her shirt all the way off. She shimmied the bra down over her head and shoulders pulling both arms through. She grabbed the bottom of it, lifting it down over her bare breasts, smoothing it out. Her shirt went back on next; then she pulled a black, lightweight waist-length jacket from the same bag. She felt around finding the tag, then pulled it off. She put it on, then reached into the smaller bag, pulling out a black stretch beanie. Off came the tag. She'd bought an extra large. She needed the length so that when she put it on it would come down past her chin. She slipped it on, reaching up to her left eye, pinching the fabric with two fingers. She pulled it back off, holding it by the pinch, then looked over at Dimitri. He handed her a small set of scissors he'd pulled out from a manicure set he'd purchased earlier. She cut an eye hole then repéated the procedure on the right eye. She tried it out. It worked well enough for her to see with it on. She pulled it back off, waiting.

Dimitri had pulled out the bag from the sex shop. He couldn't find any duct tape at any of the concourse stores, so he bought the only tape he could find. He'd already pulled the rolls of black Fetish Fantasy Pleasure Tape out of their wrappers. It would have to do. He felt one roll with his fingers gauging how tacky it was. Not very, but if he wrapped the tape around again and again a bunch of times it would do the trick. He bought four rolls just to be sure. While Sami was getting ready, he'd already pulled the tag off his own black jacket and slipped it on. He stuffed the pockets with the items he'd need.

Sami looked over at him handing him an extra large beanie she'd bought for him too. Dimitri went through the same steps she did to cut out the eye holes. Finally, he pulled out two pairs of black gloves handing the smaller ones to her, tag already gone. She tried them on, good to go. He slipped his pair on and was ready. They didn't have the beanies on yet.

They looked at each other.

"We go in the back, or in the master bed door, if there is one," Dimitri instructed.

"There's going to be an alarm. But it's going to be silent. If not, we abort. A blaring siren kills the surprise. We find the master suite and get what we came for, then out the way we came in. Or, you just follow me if I think another exit is better. Security won't be able to respond as fast as I intend to get what we came for."

He could see her nod.

"You do your part fast. And Sami…" He hesitated.

"What Dimitri?"

"Don't be shocked by what I say or do. I'm doing it for a reason…I would never hurt their children."

He could see her nod in understanding.

"Keep up with me on the way back here. If security does get here fast, the route I take will be circuitous."

"Understood. Let's do it," she said.

They walked the two blocks to the house pausing when Dimitri thought they needed to. Dean Tremble actually had one of the smaller houses on the block. It was one level with a modest sized yard. No air cars were parked in the drive on the right. A walkway led down the left side. The front was lit up with yard lights projected up its facade. The street was quiet. It was almost 10 midnight in a working class neighborhood. People were asleep. Unfortunately, Dean Tremble wasn't one of them.

"He or his wife are still up," Dimitri observed, stopping across the street, scanning the front windows. He could see lights were on in two front windows.

"Or, maybe it's his kids. Follow me."

He pulled on his beanie; she followed suit. They crouched and rushed across the street, Dimitri leading the way down the walkway on the left side of the house. He paused at the side door and looked in. The kitchen beyond was dark. He decided this might just work in their favor. The security system probably hadn't been set since they were awake.

He reached in his jacket pulling out Jennifer's laser pistol. Speed, not subtlety, was next. He was about to fire through the window so he could break it, then reach in and pass his hand over the scan pad next to the door to open it, when he felt something. A puma kitty rubbed up against his leg purring. He looked down as it continued to circle and purr. There was a kitty door it could use. Dimitri bent down petting the kitty a few times, then reached in through the little door trying to wrap his arm up to pass it by the scan pad—no use. His arm wasn't long enough. When he tried to extract his arm from the swinging little door, the fabric on his jacket got caught in the closing door. He pushed the kitty door further open with his free hand so he could pull his arm out. Once he did, he grabbed the kitty, stood up, and handed it to Sami.

"When I say, shove the little guy through."

Sami nodded. The kitty's little tractor engine was even louder in her arms.

Dimitri bent back down and flipped the selector on the laser pistol to NL. In Non-Lethal mode, the laser beam was a quarter of it's full strength. He bent on one knee looking inside the kitchen through the open kitty door he had propped open with his fingers. He thumbed the laser site reticle painting the far side of the kitchen looking for the right angle. Sami figured out what he was trying to do. She leaned closer to the window looking in. Once Dimitri saw what might work, he tried it.

"No, too far right, try again," she whispered.

He'd painted the side of the coffee maker on the other side of the kitchen trying to bounce the site beam off it back to the scan pad next to the door. He picked out a round, shiny cabinet knob above the coffee maker.

"Too high," she breathed, as she peered in through the window.

There were several pans hanging over the small island in the center of the room. He tried the first pan, no joy. He painted the second one with the site beam, and bingo, it hit the scan pad.

"You got it, Dimitri. Hold it steady…" She bent down and waited. He locked eyes with her and whispered.

"On three—one, two, three." He aimed, fired, and she shoved the kitty noisily through the open kitty door.

At the same time, the *Zint* from the laser pistol tinged off the hanging frying pan, ricochetting back hitting the scan pad. The door started moving aside; Sami grabbed it slowing it down. The puma kitty turned in front of the opening door waiting for a leg to rub. The two of them eased inside and waited, listening. Sami pulled the pocket door closed quietly. No stirring in the house, Dimitri looked down at the puma cat and mouthed, "Nice job, Tygre." The little diversionary sound of the swinging kitty door seemed to have worked.

On his way past the puma, Dimitri reached down stroking the kitty once, then crept out of the kitchen toward the front room. As soon as he cleared the kitchen threshold, he saw the back of a man's head sitting on a couch watching the large vid screen that hung between the two front windows. The room was lit up by a few overhead cans splashing light down on either side of the vid screen to prevent glare. He pivoted, brushing past Sami back through the kitchen. The puma kitty just stood in front of its feeding bowl near the back door watching them. *On down the quiet hall to the door at the end. Should be the master.* Dimitri turned, Sami nodded.

Silent but fast, Dimitri pushed the door aside, Sami following him in, pushing the pocket door closed behind her. Dimitri stopped at the foot of the bed looking at the woman sleeping under a light sheet. Sami brushed past his back making her way down the left side of the bed stopping next to the woman's head. When she looked over at Dimitri, he was holding a roll of the black pleasure tape signaling that he was going to toss it to her, which he did. She caught it, pulled the lead out about 12 inches, then glanced back at him waiting.

He mounted the bed in a blur straddling the woman's chest already pulling both of her wrists together. Sami shoved her hand down over the woman's mouth hard as her eyes shot open in surprise. She wrapped tape over her mouth lifting her head encircling her mouth 10 times. Dimitri wrapped tape around her wrists fast and efficient, encircling at least 20 times. Dean Tremble's wife wasn't going anywhere. After a mere 10 seconds of binding her, Dimitri scooted down onto her feet with all his weight.

Sami then brought the fear. She bent down, the two haphazard shaped cuts in the beanie eye-slits inches from the woman's face.

"When you're abducted by slavers, they start by taming you like this."

She turned her head. As she did, the terrified woman's eyes followed hers down to Dimitri who had moved toward the foot of the bed. He grabbed the woman's ankles with his powerful hands spreading her legs. She tried to resist, but that was the whole point. She couldn't. It made for an immediate and terrifying realization of how vulnerable she was. Sami reached over to the laser pistol tucked in his belt pulling it out and looping it up under the woman's nightgown pointing directly at her privates.

Sami's voice was a low growl, more like a painful breath of something evil from her past.

"I'm not going to do that to you."

The woman's eyes rolled back, and she shook her head, guessing what was coming next. She was so scared she was forgetting to breathe.

Dimitri yanked her by the ankles down the bed toward him. She slid easily until the barrel of the laser pistol Sami held impacted the tender skin between her legs hard. She gasped and started to cry.

Sami reached behind the woman's head jerking it up so she'd look at Dimitri.

"This is what we are going to do to both of your children this evening. If they're alive after, *then* they go to the slavers," Dimitri threatened.

The look of panic on the woman's face hurt Sami's heart, but this was the only way. She reminded herself that they'd not hurt the woman yet. It was just the flood of painful memories that made Sami so upset. She didn't even know where she had summoned the evil voice she'd used to scare Tremble's wife. The voice was buried in a part of her she thought she had locked the cage on forever.

"Talk to your husband. Convince him this isn't what you want," Dimitri growled. He let go, but quickly wrapped her ankles in 15 loops of the tape. The woman went limp, already exhausted with fear. He rushed back out of the room—

—The instant he did, Sami heard a muffled *Zint* out in the hallway that was higher pitch than Dimitri's shot earlier. A laser spark ripped through the open bedroom door zipping past Sami's head impacting the synth glass window behind her breaking it.

A muffled thud, a softer *Zint*, and what sounded like a brief struggle, then silence.

Dean Tremble frog marched in through the bedroom door, his right arm held high up behind his back by Dimitri.

"This man owns a lot of firearms," Dimitri said. Tremble and Dimitri came to a halt, with Tremble trying to keep his balance on tippy toes with his arm being jammed up between his shoulder blades painfully.

Dimitri's black, threatening hood looked at Sami.

"Go take care of the kids; they've worn out their welcome thanks to their father here."

Sami disappeared out past Tremble and Dimitri almost before he finished his sentence.

The mother convulsed on the bed trying to scream. Dean Tremble looked over helplessly at her. The voice Tremble heard in his ear was one that spoke finality, ultimatum.

This is the end, and the end is mine to decide and mine alone.

"Name and address of the referral you gave Bonisabella Brigham for the 21k you got paid for the client lead to the hunting resort. You tell me and your kids don't go to the slavers tonight. You don't tell me, well, let your wife explain."

Dimitri wrenched Tremble's arm up higher, tears started to leak out of his eyes from the pain. His wife heard and stopped struggling. She was able to bend at the waist and sit up in the bed. If Tremble saw the desperate pleading that ejected from the back of his wife's terrified eyes, he would know he was beat. He shifted his eyes choosing not to look at her.

When the answer didn't come, Dimitri waited. He hated what was going to happen next, but his inner chrono had just hit 50 seconds. Any second now—

—And there it was. It was the shattered shrill of a young girl screaming from down the hall. Dean Tremble deflated, the vibrato of defying a home invasion a silly thing of the past now.

He gulped.

"I referred John Paul Sark to Bonisabella Brigham. He lives out near the Shavertooth WA. Not sure of his exact address because I only spoke to him a few times when he was in the store. I can get it. Don't hurt my kids; I took the payoff, your argument is with me." He said it as manly as he could given the circumstances.

One last question.

"How's the lead qualified?" Dimitri lessened his grip on Tremble's arm but not enough for him to think he had a chance to break free.

Tremble let out a painful cough, gasped in a lungful of air, then licked his lips.

"Firearm sales on a host of planets and space stations are tracked. Only when a buyer returns for the twentieth time to purchase ammunition do they qualify as a lead. At that point, the person comes to Brigham's attention. She applies certain criteria to discover if they fall into the category of an Ideal Customer Profile which includes things like net worth. If they pass the ICP criteria, they would then be cleared for direct marketing. That's done by me, at the store where the ammunition was sold. I approach the buyer about the hunting resort idea when the buyer returns to purchase ammunition the 21st time. In this case, John

Paul Sark. I get the 21,000 creds whether the client accepts a face-to-face meeting with Approach Logic or not."

Tremble's eyes kept flicking back and forth at his wife as he said all this. He could see her terror was steadily being replaced by anger at what she was hearing.

Dimitri pistol whipped him, not hard, and off to the side of the shoulder over Tremble's clavicle, just hard enough to get him on his knees. Tremble grunted, falling to both knees, careful not to make any moves that would initiate a harder smack. He knew it was an attention getter, nothing much more.

Dimitri poked the barrel into the back of Tremble's neck, hard, several times.

"Hands straight up over your head."

He did what he was told, and in no time Dimitri had wrapped his outstretched wrists in a cocoon of black fetish tape. He started on another roll using half of it too. Dimitri kneed him forward, Tremble crashing onto his chest, all the air in his lungs rushing out in a low grunt. Dimitri did the same to Tremble's ankles, and was well into the third roll of pleasure tape, before he was done.

Dimitri looked at the wife's enraged stare fringed with a mothers's terror for the safety of her children and said, "Have your husband explain why this was necessary. I'm the one trying to save lives. Dean's recruiting hunters to take them on a resort that kills people for sport. Don't let him talk his way out of this one. He knows exactly what he was paid the 21k for. Disgust is not even strong enough a word—maybe *slavers* is. If something like this happens again, if Dean refers another client to Approach Logic…just think how easy it was for me to be here Mrs. Tremble. I'll take it a step further with Dean if he calls security forces in on this. He'll be the one bound by law. I have access to cyber skills he could only dream of. Consider that when your family is alive and back together. Is revenge against the humiliation and fear I caused tonight worth slavers in your children's lives and prison time for your immoral husband?"

Dimitri turned on a heel finding Sami standing in the hall waiting for him. He strode past, turned through the kitchen, her right behind him. Out the kitchen door, across the street, they jogged without incident back to their air car.

Safe inside breathing heavy, he fired up the grav gen nudging the air car around a few corners back toward the city. He picked up speed; only then did they pull off their beanies.

Sami ran her hands through her hair. She was sweating.

"Tremble tell you what we needed?"

Dimitri nodded.

"Yes, he would have been crazy not to take our threats for real."

Sami was silent. He could tell she had conflicting feelings about hurting one of their children. He let it go. The damage was done, but so was the reward. It could have gone a lot differently, especially with Tremble trying to blow a hole in him with a laser pistol.

This time Dimitri reached over into Sami's lap resting his warm hand over hers. He squeezed it. She glanced at him heaving a sigh that seemed to release years of hurt she was tired of carrying.

"I have it in me to do the things that were done to me by the slavers. I hate that I do, but I remember every time I was tortured. I could've had that young girl stand on one foot doing circles trying to stop me from hurting her any more."

Her shoulders sagged. Dimitri spotted an all night Quick Mart and pulled in far enough back from the entrance to be alone while they talked. He powered down the grav gen coming to a stop.

He pulled his hand away and waited. Sami's chest rose and fell for a few moments. Her head lifted. She stared out the front window expressionless. One thing Dimitri had learned growing up was that if you didn't know what to say, it was best not to say anything. Opening your mouth in a warrior caste society could get you into deep trouble—fast. She'd start getting past it when she did. He was patient.

Dimitri looked her over and realized that she'd developed a way that worked for her and was using it now. The only way Sami knew how to put the terrible things she'd experienced behind her was to leave them where they were. Unfortunately, he had made her bring them along into Dean Tremble's home.

Dimitri rubbed his temples. "I'm sorry I had you do that to one of the kids. I just couldn't think of another way to get the information we needed so fast. I couldn't be in two places at once—in Dean's bedroom and in the kids' room." He realized he was rationalizing and it made him feel small, small and effete. *And yes*, he thought to himself in that moment, *I'm getting sentimental with this woman. I know I care, but do I care this much? I sure must*, he concluded. And he did.

Her expression was so neutral Dimitri felt she had to be controlling it.

"And you, Dimitri? What do you do?"

He didn't know what to say again.

"What do you do when you want to get past the bad things that've happened to you?" She asked gently. "I can see how much you care. Care for Jennifer or me, I don't think you can separate the two."

She was wrong. He was very glad that she was. He'd been rapped in the mind directing comfort of his Auto Adapt ability since before Sami even came to meet him at the Tight Beam Lounge. The Auto Adapt was a guiding presence that had been focusing his attention on what they had been doing all night. He had no need to control it. It led him without conscious thought. It was so peaceful, he knew that was the reason that he was so maudlin. But that was genetics, his genetics. He had to go covert to accomplish what they did in such a short period of time. That was how his Auto Adapt always supported him. The gene mechanism bracketed his goal so that he didn't deviate from it. It never clouded his true self though—never.

"I can separate the two, Sami." He said after a few moments.

"I can, too. I mean, I want to help Jennifer because I love her. But…" When she hesitated, he imagined she was going to figure it out very soon. It was right there, that was why she felt he couldn't separate himself from his Lord. If she did pin it down, she would be one of the few people he'd known that had.

Dimitri waited, raising his eyebrows, "But what, Sami?"

She looked back at him with an odd combination of admiration and attraction.

"You're obligated to be faithful to your Lord. But you can feel anything you want and still be loyal." She smiled. *Like*, he thought, *she did know*. Then, "You're not using me. You could have asked Adrianna to help you tonight. You wanted to be with me so that we would succeed together. You're falling in love with me, aren't you, Dimitri?"

He was a man, and his man's heart skipped two beats. His warm smile confirmed it all, almost. "No, I'm not."

Sami looked shattered, but just for an instant until he said, "No I'm not falling in love with you, I *am* in love with you." He sat back in his seat still looking into her eyes. "I have been for quite some time now, Sami."

Her grin looked like it hurt her jaws. Then she said, "You'd never let us do anything that would dishonor Jennifer or ourselves, would you, love?"

"Right now, the two children you kept separate from their parents are untying the tape we bound them with. They're hugging each other so hard I'll bet it hurts. Dean Tremble has learned a lesson that only took a few bruises and a strained shoulder to learn. You and I just stopped a man that was capable of sending more hunters out to kill. Is that the definition of honor? You tell me…?" He smiled.

She looked back at him, her checks flushed, figuring out even more of it, not understanding why she'd not seen it earlier.

"This is always the motivation behind what Jennifer and her crew have done isn't it?"

He had to be honest, "Not always, but certainly now, the past few years, definitely. And to answer your question earlier, I fall back upon my privilege to honor and serve such a worthy liege lord. That's how I get past the bad things that have happened to me. Jennifer's motivations have changed a lot in the past three years, Sami. You didn't do anything dishonorable tonight. That girl you traumatized is young. She'll heal, get past it. Ask yourself this: What would her life be like if her father was in prison? Worst still, that he was in prison, and she understood why. What would be dishonorable would be if we subjected that young girl you hurt to that."

Sami blinked.

"Yes, you have the ability to do the things to others that were done to you by slavers. That's part of who you are. But using them with discretion, and without joy, proves your motivation. I know you may not be able to see it, but missions like this seem to always start the same way. You offered to help with something that will end up uncovering bad people, Sami. I speak from experience when I say I've seen it go that way more times than not."

"I didn't realize all this, Dimitri. I was blinded by my urge to help someone that saved my future the way Jennifer did when she rescued me from the slavers."

She took in a breath deciding something.

"But I see it now. I also see that you'll look out for me." She leaned over the console watching Dimitri, her eyes focusing on his, then dropping momentarily to his lips, and moving back to his eyes again.

He leaned closer, their faces inches apart. He could smell a hint of her breath, definitely a sexy, womanly smell from the jog back to the air car earlier. He inched his head further and kissed her. She accepted the kiss, embracing it.

After a moment she drew back and looked at him.

"A few minutes ago I hated myself for being who I was."

He shook his head. "That wasn't you. That was your past." He blinked. "Sorry, I'm not interested in her."

"You really think you'd be interested in what's in front of her?"

He looked at her face, back into her eyes.

"I've liked what I've seen every day I've known you. You can't be that modest." He looked down her open coat at her chest with something like hunger.

"Modest about what?"

"About how much you're going to enjoy me *looking out for you*."

She grinned, then leaned forward and kissed him. The kiss was better this time, more passion, and a familiarity that surprised her.

They settled back in their seats, the hum of the grav gen urging the air car out of the lot, turning right toward the city. She glanced back over at him. Dimitri was smiling. Sami leaned back looking out the front window smiling too.

***

Sami and Dimitri made their way back through the city to the hotel. The hotel was in a good section of Minos, only about two blocks from the TBL they'd used earlier that evening. After parking their air car in the sub lot, they caught a lift tube up to eight, where Jeffrey had gotten a suite.

Dimitri came up to the door of the room, rapping lightly, waiting. He and Sami were tired. She leaned against him her left arm interlocked with his. The door moved aside, Adrianna smiling a welcome as they both entered.

Jeffrey was standing with an elbow resting on the kitchenette counter. He said hello as Sami flopped down on the low couch in the middle of the room. Two couches faced each other situated perpendicular to the closed curtains on the far window. Dimitri took a right turn behind the couch to find a bathroom. Adrianna was in black leggings, black socks, and a loose fitting grey night shirt. She hopped up on the couch next to Sami, pulling her legs underneath herself.

"Busy night?" She asked.

"Productive," Sami countered. She leaned forward pulling off the black jacket laying it beside her on the couch. This was the living area, with a bathroom and bedroom on both sides left and right.

"How's Jennifer?"

Just then Jeffrey handed her a synth glass tumbler of ice water. She took it gulping down half the glass.

"She's been resting since we got here. She's in that room." Adrianna pointed in front of her toward the leftmost room.

Jeffrey walked over to the other couch and sat down facing them both. They all waited, hearing Dimitri finish up in the bathroom. He came out and Jeffrey nodded to the synth tumbler of water he'd sat down on the coffee table. Dimitri said thanks and grabbed it sitting down next to Jeff. He drank most of the water then looked at Jeffrey.

"Jennifer okay?"

"She's fine, sleeping hard. I got some food in the kitchen if she wakes up hungry. I figure we can let the two ladies have the other room, and you and I take a couch," Jeffrey said.

"About tonight," Dimitri looked over at Sami while he took off his jacket and placed Jennifer's bum bag on the coffee table. "Sami can fill you in."

"The indirect approach worked well," Sami said. "We started at Brazzy's Bazaar. I gave their best hacker the stolen air car I boosted earlier today to tell us about how this hunt takes shape and about how client leads are generated." Sami explained everything Murphy told her and who they went to see next. She looked at Dimitri.

"We visited the owner of Tremble's," Dimitri continued. He explained the details of their home invasion, wrapping it up by telling them how the leads are generated and placing special emphasis on the potential scale of the off-world operation.

Jeffrey wasn't surprised. Adrianna too seemed resigned that this was going to be much more than just trying to find Krachy and get him back alive. When they were finished discussing the possibilities and scale of what they might be facing, they all agreed that sleep was needed. Jeffrey and Dimitri would watch after Jennifer and let Adrianna and Sami rest in their room.

When Sami and Adrianna had gone back into their bedroom, Jeffrey looked at Dimitri.

"We meet DA Altimer at 8 am. That'll give us time to have breakfast and plan how to handle him. He's going to be floored at how much we've uncovered already. Do you think Tremble is going to, or already has, called in security forces?"

"That's the real question isn't it, Jeff? I guess we won't know until we first see Altimer's face tomorrow. I will tell you that the fear of reprisals we put in him, his wife, and their children should give him definite pause. We didn't leave them damaged—just humiliated. My take is that Tremble will be so busy trying to square what he's done with his wife, he won't want to add an investigation on top of it. Besides, if his misdeeds are uncovered, it could risk his business and even prison time."

"You realize at the very least Tremble's going to contact this Bonisabella Brigham from Approach Logic and tell her what happened tonight," Jeff smiled cruelly.

"Oh yeah," Dimitri shot him a similar look back, "I'm counting on it."

"I think that's the entry point for Altimer, don't you?"

"I do. Altimer's the one with off-world pull. Let's see if he really is serious about using it on this."

"Given that you and Sami did two weeks worth of investigative work in one evening…"

"Sami was good. For just jumping into something like this, she got past some deep fears to play the roles I ask her to. I was impressed."

"I told you she and Adrianna were grown ups. They have street smarts you and I don't."

"Sami has something else too, Jeff."

Jeff rose an eye brow.

"She's got this," Dimitri patted his chest a few times with his closed fist, "It all came out tonight, but I've been hoping it would for a long time."

Jeffrey smiled patting Dimitri's shoulder a few times.

"You know, that might be the best medicine Jennifer could ever get."

"I hope so—no that's not fair. Jennifer's going to be thrilled with it. She only wants the best for me. This is as good as it gets, don't you think?"

"I do, Vassal Volodya, I do," Jeff agreed.

SIX

It was important to keep Detective Agent Channing Altimer somewhat off balance. Altimer still may not realize what he had gotten himself into. Until he did, he was a liability. After Dimitri and Sami invaded Tremble's home, it was certain that things were going to escalate not because Tremble was going to call in Minos Security; things were going to escalate because the people that ran the hunting resort had been notified. Jennifer's team had to assume that now. Jennifer was filled in on everything that happened during the home invasion over breakfast in the hotel cafe. Her five member team got an early start and still had over 45 minutes until they had to meet Altimer.

To change things up, Dimitri and Jennifer would meet with Channing Altimer. Jeffrey, Sami, and Adrianna would run cover. It had to be done that way to have overlapping eyes. All of them agreed that they were now vulnerable to assassination. Dimitri had concluded that if a human hunt was being organized then the price to buy into that hunt was high. If the buy-in price was as high as they'd discussed, that meant the people that ran it had a lot to lose if it was shut down. That was why assassination was a real concern.

Dimitri and Jennifer set up down the street from the Tight Beam Lounge they'd used the day before. The TBL wasn't a nexus for a hit team to pinpoint their location yet. Tomorrow it would be, but not today. When they'd been there last evening, Dean Tremble had not been approached. Now that Tremble had been approached, any place Jennifer's team visited more than once was a choke point. It was now going to be too dangerous to use the same hotel again or the same meeting place again all because Tremble was now in play, so to speak.

After leaving the hotel cafe, Jennifer and Dimitri ran a thorough counter surveillance route to the TBL. They changed air cabs twice, walked through the lobbies of three buildings leaving through different exits than they entered, and retraced their route for 10 minutes just to be sure. There was only one problem: between the five on Jennifer's team, they only had one weapon.

The decision was made that Dimitri would carry. The laser pistol was not a long distance weapon. If a threat to Jennifer was close, then it would be useful. Any long distance danger would have to be identified by Adrianna, Jeffrey, or Sami. All five of them called into a group conference call on their burner hand comps. They all slipped an ear bud into one ear so that they could talk to each other real time and alert each other if something was wrong. It wasn't a foolproof plan, but it was reasonably solid, as solid as they could make it given the lead time to prepare.

Jennifer was taller than Dimitri, so she saw Channing Altimer enter the TBL from a doorway a half block down the street from the entrance. Foot traffic was fairly heavy; people were just getting to work in the city. It was a few minutes before 8 am. The plan was to let him wait to see if Altimer had been followed.

"Nothing so far," Sami sounded off in Jennifer's ear. She was watching the Tight Beam Lounge rear exit. "Looks clear around back."

"I'm around the corner from Sami watching the approach to TBL opposite Jennifer. All clear here," Adrianna confirmed.

"I'm stationed directly across the street from the entrance. All clear here," Jeffrey chimed in.

Dimitri stood beside Jennifer scanning the street. After 15 minutes, Jennifer reached over tapping Dimitri on the arm. They waited for a break in the air car traffic, then jogged across the street. They turned left walking at the same pace as everyone else until they were in front of the TBL. They entered not overly worried that someone had set up early inside. Adrianna had left breakfast just after 6 am. She scouted the TBL alone while Jen, Dimitri, Jeff, and Sami ate. Adrianna had breakfast at the TBL instead. No one came in and stayed that set off her internal alarm while she was eating. She left once Jennifer and Dimitri had taken up position down the block from the entrance. Then Adrianna hurried to her vantage point around the corner from where Sami was watching the rear exit, again not foolproof, but decent.

As soon as Jennifer stepped inside the lounge, Dimitri's thunderous voice behind her yelled, "Down!"

All things considered, Dimitri thought that falling to the floor scrambling for cover with Jennifer was a bad idea. With laser bolts cracking off the windows behind them, it seemed essential at the time. The woman assassin had a clear shot at them, and there was nothing they could do but get low and scurry behind a passing servo droid and pray that a well placed bolt didn't find them first.

Dimitri thought the stalled droid ought to offer some protection, but he saw the woman move to take aim again. The droid stopped because it sensed a customer.

Or maybe it was fate.

Whatever, he rose up sprinting for what seemed to be the closest cover—and not nearly close enough—so he could draw her fire. Momentarily confused, the woman standing at the back of the room in front of the entrance to the kitchen glanced at Dimitri's legs pumping hard. The distraction gave Jennifer a split second to pull herself up behind the waist-high droid making herself as small as possible.

When Dimitri tried to put the brakes on, things got worse and momentum pitched him forward over a low couch on his face. Or maybe that wasn't so bad; he wasn't shot yet.

In retrospect, it hadn't been a fall as much as it had been a dive. After flying eight or nine feet in a free falling arc over the couch, Dimitri landed on his belly, hands outstretched to catch himself against the ankles of a shocked Detective Agent Channing Altimer sitting at a table. A white hot bolt of energy zipped past Altimer's nose; Dimtiri looked up at him and yelled, "Morning, Channing, please return FIRE!"

The woman read Dimitri's mind, or probably heard him bark, and side stepped a few paces to get a better shot. Channing was too slow pulling his pistol out, but Dimitri didn't really care. He couldn't get his LP out fast enough either. So he did the only thing he could think of. He exploded up pushing hard with his legs slamming his back into the round table above him. Dimitri twisted at the waist grabbing the flying dura steel table when it came loose from the round pedestal anchored to the floor. The impact hurt like hell thumping it off his upper back, but he managed to deflect two cracks of energy with it as he peered over his temporary shield as the woman took dead aim at his face.

Knowing how bad it was going to hurt, Dimitri let gravity do its thing. He reached out, grabbed a fist full of Alitmer's shirt as he fell backward, pulling Channing down with him. Still gripping the table in one hand, he smacked the hard floor head first.

Jennifer burst from cover, triggering a *Zint* in her direction. Her opponent dropped to one knee, squeezing off a hot bolt of death that missed because she dove behind a low couch slamming her shoulder into it grunting loud. It was only a matter of time now.

Dimitri was unconscious, and Jennifer was in no position to offer resistance when the woman came around the side of the couch to finish the job. She thought of Krachy, and *how nice it would have been to be his wife.*

Then, finally, a high pitched *Zint* off to her right sounded. One shot was all it took from DA Altimer. The bolt caught the woman in the side of the head, just below her jawline, almost taking it off before she fell.

Jennifer took a moment to discover she was still alive, and then she picked out Channing crouched on one knee on the far side of the lounge, his laser pistol gripped in both hands.

Oh no, what happened to my vassal? was all her panicked mind could process. She jumped up and ran toward Dimitri's inert body. Channing glanced down at Dimitri, but didn't try to help him; he instead stood up and walked slowly toward the assassin's body never taking his aim or eyes off her as he did.

Jennifer weaved around several tables, knelt down, and searched Dimitri's face for signs of life. He was breathing. The relief she felt caused her to miss what happened next. She never saw the second gunner, a man, aiming at her back from the entrance of the lounge. She did see Channing out of the corner of her eye turn fast, his eyes shooting open in surprise.

For some reason the pain of an energy bolt never came. Jennifer wheeled around, plopping down on her backside to see Jeffrey Jansen standing over the hard case lying on the floor in front of him. Jeffrey had just saved Jennifer's life.

***

Only pain told Dimitri he was still alive, and at the moment his head hurt everywhere. Despite the ringing in his ears and sounds of muffled voices in close proximity, he could hear Jennifer say, "Welcome back."

She was leaning over his hospital bed smiling down into his eyes. Jennifer knew enough to keep the room dim. She was pretty used to what made a concussion worse.

"Feel like shit, don't you?"

"Hmm…" Was all Dimitri could manage, closing his eyes hoping the pain would ebb.

Jennifer stood up, glancing at the door to the ICU room. Channing Altimer was waving her and Sami out into the hall. Sami stepped closer, touched Dimitri's arm squeezing it, before following Jennifer out of the room.

Channing jerked his head toward the waiting room. The two women followed him out the auto doors, making a right. Jeffrey was planted in the hallway, his back to them. He was taking first watch not giving another set up team the chance to finish their work.

Adrianna was looking out the window of the Surgical Trauma Intensive Care Unit waiting room watching an air ambulance set down on the air pad bringing in what must be another person that needed care. She turned seeing Jennifer, Channing and Sami enter the room. The four of them made their way to the closest table pulling out chairs and taking a seat.

Channing scanned the three women's faces.

"The assassin was a cook at the TBL. Just started this morning."

"That's why I missed her." Adrianna's voice was husky, blaming herself.

"How could the assassin have applied, interviewed, and got on shift so fast, Channing?" Jennifer asked tightly. "How did she even know who I was?"

"Isn't it clear, Jennifer?" Channing let out a breath, sitting back in his chair shaking his head.

"Isn't what clear, Channing? Don't turn yourself back into the puzzling, confusing, ass you have a tendency be, all right! Dimitri just saved both our lives back there!"

Jennifer's head started to pound between her ears. Getting angry was a real bad idea, but she couldn't help it. When her temper started to rise, she knew it was hit or miss if she could control how high, especially now, given her current condition.

"The assassin applied online, while you were there last night, Jennifer. As soon as all of you left, she was interviewed by the owner. They let her start this morning."

Jennifer shot a look at Sami then Adrianna. That meant, "Krachy wasn't the target, I was." This made Jennifer feel so bad, she started to shake. Sami stood up and moved beside her leaning down next to her wrapping an arm around her shoulder.

Channing felt terrible. He was slow. He had not listened to Jennifer, to all of them. He had not taken things seriously when he was openly warned. There was nothing he could say that proved he was able to do anything constructive. He looked at Adrianna. She squinted her eyes, coaxing him to try.

"Jennifer, I'm sorry. I am. You were right, this is just starting."

"Channing?" Adrianna grabbed his arm while he was looking at Jennifer. He turned.

"What?"

"We thought the TBL might be a choke point, just not today. Part of this was our fault. We went back to the same damn place as last night. Dimitri didn't even have time to pull out his LP. All our recon work didn't mean anything." Adrianna shook her head.

"So why didn't they take Jennifer out before? They had to have been tailing her for days. At least since she left the hospital," Channing reasoned.

Jennifer pulled her head off Sami's side. Channing looked at her.

"Because, Dean Tremble was the trigger. They set up in a known choke point but didn't act until Tremble contacted Brigham. We started to get close, so they figured that I wasn't so valuable after all. I'm only one person to hunt, not worth the price of their entire operation being discovered. These people have a lot of resources. Hell, I'm afraid to leave Dimitri with the nurses in the STICU tonight." She sat up straight, looking up a thanks to Sami. Sami stepped back releasing her.

Channing believed it all now. How couldn't he?

"But if you were the target all along, why take Krachy in the first place?"

"It was a mistake, Channing."

Jennifer's look was fierce, the drive to get the people behind all of this strengthening her and her resolve.

"Taking Krachy instead of me was a mistake that cost the lady that slammed the air car into my head her life. The air car driver probably checked and thought I was dead on the top of that mountain. Or, didn't check and assumed wrong. She kidnapped Krachy to cover her ass. For her, it didn't rate with Brigham. Brigham had her killed anyway."

Channing heaved a sigh.

"I should have known that hit teams always travel in pairs."

"You?" Jennifer asked, upset she didn't know better either.

Just then Jeffrey came through the entrance off to Jennifer's left. He stopped short of the table.

"My Lord, we can't stay here any longer. They tried once; they know Dimitri is here being treated. We have to go."

Jennifer's look was desperate. She wanted to stay so bad it hurt.

Jeffrey saw it in her face. "Adrianna can stay to look out for Dimitri."

Not hiding what Jeffrey was doing, he reached behind his back under his quarter zip pullover, grabbing the laser pistol out of his belt. He handed it to Adrianna.

Channing's eyes widened a bit, but looked resigned to let it go.

"Okay, Jeff," Jennifer said, "I'm just going to duck back in and check on Dimitri once more."

Jeff nodded, reaching down under her arm, hurrying her along. They left the room. Channing turned to Adrianna.

"I'll have hospital security put a man on Dimitri's room. That way you'll have at least one backup."

Adrianna nodded standing up. She slipped the pistol in her waistband as she left the room. Sami sat down in Jennifer's chair.

"That leaves you and me to run down the next thing on the list, Channing."

The look in her eyes was chiseled dura steel. Sami had a lot of things taken from her in the past, her dignity and virtue among them. She thought she now knew how Jennifer felt. Moments after Krachy proposed, he was taken from her. The next day after Dimitri told her that he loved her, he was almost killed. This was where it ended. Channing didn't know what he was seeing in Sami's face. It could have been a part of her she never let anyone see. All he knew is that it worried him.

"John Paul Sark, right?"

"Brigham's going to know that's where we're headed next, Channing. You know we're chasing the tail on this dog now, don't you?"

"I know. What do you suggest we do about it?"

"Cut the fucker off!" Sami spat. Something in her changed it seemed. The determination behind her young face didn't look young anymore. It looked like a woman that had taken despair and beaten it back into submission.

Channing didn't understand. He was out of his depth the more this thing moved along. He hated that he was, but he was over matched. Jennifer's team over matched him, and Brigham's team overmatched them all. Or did it? Then there was the huge question on his mind that he knew Jennifer didn't have the energy to say out loud. *Was Krachy even alive after all this?* The only saving grace had to be Krachy's soldiering past. He was at least as experienced a commando as Jennifer, therefore worthy to hunt.

"He's alive, Altimer," Sami stood up. "If you start giving up," she leaned down breathing into Channing's face, "I'll kill you myself." What he saw in her dark brown eyes was reptilian.

"You signed on to this thing. We go all the way."

Her muscles were so taught they rippled under her sheen black shirt. *Where did these people come from?* He thought to himself. *What had been done to them to make them like this?*

"I'm no leader here, Sami. Me trying to think ahead of these people might get all of us killed." He flicked a skittish look at the entrance to the waiting room like he expected a hit team to step through it at any second.

Sami straightened still drilling him with a stare.

"That's the edge you need. Let's go, I'll explain on the way."

***

"We're not going to use the one at your office." Sami looked over at Channing as he pulled his air car into traffic leaving the hospital.

He glanced at her then decided not to ask why.

She exhaled patiently. If Channing was going to be a part of the rest of this, she needed to tell him.

"Let me ask you this, Channing. Do you trust every person that's in your building at Security HQ?" She pulled her hand comp out fingering the screen.

"I don't know every person in the building at HQ."

"That's kinda my point. If Brigham's people can track Jennifer down, how easy would it be to know you're assigned to Krachy's case? How easy would it be for them to get someone in the building to stop you from finding out who they are?" She glanced up from her comp.

"The place we're headed to is near Central Plaza." She looked over at him. "You know where that is, right?"

"I do." He nodded, making a turn at the next stop crossing.

"So at this point, you're saying that I shouldn't even go home tonight."

Sami smiled. It was a nice smile, not the dark leer he'd been the recipient of 10 minutes earlier in the STICU waiting room.

"Not to belabor things, but yes, you mustn't go home tonight or any night until this is over." Her look turned gentle.

"You have family that may need to…" She trailed off, not wanting to pry, but it had to be discussed.

He shook his head. "Not married…"

"Do you have someone in Basley Space Ops that you trust? Someone you're comfortable contacting for help?"

They were at a stop crossing. Channing turned to face her, studying her face, searching for the drive behind it, the reason why she was putting so much on the line to get the results she wanted. Sami was young, at least eight or nine years younger than him, maybe more. He was 34.

"Before we go there, can I ask you something?" He looked both ways, making a left then nudging the air car higher in his lane to slot two. Slot two was more like a high occupancy level air cars could use if there was two or more people in the vehicle, less traffic than closer to the ground, slot one.

Sami had been expecting this. She knew how to read men, especially ones older than her

"Sure, go ahead."

"How do I phrase it, Sami?"

She knew what he meant.

"If you're going to trust me, Channing. If you're going to trust any of us, you want to know motivations. You want to know why I went so far as to threaten you."

Channing kept his eyes on the slot, not looking over at her. He wasn't so sure he wanted to see her eyes. All the people he'd met that Jennifer surrounded herself with had a large capacity for, how could he put it? *Extreme measures* was the only way to accurately sum it up. It bothered a person like him because he was sworn to prevent people from getting to that point. That was a default part of his job, even a default part of who he was. Channing had killed a person today. Another was dead from a blow to the head delivered by Jeffrey Jansen. Jennifer's team moved past it like it was a strong wind they had to brace themselves against until it passed so they could go on their way. It wasn't common. He decided he didn't know how to phrase his question. *What do you ask someone you know nothing about?*

They were in the Central Plaza part of Minos City now, a nice area, with a different Tight Beam Lounge than the one they'd been at that morning when the assassination attempt took place. Sami wanted to make an off world trans. She could wait for Channing's question; there was some time.

"You see it up on the right?"

"Yes."

"Can you pull past the TBL and find an underground air car lot within a block or two to park?"

"Yeah."

He slowed, waiting for a break in slot one below him. Once a gap opened, he dove down, gliding back into slot one passing the TBL, making a right turn. On the left ahead was a sub lot. He waited for a break in oncoming traffic then banked the air car in, dropping down into the underground lot finding a parking slot. He pulled in and cut the grav gen.

The quiet in the air car was only punctuated by both of them breathing. Then Sami turned to him. The dim light in the underground lot seemed foreboding to Channing for some reason. The look on Sami's face did as well. He thought carefully about what to ask her and how to do it. He decided that he must.

"Why would you kill me for not helping Jennifer?"

Sami considered his face, almost like she was studying it to see if he deserved to know.

"Jennifer didn't even know who I was. Just like you don't. But she risked more than just her life to save my worth as a human being."

Channing breathed in, holding it for a moment. He let out his breath, drawing down his brows, blinking. *What was this?* Maybe it was what he sensed about Jennifer before.

Sami's features softened, like what she said was as much a very fond memory as it was a reward, a favor that was given to her to allow her to live clean.

"You can't understand unless you've been me, been there. I'm no murderer, Channing. I don't want to hurt you. I don't want to hurt anybody." She tilted her head to one side then back.

"I only want to do the right thing. I've had so many wrong things done to me; I only want to pay what Jennifer did for me forward for the rest of my life. I feel that has to be why I'm helping her."

From open hostility to calm resolve, this woman was strung very taut. It was not going to be wise to say anything about Sami's past. He knew that much. Just like Jeffery Jansen had reminded him, Jennifer too: He hadn't been there, hadn't seen what they had. That was fine with him though. He didn't want to be.

"You don't have to watch your back around me, Channing. If you can't see it by now, the only ones that need to do that are the people that took Krachy. Plus any idiot that gets in the way." She smiled mirthlessly.

Despite himself, Channing returned her look. The confidence that this mess could be conquered with such few people, and limited firepower *was* inspiring. Sami must believe it. It was anchored in everything she did and said. Channing was finally beginning to stop doubting himself, to stop underestimating that this could be solved like any problem he'd solved before, just using a more deliberate approach than he was used to. It could even be interesting, if that was even allowable to think. The intensity of these people around him made for intense drama at the very least. *Oh no*, he reasoned to himself, *I'm starting to think like them.*

"We good?" Sami quipped.

How Sami could bounce back from wherever her memories had just been made her the person she was. Channing couldn't help but try to catch up.

"We are good. Let me scout the TBL before you go in. I can throw my emblem around and check the staff. It can't hurt to look a few of them in the face after what happened earlier at the other one. Agreed?"

"Agreed. Here," Sami fingered her hand comp then looked back at him. "Turn on your sync mate; I'll give you my burner number so you can call me."

Channing pulled his comp out of his pocket. A few touches later it pinged signaling her contact file was received. He thumbed the auto door and got out walking fast around a corner and up the ramp out of the sub lot.

The door closed, and Sami let out a ragged breath. She held up a hand to find it shaking. She snapped it closed into a fist setting it down in her lap. Anytime she skirted the horrific boundaries of her past, no matter what the setting, she felt like this. Thinking about Dimitri lying in the hospital only made it more severe. *Not to worry though,* she thought. *I'm not alone in this. Not even by a long margin, I'm not alone in this.* Sami smiled and waited for Channing's call.

The call took longer than she thought it might, but that seemed good. *Channing must be using caution. Not a bad idea, now that both Dean Tremble and John Paul Sark, whoever he is, are in play.* She held the hand comp to her ear telling Channing she'd be there in a minute.

Inside the TBL, Channing waved when Sami entered. He was standing in front of the booths. This TBL was much smaller than the one earlier. Only two booths were on the right wall; six or seven small tables with chairs in the center of the room were not occupied. On the left wall there were four comp desks, two people huddled around one screen sharing it. Auto vend machines on the back wall substituted for servo droids passing out food and drink. She weaved past the tables dipping her head at the closest booth. The tight beam trans booth was big enough for them both to enter, the hatch swooshing shut behind them. They were almost shoulder to shoulder as the auto lights illuminated. An auto bench on the left bulkhead extruded, extending itself in front of the closed hatch behind them, locking into place on the other bulkhead to their right. They both sat down, Sami already holding up her hand comp to the scan pad to the right of the vid screen so that her creds for a tight beam trans could be deducted. The ID number for her trans was imbedded in her payment. After a minute or so, the vid screen crackled to life, the auto lights inside the booth dimming.

A tan woman with very black hair was staring back at them. The corners of the woman's mouth rose, slight wrinkles in the corner of each eye creased, revealing a person that spent a great deal of time working on that tan.

"Hi Sami, hello Detective Agent," the woman said. Then more concerned, "Is Dimitri okay?" When the woman asked that, her dark brown eyes locked on Sami.

"Concussion," Sami smiled, "No bolt holes in his body, thank God." Channing could tell the relief in Sami's reply signaled there was more to her feelings than just a person on her team avoiding serious injury. He glanced sideways at her; she was almost beaming with delight to tell this woman that.

"I've mobilized a remote team to help. It's only me here on SV's ship. I have information for you." Sami knew what the acronym SV stood for. The woman was using it not to reveal the identity of the person it referred to.

"Jennifer and Jeffrey left the hospital for a location I don't even know." Sami filled her in. "Best to do it that way; what happened this morning was nearly a disaster. Adrianna is watching out for Dimitri while he rests."

The woman turned to Channing.

"DA Altimer, my name is Donina Draper. Thank you for what you did this morning. I'm sure if there'd been another way, you would have used it." She smiled thinly.

Channing fought the urge to be confused. He was getting with the program now; the people Jennifer Bane had at her disposal were multifaceted. How this woman knew his name and what took place earlier wasn't clear. To his knowledge, Sami had never left Dimitri's side to contact Donina, or anyone else for that matter.

"Nice to meet you, Donina," he offered instead.

Donina looked at Sami. "You may want to record this."

Sami reached in her lap, fingering her hand comp's sync mate. She nodded for Donina to go ahead.

"John Paul Sark was reachable up until late morning your time. After that he wasn't. It was clear Sark was traveling to something called a *Gather*. He didn't define it to himself. He was just excited he was a part of it again. Even more so that he didn't have to pay to travel to it this time. Sami, this man is part of his second Gather. He has taken part in what you're trying to stop more than once."

"A Gather," Sami's eyes narrowed.

"Yes, it had a number. It was Gather 14. My team went over this matching it with the length of time this person Bonisabella Brigham has been using her bank account to pay for leads. We think a Gather is the name Brigham gives to assembling the kidnapped prey group they intend to hunt."

"They've run this hunt 14 times?" Channing had to ask.

Sami looked at him.

"Brigham has been paying the owner of firearm stores 21,000 creds for referrals to her hunting resort. She travels dirtside once the lead is qualified and meets the perspective client face-to-face. She's been doing this for seven months now, Channing." She looked back at Donina.

"My team thinks that each Gather takes approximately two weeks, maybe more, maybe less," Donina explained. "That's why we matched the timeline of seven months with the payoffs. Seven months, about two Gathers a month, that's T months mind you. Not the 32 days Basley takes to complete a month due to your eight-day-week." Terran time—T time—had been first established on old Earth as a baseline for a seven-day week. Time had been calculated in that way since the first colonists took to the stars.

Channing turned from Donina and stared at Sami, "You found all this out in a day?"

Sami didn't want to rehash everything for him. Channing had not used the techniques she and Dimitri had. His indecisiveness was apparent when Dimitri almost died at the TBL during the assassination attempt earlier. All she did was nod.

"The most important thing we found out, however, was what Sark kept bragging to himself about," Donina continued. "Sark was really full of himself, so pleased with himself that because of what he knew, he'd be back again and again to the hunting resort to hunt more people. His cockiness about how foolproof it was, and how happy he was that it was offered, made me sick to my stomach, Sami." Donina's look turned dark, and not because her face was so tan.

"Tell me," Sami said.

"This hunting resort offers a *Guarantee*. Sark was all around it, rolling it back and forth in his mind, even laughing to himself while he traveled first class on a private shuttle to the resort. The only thing Sark didn't do was define it. My team couldn't pull the definition of it from his thoughts."

Then it hit Channing. Everything Jennifer said about telepathy was true! What Donina just said was the only explanation. He pursed his lips having the good sense to just listen.

"Donina, Brigham has local muscle. There is no way that she could have deployed a team from off-planet to get to Jennifer as fast as she did. Dimitri and I just spoke with Dean Tremble 10 hours ago."

"That's right, Sami. Brigham has local resources, but we've not been able to pitch into any other person's mind that's dirt-side setting up to try to assassinate Jennifer again. Jeff and Channing must have taken out the only two resources Brigham had. My team can't pitch unlimitedly, you know that. But as of now, what we know is that the two assassins that were killed in the TBL earlier were the lone assassins she had. My team's telepathy is not foolproof. You understand that, right?"

"I do," Sami said. "I know you'd have already told me if you knew where Brigham's hunting resort is, where Sark is headed."

Both women looked at Channing at the same time. He saw it happen, then realized they were waiting. He thought he knew what for.

"Sark's shuttle had to clear orb control after he lifted off," Channing said, knowing that might be one way to track him.

They waited, much like telling him, *Hey, we got us this far this fast, start being useful or we'll do it without you.* But Channing did have a very clear idea what to do. In fact, he'd already got it started.

"I contacted my guy in Basley Space Ops after I left the TBL this morning. I asked him to be ready for a tight beam from me today. I have his ID; is it okay if I bring him online with us?" He reached for his hand comp snapping a glance at both women in turn.

Sami nodded and Donina answered, "Please do."

Channing held his hand comp in front of the scan pad. The screen split in two. After about 30 seconds, the grey static on the left side of the screen was replaced by a man sitting at a desk pulling a sandwich from his mouth, chomping hard. The man reached back from the screen, having just hit the accept button for the tight beam.

"Hey, Channing, who's the pretty lady?" He managed around his mouthful.

Rand Fullrider was a husky middle-aged man with bushy brown eyebrows, playful eyes, and a round, friendly face. His temples were grey, the rest of his greying brown hair ran up under a blue ball cap with BSO slanted in orange letters above the bill. Fullrider continued to munch away waiting.

"Rand this is Sami. She brought in Donina on this, too. I'm going to pipe Donina's feed in now."

"Hello Rand, I'm Donina." Rand was on the left, Donina on the right on the three-way tight beam now.

"Hi, Donina and Sami, Channing told me—" Rand took a swig out of the cup in front of him, clearing his throat. "—that he'd be calling today. What's going on that you need Space Ops' help?" He took another bite of his sandwich, fingering some stray lettuce into the side of his mouth.

"Rand, we have an off-world resort that's kidnapping people so they can be hunted for sport," Channing said without preamble.

Rand froze as he was pulling the cup to his lips for another drink. He set the cup down slowly. It seemed this man had seen it all because while he looked somewhat surprised, his look started to turn angry. He waited chewing slower now.

"It's all been confirmed in the last day. Sami and Donina here are neck deep in this. Two assassins tried to kill their friend, Jennifer Bane, who had been targeted for abduction to act as prey. Her fiancé, Krachy Bantor, has already been kidnapped. A hit team missed Jennifer this morning; I shot one of the hard cases and the other was killed by Jennifer's bodyguard. We don't think they have more hitters lined up to try again, but this has escalated to the point now that an interagency force is required. We think a man named Sark departed on a shuttle today headed to the hunting resort."

Sami watched as Channing finished laying it out, and for the first time she was impressed.

"I see." Rand finished swallowing his mouthful. He was quick on the uptake. "You need help finding the resort."

"We do," Channing confirmed.

"I know where to start," Rand said, setting down his sandwich, rubbing his hands together several times before grabbing a napkin and using it. "Is this a public or private shuttle that this man Sark used?" He asked.

"Private, possibly chartered. This client is wealthy," Donina pointed out.

"That'll narrow it down. There can't be that many private shuttles leaving orbit today. Understand, the private shuttles are just that. They aren't required to say who's on board. As long as the shuttle clears orb control, they can go on their way."

Rand looked down like he thought of something else that might help.

"There's an off chance Sark's shuttle refueled in high orbit. The smaller shuttles like the one this guy is on only have enough fuel to launch from the surface, push through the gravity well, and insert into orbit. They need to refuel at one of the orbital equipment stations to have enough juice to get to their final destination."

He hesitated looking at the screen thinking to himself.

"Sometimes they meet up with a bigger ship if the destination is out of their range to transfer the passengers over for the rest of the trip. Hmmm…" Rand said to himself.

"What is it, Rand?" Channing asked.

"The orbital equipment stations are independently owned and operated. As long as they play by the rules, I can't board and search without Tribunal approval."

Rand was a man that didn't like the word, "No." He was forming a workaround. They could all see it. Actually, Sami already had formed a workaround. She was not going to be slowed down by something as trivial as proper procedure.

"I know people on all three of the equipment stations. I can do some informal inquiries to see if they want to help me out. It's a start, but maybe another approach will work better." Rand's round face brightened, a grin edging his lips.

"Basley Space Ops man defense pickets. The defense pickets cover the most common approach vectors to the planet and monitor all traffic coming and going. The pickets pull transponder IDs on all of the spaceships. I'm going to start there. I have control over the defense pickets and what they can tell me. If I have to fall back, or confirm a lead with any of the equipment stations, I will." He looked off screen then back, "Can you give me 90 minutes to find out more, Channing? I should have something by then."

"Can you get the shuttle's transponder ID from orb control so you know which one to look for?" Channing asked.

"Yeah, I think so. Like I said, can't be that many. I'll feed what I find to the defense pickets and see if any of the IDs match. From what you're telling me though, this is a highly secretive and illegal operation. I wouldn't be surprised if a transponder refresh is part of their standard operating procedure once the shuttle leaves orbit. The 'ponder ID only has to match a registered ship—any ship. There are so many ships coming, going, active, inactive, it's difficult to track them from origin to destination. Besides, once they get past the defense pickets, space gets vast. Basley Space Ops guard the frontier and do it well.

A small shuttle is not an imposing threat, per se. You feel me, Channing?" Rand's eyes opened wider.

Channing smiled. He'd known Rand a long time and worked with him many times. He had confidence in him. Regardless how far Rand got, having him and his resources on this would be a huge boost.

"I feel ya, Rand. You're a good man. I know you'll do your best."

Sami was surprised by the familiarity which he and Rand spoke. It was welcome though, and could only help.

"Rand, I have a few leads I'll run down here with Channing's help. Let's give it at least two hours before we get back with you, okay?" Sami proposed.

Rand smiled, "Sure thing, pretty lady. Two hours, Rand out." He cut his feed, Donina still online.

"Donina, you okay with two hours?" Sami asked.

Donina shook her head, "Sorry, Sami, It's after 3 am ship time here. I need some rack time. I've already put in a pretty full day."

"I understand. I'll try to check back with you after you get some rest."

"Nice meeting you, Channing," Donina smiled at him. She looked at Sami, the smile fading, her look turning serious. "I don't have to tell you to watch yourself, right?"

"Oh no, Donina. Thank you very much for all your help. Tell your team we appreciate it." Sami's look turned playful, "And tell your Cling-On, Hi."

Donina smiled, then cut her feed.

Outside the TBL clouds had moved in bringing rain. Sami didn't have the black jacket she'd picked up the night before. As a matter of fact, she didn't have any luggage with her that she'd brought dirt-side. She'd left her other two outfits behind in the hotel suite this morning. She ask Channing to circle the block a few times after he got his air car and pick her up near a boutique she'd spotted across the street from the TBL. She didn't run through the rain. It felt good on her body. So much time in space made little things like rain welcome.

Inside the boutique, she picked out a pair of straight leg, dark brown slacks, a matching belt, and a brown knit long sleeve top. The boutique didn't have any bras, so Sami stuck with her sports version. She left her old clothes in the dressing room. She added another light black, nylon zip jacket, and she was good to go. The jacket had a hoodie insert you could zip into its interior. She flipped the hood over her head as the rain starting coming down harder. Channing pulled up to the curb seeing her leave the boutique.

It was just coming up on 1 pm in the afternoon. Inside the air car, Sami felt she was right on time. She reflected for a moment on how exhilarating it was to know that Jennifer needed her help, and gave her the freedom to search for the answers she needed without questioning her. This was how she'd been treated by Jennifer and her whole crew from the moment they first rescued her from the slavers.

Channing looked over at Sami and she was smiling.

"What gives?" He asked, seeing it.

For the first time Channing had been around Sami, she actually blushed.

"Nothing," she cleared her throat, grabbing her hand comp fingering the screen.

Channing let it go. Sami was in her own thoughts; it beat the hell out of threats. Not to mention, she was an attractive young lady. It didn't suck to work with her.

"I sensed you had another idea when Rand was talking earlier," he prodded.

"I do," she held the hand comp up for him to see. "Can you take us here?"

"I can, but you know that's not the best part of town, right?"

"Sure I do. I know someone there that's not going to mind seeing me again." Sami looked out the front window. "Make a right in two blocks."

The trip was quick, less than 10 minutes. Channing pulled down the alley to the chop shop Sami had used the day before. The rain was sheeting down sideways now.

"Pull up in front of the door," she instructed him.

Channing eased the air car over to the far side across the alley from the roll-up door in front of the chop shop and stopped.

"I'll be in there for a few minutes; it shouldn't take long."

"You gonna share?" He asked.

"I need some more *incentive*. Trust me." Sami grinned and got out pulling up her hoodie as the auto door closed behind her.

Channing watched her walk up to the sound door and bang on it several times. He noticed a small vid cam perched up high on the right side of the roll-up door. To confirm what he thought, Sami pulled the hoodie off her head, looking up towards the vid cam. The rain pelted her brown hair soaking it. On queue, the roll-up door starting rising. She didn't pull her hood back up; instead she lifted her head and let the rain pour down on her upturned face. When the door was chest high, she ducked under it and disappeared into the dark garage. Channing couldn't see what was inside. The door started back down too fast.

Not five minutes later, the roll-up door started rising again. Sami was standing beside a young black man talking to him as she used a white towel to dry her hair. It looked like the two of them were long-lost friends. The guy was smiling and pointing to the back of her head. The young man reached up and grabbed the towel; Sami turned her back to him, and he used the towel to dry the back of her head. She turned around, and smiled, bumping fists with the guy, but Channing could tell he didn't want to leave it at that. Sami didn't push back when the man pulled her close to him, his arms around her waist. He leaned forward whispering, talking, whatever, in her ear. She listened not looking the least bit uncomfortable. After 15 seconds he pulled back and her right hand came up to his cheek touching it. The guy was all about that; he smiled hard. Sami nodded, pulling her hand back, the hood came up, and Channing watched her walk over to the air car. She got in.

"Brazzy's Tech Bazaar, we might be right on time." She looked over at Channing, pulling out a wide tooth comb the chop shop guy must have given her. She started combing her drying hair. Sami stopped combing looking over at Channing, then scooted her butt and head forward and back urging him to go, as if to say, *Get a move on, let's go!*

Channing pulled the air car out of the alley, making a right, not asking. Sami knew what she wanted. Smelling her scent, the drying rain accentuating her womanly aura in the small air car, once again, didn't make for such a bad drive to the Bazaar.

Channing pulled into Brazzy's Tech Bazaar, the same place Sami had visited the night before with Dimitri.

"Pull around toward back, stop where you can give us a view of the back door," Sami instructed.

He did. What looked like a few employee air cars were parked in the lot 'round back.

She looked over at him.

"The black air car belongs to a chick that helped Dimitri and I last night. It's gotta be just about lunch time; she'll be coming out the back door any time, I hope."

Channing waited.

"The woman that helped us is a hacker. Maybe the best I've—no she *is*—the best I've ever seen. Grant it, I've not seen that many. But, in about five minutes she dismantled Bonisabella Brigham's evil intentions. The girl is pretty hardcore and kinda evil herself. She saw what was happening like she would have done it the same way herself. Anyway, we follow her to lunch. I'm gonna talk with her again." She flashed a half grin at Channing.

He lifted the corners of his mouth in response.

They both turned to watch the back door.

Just after 2 pm, a thin black-haired woman with a white hoodie on ducked her chin when the back door opened and rain was pelting her. She zipped over to the black air car and climbed in fast. Once in, she pulled out heading for the back lot exit. Channing fired up the grav gen and followed at a safe distance. After a few minutes, the woman in the hoodie banked her air car into a small side lot next to a rib shack. There were a few other cars in the air lot, but it seemed to be off the beaten path for eateries. The woman got out and made a right in front of the building then another right entering the restaurant.

Channing looked left across the street seeing a surface air lot. He swung in, then pulled into a slot that gave him a view of the rib shack.

"Stay here, Channing. I don't think she's gonna stay that long. I saw a mess near her workstation in the back of Brazzy's warehouse. Looked like she grabs and goes back with food all the time." Sami got out, waited for a break in traffic, then crossed the street.

Channing watched Sami go in the entrance on the left of the eatery. Tables were lined up in front of the synth glass windows to the right. The black-haired woman sat down at a table near the window looking out the front watching it rain. A waitress didn't come over to her table, and the woman didn't seem to be fingering her hand comp to order. Sami was right; in all likelihood, take-out. The woman couldn't see Sami enter; there was a wall just inside the entrance creating a hall that funneled guests deeper into the restaurant to the cashier. Sami stopped at the cashier talking to him. The guy nodded and Sami handed him her hand comp. The cashier liked what he saw, smiling. He pecked a few keys into his hand comp then lifted it up and pressed it against Sami's hand comp. Sami waited, not rounding the corner to her right, to go sit with the woman.

The woman's take out bag was ready. The woman must've heard the cashier call out; she stood up, turned around, and walked toward the cashier. When the woman turned left to grab her bag of food sitting on the counter next to the cashier, she spotted Sami. Both ladies smiled. Sami stepped toward the woman extending her hand, the other woman accepting it in a hand hug. The two women chatted for a few moments, the black-haired woman pointing in the direction of the parking lot where her air car was a few times as they spoke.

The black-haired woman pulled out her hand comp to swipe it over the cashier scan pad to pay. She did, then hesitated, pulling the HC back staring at the screen. The cashier tilted his head in Sami's direction and the black-haired woman's head followed his eyes landing on Sami too. The black-haired woman looked a little stunned, maybe confused. Sami then reached down for the woman's hand comp still gripped in her hand. Sami pulled the HC closer, then tapped her own hand comp against the woman's HC. The black-haired woman, it was clear, didn't know what she'd just been given. Channing could almost read her lips ask, "What's this?'

Sami smiled, pointing toward the air car lot a few times while she explained, then waited. Channing saw the grin on the woman's face. Sami explained a few more things, every so often the other woman nodded. Sami reached out and patted her on the shoulder; the woman smiled, then Sami nodded and turned down the short hall to the exit. Hood up, Sami jogged across the street hopping back into the air car.

The black-haired woman exited the eatery, glanced at Sami seated in the air car across the street, then lifted her hand gesturing to Sami with Hook 'Em Horns. Sami gestured back with a two finger Hook 'Em Horns of her own and smiled. Sami turned to Channing.

"With Rand doing his thing, and Murphy doing hers, I think we're covered." She pulled down her hoodie getting comfortable in her seat.

"What was the incentive?" Channing couldn't help asking.

"I gave Murphy the black air car you saw her driving for the help she gave us last night. I picked up a Restomod Cert at the chop shop a few minutes ago she can use to gut the interior and upgrade it with anything she wants. I paid the chop shop extra so that the restoration would be finished in one day," Sami explained.

Channing didn't ask Sami where she got the air car. It was pretty clear it was yesterday's boost to divert him. He got past it fast, instead saying, "You bought Murphy lunch, too."

Sami turned to him. "I looked at Murphy's bill, multiplied it by the number of work-days in a year, and bought her lunch for a year," Sami smiled. "So yeah, I did buy her lunch." She fingered her hand comp not finding what she wanted. "It'll take Murphy a bit to get the source."

Channing glanced at Sami's hand comp screen then back at her, "What source?"

Sami scratched the side of her head, as she did it, she tilted it toward him.

"I want to know which company John Paul Sark chartered his shuttle from."

Channing understood how valuable that information would be. He thought that Rand might come up with that same information as well. The doubt that using Murphy to find that out showed on his face. *Why use Murphy when we have Rand*, he thought.

Sami turned in her seat; the rain was easing up outside. She looked out the front windshield then looked back at Channing, pulling her legs underneath her, reaching up to flip her hair back off her wet hood. She pulled her jacket off and dropped it in the foot well. Sami's posture looked like she was preparing for what she was going to tell Channing next, or what the two of them had to do next, he couldn't tell. He forced himself not to let the trepidation he felt show on his face. Channing realized that what Sami had just done with Murphy was not only to get the name of the shuttle company John Paul Sark was using to travel to the hunting resort. It was much more than that.

"Channing, Donina said that Sark didn't have to pay to travel to the resort this time. He didn't buy his first-class shuttle trip."

"Sark is a repeat customer," Channing reasoned. "If he didn't pay for his trip..."

Sami's head dipped, her lips thinning, "If he didn't pay for the trip, Brigham must have."

Channing blinked.

"One of the sources I'm talking about is Brigham's payment source. Murphy might find it or she might not. If she does, great, if she doesn't, well that's not that bad either...It'll be less painful if she finds it, but either way you and I are going to find it."

Channing couldn't read the look on Sami's face. The lone word that came to mind was *unavoidable*.

Sami nibbled her lower lip, like she was undecided about something.

"It bugged me when Donina said how Sark was so full of himself. It bugged me more that he wasn't paying for his trip. Then I thought that if he isn't paying for his trip, *why* wouldn't he be? He can afford it. But no matter how rich someone is, they always like free stuff. Sark was all about what was going on, about enjoying himself, being carefree. Being carefree prevented Donina and her team from finding out why. Preventing them from finding out what he was thinking, because it was spoon fed to him. Sark didn't have to think about it. If he didn't think about it, Donina's team couldn't pull it from his thoughts. But I think that Donina and her team were so focused on him, they missed something important."

Channing couldn't picture it; he tried, but it wasn't coming.

"You may think I'm crazy, but I think Sark got a free ride to the resort because he referred a friend. Brigham gave him an all expenses paid trip back to the resort. The key is 'back to the resort.' He's visiting for a second time—Brigham's building relationships, Channing. It's the most basic thing a company does when they want to insure repeat customers. She floated him a free trip to his second hunt. He *and* his friend are traveling to the resort together. On the same shuttle." She nodded imperceptibly. "I asked Murphy to look for two people getting on the same chartered shuttle. This will double our chances."

"You said it would be less painful, but either way we're going to find it," Channing said, frightened at what her response might be.

"I did." Sami let out a breath coming to a decision, a decision he sensed was unavoidable for the both of them. He saw it in her eyes; he was certain of it.

"Rand Fullrider was right, this is an ultra secret and illegal operation. Therefore, Brigham has people on her payroll to do the things she needs done covert. Sure, Rand finding the 'ponder ID of the shuttle Sark is on is a good start. His defense pickets guys might even be able to track Sark's shuttle, to an extent. But Brigham made a mistake. As hidden as she wants all this to be, she's traveling a lot, meeting perspective clients, and talking with existing ones. She'd not dumb enough to send messages out in the open, or risk tight beam transmissions being intercepted. The shuttle company she's using over and over knows who Brigham is. This is just one of the planets she's marketing too. She's got a trusted travel partner here and she uses it. *That's* the source I want, Channing." She fixed him with a glare. "The owner of the shuttle company will tell us where Brigham is going. He knows because he has to know. His shuttles go back and forth to her resort. He has to use shuttles that are capable of completing that journey safely."

"So he can get paid," Channing concluded.

"So he can keep getting paid. The guy that owns the shuttle company is a greedy bastard and when I said we're going to cut the tail off, I meant we're going to cut his tail off! You threaten a person in the right way, Channing, and they'll sing a tune, roll over, and bark if you want." The look on Sami's face seemed to return to the place in her memory where the source of all her pain lived.

"I know this because it's been done to me. And you're going to help me do it to him."

Channing was so troubled about what she was asking him to be a part of, he got flustered.

"What if it's a woman that owns the shuttle company?" This was the only lame question Channing could think to ask.

"I was a girl when the slavers did it to me, Channing. I never thought I'd live long enough to become a woman."

From where Channing stood, the Detective Agent felt exposed. This present mission laid outside the sheltered realm of his profession, treading on the quicksand of criminal conspiracy. He was only going to go so far. He knew that, and he sensed she did too. He intended to help her, and he'd live up to that obligation. But there was a moral threshold he was not going to cross. Staring into Sami's determined eyes didn't sway his compass in the wrong direction. He had his principles and he valued them. Here he was following a woman that he didn't even know anything about. He didn't even know her last name.

"What's your last name, Sami?" He finally asked.

She blinked, "Sami is all I remember."

SEVEN

The compromise they agreed on to approach Parten Trask, the owner of the shuttle company Bonisabella Brigham was using to transport people to the resort, was only a shade south of the off-limits boundary on Channing's moral compass. The dread he felt picking up the gear they needed to carry through with their strategy gave him time to think. They'd also stopped for lunch which calmed his nerves even more. It was only when they were parked across the street from the school that Channing knew he wasn't going to be forced to act shamefully.

Sami turned to him from the passenger seat.

"Don't be shocked by what I say. I'm doing it for a reason, Channing. I could never live with myself if we hurt Trask's son. All he has to do is believe we will. You understand?"

Just the night before Dimitri had to tell her the same thing. She remembered how awful she felt after what she'd done to Tremble's daughter. The strength in Dimitri's eyes, the trust that he displayed in her, convinced her that they were doing the right thing. She was making every attempt now to convey that same confidence to Channing.

Channing's features hardened.

"Sami, I'm not going to blindly follow your orders. You understand that don't you?" He snipped, an immovable barrier evident in his response.

"I do."

137

"Good, now let's go over this again. When kids start spilling out the front of that school, I want to be damn sure we're on the same page. Things are going to happen fast. We don't know where Trask is going to take his son after he picks him up, if he even picks him up at all. We may not even get a chance to isolate Trask and his son for any of this to work." He flipped a look at the school out the front of the air car windshield, then back at her face.

A lot had happened in the last hour. Channing checked in with Rand Fullrider from Basley Space Ops to cancel their upcoming tight beam trans. Fullrider told him that he could use the extra time to confirm what he'd found out about a private shuttle departure early that morning. Private shuttles had their own terminal from which to depart. The shuttles were kept in private hangers as well. Finding out who was on the private shuttle was proving difficult, however.

Fullrider did find out which high orbit equipment station Sark's shuttle docked at to refuel. His defense pickets were tracking its movement out-system now. All that was working well. Fullrider just couldn't confirm who boarded it. That was private information that he didn't have access to.

The help Sami enlisted filled in the gaps that Fullrider couldn't. Murphy *was* an evil genius. She didn't even bother with public or private records at all. She accessed vid cam footage at the places she thought John Paul Sark would be. The entrance to the private terminal at Minos Space Port was monitored by security vid cams. Finding a public photo of John Paul Sark was easy enough. Sark kept a somewhat high profile as a private citizen donating money to several local philanthropic organizations. Murphy pulled his face off newsy vids and ran it against the facial recognition app on her workstation. She got a match that morning at the Minos private terminal security entrance.

John Paul Sark and another man were checked in by security and allowed to board a chartered shuttle at the space port. Finding out the name of the charter shuttle company was easier. The name of the company was stenciled on the side of the shuttle Sark and his friend boarded. It was all captured on vid cam, as were all the activities at the private terminal. Parten Trask was the owner of *FleetUp Transport*.

Murphy sent a picture of Trask to Sami's hand comp. Trask owned the company and his picture was on the inside cover of FleetUp's latest annual company report. Murphy scanned all the public and private school registries in the immediate area of Minos and found that Trask had a son enrolled at Barten Elementary. Murphy provided the ID number on Trask's company air car to Sami. All Channing and Sami had to do was wait to see if Trask came to pick up his son after work. They could verify the ID Tag on his air car with the one Murphy provided, and try to match the pic they had of Trask with the driver. The plan wasn't foolproof, but Channing flat out refused to participate in a home invasion at Trask's home later that evening. Sami had suggested it, but he wouldn't cross that line. Actually, she was fine with that. Not only did Sami not want to try to get into the man's house, she didn't want to wait that long. If Trask came to pick up his son, they might get the information they needed sooner. Maybe…

Sami was about to answer Channing when she looked over spotting several air cars queuing up to pick up kids exiting the front of the school. Two teachers dropped their arm in front of the kids coming out the front entrance. Kids had to be stopped so that a teacher stationed next to the curb could check the person's ID inside the air car before letting a child get in the vehicle. The teachers were making sure a child only got into an air car they were supposed to leave in.

Channing followed Sami's gaze spotting the air cars queuing to pick up kids.

"What was the ID again?" He asked.

"G7F4531." Sami said, not taking her eyes off the ever growing line of air cars inching their way up in front of the school.

"Don't see it yet."

"Me either."

After five minutes, they spotted it. The tag on the back of the air car matched the ID Murphy gave Sami. Only problem was, the person driving it was not Parten Trask. The driver was a man, but definitely not Trask. The guy behind the controls had on a suit. He pulled up to the curb opening the passenger auto window leaning toward the teacher looking down into the air car. He pulled something from the dash in front of him and handed it to the outstretched arm of the teacher. The teacher, a woman, looked it over, nodded, then swung around yelling something at the two teachers herding the kids that were exiting the school. What looked like a seven-year-old boy, pushed his way past the other kids waiting for their rides, and ran down the short sidewalk toward the waiting air car. The auto door rose and the child jumped in, the teacher standing at the curb smiling at him as the auto door shut.

Trask's air car nudged its grav gen away from the curb and Channing let it merge into slot one before pulling out to follow. The weather had cleared, but the streets were still damp with puddles in some places. The grav gens of the moving traffic pushed puffs of water out from under vehicles close to the ground in slot one. Trask's driver gained altitude in the next block past the school, inserting himself higher from the ground into slot two. Channing did the same when the slot above was clear. He hung back leaving several air cars between himself and Trask's vehicle.

After a bit of a circuitous route, Trask's driver slowed, dove lower into slot one, then pulled to the curb. Waiting at the curb was a slim man in his late forties with grey slacks and a button-down light blue shirt—Parten Trask.

Trask watched his driver pull the air car to the curb, his smile widening when he locked his eyes on the passenger side. Trask's son climbed out of the air car after the auto door swung up and back. The boy ran over to his father as Trask kneeled down to swing his arms around his son. Trask stood up and looked down into the air car saying a few words to the driver. The air car banked away from the curb with Trask grabbing his son's hand and walking toward the low park behind him.

The low park was the size of a city block. Street level on all sides were bordered by meandering sidewalks that weaved around neatly trimmed trees, shrubs and sitting areas. Randomly placed pergola shelters lined the periphery of the park occasionally covering the walkway to provide filtered shade for people to sit under. Breaks in the sidewalks led to steps that went down to the low park mezzo. The mezzo was five feet down from street level and contained a large rectangular fountain pool in the center. Vendors were dotted around the fountain selling food and drinks. Trask led his son down a set of stairs walking over to a vendor.

Sami snapped a look at Channing as he pulled the air car to the curb.

"I'm going to approach Trask before his driver parks the air car and comes to join them." She rested her finger over the auto door switch on the center console preparing to get out. Before she did, she scanned the far side of the low park out the front windshield spotting what she wanted after a few moments.

"You see the two air cars parked over there?" She pointed and Channing nodded looking that way. "Pick an open space and set up."

She glanced back down into the mezzo; Trask and his son had finished buying something to snack on and had made their way to the bench that outlined the fountain to sit down.

"Your aiming point is the water just behind them, okay?"

Channing flicked a glance at the fountain and shook his head.

"No way, it'll ricochet off at that angle." He looked behind Sami through the back window of the air car.

"Too many people milling around over there. Pick another one," he argued.

Sami studied the area around Trask, coming to a decision.

"You're right. I'll lead him over to the right side of the mezzo. You see the bench near the stairs?"

Channing adjusted in his seat, straitening up looking for what she said. His eyes narrowed and he nodded.

"Yeah, I see it."

"The tree to the left of the bench, think you can hit that from the other side of the mezzo?"

Channing shot his eyes open looking like he was insulted, snorting a puff out his nose.

"Get real."

She pursed her lips, "Sorry, just checking."

Sami pushed the ear bud she was holding into one ear, fingered the auto door, and got out. She hustled to the closest stairs leading down to the fountain mezzo. Channing popped his ear bud in. He could now hear everything in realtime.

The auto door closed and Channing urged the grav gen forward making a right at the stop crossing, swinging around the far side of the low park. There were three open parking spots. He banked the air car right into the second one, and cut the grav gen, leaving an open spot in front and behind. After a push of the auto dim, all the windows in the air car darkened.

Channing took in a long breath, then swiveled around reaching into the back seat. A flechette rifle with laser auto scope and muffler was laying across the seats. He picked it up and heaved its weight over the passenger seat back. With the windows auto dimmed, he could see out, but no one could see in. He glanced out the passenger window waiting until two people walked past. Once they were clear, he reached down to the center console to press the button lowering the passenger auto window. He lifted the rifle to his shoulder adjusting it to get comfortable, making sure the barrel was well back from the five-inch gap in the window. He listened and waited.

Sami approached Trask and his son sitting on the fountain bench. She weaved past a few people, then stopped short. Trask's little boy was a doll. His brown hair was wavy, his eyes were blue, and he was in a little pair of blue trousers and a white short-sleeved button shirt. The boy noticed Sami stop first. He had just taken a lick from his ice cream cone. His dad saw his eyes stop on Sami and turned his head pulling the cone down from his mouth looking at her too.

Without delay Sami said, "You're providing transport to people that are hunting human beings for sport, you total piece of shit!" She placed her hands on her hips breathing hard not moving an inch.

Trask's casual demeanor fell off his face like a light being turned off. His eyes darted back and forth between his son and Sami at least three times. He was speechless, but started to stand up.

Sami's eyes were piercing slits. "Look down," she growled.

Trask was halfway standing when she said it. He went ahead and stood all the way up inchmeal. His face looked like he had expected this day to come eventually, and he had been dreading it his whole life.

Sami took a step closer. Trask's son looked up at his dad and said.

"Look at what, Daddy?"

When Trask looked down at his son he saw it. It was centered on his son's chest. Trask gulped then turned to Sami, his eyes so submissive and pleading, her heart actually began to hurt. This was a terrible thing to threaten, but Trask was a terrible man. As if reading her thoughts, he eased himself back down onto the bench, his ice cream beginning to melt and drip down his hand onto his pant leg. What he had just seen was the red laser reticle that Channing painted in the middle of his son's chest.

"Daddy, your ice cream is melting," Trask's son said then took another lick of his cone. He looked at his father not understanding. "Don't you want it anymore?" The boy asked, then, "What's she want us to look at?"

Trask gulped again. As soon as he did, his son looked at Sami and asked, "Who is hunting, Daddy?" The boy licked again, just like an innocent child should, just like all children should have the pleasure of doing with their dad on a nice afternoon in the park.

Sami jerked her head toward the bench off to her right, swiveled, then strode in that direction. Trask dropped his cone next to his feet, grabbed his son in his arms and lifted him up on his hip.

"You don't like your flavor?" His son looked back at the fallen ice cream cone next to the fountain as Trask walked over toward Sami now sitting on the bench by herself.

"No, Daddy isn't hungry, Tiger, let's go sit over here and talk to this nice lady."

Trask reached up with his free hand brushing the hair on the back of his son's head. He approached Sami and his eyes weren't pleading; they were hopeless.

Trask opened his mouth to say something, but Sami barked, "Sit!"

Trask eyed the bench beside her with eyes that begged her not to harm his son. He sat.

"What's your name?" The boy's huge innocent blue eyes looked into Sami's and her breath almost caught. She dug deep, remembering what the man holding him was doing to make money.

Sami turned to her right staring at the tree next to the bench.

Trask tracked her eyes and as soon as they landed on the tree a sharp *Pifft* exploded a small jagged hole in the bark.

Channing had refused to use the fountain water behind Trask and his son as an aiming point with the flechette rifle. He rightfully predicted that if he shot into the water, the dart would skip off the surface ricochetting toward some other innocent person. That's why Sami picked the tree instead to make her point.

"Where's your hand comp?" Sami asked as Trask looked from her to his son and back.

"In my left pocket."

Sami extended her arm and pressed her hand comp against his pocket. Both of them heard the audible ping.

"I'll expect the answers to those questions within 20 minutes. Just to encourage you not to take any longer—" The instant she finished her sentence another sharp *Pifft* exploded the bark on the tree an inch above the first shot.

Before Trask could reign in his fear, Sami was up, turning on a heel, taking two steps at a time up the stairs behind him out of sight. At the top of the stairs she cut left, pumping her legs hard, like she was trying to run away from what she was and what she'd just done.

The picture of Trask's little boy asking her name was burnt into her vision. Sami was having a hard time seeing and had to blink several times. She picked up speed, then at the end of the block, she cut right at the stop crossing in front of several air cars that had to slow to let her pass. She was almost frantic now, huffing, digging hard with each stride, looking for something, but she didn't know what. Up ahead was a sub lot on the opposite side of the street; she dodged left like an athlete making a cut to avoid being brought down from behind before she scored. Arms pumping, Sami sprinted into the sub lot garage, down into the dim first sub level, then pulled up, stopping short in front of a ceramacrete pillar. She looked back wildly like someone might be following her, then her stomach lurched and she pitched forward, hands on knees, vomiting up all her lunch.

"Sami, where are you? Sami, come in, do you read?" She heard for a split second before she reached up ripping the ear bud out of her ear, trying to give herself a moment of peace she feared would never come. Her legs gave way and she landed on both knees, tilted forward, catching herself with outstretched hands, and vomited again. She could barely breathe. Her heart was pounding in her chest; then after a bit, she rolled herself to one side and sat down on her butt, leaning up against the pillar exhausted.

Sami didn't know how long she stayed that way. She did know that she reached into her pocket to mute the hand comp. Alone, that was all she wanted to be right now. Then she started to shiver. She curled up, pulling both knees to her chest. She wrapped her arms around her legs and let her head sink.

***

A soft touch on the back of Sami's head gave her a start. She opened her eyes and looked up. Jennifer Bane was down on one knee looking into her eyes. The corner of her lips curled and she said, "You're okay now. I'd never leave you, Sami."

Sami wasn't quite sure she was seeing her at first. Then Jennifer reached her long arm down around her shoulder as she sat down next to her against the pillar, pulling her against her body. Sami sagged breathlessly into her grasp and started to cry. Jennifer reached up with her other hand pulling her face against her breast letting her gasp and shudder until it subsided. After it all, Sami's face still looked young and alive. Jennifer smiled.

"You're not even a mess after all that," she chided. Jennifer's head turned and she spotted the hardening pool of upchuck in front of them.

"Lunch didn't agree with you, huh?"

Sami grinned but didn't try to extract herself. There wasn't another place she could think of she'd rather be than right here. Jennifer didn't press; she let her sag back against her and catch her breath until she started to calm down. Jennifer stood up first offering a hand to Sami pulling her to her feet.

Sami wiped her mouth with the back of her sleeve, then spotted Jeffrey standing 10 feet away with his back to them. He glanced over his shoulder, nodded, then turned his stare toward the up ramp to the sub lot leading to street level.

"Thanks for not turning off your sync mate," Jennifer said.

"What?"

"I knew where you were." Jennifer held up her burner comp jiggling it.

"You even have a signal down here," she smiled.

"I don't know what to say. It hurt to get the information I got, Jennifer. I'm so sorry, I'm not strong like you."

Jennifer's breath caught. Sami didn't understand why.

"You and I need to spend more time together. You don't know how weak I really am." The look on Jennifer's face was almost forlorn, like she was so tired of always having to act strong when in fact she was beaten down from the performance.

"Please don't think you have to apologize to me for who you are, Sami. You don't have to prove anything to me…ever." She offered her hand out. Sami reached for it.

"C'mon, let's go. You and I are going to spend the night in the hospital, doting after Dimitri until he's sick of us." She beamed. Jennifer looked alert; she was wearing black slacks and a light green, long-sleeve casual knit blouse.

Sami's eyes brightened. "We can stay in the ICU all night?"

"Dimitri's already been discharged to the step-down trauma ward. The bump on the back of his head was bad, but not so bad he didn't pass concussion protocols."

Jennifer pulled Sami closer, then interlocked her arm in hers.

"He told me you guys have the hots for each other. Supertastic!"

Her grin restored hope in Sami's heart that she might start to forget the vision of Trask's son looking into her eyes.

Jeff heard the two women come up behind him, and walked ahead of them up the ramp. Out in the sun, he swung his arm back halting both women, then scanned the surface street just to be sure. He turned around, looking at them both.

"Please turn off your sync mates now okay, ladies," he instructed. Burner hand comps or not, there was no need to have the devices powered on painting their location for anyone determined enough to try to find them. Both women complied, then

Jennifer pulled at Sami's arm taking a few steps back from the street waiting for Jeffrey to summon an air cab on his hand comp.

While they were waiting for the air cab, Sami looked up at Jennifer.

"I left Channing without an explanation after I saw Trask and his son," she explained.

"Hey, no worries. Jeff already called him. You're covered."

Sami smiled and sighed. "Thanks."

"No problem, Channing wasn't pissed."

"No, thanks for coming for me. No one has ever done that before. I didn't even recognize you at first, Jennifer."

"Get used to it. Let's go." Jeff motioned for them to jump into the back of the air cab that had pulled up to the curb, and they did. The air cab pulled away from the curb heading for the hospital.

***

It was strange; watching Sami napping in the recliner next to Dimitri's bed with her hand outstretched resting on his arm as he slept, the hospital room felt almost like a haven. Jennifer watched the two of them and realized that what she felt earlier when she first found Sami in the sub lot was true. She was tired of always having to act strong when in fact she was beaten down by the performance. But also, some part of her, perhaps, just wanted to feel safe, to feel like she was in a sanctuary, independent of the evidence of the outside world. She had listened to the signs, and left privateering because she had grown less well adapted to the game, and less able to survive it without harm—but the game wouldn't relent. The game wouldn't stop chasing her, no matter what she did to try to escape it. Its pursuit was exhausting, indefatigable, and above all, cruel.

Jennifer leaned on the wall just inside the door to Dimitri's room with her arms crossed over her chest listening to the sound of them sleeping. She knew there was at least a theoretical possibility that Krachy was dead. It had been over two weeks now since he disappeared. In a very real way, her gut told her to cut her losses and pull these people that meant so much to her out of this and run away. They would be safe; they were also the only family she had and would comfort her for what she didn't do— for not saving Krachy, for leaving him alone to his own fate.

The warm hand on Jennifer's shoulder pulled her out of her reverie. She straightened, uncrossing her arms, taking in a breath to center her thoughts, and turned.

"Here," Adrianna extended a steaming thermo cup of black coffee to Jennifer when she turned.

Jennifer glanced down at it then back into Adrianna's dark eyes smiling thinly, "Thanks." She took it and followed Adrianna out into the hall taking a few tentative sips. Jeffrey, as usual, was not far away, the ever-present sentry standing not five feet from the door.

"She's pretty worn out," Adrianna said referring to Sami.

"Yeah," Jennifer took another sip, "but she looks adorable resting her hand on Dimitri's arm. I feel like a mother watching her kids sleep in their bunk beds after a tuck in. Silly, isn't it?"

Adrianna shrugged. "You look out for all of us, nothing silly about that." She had on grey leggings, a soft looking black quarter zip woman's pullover, the sleeves rolled up. She looked nice no matter what she wore, especially since she always pulled her hair back from her face. It was pulled back in a ponytail now. Jennifer noticed Sami's hand comp in her hand. Sami had given it to Adrianna when they first arrived at the hospital two hours ago.

Adrianna followed Jennifer's eyes to her hand holding the comp, then looked up at her. "Yes, it tells us the general location of the hunting resort, Jennifer. Trask couldn't have given more details than he did. Whatever Sami and Channing did, it worked."

It was a terrible feeling, but Jennifer almost didn't want to know. She'd refused to know the outcome of the mission a year ago to protect herself. But Krachy knew, and with the exception of the day that mission ended, he never hinted the outcome was a burden in all that time. She could only admire how much he cared and protected her by doing that. Now she was actually thinking about giving up on him.

Adrianna saw the indecision in Jennifer's eyes, and understood. She was a front-line observer to the entire mess that'd been discovered last year. She knew how that mission had affected Jennifer. But there was one important thing that none of Jennifer's team could have anticipated that was on the hand comp. The information had come in from a person named Murphy.

Jennifer didn't know the details, of course, but then she didn't need to.

"What else is on that hand comp changes everything doesn't it, Adrianna?"

Jennifer had been through this all too many times. It was destined to happen at some point, something that made the situation boundlessly more complicated. Just looking into Adrianna's troubled eyes said it all.

"Yes and no, Jennifer," Adrianna said firmly, "it changes things for us, but not for you this time."

Jennifer didn't understand. This is not what she was used to hearing.

"What?"

"You're not going to solve this yourself, Jennifer. We intend to do it for you."

Jennifer was quiet for a moment, processing this bizarre idea, not liking it.

"I fight my own battles, Adrianna. I don't do that by sticking my head in a hole and hoping they get solved for me." Her chest inflated, the animal within probing the fence line holding her anger inside, looking for a weak spot to get out.

"The kidnappers were after me not Krach—"

"—Shut up!" Adrianna barked much more loudly than she intended to. "Will you just listen for once? Will you? Can you? Can you just let me explain and not point your damn flame thrower at me burning me to a crisp with your temper? Can you just do that, Jennifer?" Her features softened, but only marginally. "Please." She was breathing hard, her face flushed.

Jennifer heaved a shuttered sigh trying to control herself. Finally, she agreed.

"Okay, Adrianna."

The tentative submission felt shitty, and her head was starting to return to its well rehearsed painful pounding. God it sucked to be head strong, and not having a fully functioning head to do it with. Jennifer glanced back at Dimitri's door, like she didn't want him or Sami to hear any of this conversation. She was protecting, always protecting, always bleeding energy from herself in the process.

"Come sit down with me." Adrianna pushed at Jennifer's arm, motioning with her head down the hallway toward the auto doors. Jennifer turned reluctantly, but said nothing. She passed Jeffrey, then Adrianna did, and as she did, she snatched the laser pistol he handed to her. Adrianna stuffed it in her waistband under her shirt. Jeffrey stayed outside Dimitri's room motioning to Adrianna with a finger touched to his ear. Adrianna nodded, promising to leave her ear bud in, and connected so he could hear if there was any sign of trouble.

Just through the auto doors several chairs were lined up against the left windows. To the right around the corner were the lift tubes. They sat down, setting their drinks down on a small coffee table between them. There wasn't any light spilling in from the windows behind them. It got dark early on a 20-hour-a-day planet. Besides, the windows only looked out to a rectangular vertical shaft, on all sides just ceramacrete walls. No view of the city, just an open shaft that was probably for maintenance.

Jennifer twisted and looked emptily out at nothing beyond the windows anyway, grabbing her coffee, taking several sips, then setting it back down.

Adrianna squeezed Jennifer's arm until she looked over at her. Jennifer's eyes were tired.

"You've got all this help, but you just refuse to let us *really* help. Is that not the most ridiculous oxymoronic thing you've ever heard, Ms. Bane?" The corners of Adrianna's lips rose imperceptibly.

Jennifer twisted her mouth. "Are you calling me a moron?"

Adrianna's eyebrows rose toward her hair line.

"I think the least you could do is let us apply our appallingly inadequate skills to get us to the hunting resort, so we can then figure out how to get your short man hunk back." She didn't smile when she said it.

"Piss off." Jennifer didn't smile either, and, she was trying to picture being led around by a collar and not doing the leading. The vision she saw looked dumb.

"Does the thought of you *advising* and not *leading* make you piss in your pants, Jennifer? Sure sounds like it does."

"That was just a gut reaction to you hinting I'm stupid. You don't have to do that. I know I'm stupid…"

"…Sometimes, right?" Adrianna agreed.

"Yeah," Jennifer stood up taking a few paces away then turned back to face Adrianna, "Sometimes I am. Like now, but I'm not making excuses. Look," she sat back down studying Adrianna's face, "I don't want to be blamed when one of you ends up…"

"What Jennifer, when one of us ends up what?"

Jennifer bit at her lip, her head throbbing, but not in an angry way. She was trying to be honest here.

"I don't want to be responsible. I don't! You get it, Adrianna? I came after Sami today because I was scared she was hurt. Sami didn't see it, but my knees buckled when I found her safe."

When Adrianna looked back at her mocking Jennifer's look of concern, it pissed Jennifer off to be read so completely, and to be so ignored while doing it.

"Up yours, okay? Okay Adrianna, I don't need this on me."

"What don't you need, the blame, Jennifer? Is that what you don't need? You don't want me to blame you if I willingly volunteer to help you. Is that what you're telling me?"

"What? That's not what I'm saying. You're twisting my words. You know, you can be a real bitch when you want to."

"You didn't know what I was when you pulled me off that pleasure base so I wouldn't spend the rest of my life being violated by slavers."

Jennifer gulped.

Adrianna had a corner of herself where she carried her horrors, but she wasn't afraid to use their influence, their severity, to get her point across.

"You can call me whatever you want. I've been called a lot worse than a bitch. That's pretty much a compliment from where I stood before you and Marco showed up and rescued me."

Jennifer blew out a breath.

"Look, I'm sorry I said that. The last thing I want to do is cause you any more pain. Don't you see that?"

"And you think helping you is causing me pain?"

"You're. Doing. It. Again!" Jennifer huffed.

"Doing what?"

Jennifer shook her head. It did hurt now; this damn woman was spinning everything she said around in circles.

"I didn't save you from all that so you could psycho-analyze me!"

"So now you're saying you wish you didn't save me?"

Jennifer's eyes exploded open.

"What the hell?!" She started to stand up and leave.

Adrianna was a strong young woman; she shot her hands out grabbing both of Jennifer's wrists. It was quite impossible to stand up now. All Jennifer could do was look into Adrianna's dark brown eyes.

"Let me ask you this. This one last thing, then I'll leave you alone. I promise I will. You're mad at me, I know you are. You can't believe for one minute that I want you to be mad at me. I'm doing it for a very good reason. Just like you don't want any of us hurt, we don't want you hurt either. It's a two-way street that you're not allowing us to travel on. You're hogging the street. That's the only point I'm trying to make here. So here it goes, you ready?"

Jennifer's brows drew down. "Ready, what are you talking about?"

"I'm asking if you're ready to have one last question asked of you, that's all. That's it, no more arguing, you ready?"

"You're treating me like an effin' child, Adrianna. Say what you have to say." Jennifer rolled her eyes.

"I asked if you were ready."

"I'm ready already. Get on with it!" She looked down at her wrists, "And let go of me!" She spat.

Adrianna released Jennifer's wrists. She reached in her pocket pulling out her hand comp, touched the screen, then turned it toward Jennifer. A man's face was on the screen, the video played.

"Will you please let Adrianna, Jeff, Dimitri, Sami, and Channing get Krachy back for you, Jennifer?"

Jennifer saw who it was, then looked over at Adrianna angrily for being manipulated so premeditatedly. She was at a loss for words. One of her oldest friends and first officer of her spaceship *Viper II*, Ian McKivey, was always the one that could get through to Jennifer when she thought she couldn't find her footing. When she was ready to submit, Ian was always the person she had leaned on for help. He had covered her back longer than any person she had ever known. Jennifer trusted him more than anyone, period.

Adrianna pulled back her comp and tapped the screen again, then turned it to Jennifer so she could see it. On the strength of her oldest friend's request, Jennifer was now resigned to let this play out. She knew that if Ian thought it was best to let them do it, then she'd better wait to see what Adrianna had to show her next. Adrianna looked at her while she held up a picture of someone Jennifer didn't know.

"We have a real advantage now, Jennifer. This man was on the private shuttle along with John Paul Sark this morning heading to the resort."

Jennifer didn't understand; she had no idea who the man was. She was certain, however, that it'd be explained to her.

"His name is Lev Babinot. He's the Commissioner of Minos Security Forces."

Jennifer glanced over at Adrianna's face, then back at the picture, not quite sure she had just heard that correctly. Her gaze went back to Adrianna again.

Adrianna nodded. "That's right, John Paul Sark and Lev Babinot are going to hunt people for sport together."

"But I don't understand, how does this guy being involved give us an advantage, Adrianna? This guy is the most powerful law enforcement agent dirt-side. Us going up against him is suicide. Even Channing works for this guy, indirectly, but he does. All security forces do. This is way beyond what we can handle now. This is a full blown conspiracy. All I want is my short man hunk back. All of us'll get killed trying to fight our way through this guy to get Krachy back. Don't you see, I don't want any of you to get hurt on account of me. I couldn't live with myself if that happened. Now you get Ian to gang up on me too. This is not an advantage; it's a disaster!"

Adrianna shook her head. Jennifer was so used to trying to be the lone apex predator she couldn't see it. This was pack predation, the most effective way to hunt what you were trying to kill.

"No, Jennifer, this is not a disaster, this is the break we needed. A man that is the head of Basley Space Ops named Rand Fullrider has already agreed to work with Channing on a joint task force. When Rand Fullrider learned that Lev Babinot was involved, he deployed his Space Ops team to help. Fullrider's a good man, Jennifer; he's going to help put an end to this hunting resort."

"But Fullrider'll be going up against this Babinot guy, too. Isn't Fullrider going to side with Babinot and shut us down, and not the resort? How could Fullrider believe just us? All we have is a picture to show him."

"Oh no, we have much more than that. Vid cams caught John Paul Sark and Lev Babinot leaving on a chartered shuttle from Trask's company this morning at the private launch pad at Minos Space Port. Rand Fullrider was already tracking that same shuttle out-system when he was told who was on it. Then Fullrider was given the approximate location of the hunting resort from the information Sami and Channing got from Trask this afternoon. The private shuttle Fullrider was already tracking was heading in that direction. When Fullrider found all this out, he was furious. He's on his *own* mission to stop this."

"Sami got all this information?"

"Sami got help from others, but yes she, Dimitri, and Channing got all this themselves since yesterday."

"Who gave Fullrider all of it?" Jennifer asked.

"DA Altimer did—they're comrades, Channing lived up to his promise to help after all." Adrianna smiled.

Jennifer finally smiled too. Channing could be counted on after all! And she now realized that he was going to help. She liked it, even more so since a force as formidable as Basley Space Ops was now a part of this mission. That meant that her team didn't have to do all of it themselves. Therefore, they very well could live through it and emerge out the other side alive.

"You know, you could have just started with all this instead of pissing me off so much. I would have listened."

"Oh really? You would have?"

Jennifer twisted one side of her face like she'd bitten into something sour.

"No, probably not…"

"Yeah," Adrianna stood up extending a hand to Jennifer to help her up too, "probably not," she smiled. She pulled Jennifer up then let go, the both of them ready to turn through the auto doors towards Dimitri's room.

"It takes a lot to get through to me," Jennifer admitted. "Sorry you had to work so hard at it. I can't believe you had to ask Ian to get involved." She shook her head.

"Jennifer, Ian contacted me."

"The hell..?"

"He knows you, remember?"

Jennifer stood there dumbstruck. Adrianna nudged her with her hand.

"Forget about it…"

"I said a few things to you. You know I was just pissed. You got me that way!"

"I said forget about it. I said some things, too. You're not holding them against me are you?" Adrianna asked.

Jennifer smiled. That said it all. "You know you actually do have a set of appallingly inadequate skills."

"We, *we*, all of the people here to help you, have appallingly inadequate skills." Adrianna dipped her head toward the auto doors. "Let's go get your short man hunk back." She grinned.

EIGHT

"She's the one that warned me."

Detective Agent Channing Altimer jabbed a thumb in the direction of Sami seated next to him. He was looking at Adrianna and Jennifer across the table when he said it.

They could feel the light cruiser changing course under their feet. Basley Space Ops Commander Rand Fullrider's ship was breaking orbit over Basley, heading out-system. The four of them were alone in the mess hall at one of the four rectangular tables that occupied the small galley. Rand Fullrider's ship might even be called a sub-light cruiser. It was built mainly for speed. Space that would normally be allocated to crew gave way to armament storage. Engineering was larger than a normal light cruiser as well, accommodating a bigger, more powerful fusion drive. Damage control was stout as well, more capable to keep up with battle repairs and injuries.

Jennifer turned to look at Sami. Sami shrugged, not saying anything. Jennifer had to ask, "How is it you know so much about how these people think that we're up against? I'm the one that's not suppose to trust anyone."

Sami thought about it for a moment. Her look turned deliberate, almost formidable.

"I learn fast." Her lips thinned. "Plus, I wanted Channing to live through yesterday so he could help you," she said deadpan.

Channing was looking at Sami when she said it; he could tell there was no sarcasm in it. She was right, nonetheless. If he'd gone back to Minos Security HQ before this morning no telling if he would have made it out of there in one piece. Now that Lev Babinot, the highest ranking security official on the planet, was involved in this illegal hunt, all bets were off. But that still didn't mean what Sami said didn't bother him.

"That the only reason?" He scanned her face, hoping it wasn't.

"I watch your back, you watch my back. Don't forget you helped me get the information that made this whole trip possible, Channing. You did a good job. You want me to list a few more things?" Her eyebrows drifted up. "By the way, thank you," she said, looking pleased.

It was something, at least. Channing returned a wry grin, "You're welcome, I think." He turned back to Jennifer and Adrianna blowing out a breath through puffy cheeks, "Tough crowd."

Adrianna reached across the table when Channing's head sagged. She nudged his hand. "Hey," he looked up at her, "It's not your fault Babinot's involved."

"What?"

"This was always going to get complicated. We talked about this, remember?" Jennifer's eyes widened.

He shook his head. "You don't have to remind me that I didn't take this thing serious enough."

"Channing, I'm not doing that. I'm just suggesting…"

"Suggesting what? You call *me* a puzzle, say what you mean." This was already an explosive situation; he didn't need these women being cryptic about it.

"Rand Fullrider allowed us to be a part of this mission because we provided information he needed to kickstart this thing. Rand's also kept this operation off the books, so to speak, because Babinot's a part of this conspiracy. I'm suggesting that you remember not to underestimate yourself. You're starting to feel some of the dread realizing what's at the end of all this. We've all been there, Channing. You're not immune."

Channing eyed Sami. She nodded with a look that said, *I don't like it anymore than you do.*

He turned back to Jennifer.

"You're finally going to see some of the things we have. To know the kind of people the three of us have been forced to stop. I never wanted it either, but here we are," Jennifer explained.

And they were here, on a ship, heading to the hunting resort. She was thrilled though that Rand Fullrider was the kind of person he was. He didn't give it a second thought when Jennifer asked for Dimitri to come with them even though he wasn't a hundred percent after hitting his head so hard at the TBL the day before. After Jeffrey stood sentry almost a day-and-a-half, he had to rest. He and Dimitri were sharing a crew cabin. There was a first rate Medico team on board, but really all Dimitri needed was rest, so he and Jeffrey were assigned a cabin this morning before take off as was the newest member on Jennifer's team. She was bunking with Sami.

Channing looked at Sami. "I'm still not so sure it was such a smoking hot idea to let her come along."

"She wanted in. Besides, I didn't have final say on it anyway. Fullrider cleared her to come aboard his ship. I only strongly agreed," Sami thinned her lips innocently.

"Strongly agreed, yeah, you spent ten minutes strongly agreeing her right on to the ship. You can be pretty persuasive when you want to be, Sami." Channing said having seen it first hand—very, first hand.

"So you don't think she can help us?"

"Help us what?" Murphy parked herself behind Channing having just entered the mess hall like she owned it. She had on soft sole, white low boots, loose fitting blue trousers with holes on each knee, and a white T-shirt under a black hoodie not pulled up over her head at the moment. She could move as silent as a puma cat; he didn't even hear her come through the hatchway behind him. She placed a hand on his shoulder.

"Don't think I can help with what, Channy?"

Channing turned in his chair looking up at the young woman. Her dark, almost black eyes were burning into his.

"My name is Channing, not Channy," he snipped peevishly.

There wasn't a free seat to Channing's right, Sami was in it. Murphy looked down at Sami.

"Mind if I sit there?"

She didn't wait for Sami to start moving; she shouldered herself down scooting her butt onto the seat forcing Sami to stand up and pull out the chair at the head of the table to sit back down. Sami didn't say a word.

"Go ahead, Chazzy, tell me what I can't help with."

She dropped her elbows on the table crossing her hands looking at him. When she did, the rings on her pinkies clanked on the tabletop.

Channing was cornered. All these women were reaching in through the slits on his cage poking at him with their sticks. He was getting good and damn well tired of it. His pissed off expression showed he was very tired of it.

"For someone that's supposed to be so smart, you can't even remember my name. You're here on a pass, Sweetie, don't push it, or I'll make you sit in the corner until playtime is over." He ground his jaw, feeling much better.

The other women at the table let it happen. Jennifer was even enjoying the show.

Murphy bumped him with her shoulder when Channing refused to look at her. She did it again. He still stared straight ahead, focusing on the open galley behind Adrianna and Jennifer. She nudged him again leaning closer, breathing into his ear.

"Did anyone ever tell you that you're really hot?"

Channing's eyes widened. He turned his head. "Why no, actually."

Murphy's lips curled, "They never will."

He looked shocked at first, then his mouth crinkled into a reluctant sneer. He eyed her face, then let his leer travel past the tattoos down her neck, over her small breasts, then landed on her crotch. He openly started at it for what seemed like 10 seconds, as though no other person but she and him existed in the entire universe. He finally pulled his gaze up stopping on her lips. After hovering on them, smirking back a grin at him, he looked into her eyes.

"Up yours, bitch."

"You disgust me."

"And you have nice lips, Emo skank."

The force with which Murphy lunged her open mouth at Channing's could have broken teeth. She swung her arms around his neck, slurping in his tongue with an urgency to repopulate the human species before dinner. His hands grabbed both sides of her head caressing her buzz cut above each ear kissing her back passionately.

Sami snickered, Adrianna laughed, and Jennifer shook her head. *Who would a thought? Oh well, we all have something that sets us off. Smart, dirty talking grunge babes did it for Channing.*

"You guys don't have to rent a room, ya know?" Jennifer snorted. "No fee for the cabins on this boat."

Murphy extricated her sucking lips from Channing's looking over at her.

"He tastes like raw lust. You ever been lucky enough to taste that, Jen?" She fluttered her eyebrows several times. Channing looked over at Jennifer too, like he was quite interested in what she had to say on the subject.

"Wait until you see me get my short man hunk back. Lucky won't begin to describe it," Jennifer smiled.

Channing pulled back from Murphy and cleared his throat.

"Now that we got that out of the way," Murphy sat back in her chair next to him, resting a hand on top of his. He could feel pockets of warmth. All the rings she had on each finger were cool, only the skin above or below each one let her body heat through. Her long sleeve hoodie had a hole for each thumb, the sleeves pulled down to mid-palms because of it.

Jennifer thought Channing might cross his legs to hide what looked like a pretty hard stiffy. He didn't. He looked relaxed when he sighed. He glanced at Murphy, then over at Sami.

"She'll do."

A corner of Sami's mouth turned up. "So you're saying she meets with your approval now?"

Murphy answered for him. "I'll let you know afterwards." She glanced back toward Channing. He smacked open his lips, then closed them. He agreed it seemed.

"So, Adrianna," Murphy said looking at her across the table, "since we don't know the exact location of this hunting resort, I was thinking we need someone to infiltrate it. What do you think?"

It was going to take a bit of getting used to Murphy. She didn't have a filter, on her mouth or her emotions, that was very clear. She got straight to the point. Channing was just the latest recipient of that, the point.

Murphy and Adrianna had reviewed the information Parten Trask had given Sami yesterday when she and Channing threatened his son at the low park back on Basley. Shuttles from

Trask's FleetUp company were not allowed to travel all the way to the resort. They dropped off hunters at a deep space pleasure base for staging, and as a precaution to hide the actual location of the hunting resort. It wasn't as easy as just following the private shuttle John Paul Sark and Lev Babinot were on straight to the resort. They had to find another way to zero in on its exact location.

"If we get discovered following Sark and Babinot, or get discovered docking at the pleasure base they use for staging, we're bound to fail. How can we infiltrate someone onto the resort? I mean, how do we get the resort to want someone who's not a paying client to come there?" Adrianna asked.

Murphy shrugged. "A legend might do for starters," she suggested.

Adrianna glanced at Jennifer, she inched closer to the table leaning forward.

"A legend?" Adrianna turned back to Murphy studying her.

Murphy confirmed. "A legend is a fake background or backstory I can attach to myself that turns me into a different person. Kinda like an alias supported by all the history to make my new identity look real."

"Yeah, that could work," Channing said. Murphy sat back content to let him think it over. She pulled her hand off his then dropped it under the table rubbing his thigh. It didn't seem to phase him.

"Just need to think of who they need, and need pretty soon." He looked at Murphy, the two of them already on the exact same wavelength. They didn't mean for it to, but it left the other three women completely out of their knowledge bubble.

Murphy didn't care, she was wired that way. And she wasn't being rude, she just knew what would work and pushed it out into the open past her filterless thoughts. She nodded.

"It would have to be someone already scheduled to go there, then maybe the old Switch-Er-Oooo! Fun, don't you think?" She leaned over against Channing, edging her chin up onto his shoulder staring into his eyes. Their noses were touching, the swooping black lock of her hair arched down over her forehead brushing the tip of his nose. She liked he was following her; she was almost squirming in her seat with it.

Channing half smiled at her then swiveled his head toward Jennifer.

"She's on to something here—" As soon as he said it, he tensed jerking his butt back in his seat. Murphy's arm was taut where she'd goosed him under the table.

"Hey, Grapple Woman, hey!" Jennifer pooched out her lips making a sound trying to get Murphy's attention. "Yo!" She reached across the table snapping her fingers next to Murphy's ear.

Murphy blinked, then turned to Jennifer pulling back from Channing but not before getting another grab in as she did.

"Hi-yah!" Channing's knee flinched this time hitting the underside of the table. He didn't blush though. *Good for him,* Jennifer mused.

Murphy's contented stare landed on Jennifer. Her eyes went back and forth between her and Adrianna as if to say, *Let me go ahead and set up the infiltration to the resort real quick, so I can get back to more pressing matters.*

Sami grabbed her forearm; Murphy turned to her.

"Look, I realize you have this fundamental itch that only Channing can scratch, and hey, good for you, really. I was wondering if he was pelvis-worthy too. But, can you please focus for a few uninterrupted minutes to clue us in on your revelation, oh, Mistress Wonder of the Key Pad, Murphy?" Sami smirked.

That seemed to get through to her. Murphy returned the haughty look.

"Of course, Lady That Giveth Air Cars to Hackers Extraordinaire."

Sami let go and sat back waving an arm across the table asking her to get on with it.

Murphy turned, her demeanor changing. She was intense now, seeing obstacles that weren't obstacles at all, just small hurdles to jump over on her way to total victory.

"At the staging pleasure base, we find a person that's headed to the resort. Headed on the next supply shuttle, a shuttle attendant, or maybe just a janitor that's taken a few days off from cleaning WC's on the resort and spending some free time on the PB. Whatever, but there has to be someone like that. I create a legend for me. I put my claimed background and bio in their place, supported by all the docs, certs, and details, which I memorize, then take the person's place. Switch. Er. Oooo."

Channing nodded; Sami tilted her head trying to believe that could work. Adrianna blinked several times.

Jennifer knew she heard her right. "You sure about that?" She asked seriously.

Murphy knew what she meant. "I am."

Jennifer waited.

Murphy focused on Jennifer.

"You folks have been plastering your faces around Minos for the past how many days, weeks, trying to run down some really bad people? Your faces are known—out there. You almost died because of it, so did your friend Dimitri. Meanwhile, I've been sitting in the back of a warehouse, reconfiguring cyber limb neural implants, polishing pleasure droid helmets, and generally not doing fuck-all-anything worth my outrageous talent. Then," Murphy looked at Sami briefly, then pulled her glare back to

Jennifer, "Miss Generous to the Point of Being Lavish over here, shows up, and snap! I finally get my heart rate pumping on something that's important. Not only that, something that even I don't like to see happening." She glanced at Sami. "Yeah, that's right, I do care about something." She frowned a bit, then continued, "But don't tell anyone." She smiled then turned back to Jennifer. "I don't have to worry about eating for the next year thanks to your weird friend here." She smirked referring to Sami. "I've got lots of time-off built up from my painfully tedious non-job. So hey, what's to keep me chained to that damn boring workstation in the back dungeon of Brazzy's? You didn't actually think I was going to let you have all the fun did you?" She pierced Jennifer with a look.

Sami blew out a breath and sat back. She scanned the others at the table.

"Yeah, I think Murphy understands how dangerous this is. Any questions?" Her brows inched toward her hairline.

"What about Space Ops Commander Fullrider? What do we tell him?" Adrianna asked.

Murphy shrugged an arm. "I'll explain it to the guy. He let me hop on his ship this morning didn't he? Fullrider couldn't have thought I was just eye candy to feed Channing's insatiable desires." Her eyes opened wider. "Hey, I know I'm a smokin' hot skank-ho, but Fullrider had to think I might be worth more than just a few In-Outs." She flicked a look at Sami.

"Yeah, I did mention to him that you were worth more than just a few In-Outs. I specifically told Fullrider that." Sami said straight-faced.

"See." Murphy looked at Adrianna, then Jennifer.

"Murphy, you still haven't mentioned you're the main reason we're as close as we are to finding my short man hunk," Jennifer commented with a wry smile.

"I'm also very modest," Murphy smiled thinly. She sat back crossing her arms looking bored.

"Look, you can search for a way to get access to that resort all you want. I can smell your burning brain cells doing it right now. Or, you can let me do what I do. You can hop on board for the big win. You know, join the team, jump on my shoulders and let me carry you malevolents to . . .," she glanced over at Sami, "What's the mini hunk guy's name—?"

"Krachy…" Sami said.

"—Let me carry you to the promised Krachyland." Murphy finished, looking pleased with herself like she had just split the atom for the first time, discovering a new form of energy in the process.

Jennifer shook her head matter-of-factly, "Can't argue with a confident skank-ho."

"You know, you're not as headstrong as Addy said, Jen." Murphy looked at Adrianna. Jennifer rifled a sideways look at her too, but her stare fizzled knowing she deserved that comment. "You don't mind me calling you Addy, do you?" She asked Adrianna.

Adrianna held up her hands. "Hey, whatever…"

Murphy uncrossed her arms, leaning toward Channing. Not looking at Adrianna, she said, "Good, because I like calling him, Chazzy. Has a certain grind to it. Don't you think, Chazzy, dear?" She purred into his ear, extracting her tongue touching its tip on the exact bottom of his ear lobe for the briefest of seconds.

Channing was trying to focus on the galley behind Jen and Addy. His attempt to ignore Murphy's force of personality hopeless.

"My name is *Channing*," he snipped, biting his lower lip to keep the corners of his mouth from arching up.

"Channing, I have this wet spot I need cleaned; you think you could please help a skank-ho out?" He grabbed her hand before she could finger his junk again.

Yes, Murphy was going to take some getting used to. But what she wasn't, was wrong about anything she'd said. Channing turned to look at her.

"You know, I'm just starting to like you. It'd be nice if I thought you'd live long enough to like you more. You just said people almost got killed working on this thing. You're not going to throw yourself at this and forget who you're dealing with are you?"

Murphy pulled back beaming. She pushed her steepled hands together, placing them on her cheek dramatically, acting like she was just asked out to upper-school prom.

"Yes, I will. I will marry you, Chazzy!" She batted her eyes for good measure.

Channing blew a loud sigh, submitting.

"She has my vote. I'm on board for the big win." He raised his brows looking at the other three ladies. "Any objections to taking this to the next level?"

With no dissension evident, Channing stood up.

"Before I—I mean *we*, go," he looked down at Murphy then back at the others, "who's going to take a first crack at Rand Fullrider to explain some of this? She's going to be busy in the immediate future," he noted referring to Murphy.

Adrianna stood up. "I said we'd keep this moving, and I meant it."

Jennifer didn't object. She was happy to let these people help now. Her former first officer, and close friend, Ian McKivey was always right. He asked Jennifer to let her team help get Krachy back. Jennifer was starting to see the logic in that simple request. It may be an odd mix of personalities, but the focus was there. Besides, she was keeping a few things in the back of her mind that comforted her. Sami was so driven it was like she was on auto pilot. She'd accomplished so much in such a short period time; it was impressive. She'd also found someone like Murphy. And, for all Murphy's quirks, she was intelligent. Genius came in lots of forms. Her package wasn't so unexpected. The logic behind her approach was deviously simple. Beyond all of that, once they found the resort, if Space Ops Commander Fullrider went in shooting, Krachy would be as good as dead. That sobering thought made it easy for Jennifer to hop on board for the big win.

***

"Right there, stop the vid right there, Adrianna," Channing instructed her in the small briefing room off the bridge of Rand Fullrider's light cruiser *Brandish*.

Rand sat at the head of the narrow table. He heard what Donina Draper said on the vid screen being played on the far bulkhead. He grabbed the bill of his cap pulling it off his head and scratching at his thick greying brown hair with a pinky. He popped his cap back on looking over at Channing sitting to his left. Adrianna was seated next to him. Murphy sat across the table from them to Rand's right. It was best for all involved to separate Channing and Murphy in Rand's presence. Adrianna convinced Murphy that Rand might not have the same kind of patience with her outbursts as everyone else did. It seemed to be working so far.

"Donina said her telepathy team was able to track John Paul Sark up until late morning yesterday after he took off in the FleetUp shuttle. After that it wasn't."

Rand repeated what Donina Draper had told Channing and Sami when they had their tight beam trans together at the TBL back in Minos. Sami had vid recorded it and they were all going over what Donina said again. It was Adrianna's idea to give Rand as much information as she could so he could see the logic of hopping on board for the big win. That had to mean something specific for a man like Rand Fullrider. He was risking his ship and crew on all the hopping. It wasn't that Rand didn't agree with Murphy's approach. Adrianna was a just a better spokesperson for the group. Adrianna had decided to wait and meet with Rand when both Murphy and Channing were done with their bonding. As long as Murphy kept her self-pride in check, this meeting would get them some answers and some practical ideas on how to get the big win accomplished.

"My defense pickets tracked Sark and Babinot's shuttle until it entered hyperspace leaving our control area. Do you think that's what Donina meant, Channing? Once a ship goes into hyperspace, comms are lost, etcetera?" Rand asked.

Channing looked sideways at Adrianna. "Can you answer that? I don't know how your friend Donina does what she does."

Adrianna leaned forward.

"Donina's telepathy skills don't work in hyperspace, but Sark's trip in hyperspace was short, like all planned jumps using a known jump point are. So she would have continued to have her team deployed when he came out the other side of hyperspace. I know it'd be easier if we just asked Donina via tight beam, but she and her team are on their own mission and have gone dark for the time being. That's not possible right now."

Murphy was making an attempt to be polite. It was warm and fuzzy in a grown up, that's not really a grown up, sort of way. "I know what Donina means." She said without emotion.

The three others looked at her.

"Before I explain that," she turned to Rand, "what direction, what jump direction was their shuttle headed when it translated into hyperspace?"

"My pickets lost it heading toward Basley's Kuiper belt. It's not one specific place because of how vast space is in that direction. But there are a lot of rogue outposts, pirate bases, and several legit pleasure bases as well, including the one that Parten Trask gave us," Rand reasoned.

"If you pick the closest pleasure base on that trajectory, that's where Sark and Babinot are. We already have the location from Trask. We know which one." Murphy leaned back, extending her legs and crossing them under the table. She folded her arms glancing around the table. "The two of them are already on the pleasure base, both Sark and Babinot, but both of them are already encased." She pursed her lips, making a pretty good attempt not to be impressed with herself. She was even pulling it off.

Rand's mouth twisted, "Encased?"

"Yes, Mr. Fulltimer," Murphy smiled, then Channing kicked her under the table. She uncrossed her arms and sat up. "I mean, Mr. Fullrider." She turned to Adrianna. "You're psychic friend Donina can't pitch her telepathy through certain materials or even certain radio wave lengths. Sami told me this; I asked her. Therefore, just on the other side of the jump point, where Sark and Babinot exited hyperspace, a ship was waiting for them. I mean a ship was waiting for them or they just locked themselves up inside it on the same shuttle they were on. It all amounts to the same thing."

"What amounts to the same thing, Murphy?" Rand asked.

Murphy leaned forward looking as though she was forced to be patient with people that could not capture the moment, field the ball, and jump on the winning side fast. She dealt with the entire population around her not being able to keep up. To-day was yet just another day of the same.

"I will slow this down. When harmful radiation travels through space, the outer shell of a ship has to be designed to shield the people inside from it. Donina's mental telepathy works in a similar way. While it's not harmful, it does travel through space toward its intended target. Just on the other side of the jump point Sark and Babinot used, was a ship waiting for them to encase them in a telepathy shield so that they couldn't be tracked. Or, the private shuttle they were on had a small room inside it that they entered and closed the door on that did the exact same thing, encase them in an impenetrable cocoon that prevents mind monitoring. The jump wave that follows a ship as it exits hyperspace lasts for minutes. During that time, either a ship or a room on their shuttle was used to encase them so that the next part of their journey to the pleasure base that Bonisabella Brigham is using for staging clients would be undetected. The hyperspace trail that follows a ship gives them plenty of time to enter a room or even get on another ship. No one would know it's happening because the jump wave masks it. It's a simple, yet elegant solution, and would have been quite foolproof except for the human factor in all of it—namely Parten Trask. Trask knew the exact location of the pleasure base because he had to design the ships to get them all the way there. Given that alone, my money is on a small room on the FleetUp shuttle. Those two men hopped inside some sort of telepathy shielding room to hide themselves from prying eavesdroppers."

"Then that means…" Adrianna was following now.

Murphy smiled. She liked that all of them were following her now.

"That means that this Brigham person who runs the resort knows telepaths like Donina Draper exist. Brigham is a very smart person, and is trying to be as thorough as possible to hide the location of her operation. She figures that starts as soon as the last jump is made into the immediate vicinity of the pleasure base she uses for staging customers like Sark and Babinot. While I don't want admit it, Brigham may be as smart as me. If there is even a thing possible." She snorted, but did mean just that.

Channing smiled at Murphy and she smiled back rubbing his ankle under the table with her foot. He could tell she was seeing it now, seeing how formidable this was, the force she had agreed to go up against. It was even throttling her ego some.

"That explains why Donina's team couldn't track Sark and Babinot to the PB, but that doesn't explain how we select a person on the pleasure base for you to trade places with, Murphy," Channing offered. He noticed Murphy was fighting it, he could see it, but he could also see she was on her best behavior at the moment. He liked her energy, her drive. He even admired it. At last, he said, "Go ahead, Sweetie, tell us how we select the right person on the pleasure base for you to trade places with."

"Thank you," Murphy responded, then took in a breath. "I believe our best bet is to look at this problem from this point-of-view. I just mentioned that Brigham is smart enough to use a telepathy deadening room to encase her clients in on the last part of their journey to the pleasure base she uses for staging. Okay, that's a given. What's also a given is that she also has to encase her resort in something that makes it undetectable as well."

Rand Fullrider sat back in his chair, pulled off his cap, and wiped the back of his hand across his forehead. He wasn't sweating; he was just a bit overwhelmed by the concept. *How do you encase an entire place in space that has to be very large? How do you do that and make it practical? And, most importantly, how do you do it without spending too much on it? Lest we not forget, this resort is in business to make money off hunting live human beings. It already cost a fortune to kidnap the prey. Add the cost of getting leads on clients, and the amount of creds involved start to look ominous.* He looked over at Murphy who he could tell was waiting.

"How?" He asked.

Adrianna and Channing shifted their gaze from Rand to Murphy. Again, Murphy liked solving this problem, they all could tell. But something in her face said that what she was thinking was more than just a simple Switch-Er-Ooo.

"The resort is encased by some very sophisticated and expensive directional satellite components. These light sats are directional. They direct a bubble of impenetrable technology around the resort so that it's encased from outside penetration. Right now, Sark and Babinot are on the pleasure base, or on their shuttle locked up inside their cocoon at the PB. They won't be allowed to exit it until they dock at the resort, which in turn is shielded from outside monitoring by light sats. Once Sark and Babinot enter inside this tech bubble, they're safe to start the safari, or whatever they call it."

"...And?" Adrianna questioned, "How are you going to select a person to get in this telepathy shielding bubble, Murphy?"

"I just make up a legend for the simplest, most demeaning job every ship needs. I'll trade places with a janitor, a toilet cleaner. I can find the person that does that work on a cargo ship easy enough. There has to be a cargo ship that's delivering spare parts to the hunting resort. Very expensive, delicate components that are headed for the resort. Parts to keep these light sats operational so the impenetrable shield stays up. The resort doesn't own their own cargo company, or cargo ships. We've already discovered Brigham has to pay outside companies like FleetUp to transport people there. Brigham pays cargo carriers, too. There can only be one cargo ship on the PB that has this type technology on their manifest. I should have no problem finding that specific cargo ship once I get access to the PB's net. Then there's the huge problem I haven't mentioned yet." Murphy crossed her hands, her rings dinged the table top.

"You make it sound like trading places and infiltrating the resort isn't much of a problem," Adrianna said. "What's tougher than that?"

Murphy scanned the faces of the others in turn, and sighed. She shook her head like what she was about to tell the others was so unbelievable she couldn't even believe it herself.

"I know what the *Guarantee* is that Brigham offers her clients."

"What? How did you get to that out of all this, Murphy?" Channing's eyes rounded. This leap was a bit much even for her. He hadn't even given much thought to what the hunting resort was offering their clients as a *Guarantee* since Donina mentioned it during their tight beam trans yesterday.

"It changes everything, Channing," she said with the most serious look Channing had seen on her face in the short time he'd been around her.

"Tell me," Channing prodded.

Murphy looked at Adrianna, "The most important thing your friend Donina discovered was what Sark was bragging to himself about. We just heard her say it on the vid recording. The guy was full of himself, confident he could go back to the resort again and again. A foolproof guarantee to keep hunting and killing human beings." Murphy dropped her head, picturing what she knew and how awful it was. Her head came up and she looked into Channing's eyes.

"Donina was sick to her stomach because of it and I have to say so am I." Murphy searched his face, looking at him as though what she found out may mean that this was even too difficult for her to defeat. "What is a foolproof guarantee that allows inexperienced hunters to hunt highly trained soldiers as many times as they want without the fear that they will die doing it?"

The other three looked at each other without an answer.

Murphy swallowed. "The hunting resort has the capability to reset the day," she explained.

Rand tilted his head, eyes narrowing. "What?! Come again..."

Murphy swung her gaze toward him; she looked tired all of the sudden.

"The technology bubble that protects the resort from mind monitoring also allows it to travel back in time." She sat back nodding, and crossed her arms.

"Brigham has built a time device around the resort to guarantee that when her clients get killed they are alive after a reset so they can keep hunting."

Adrianna gulped. "That means even if a hunter is killed, a client is killed, they are alive once the time is reset. What you're saying is that the entire day doesn't have to be reset and that increments of time can be reset if the hunters encounter a problem or obstacle of some type. The hunters can reset resort time just a few minutes before a problem occurs until they overcome the obstacle. So Krachy may be able to kill a hunter once, only to face that same hunter again the next day, again and again. Oh shit, this is..."

Murphy looked at her. "...The biggest problem for me too, Adrianna." She sat up uncrossing her arms. "Once I infiltrate on the resort, I have just one cycle, one day, whatever, to shut it down so Rand can find it, for me to unmask the tech bubble so Rand can find it. If I take too long, the day will reset. If the day resets, I'll be found out because the sabotage work I started before the reset will already have been discovered. I have to start the work all over again; I'll have to start the next reset from square one again. The resort workers will have discovered the progress I made up until the reset. Since they'll know the progress I made, there's no way I can go about it the exact same way and try to begin again."

NINE

Rand Fullrider was experienced. He was just south of 50 years old, and had not always been with Basley Space Ops. In his former life he was the captain of a bucket-of-bolts merchant ship held together by himself and a few crew members. Dealing with the type of people that offered, or were the recipient of, his illicit cargo was commonplace for him. He'd seen just about every type of unsavory character there was. That was one of the reasons that now, in his current job as head of Basley Space Ops, he was so effective. He knew how his enemies thought because he had dealt with them up close and personal for almost 15 years.

The other reason Rand was so successful at his current job was that he was very comfortable wearing the mantle of command. He was a cagey veteran that was used to leading, was used to taking risks, and that was used to succeeding when he did.

Rand was exercising his mantle of command now. After the conversation with Channing, Adrianna, and the spirited Murphy, he made a decision on how to proceed with the mission. The intel he'd received from them was not something that he was un-comfortable with. He'd sat at the table with more unusual people than he could count. He always accepted the people he dealt with at face value. The most prized lesson he had ever learned was that you could *never* underestimate the man on the street. The diversity he saw in the team of people Channing brought with him to help shut down this illegal hunt was an advantage. Granted, Rand was not totally convinced what Murphy said was 100% true, but that didn't make it untrue either. The approach he decided on how to proceed with the mission would help get them closer to the truth one way or the other anyway.

"They didn't want a landing fee paid in creds," Rand took another pull on his Pinaten ale. The drink came from one of the moons around the planet of Pinat and was considered a "Black," a dark stout that had a rich, one-of-a-kind taste. He always had one when he could find someplace that served it. It didn't matter that it was beyond expensive for a mug of it. That could only be expected. This was, after all, a pirate base bar. Everything was about profit here.

"What did the pirate base landing control want?" Adrianna looked at him sipping on her own mug. The creamy brown, thick foamy head of her P ale left a tan mustache on her upper lip. She didn't realize it.

Rand gave her a half smile. He motioned with his finger up and down under his nose while looking at her.

Adrianna squinted seeing his signal then reached up with the back of her thumb wiping the 'stash from her upper lip. She smiled. She liked the beer and company too. Rand was an interesting man, and Murphy was proving to be much less over-bearing now in the presence of people more of her sort, name-ly—pirates and criminals.

"I had to give the pirate base two missiles and 20 rations of food. They need food and weapons," Rand reasoned, shifting his eyes toward the entrance to the small bar behind Adrianna. The three of them sat at a table in the back. Rand never picked a seat in a place like this where he couldn't see the entrance. He would never have his back to it, too dangerous.

Everything about this mission so far had given Rand pause; he felt like things could get out of hand at any moment but was afraid he wouldn't see it coming until it was too late. The bar did nothing to calm his nerves. It was a dark place, in what looked like an old cargo storage pod on the pirate base, identifiable only by a burnt-out neon sign reading "DRINKS" over the entrance. The pirate base was an old equipment station, well off main space shipping routes. It was a little after 11 in the morning base time, and the place was crowded with freebooters that all seemed to be waiting.

The bar itself lined the back wall to Rand's right. Their table was tucked in the corner on the right wall just in front of it. The tables were beat up and set pretty close together, and as near as Rand could tell, the way they had come in was the only way out. He glanced at Murphy fingering her hand comp in her lap next to him. He hoped she was as smart as she seemed to be.

Murphy was deliberate, that was certain. Before leaving Rand's ship, she went through what could only be described as a transformation. She had him distress an old blue crew flight suit. He helped her put it in an auto clothes dryer with some spare machine parts running in it for an hour to, more or less, beat the hell out of it. The flight suit Murphy now wore looked as old and ragged as it possibly could. It was also over-sized for her, making her look, for lack of a better term—frumpy. She topped it off with a dirty engineering ball cap, also too big for her head. She used some dark eye pencil Sami had given her to give her eyes a dark outline. Added on top of that, Murphy even placed soap in her eyes to make them bloodshot. A few smudges of dirt and grease here-and-there and she looked about as menial as a 25-year-old could. No more rings on her fingers, no more attitude. Murphy was acting, and it was impressive.

The only hint Murphy had brain one in her head was the hand comp in her lap, not a problem to conflict with her legend though. Every person in the bar had either a hand comp or a slate clipped to their belt—had to. These devices were the backbone of human and financial interactions, and the first thing everyone owned no matter what socio economic status they subscribed too. Poor or not, *everyone* had one.

Besides, everyone in a place like this minded their own business. And everyone in a place like this wore a sidearm. Rand and Adrianna had on a laser pistol. Murphy declined, but that was by design. She had a role she needed to play. A person with her legend couldn't afford one.

"No one turns off their synch mates around here. Crazy cool," Murphy whispered, still looking down at the small screen pecking in commands.

"Of course not," Rand said, "if they turn it off they wouldn't be notified that a contract was out for hire. They don't have a Mercenary or Merchant's Guild on a place like this. Word of mouth or synch mates do the trick, no need for the Guilds." Rand wore a rugged looking flannel long sleeve brown shirt, and multi-pocket thick trousers cinched with a worn out faded black belt to clip his LP holster to.

As usual, Adrianna had her hair pulled back from her face in a single ponytail. Nothing fancy, but her profile did garner attention. Two men a few tables over were looking her way and had been from the moment she stepped into the bar. She had on her casual women's black long sleeve quarter zip pullover and black leggings. Not a suggestive outfit, and pretty plain, but she was young and pretty nonetheless. Even without any makeup on, that fact was obvious. She knew what was going on, and felt the stares.

"I'll walk over and sit with the guys that have been staring at me for a bit. See if I can get anything from them we need." She rested her elbows on the table cupping her mug looking at Rand talking lowly. She, Rand, and Murphy only spoke in hushed tones at their table.

Rand nodded, indicating that was a good idea and that he'd watch her back.

Adrianna nodded back.

"Besides, no use you spending all your creds on my beer, right?" She got up and walked over sitting down with the two men seated at a table in front of the bar. One guy pushed a chair out for her.

"Oh yeah, yeah, yeah, ah huh, mmm, yep, yep..." Murphy mumbled to herself inching closer to what she was looking for on the pirate base's net.

Rand had decided to flank the pleasure base Brigham was using to stage clients to travel to her resort. He knew he couldn't dock on the staging pleasure base without giving their identity away, so docking on this pirate base would be the best strategy to attempt to get Murphy on the staging PB using this base as a departure point. Another thing Rand learned early on to cover his tracks was that is was always best to put layers, always layers of camouflage between you and your target. The stop at this pirate base was just another layer to camouflage them from their true, intended target—the staging pleasure base.

"Find anything yet?" Rand asked Murphy, not taking his eyes off Adrianna.

Adrianna was quite at ease, even emboldened it seemed, working the two men for information. Rand didn't know that much about her, only what Jennifer had told him during a brief conversation before they left his ship. What he did know was that Adrianna had a background with slavers. He knew plenty about them. So watching her handle herself with ease, averting a stray hand trying to grope her now and then, looked practiced but not bitchy. She was working the two men, hanging her fruits out close to their touch, but not bending her tree limbs allowing them to pull off the ripe buds.

"Oh Oh! Boo-yah! Ain't no rest when you're winning!" Murphy breathed excitedly. She looked up removing the faint smile from her face. "I think I found something we can use." Her face didn't reveal a thing, but Rand cold see the animation in her dark eyes.

He waited, still not turning to face her so he could keep Adrianna in view.

"They degrade with age, so I think they're already looking for some more replacements."

"Looking for some more what?" He asked.

"Solar panels or battery packs." Murphy fought off a grin, keeping her face passive.

"Please explain."

Rand was patient. It wasn't a good idea to get ahead of yourself in a place like this. Same went for deciding what to do next on the mission. He reached over placing his hand on Murphy's arm signaling her to wait until he got back, then he stood up and walked over to the bar ordering a few more drinks. As he waited for the barkeep to get them, he leaned on one elbow keeping Adrianna and the entrance within eyeshot.

Murphy slumped a bit in her chair, pushing her hand comp into a pocket.

The woman behind the bar held two mugs of Black back against her body waiting until Rand paid. He dug in his pocket pulling out his hand comp then pressed it to one of the scan pads on top of the bar. An audible chirp told the woman his creds were debited; she then set the mugs down not saying anything. He grabbed them both then angled back over to the table, placing a mug in front of Murphy before sitting down with his.

Rand took a good pull on his ale, wiping the foam from his lip before turning toward Murphy.

Murphy acted reluctant, like she was privileged to have drinks bought for her. She reached for her mug, pulled back her hand, looked hesitantly at Rand's face waiting for his nod. Once he nodded, she snatched up her mug and downed half of it in gulps, spilling some on her chest. She burped loudly, then slumped back in her chair. She burped another gurgle, then looked at Rand. He nodded.

Murphy whispered, "The power it must take to keep the light sats pumping out their signals has to be significant." She was looking down at the table when she said it, not making eye contact with him on purpose. "Maybe even massive. I mentioned before that two frequencies at a minimum have to be at play at the resort. One signal surrounds the installation to prevent mind monitoring, or detection from active or passive scans. Another has to be used to reset the day, or cycle, whatever timeframe they pick. Anyway, this takes power. A lot of power." She glanced up to Rand waiting for a nod. He gave it to her. She grabbed her Black and downed the rest of it, spilling more and not bothering to wipe her face or chest where it spilled.

She burped into her mouth filling her cheeks with it, then blew it out down into the table. Head down she then lifted her chin, waiting for another nod. Rand was the gatekeeper, so to speak. He told her when she was allowed to speak or drink. It was all part of her legend. It was part of her anonymity too. She was a subservient, and they were both playing a part in it.

He nodded. She didn't look at him, just back down at the table top.

"Shipments of solar panels and solar optimized battery packs have been delivered to the pleasure base Brigham uses for staging. We've already estimated that her resort has been operational for around seven months. But I searched back further than that on dozens of hand comps that are on this pirate base right now. I found that as far back as nine months ago a huge shipment of panels and bat packs came through here. Makes sense because before you can open the resort the battery packs have to be installed and tested. Two months of placement and calibration sounds about right to me. The good stuff is that there is a shipment of voltaic battery packs sitting in a storage pod on the pirate base right now. They've been here for over two weeks."

Rand listened but didn't react. He took a drink being patient. Adrianna got up from the table with the two men. They stood up too, then sat back down once she turned to return to their table. When she sat down, Murphy tucked her chin further into her chest like she shouldn't make eye contact with her. Adrianna placed her mug of ale down on the table, sitting patiently looking at Rand not saying anything.

After a good minute or more, Murphy raised her face, got a nod from Rand, then continued in a low, hushed tone not looking at him, just the table.

"The way I figure it, the Voltaic BPs degrade just like the solar panels do over time, especially given how much power they must have to store then use, then store, then use, over and over, resetting the day and pumping energy into the frequency mask for the resort. I believe the Voltaics on base right now haven't been delivered to Brigham's staging pleasure base because she's waiting for the right deal on the cargo fee. I looked, bunches of cargo shipments are heading to the PB from here almost every other day. The cargo shipping fees are sky high, outrageous really. Brigham is just waiting until one of the freebooters bids the right price on the shipment. She's a stingy bitch. So her shipment is just sitting here not being delivered until she gets the right price."

"How does that help you get on the pleasure base, Murphy?" Rand asked. "If Brigham is waiting for the right deal, it may take forever. Not to mention why not just get you on one of the other cargo ships that deliver goods to the PB? Why wait for the Voltaic BPs?"

Murphy cleared her throat, then waited well over a minute to respond. She was so absorbed in her role it was scary. No impatience, no flakey outbursts, just total immersion. Rand suppressed a grin. He was liking what he was seeing from her now. She was very convincing. He was feeling good about it, until he heard what she said next.

"Because Adrianna is going to convince the two dudes she was talking to to take the cargo, and me, to the PB. That's how I'm going to get on the base."

Rand didn't let his anxiety show. To Adrianna's credit, neither did she. It seemed like she was used to hearing that she didn't have control over her own fate. It bothered him. Maybe more than it bothered Adrianna, he just couldn't tell. Her expression didn't change in the least. She just took a pull on her mug, wiping her lip, waiting.

It took another two minutes for Murphy to continue; she went through the non-eye-contact-wait-for-a-nod-from-Rand routine then finally responded.

"This gets me close to equipment, the Voltaics, that are ultimately going to Brigham's resort, the high tech stuff I figured she might need. Those two guys have a cargo ship that can handle the cargo. They've been on this base waiting. Adrianna just needs to broker the deal with the pirate base boss woman. Nothing moves without her getting her cut. Adrianna can offer me up as a free crew hand, shit scrubber, whatever. I'll mumble my way on to their cargo ship then infiltrate the PB. I'm my own Switch-Er-Oooo. Once I'm on the PB, I'll take out the two guys, refresh their 'ponder, and snap, I'm now the captain of my own ship. Captain of a ship with cargo we know will ultimately go to the hunting resort."

Murphy's monotone explanation didn't reflect the gravity of what she was proposing. That was almost as scary as her admission that she intended to volunteer to kill the two men to get herself on the resort.

Adrianna took a drink looking at Rand then she set her mug down.

"She's right. They are waiting, and their cred reserves are about dry. The two guys apologized to me that they couldn't buy me more than one round. Rail Thin Man even asked me if we had any food rations we could part with. His hands were shaking, Rand. The guy is starving I think. No one on the base cares if he keels over and dies. That's just less competition for the limited runs being handed out by Bonita Boss. Yeah, Bonita Boss has all these guys on the base playing themselves off each other for the runs that are doled out. I can speak with BB. Murphy's idea to throw herself in to get some cargo off her base may just work. I don't think Rail Thin or Wary Eyes Man even knows that some cargo is ready to be moved for Brigham. Bonita Boss hasn't been offered a big enough cut so she's just sitting on it."

"Then what makes you think that low bidding will get the cargo moved, Adrianna?" Rand asked. "Rail Thin and Wary Eyes get a free ship hand, but what will Bonita Boss get if the price is low?"

"Me." Adrianna blinked.

Rand couldn't let that response go. This was not what he wanted, what he wanted to happen to Adrianna.

"The hell you are!" He spat.

No one seemed to notice, or if they did, they didn't look over at them. The low hum of conversations in the bar remained static. But Rand's temper was not. He was not liking this now. No way—

Before he could respond again, Adrianna reached over placing a hand on his.

"—It's okay, Rand. I can do this, I've done it before." The calm reason with which she said it made Rand even more upset. Adrianna was offering up herself as a fee for getting to the end game on this crazy scheme. He wasn't going to allow it.

"Like hell! I say what we do or don't do." Rand's round face was flush now. He pulled back his hand from her grip, his green eyes not giving an inch.

"Hear me out, Rand. Just listen, will you?" Adrianna cupped her mug with both hands not showing any emotion, none.

He exhaled a long breath, looked over at Murphy who hadn't moved a muscle this whole time, then looked back at Adrianna. He nodded reluctantly.

"Listen," she started, "on Basley, Sami, Dimitri and Channing did all of the heavy lifting. For the most part, I stayed out of sight. I didn't put my face out there, so Brigham doesn't know me. From that perspective, I'm covered. When I go to Bonita Boss I'm going to offer her me as an incentive. But the incentive is that I intend to tell her the truth about the hunting resort, all of it. I'm going to let BB get a vision of the resort, and what it might mean to her. I've dealt with people like her before, Rand. I've been around them all of my adult life. You hear me? I know what motivates them. If I tell her that I'm going to shut down this resort, *and* I have the backing of Basley Space Ops doing it, what do you think she's going to think?"

Rand shook his head. "You're dreaming, Adrianna. You think you can offer her that and she'll buy it? Really?"

"Of course she will, because you're going with me to explain it."

Rand blinked. He had been out of the freebooting business so long he wasn't seeing it until now. The logic of it etched the features of his face, but he suppressed his grin.

"Bonita Boss will think that she'll get the resort when all this is done, that's what you're saying."

"Basically yes, but she'll not want to run it. Not like Brigham, not a person like her. All Bonita Boss will want to do is to carve the resort up into little pieces and sell them off one by one, so she can sit on her ass here making an enormous profit in the process. When I serve it up to her, we serve it up, she'll bite because there's no skin in the game for her. I'm the one risking myself on the takeover of the hunting resort, not her. Further, all BB's risking is one cargo run fee to get that kind of return. It's a total win for her. You see?"

"But a guarantee, Adrianna, what are you going to tell BB when she asks you how you're going to guarantee she gets what she wants? What's to make her think that once you get the cargo and leave you'll follow through with any of it?"

Adrianna's smile was faint, but it was there. She knew the answer. So did Murphy. After the gesture-wait-nod-act from Rand, Murphy said.

"She gets *The Guarantee*, Rand. Bonita Boss gets a time machine."

Rand pulled his upper lip behind his bottom teeth fighting to understand the clarity of it, the simplicity of it even. Adrianna's play was, he could see now, very clever. If Bonita Boss had a time device, what wonderful things could she do with it? Moreover, how much money could BB make if she knew that she could reset the clock always knowing the future to come.

"You two are bold bitches, I'll give you that." He let the corners of his mouth inch up a bit.

"Now do you see why it'll work?" Adrianna asked.

"You say that, but this Bonita broad will have something no one like her should have, Adrianna. What do you say about that? How can I let a person like her own that power?"

"We win the battles that threaten us the most, Rand. Tomorrow is another day, another chance to decide how to deal with Bonita Boss. For now, we attack what's in front of us. By doing that, we save the lives of people that are being systematically killed as trophies on the hunting resort. Don't you want to see that end?" Adrianna reasoned.

"You're playing me, Adrianna. Appealing to my soft side. Both of you are."

"Yes," Adrianna agreed. "But I know you don't like that Brigham is taking people off your home planet to be chased down and slaughtered."

Rand took a long breath in, then let it out looking around the bar considering what all this meant before responding.

"How do we approach BB?"

He sensed Adrianna was right. He'd been around people like Bonita Boss before as well. At least Adrianna and Murphy were honest. He liked that; he liked that in both these women.

"Follow me," but before Adrianna pushed back from the table, she looked at Murphy then Rand. "Stay in character; Bonita Boss will look us over real close and run our backgrounds. She won't find anything for me. I'm a ghost from my slaver days and have been ever since with Jennifer because her CRS has hidden my every move, financial or otherwise. Murphy's legend will speak for itself, but she'll know who you are, Rand, which is what I'm counting on. Follow me when we start talking with her. I may lead her in a few directions you might not understand at first, but I have a reason."

Rand nodded. "Okay, I can do that. But I'm going to tell you now that once BB thinks she has something we want, and is holding something over us, she's not going to stop until she milks us for everything she can get for it. You realize that don't you? I mean you have to know that's how this is gonna go, right?"

"I think that's going to be something for you to worry about much more than Murphy or myself."

"What?" He asked.

"Rand, I told you I know how these people think. You have this swagger, this confidence you exude toward everyone around you. Can't you just trust me on that—?"

Murphy murmured a snicker. "You do, Rand. You got animal magnetism, roll with it…"

Rand flicked a glance at Murphy, but she was back in her immovable role of servitude. He wheeled his face back toward Adrianna, but her face was unreadable yet again.

Adrianna pressed on. "You ready to go?" Her head dipped.

He twisted his lips and stood up, realizing he would have to just adapt as they went. Adrianna stood up next, but Murphy stayed seated. Rand patted her shoulder and she stood up, eyes downcast, following the two of them around several tables, then out through the exit.

Bonita Boss' pirate base was haphazardly laid out. The overall effect was to make people spend more time on it so they'd spend more creds. The corridor the three of them came out into was slanted causing them to walk further left to avoid hitting their head on the sloped hallway wall. They turned a corner and the shape changed again with three choices to pick from, two rectangular corridors and a rounded one in the center. Adrianna strode down the left rectangular corridor, and in no time, it bended left, then right, then opened up into a large, high room.

This room was circular with three levels. They entered on the bottom floor and stopped just inside the entrance way. The room was about 30 feet in diameter, and got more narrow the higher it went up. It was shaped like an upside down funnel. Level two was only around 15 feet in diameter, and the top level a mere seven or eight feet round, ending in a point above it. No guard rails lined the upper two levels, just a few hand holds were sticking out of the walls you could grab to keep your balance on the narrow balcony floors. A few hatchways led off levels two and three.

Adrianna seemed to know where she was going. There was a man on level three next to one of the two hatches on that level. He was perched in a seat that was built into the wall next to one of the hatchways, his legs dangling over. He had a flechette rifle on his lap and was looking down at them when they entered below. The two hatches on the level where the man was seated were slanted built into the steep slope of the walls.

Just then a woman came out of one of the hatchways on the ground level to their right with a man trailing along behind the woman on a leash. They walked right passed Rand, Adrianna, and Murphy, then a hatchway on the left opened and she and the man went in and it shut.

Adrianna looked up to the man seated on the third floor and waved. The man waved back, leering a stare at her, then spoke into a hand comp. After a minute or so, he motioned for her to come up.

"Just you, they wait! It'll give us more time." The man yelled his instruction, grinning like his performance was for the benefit of the two people with her.

Before Rand could reach to stop her, Adrianna nodded taking a step forward. She pulled her laser pistol from her holster and held it up so the man could see it. She held it down by her side by the barrel, not putting her hand on the grip. On the other side of the room she clutched a lift pulley hand grab. The thin belt started moving upward. She held on to the grab waiting for the foot peg to exit the hole in the floor. She slipped her foot in the curved foot peg leaning into the pulley belt to keep from being forced off the grab lift the higher it went. The room was canted, making the grab lift swing out into the center of the room more and more as the altitude increased.

The grab lift stopped beside the hatchway where the man was seated. Adrianna handed her LP, grip first, to the man. He grabbed it and jerked his head at the hatchway. The hatch opened; Adrianna stepped off and grabbed a hand hold in the frame of the hatch, then pulled herself inside. As she did, the man made it a point to pat her backside like everything inside would be a real treat for her. The hatch shut.

Someone came up behind Rand and Murphy as they watched Adrianna disappear through the hatch on level three. He and Murphy were blocking the entrance leading into the Funnel Room. He wheeled around not seeing anyone at eye level. He lowered his gaze to find two creatures.

The tan creatures were insect-like. They were about three-and-a-half-feet long. Wrapped around their abdomens was a small vest-like piece of clothing that held a laser pistol. Two sets of legs extended from their thoraxes and another set from their abdomens. Their thorax tilted upward keeping the creature's head angled up as they moved.

This was the first time Rand had ever seen anything like this in his life, but he could sense all the two creatures wanted to do was get past them and into the Funnel Room. He grabbed a handful of Murphy's flight suit and jerked her out of the way of the entrance. The instant they shuffled sideways out of the way, the two creatures rushed in past them. They scrambled to the far wall, and for lack of a better term, walked right up the wall stopping next to the man on the third floor, their six legs a blur doing it. The creatures pulled their laser pistols off their vests with one of their legs, tossed them to the man, and he dipped his head. The hatchway Adrianna had just entered opened, and the creatures scurried in so fast Rand would have missed it if he'd blinked.

Rand didn't bother a glance at Murphy; he was just thinking how much danger Adrianna had to be in alone with those two insects, not to mention the degenerates that might be in there as well. *What's going to happen to her?*

He didn't finish the thought as the man yelled down at them. "Come up! Let's go!" The guard waved.

Rand rushed across the room to the grab lift pulley not waiting for Murphy. He clutched a hand hold, secured a foot in a curved peg, and up he went. About half way up, he could feel the tension on the belt where Murphy must have gotten on. He stopped next to the guard and before he could ask the guard shouted, "Gimme your pistol, A-Hole, no effin' around!" The guard extended his hand, and Rand handed it over as the hatch opened. Rand leapt inside not waiting for Murphy.

Murphy was fast on Rand's heels, but just inside the hatch she shuffled off to one side and dropped her head, motionless, almost like she was content to let the grownups talk and take care of business while she passed the time pretending not to hear anything they said.

The rectangular room was two cargo pods that had been synth welded together. The room was narrow and deep with one window cut out of the far wall so Bonita Boss could see out.

Anti grav pallets and containers of haphazardly stacked goods were against the left wall running about half way down it. Just past the boxes was a tired looking black auto couch folded out. Nothing was in front of the window, but to the right, angled in the corner, was a utilitarian dura steel grey desk with a woman sitting behind it.

Bonita Boss was a tall dishwater blonde. She wore her hair pulled back revealing dark roots. Her oversized breasts strained against a white T-shirt with the words *Space Ain't For Pussies* on the front. She may have been pretty once, but now her face was etched into a constant suspicious sneer. You could tell she had seen and been through it all, finding most of it shitty.

Adrianna was standing off to Rand and Murphy's right next to a small bar along the wall in front of Bonita Boss' desk. There were three men in the place, all of them in dirty coveralls with semi-long matted hair; two of the men had beards. The three men sat at two small round tables tucked in the right corner of the unscrubbed dura steel floor near the bar.

As Rand's eyes got used to the dimness, he tried to find the two insects that had just come into the room but couldn't see them anywhere. Just then he heard some scraping noises above him and looked up. The two little creatures were perched upside down on the ceiling. They were moving in random agitated little circles around each other but otherwise staying pretty much where they were. Rand noticed the sweeter smell of the euphoric drug Gleam cutting the musty odor of the room. One of the bearded guys slumped in his seat had a vape stick in one hand that was still smoldering from one end. Both he and his bearded buddy were staring at Adrianna's body.

The fat non-bearded man closest to Adrianna stood up holding his mug and walked over to Adrianna setting the mug down on the bar. He turned to grin at his two buddies as if performing for them or on a bet. The other two guys sneered back, licking their lips. They had a good idea what came next. It was like they had seen this before, still it was always a treat, sort of like a fond trip down memory lane. Fatty was looking Adrianna over just like his buddies were, but shrewdly, like a meat inspector grading a piece of choice.

Fatty drained the rest of his Black, set his mug back down, then wiped his mouth with the back of his hand.

"You're looking lonely, wench."

"I'm not lonely," Adrianna grimaced. "And I'm not a wench."

Fatty was grinning now, but his voice turned icy.

"You could be." He jerked his head back toward his two friends. "Nothing we like better'n strange grab. I give the word and you're face down. You'll get the damned ride of your life, bitch." Fatty shrugged. "Some hos like that, takin' it. You must be that kind, huh?"

"What kind is that?" Adrianna asked levelly.

"Someone who needs what Jammy has."

Adrianna looked him top to bottom. "Jammy?"

"I'm Jammy." He poked himself in his flabby chest looking proud, like a gold medal winner who had just won the role-down-the-hill-drunk race.

"Yeah," Adrianna drawled, with enough volume for everyone in to hear. "You're about the Jammiest piece of shit I've seen in three planets."

Jammy's face darkened. Bonita Boss was smiling with glum satisfaction from behind her desk; she was going to enjoy what happened next.

Jammy grabbed Adrianna's left arm above the elbow, digging his fingers into her bicep. He may have been fat, but was strong and it hurt her. He had to outweigh her over two-to-one.

"You hear me good, bitch." A fleck of spit landed on her cheek. "We're making it, me and you. You see that couch over there?"

"Where?" Adrianna asked.

Jammy scowled, then turned his head toward the auto couch.

Adrianna grabbed his empty mug slamming it into the guy's nose. The heavy thick mug did not shatter, but Jammy's nose did. He howled, buckled at the waist, and slapped both hands over his nose, blood pouring between cupped fingers. Adrianna rabbit-punched him with the large solid mug at the base of his skull and the guy tumbled to the deck smacking face first. His legs drew up instinctively into a fetal curl, his body remembering the last time he'd been stomped.

Adrianna drove her foot into the guy's face. Jammy tried to cover his head; when he did, she stepped over him. His flab would have cushioned the next kicks, so standing behind him she wound up and kicked him viciously in the kidneys twice.

Jammy lay quiet, but still breathing. The ordeal lasted maybe 10 seconds.

Jammy's two friends' eyes shot open.

"Damn, bitch!" The closest guy not smoking Gleam started to stand up.

Adrianna twisted at the waist unleashing a well placed round kick to the guy's cheek. She powered through it with her arms corkscrewing nicely snapping the guy's head sideways. The smack was audible in the closed room. His legs buckled, and he fell straight down on his knees teetering on them for what seemed like two seconds before pitching forward on his face. The second smack was more of a wet *sput*, where his nose took the worst of the impact.

"Enough!" Bonita Boss leapt up from her desk, the chair tumbling back from her legs hitting the wall then falling over noisily.

Adrianna wasn't even breathing hard. She eyed Gleam Boy who had tensed his legs until he heard Bonita Boss. Gleam Boy thought better of it. The look on Adrianna's face said there was plenty left in the way of lessons if he cared to sign up.

Adrianna turned looking at Bonita Boss holding a laser pistol pointed her way. Bonita looked more amused than threatening, however.

"You want a drink, Butch?" She moved out from behind her desk strolling over behind the bar. She placed the LP on top, still holding it, waiting for Adrianna.

"Sure—" Adrianna barely got out.

"—I know damn sure I want to get one for him!" Bonita was leering straight at Rand, with what could only be hot lust on her mind.

"He's a stud, isn't he?" She said reaching for two mugs, then holding them in one hand, pulled back on the tap pouring two Blacks letting the foam spill everywhere.

"Sit, sit." Bonita dropped the two mugs on the bar. There were two narrow worn, rickety stools in front of the bar. Adrianna stepped past the closest one hitching her rump up onto the furthest one so Rand could climb on the other one. He did.

Bonita Boss could not take her eyes off Rand. Rand saw it; he knew what it meant, and he would definitely get Murphy and Adrianna for not warning him better than they did. They knew earlier, and it had zipped right over his head. He sighed as he grabbed his mug. It sure was going to be more of a problem for him than Adrianna and Murphy.

Resigned, Rand nodded his thanks.

"You may need some more useless peons." He glanced at the two lumps on the floor. Gleam Boy was sitting upright staring at Adrianna, grinding his teeth.

"I think I found what *I* need." Bonita Boss reached over the bar with her free hand, slipping her wet fingers under Rand's holding them. She had rough hands, like she had moved every container that was ever delivered or left the base herself. She smiled. It was a tight smile, like she didn't have much practice doing it.

"And, you have that big job back on Basley to go with the rest of your package. How's a man like you end up on my base with a street fighter and a wart?" When Bonita Boss said wart she looked over at Murphy standing motionless where she had come to a stop just inside the hatch.

Rand glanced sideways at Adrianna.

Adrianna took a gulp of the tasty ale, and wiped her lip.

"We're going to take that load of Voltaics you've been sitting on to a resort that hunts people for sport. If anyone gets in our way, they'll end up like Fatty and Stupid. When we're done taking over the place, we're gonna turn it over to you so you can dice it up and sell if off. But you wanna know what the best part is?" Adrianna's eyes twinkled.

Bonita Boss's chest inflated. Her breasts stretched the lettering on her T-shirt sideways. She gripped Rand's hand tighter no doubt thinking he was part of the deal.

Adrianna glanced at Bonita Boss's grip on Rand's hand, then back at her face.

"Well, *besides* that." She smiled.

Rand heaved a reluctant sigh, not liking being tossed into the pot like a chip.

Adrianna waited, as she did Bonita Boss gained her composure. She let go of Rand then bounced the LP by the grip on the bar top. She knew she was going to get what she wanted; she always did. Adrianna could see the dents in the bar where she had stood many times before, doing the same tap, tap, tap, with her pistol.

Bonita Boss raised her brows.

"What makes you think I want some damn resort? Just 'cause you smacked around Jammy and Biff don't mean you have anything I want or wanna give you. Them's *my* batteries, you ain't getting anything from me, hard case." She studied Adrianna's face. "Yeah, I know where you picked up that attitude. Slavers gave it to you didn't they? You got no background."

Adrianna's face was unreadable. How she could do that Rand had no idea. But the horrors that lay behind it were there. Deep, deep, down, but there, nonetheless. He thought for a second that Adrianna was going to kill Bonita Boss for simply bringing up the subject.

Bonita Boss must have processed the exact same thought because she jerked away from the bar, bringing up the pistol leveling it at the middle of Adrianna's chest.

The hatch behind Rand and Adrianna opened, the guy with the rifle stepped inside, and it closed. BB had backup now, real backup. She relaxed noticeably.

"I know I can't get away with killing him," BB tilted her head in Rand's direction. "But you, huh, you got no past—No one's gonna miss you." She looked over at Murphy, "Or, The Wart." She walked around the far side of the bar out toward the center of the room. The familiarity with which she held the LP spoke of ingrained practice.

Rand swung around stepping off his stool, hands out away from his sides. He took a few steps toward Bonita Boss.

"Can I have a word with you?" He glanced sideways at Adrianna, then back at Bonita. "A word, it'll just take a minute." He dipped his head, the corner of his mouth on one side rising.

Bonita Boss thought about it then looked over at Rifle Man standing next to the slanted hatchway. She tossed her LP to him, then he had both his rifle and the LP pointed at Rand. He was plenty far back to cover both Adrianna and Rand. Rifle Man glanced to his right at Murphy who was too close for his liking. "Hey, go sit down, Wart."

Murphy didn't move.

"I said go sit down, Wart!" Rifle Man's eyes darted to Murphy, then back to Bonita Boss.

Rand cleared his throat. "Excuse me, she won't move until I give her permission."

"So give it to her," Rifle barked, then Bonita Boss reached out grabbing Rand's hand pulling him towards the auto couch.

"Daw, you can sit down," Rand instructed Daw (Murphy). Daw obeyed, padded over to the chair next to Gleam Boy, pulled it out and plopped down, hands dropping to her lap. She didn't make eye contact with anything except the table top.

Rand took a few steps letting himself be guided toward the couch then pulled Bonita Boss back towards him. She let it happen, pressing herself into his chest. Rand was not a tall man at five-feet-nine, she was maybe an inch shorter. She had on a pair of tan high-waist-band tummy control pants. Bonita Boss looked 50-years-old, but was probably a lot younger than that. Her lifestyle added years that weren't there otherwise. Being on her base all the time had expanded her waist and hips a good bit too, as did the need to look more threatening. She was sturdy, but not fat.

Rand eased his arms around her waist, then clutched both butt cheeks with much more than a handful in each hand.

"I was going to avoid you at first, but now I think I'll jump off the struggle bus," he said, looking into her eyes. Unfortunately for him, Bonita Boss' breath smelled like spoiled beer, *But those are the breaks,* he thought.

"This what you wanted?" Rand reached around his shoulder where she had swung her arms, and pulled her left arm down, directing her hand to his crotch. He didn't flinch when she squeezed his bulge; he just used his other hand on her butt to pull her closer for a good grind.

Bonita Boss tilted her head, doing the first thing so far that looked like a woman. His mouth latched on to her open mouth. They slurped and groaned, and grinded, and slurped, and grunted, and breathed hard, for what must have been two minutes.

Bonita Boss came up for air first.

"This isn't the best part?" She asked, referring to Adrianna's comment earlier.

Rand grinned. Bonita Boss' hands had drifted up around the sides of his face. She was holding his cheeks. Her palms were so rough he thought they might leave marks. He reached up grabbing a hand and led it back down into his cockpit again. She liked it.

"This is almost the best part. Lots more to come."

"What could be better? You know, you and me could do a lot together. A man with your background, I'd even let you keep The Wart." Bonita Boss looked over at Adrianna. "But Street Fighter has to go." She squeezed him harder then started an up-and-down motion that started to generate some friction against his zipper.

"You got a lot to offer, I see that." Rand didn't let her mouth reply. In for round two, they moaned, swallowed, gulped, and inhaled for a little while longer; then Rand went to work on her crotch with a hand. In no time she was writhing up and down humping his hand, going up on tippy toes then flat footed.

All of a sudden Rand stopped. "Not in front of the children." He pulled back.

Bonita Boss looked dazed and winded. She didn't know what he meant at first, then she looked over at Murphy. "You can't mean The Wart. She can't be your daughter."

"No, not my daughter, just a floater I helped out of some trouble. I've got a rep to live up to. You know, back home."

"What can she possibly be good for?"

"I just make sure she keeps busy. Got a soft spot in this hairy chest of mine. I can let you verify that, you want?" His eyes softened.

"You really care what happens to her?" A person like Bonita Boss didn't understand what charity meant, even less so when it didn't fight back.

"I care what you think. Isn't that the same thing?"

Bonita Boss blinked. No one ever asked her for her opinion. All she did was bark orders and take. She didn't know how to give.

"You really'd be bothered if I threw her out an airlock? Really?"

"I'd be bothered if you still had enough energy to do that after spending an hour with me. That's what would bother me."

Her eyes grew with a grin to go along with it. She snorted. "Whew, no words! I have no words for that."

"What's there to say?" Rand said. "You won't need to talk."

"Oh, honey!" She pulled back, still gripping one of his hands. She poked a look at Adrianna. "Where did you find this man?"

Adrianna shook her head. "You still not convinced? You sure you don't want to TOFTT?"

Bonita Boss's face glazed over. "What?"

"I'm sure he can give you a few. But don't you want to *Take One For The Team* while you have the chance?"

Bonita Boss turned back to Rand. His eyes were playful.

"This one," he directed her hand he was clutching back to ground zero. She looked down, rubbing it, starting to pick up the pace. "Let's go discuss this further."

She was so fixated on working it she didn't hear him.

He leaned forward and licked under her ear and whispered, "Now, like in the next minute."

Bonita Boss looked in Rand's eyes bemused, already liking what was coming next. She hooked a finger in his belt loop and pulled him toward the stacked pallets behind him. She stopped, fixing her stare on Rifle Man.

"Clean those two up and give The Wart a biscuit and beer. This is gonna take a while," she ordered, then reached over to a pallet pulling back the corner. The corner was a hinged lid, behind it was a recessed panel. She pushed the actuator and the pallets, one stacked on top of the other seven feet high, and they popped forward a few inches. With her hand, she pulled the frame of the little opening where the button was, and both pallets swung out arcing off to the left revealing a hatch.

Rand hesitated, "What about them, I mean those?" He lifted his head toward the ceiling referring to the insects scurrying above.

Bonita Boss shrugged. "What about them?" She said as she pulled him in through the hatch. It shut behind them.

TEN

Adrianna lay absolutely still. It wasn't an unfamiliar feeling, the fear she felt. She had experienced this type of fear before along with the dread that came with it. The moment Rand and Bonita Boss had left the room, she had been unceremoniously taken hostage. She had no choice but to let it happen. Rifle Man held his weapons on her while Gleam Boy cinched her bound wrists and ankles with nylon cords to the auto couch's legs. She lay stretched out now, unable to break free. The one thing that was unexpected was that they waited. They'd ripped off her shirt and bra, pawing her, but no violation, no beating, not yet at least. She wasn't even embarrassed as both men took turns groping her half naked body. They were waiting for Bonita Boss before the rest happened.

They just weren't sure if they should proceed because Bonita Boss seemed to be taken with Rand. That confused them. They knew Adrianna was with him and if they damaged her before getting approval it could be a problem. It had been almost an hour since the hatch to Bonita Boss' cabin had closed. Since they were unsure what the boundaries were on Adrianna, they figured there were no boundaries on The Wart. She was useless, that was obvious, and staring and grabbing at Adrianna's body for so long had put the itch in them both. It needed to be scratched. So they turned from Adrianna, confident she wasn't going anywhere, and looked at Murphy. She was still sitting, face fixed on a point on the table in front of her. She hadn't even eaten the small ration of food on the table in front of her.

"Stupid bitch, she can't even eat without being told to."

Rifle Man looked over at Gleam Boy. They had made their way over to the table coming to a stop in front of it looking down at Murphy. The only motion in her body was her breathing. At this point, that was pretty much all they needed to decide how that itch was going to be scratched. They'd already done what they were told to do. They gave her some food and a beer. It just sat there in front of her, the beer warm and the food solidifying, and they had Medico come get the two breathing lumps that were Jammy and Biff.

"Here, hold this." Rifle tossed the LP to Gleam Boy and stepped beside Murphy waiting for him to get on the other side of her. He adjusted his grip on his flechette rifle letting it slide down into his hand. He held it by the barrel and fore-stock.

Gleam Boy grinned as he sashayed around the other side of the table stopping next to Murphy. His laser pistol was held casually at his side. He looked over at Rifle Man.

"I think we need so see what The Wart has on under those clothes—"

Adrianna had lifted her head and was looking at the two men as they were about to take Murphy against her will. If she had not been looking at the three of them, she wouldn't have believed what happened next could happen so fast.

Murphy's left leg extended slamming the trigger guard on Rifle Man's weapon back against his body. At the same time her left hand shot out, the pinky smacking the trigger down. Simultaneously, her right hand darted out grabbing Gleam's LP jerking his wrist up firing a *Zint*. The two weapons discharged at the same time up and through the chins of each man. They collapsed in unison straight down, dragged to the deck by the base's grav gen.

"I have permission to do that?" Murphy looked over at Adrianna who was staring at her in disbelief.

Adrianna smirked. "Yes."

"Guess my plan to Switch-Er-Oooo has to be modified, huh?" Murphy stood up.

"Guess so."

Murphy didn't even look at the dead body she stepped over on her way across the room to untie Adrianna. While she started undoing the cords around her ankles, she looked up.

"Sure could have used a little backup guys!" She yelled at the two creatures still on the ceiling. Done with her ankles, she untied her wrists, stood up straight and looked back at Rifle Man's corpse.

"Most of his gooey bits shot straight up. Looks like his shirt is pretty clean if you want to use it." She helped Adrianna stand up; they locked eyes.

"Thank you." Adrianna said, rubbing her wrists.

"You're welcome. Would you believe I have another idea how to get us to the hunting resort?"

"I'd expect nothing less." Adrianna smiled.

Murphy smiled back.

The two of them jogged over to Rifle's body and took off his shirt as carefully as they could not to get much blood on it. He was a thin guy. The dark brown pullover crewneck shirt was large on Adrianna's small body, but better than nothing. Her bra was a write off, so she just rolled up the sleeves not worrying about it or the few blood stains around the collar.

"And..?" Adrianna, done fixing her shirt, turned to Murphy. She was as clothed and ready as she was going to be.

Murphy liked that she accepted what had just happened without question. She also realized she respected Adrianna. Seeing her lying exposed in a state of obvious misery that didn't even register on her face gave her pause. For maybe the first time in her life Murphy understood what teamwork might be like. This had to be it— A purpose bigger than herself, and the look of trust now on Adrianna's face. Trust that was placed in her to help them both find a way to finish what they started.

Murphy hadn't even known what she intended to do to Gleam and Rifle until it happened. She knew it was because of how mad she was to see them mistreat Adrianna the way they did, the way they had done to countless others. Now Adrianna was asking what was next. It was something Murphy had never been allowed to control before. It was liberating. Beyond that, it was undeniable, and very urgent.

Murphy jabbed a thumb in the air. "Them," she said.

"Them?"

Murphy nodded, feeling the time pressure to get moving.

"They're here for a reason, Adrianna. They're looking for their friends just like we are. Their friends have been captured and taken to the resort to be hunted too."

"What? How can you know that?"

"There isn't time to explain. We gotta get Rand and go."

Adrianna looked down, then pulled her gaze back up to Murphy trying to get her head around it. To her credit she just nodded. "Okay, let's get him and go. I trust you."

"We go, but not just with Rand. They go too."

As soon as she finished her sentence, the two creatures scurried down the wall so fast it caused Adrianna to step back when they both came to a rushing halt square in front of her and Murphy.

Not surprised, Murphy looked down at them and said, "Once we get Rand, all of us go together." She turned and made her way over to the pallets.

The pallets were still pulled aside to the left of Bonita Boss' cabin hatch. Murphy stopped short and extended a hand behind her. Adrianna had grabbed the flechette rifle and laser pistol. She pushed the LP into Murphy's outstretched hand. She took it, held it at the ready, then swung it in front of the scan pad next to the hatch. It swooshed aside.

Adrianna couldn't see past Murphy. Murphy stopped just inside the cabin tilting her head.

"Withdraw Rand, play time is over!" She barked.

Adrianna shifted to one side seeing past her; Rand had an ankle in each hand, Bonita Boss lying supine on the top of the lone table in the small cabin, her T-shirt pulled up, large breasts a bouncin'.

Rand looked over at Murphy coming to a halt in mid thrust. Bonita Boss was in rapture mode and didn't hear or see Murphy yet.

"If you'd told me we were just going to take over the base, I would've helped!" He looked down at Bonita Boss, who had finally turned her head to see Murphy The Wart standing in the hatchway pointing the LP at them both. Before she shook off her ecstasy, or even had a chance to be confused, Rand let go of her right ankle and cold cocked her with a hard left jab. Both her legs dropped straight down to either side of him limp. He pulled out and turned toward Murphy, his pants bunched at his feet, and his chub pointing right at her.

"Really?!" He blew out exasperated, "Your turn to Take One For The Team next time, Murphy. Deal?"

Murphy nodded, "Deal. Now let's go. You can use this to lead the way." She tossed him the laser pistol. "That thing hasn't even fired yet," she said referring to his joystick, then turned pushing past Adrianna leaving the cabin.

When Murphy stepped back past the pallets she didn't see the two creatures, but heard them instead. They had scampered over to Bonita Boss' desk and appeared to be going through her drawers looking for something. Adrianna came up beside Murphy and turned her head to see that both creatures had found their laser pistols and had slid them back into their holsters on their vests.

Rand was finished doing up his pants when he brushed past both of them taking a quick survey of the office. He saw the two dead guys then spun his head toward both creatures that had rushed over and stopped in front of him. For some reason he found this more or less expected because he asked Murphy, "They part of our team now?"

Murphy answered, "Yes, they have friends on the resort being hunted for sport too. All we need to do is get the Voltaics and go."

Rand turned to look at her, done cinching up his belt.

"I have an idea which ship we can use."

Adrianna looked surprised. Rand being on the ship going to the staging pleasure base, and then on to the resort, wasn't part of the original plan. She opened her mouth—

"—Look, just can it, Adrianna! Nothing is going to plan anymore. I've done more than my share. You two warriors have taken out everyone that's even a hint of a threat."

Rand jerked his head at Bonita Boss' cabin.

"Hell, I could go back in there and perform a coup de grace on Beer Mouth with a fork if I wanted to. I didn't have to do that with her; I thought I was saving your life!" His hands gripped his waist, his foot tapping, waiting for an apology for having to make it with the smelly hose beast.

"You enjoyed saving my life, didn't you?" Adrianna's damnable face was utterly unreadable again. Rand hated how she could summon that look any time she wanted to. He didn't know if she was serious or not.

As if figuring out what he was thinking, she set the rifle down against the pallets, stepped over and wrapped her arms around him.

"Thank you, stud, it might've gotten nasty if you hadn't taken matters into your own hands," she whispered in his ear, then pulled back stepping away with a grateful look on her face.

Rand wanted to not like her, and to disagree with what she'd said, but that wasn't going to happen. Bonita Boss kept insisting the whole time he was alone with her that Adrianna had to go. Bonita Boss was threatened having someone around that could fight as well as Adrianna could, and that was so attractive. She'd thought it much easier to just kill her.

Just to be sure he asked, "You messing with me? You know you can shut down your face, turn it on and off whenever you want." He waited.

"Absolutely not, Rand! I know she wanted to blow a hole in me the first chance she got. You stalled her and that gave Murphy time to pop the two remaining peons. Murphy even saved me from getting defiled by them." She reached down picking up the rifle.

Rand turned to Murphy. "You took them both out?"

Murphy shrugged, "Isn't that what teammates do? Look, I'd love to continue to discuss this. But once the few dozen freebooters on base figure out BB is slayed, they're going to want to take over and have a real nice time with us two gals. It's going to get dicey for us, and even you, in a few minutes. What say we grab the cargo we need, a ship to transport it with, and talk about all the wonderful what ifs in the universe *afterward*? You with me? Huh? Ya feel me, stud?"

She jabbed a look at his LP. "You have the weapon, you lead the way, Great Warrior Fulltimer."

She smiled. Rand was getting used to Murphy's sassy demeanor. He did have to say, she played her part up until now perfectly. Flakey or not, she was a force. One glance at the bleeding bodies near the table confirmed that.

"All right." He gathered in all of them with his eyes, including the two creatures who, seemed to be waiting, and were much less agitated now. They seemed to sense what was happening, no doubt about it.

Rand turned on a heel stepping back into Bonita Boss' cabin where she was beginning to stir. She moaned starting to come to. He stepped over next to her, looked at her groggy face and said, "Sorry," then planted a hard jab under her chin popping her back into sleepy land. He looked up at the shelf on the wall behind the table, just above Sleeping Ugly's head. There had to be seven rolls of duct tape on it. He grabbed a roll and tossed it to Adrianna standing in the hatchway. He then gathered the limp Pirate Boss up in his arms and walked back out through the hatch making his way over to the auto couch, dumping her on it.

Adrianna tossed the duct tape to Murphy, but when it was in the air one of the creatures darted a front leg out letting the hole in the tape pierce its protruding leg tip. It scurried over to the auto couch, his partner with him. Rand stepped back several paces, and almost before his feet were planted, the two insects bound Bonita Boss' wrists and legs in a blurring swirl of movements. They hopped off the couch and waited. Rand touched his hand to his mouth a few times. Before he finished tapping his lips a third time, one creature dashed up, and wound two loops of tape around BB's mouth and head. It leapt back down next to its friend waiting again.

Rand grinned his thanks, then turned back toward the cabin. On his way past Adrianna he chided, "That's how you take orders. No back talk," rubbing in the last three words for good measure. He couldn't help that the left corner of his mouth smirked up a bit. He ducked back inside the small cabin weaving past the table to the far wall. He stopped in front of a small square rug on the floor. He reached out at a scan pad on the wall, at the same time brushing the rug to one side with a foot. A panel under the rug retracted revealing a ladder heading down somewhere. He turned around.

"Her ship."

"Who gets the cargo? I mean who finds which hold has the cargo we need in it?" Adrianna asked. She and Murphy had stopped behind him. The two creatures waited just outside the hatch looking their way.

"I do, of course," Murphy said matter-of-factly, transforming her shoulders, her posture, face, and body back into Daw The Wart. She started to turn, not wasting a second shuffling head down toward the hatch.

"Hey—!" Rand yelled after her, feeling the need to plan how this might go.

"—Just call me on this if you need me, Captain Fulltimer."

Murphy pulled the hand comp out of her pocket, jiggled it, then shoved it back in, brushing past the two creatures, making a right past the pallets and out of site.

Rand looked at Adrianna.

"She can think on her feet, huh?"

"I've never seen someone kill two people so fast in my entire life," Adrianna nodded. "We better get aboard Bonita Boss' ship and strap in. Murphy will probably find the cargo hold with the Voltaics before we even circle the base to look for the damn thing."

Rand had already turned stepping down onto the first rung of the ladder. Adrianna hustled after him, as did the creatures.

***

On board one of the most basic merchant ships Rand had ever encountered, he pushed the control stick forward guiding the *Payman* class merchant ship out away from Bonita Boss' soon-to-be-up-for-grabs pirate base. The *Payman* was named that for a reason. When using it, you got paid; that was about it. You didn't travel in comfort, speed, or without risk. While the merchant ship had a nice sized cargo hold, it was very vulnerable to attack. Limited acceleration, no real top end speed, and no afterburner—it was an easy target. Shields didn't function much, most of the power that would have been used by them was always being directed to the small engine. The one good thing about the small engine was that it didn't have a sizable scan frequency. It didn't have much of a signature for scanners to paint. Rand pushed forward hard on the yoke, not feeling much of a surge, but they were underway nonetheless.

Getting the cargo out of the cargo hold was done with some pretty good military precision. After a quick call from Murphy pinpointing the hold location, Rand lined up BB's ship just outside the hold. There were two men in the cargo hold. When they saw her ship line up for touch down, they recognized the ship and let it land.

What happened next Rand didn't even have to get involved in. He popped the hatch on the *Payman* and let the two creatures storm the men instead. The speed at which they bolted out through the hatch diving headlong into both men's chests would have made any field sergeant proud. Dazed, all that was left was a little cleanup pistol whipping them both unconscious. Adrianna let Murphy in through the blast hatch, then Murphy locked it behind her.

Loading the cargo took the longest. The Solar Optimized Voltaic Battery Packs were dead weight. Even the anti grav units built into each pallet strained to shift the mass of each pallet into the cargo hold of the *Payman*. After 20 minutes they were done and on their way.

The cockpit of the *Payman* was cramped. A small pilot seat and a fold-down half table behind it just in front of a small head was it. Adrianna and Murphy mounted the two stools resting an elbow on the table wedge. The two creatures positioned themselves on the ceiling overhead, no choice really, unless they wanted to squeeze into the head, which they didn't seem to want to do.

Adrianna's elbow was touching Murphy's on the wedge. She nudged her.

"Tell me again how you knew the two creatures also had friends on the resort being hunted."

Murphy pulled off her ball cap, running both hands back and forth through her itchy hair.

"I didn't."

She reached around the small open hatch behind her leading to the head pulling a half soiled towel from the small sink. She began wiping her face.

"You didn't," Adrianna coughed. Rand grunted just behind her. They were touching backs.

Murphy dropped the towel into her lap.

"No, I didn't, hate to break that to you, Addy." She continued scrubbing her forehead pressing harder to get it clean.

Adrianna waited.

"I guessed." Murphy stopped wiping her forehead, switching to her lips and cheeks. She paused.

"Look, someone had to be decisive. I played the heavy. I figured since I just saved you from the happy hands of Rifle and Gleam, you'd let me press on. I was right."

"You played me."

"We're on Bonita Boss' ship with the cargo aren't we?"

Rand spoke up. "Yep, a bold bitch, that's what you are, Murphy…" He turned looking at them both, "Both of you!" He added airily.

Murphy nudged Adrianna back. Despite having told her a lie, she still respected Adrianna. She liked her too. She was tough and hard to rattle.

"So what's the problem? You gonna stay mad at me cause I think fast? Huh? We have what we need to finish this thing. Rand being here is only gonna help, as are our new friends. They seem to be doing fine. They didn't have to be told a thing yet." She raised her dark eyes up to the ceiling, then went to work on the black eye liner around each eye with the towel.

Adrianna's face was readable this time. She was not upset. She looked distressed.

"I've had my future dictated to me so much in the past, it's just hard for me to not keep a stranglehold on what happens next. I'm not mad. I've only said I trust you to two people in my life, you and Jennifer. You understand?"

Murphy didn't understand. She'd not been through what Adrianna had been through. She blinked.

"What I'm trying to say is look what it took for me to trust you. You had to kill two men to earn that. Jennifer saved my future as a person." She dipped her head down.

Murphy pulled the towel away, not knowing what to say. She'd never been a part of "girl talk" or anything like it, never something this deep. She was smart though, and she wanted Adrianna's approval, much more than she cared to admit to herself. After a pause, Murphy finally said it.

"I'm sorry, Adrianna." The words came out clumsy, but they were sincere.

Adrianna lifted her head, one corner of her mouth bending upward.

"I do think you're right though."

That intrigued Murphy because she'd made the decision fast and not considered all the ramifications of it.

"You do?"

"Oh yeah," Adrianna sat up straighter in her chair. She looked very confident just then, like bringing along the insect aliens could be the key to everything they needed to get to the end game on all this.

"I know where they come from. I'm not surprised they might also have friends being hunted."

"What?"

"These two creatures come from planet 0875. One year ago Jennifer and her team uncovered the link between the former protectorate of Markem, Tanner Kory, and these aliens. Jennifer chose not to know the full truth about the linkage to help save her sanity. I was there when it all happened, Murphy."

Murphy glanced at Rand who had swiveled his pilot chair around to listen. Murphy switched her eyes back to Adrianna.

"The leaders of this insect race aren't capable of space travel, but they are capable of telepathy. They are so skilled at it they can kill with it. Which they did, to a member of Jennifer's team. We tracked down their home planet, 0875, then got video evidence of the atrocities that were taking place there and turned it all over to the Prime Minister of Beltina. Since these two insect aliens are still alive, it's clear that the Prime Minister of Beltina did not commit genocide on their race. These two, as others have, found a backer, a freebooter team, to help them travel off planet 0875. Bonisabella Brigham found this out. Remember, you yourself already said Brigham is aware of telepathic threats to her resort. So, she figured she could add to the variety, the diversity, of the safari by having these aliens as a part of it. Everything I've seen from these two creatures say they are not our enemy. They want the same thing we want. Therefore, you have to be right, Murphy." Adrianna shook her head. "In your haste, your quick thinking, your instincts have to be right."

Murphy sat back, taking all this in.

Rand spoke up, "Having insect aliens as a part of the hunting resort prey gives Brigham the ability to charge more. Now she has not two races being hunted, but three: humans, pinatens, and the insect aliens," he reasoned.

"So do you think our two friends here have telepathic ability then, Adrianna?" Murphy asked.

Adrianna tilted her head considering it.

"From what I know they call themselves a Collective. They have the ability to communicate to each other. But it comes from a central source, a higher source. At least that's as far as we got until we turned it all over to the Prime Minister of Beltina. I'm not certain that each member of the Insect Alien Collective has that higher ability." She looked up. "Do you?" She asked them both.

The two insect aliens looked passive for the most part. No answer looked forthcoming.

Adrianna eyed Murphy, "They seem to understand what we're try to accomplish. They're helping, and for me, that's enough."

"It's still going to take shutting down the electronic shield around the hunting resort for any one of us, them or us, to rush the place and shut it down," Murphy reasoned.

"Yes," Adrianna agreed.

"My first officer aboard *Brandish* is trailing us at a safe distance. I gave him our flight plan," Rand mentioned. "We'll have the backup when the time comes."

It was a fair take on the state of things as far as that went. The insect aliens, IAs for short, were not the enemy; they had demonstrated it several times already. They wanted to help in their own way, it was clear. Besides, they were both armed and could have used their weapons anytime they wanted to. Rand was considering all this to himself when one of the two IAs scurried, what seemed like cautiously, down from the ceiling and came to a slow halt perched off to his right. The insect was not that large and was able to stand on its back four legs just atop the flight console. Rand arched backward giving it room.

He stared into the creature's two compound eyes but didn't feel threatened. Rand could tell it moved slow on purpose. It was almost like it was trying not to be threatening. He nodded.

"You have a say in this you know," he said to it. He continued to look into the thousands of tiny light detectors that made up the domed surface of the creature's eyes. It had many mini-eyes instead of one big eye to allow it to spot very fast movements and see in a wide angle all around its body. The reddish hue of its compound eye was not readable of course. It had no eyelid; it didn't blink.

The IA extended one of its two upper limbs and began tapping commands into the nav panel keypad. The speed was blinding. In no time the readout came up with the coordinates of Brigham's staging pleasure base. Rand had already programmed that destination in, but the IA did it again. It was then Rand realized the insect alien was trying to communicate with him. The IA was confirming it wanted to go to the PB just like he did.

Adrianna couldn't see past his shoulder.

"What did it want, Rand?" She asked from behind him. She was looking at the IA perched motionless on the flight panel top.

"It confirmed that Brigham's staging pleasure base is the destination it wants," he said with his back to her.

Murphy glanced up at the ceiling at the other one.

"I want you both to help me get to the hunting resort. We have equipment in the hold that the resort wants and I know enough about how to calibrate and install the gear to convince the gatekeeper on the PB to let me travel to the resort to install it. I want both of you to be my assistants. You understand what I mean? This will be something Brigham won't expect. But once they see how fast and efficient you both are as installers, they may just let us do it. What do you think about that?" She turned her head toward the IA in front of Rand then back to the one on the ceiling. The one on the flight panel moved inputing commands into the nav panel again.

Murphy waited while Rand read the display to her. "It input the pleasure base coordinates again. I'm taking that as a confirmation, Murphy. The creature understands you." He swiveled, glancing at her for an instant, then turned back to the IA in front of him and nodded.

Murphy chimed in, "Good, how long until we get to the PB, Rand?"

"A solid 13 hours, slow ship," he confirmed. "I'm not that worried about Bonita Boss sending a ship to intercept us. Besides, BB has no loyalty to Brigham at all. I'm not even worried about Bonita Boss trying to warn Brigham we're heading to the staging pleasure base. Even if Bonita Boss sends a starship out to try to find us, they'd have almost zero chance of tracking us. The power plant on this pig is so weak, we don't paint enough of a radar signature to even get picked up by scans. Besides, I plotted a zig-zag route to the staging pleasure base, not a direct one."

The IA seemed satisfied then scurried up off the flight panel back to the ceiling near its friend. It paused, then the two creatures did a few circles around each other as though communicating with one another. The same one that had been on the panel darted down behind both Adrianna and Murphy stopping at the small hatch at the rear of the compartment that led to the cargo hold. It waited, then did a few quick circles in front of the hatch wanting in.

Murphy picked up on this and thought she understood. She turned from the IA and looked at Adrianna and Rand. The corner of her mouth rose.

"I think it wants me to show it what I know about the Voltaics. It wants to get familiar with the solar optimized packs. If they are going to be helping me, they want to practice first." She turned back to the IA, nodded, then back to Rand and Adrianna.

"I'll take them both back into the hold and try to explain what I can."

Adrianna nodded. Rand turned and fingered the cargo hatch release. The small hatch slid aside.

The other IA followed the first one through, then Murphy kneeled down squeezing through the mini-hatch out of site. As she did, she thought to herself *that 13 hours was plenty of time.*

Adrianna watched Murphy exit through the hatch trailing the two creatures, then turned to Rand. Rand shook his head.

"She can handle just about anything. There's got to be 15 or 20 steps left to get us to the end game on this mission, but that girl is already planning her victory dance."

Rand continued, "Murphy's got to be right about the gatekeeper on the PB, Adrianna. There has to be someone that screens the deliveries that are destined for the hunting resort. The equipment that we're transporting has been sitting idle for weeks on Bonita's pirate base. The staging pleasure base gatekeeper won't care that it's late, or that the cargo is coming in on a shit box like this ship. Brigham's PB can't control every supplier, especially when pirates get involved. I don't want to jeopardize our chances with the gatekeeper on the staging PB, but my face might be recognized—even way out here. I think it's just too much of a risk to have me be seen when we dock and get boarded."

Adrianna considered Rand's statement and came to a conclusion.

"I should fly the ship in then. These controls look basic enough and we have time. Can you teach me to dock?"

He nodded, "I think so. The biggest thing you have to keep in mind is mass, inertia. This ship has almost no power and can't stop on a tenth cred. We'll spend a good portion of the last hour of flight trying to slow this thing down. During that time, there will be a communication challenge from Brigham's PB. They'll want our transponder id and docking creds. I say creds because that's what they'll want most. They won't care who you are as long as you pay the steep fees. I can help you fly the ship up until a certain point, but Brigham may send out a ship to board us, or even board us and pilot us in for final approach. PBs don't normally do that, but this one has a majority customer pulling the strings. It's a staging place for Brigham's illegal hunt, so she has to have at least a few people stationed there screening cargo deliveries."

"I'm a ghost; my background is a black hole."

"That's not going to work best, Adrianna. We'll have to get Murphy to help us refresh the transponder id on our ship and work up a believable legend for you too. Believe it or not, you look the part of a freebooter the way you're dressed. You saw how rough the lot of assholes back at Bonita's Bar looked. In that respect, you fit in, but your face is clean...I mean it's not—"

"—Worn-down? Is that what you mean, Rand?"

"You have this thing you do where you mask how you feel, painting your facial features so blank no one can tell what's behind them. You understand you do that, right?"

Adrianna was doing it now. It was like she didn't know that she was, but had to do it—had to out of some scorched earth need to deflect the harm that her eyes had seen and her body had been subjected to. She didn't answer.

Rand was scared to place a hand on her arm. She was so unreadable that there was no way he could tell if she understood, didn't understand, didn't care, or cared so much she wanted to kill to protect it. He decided to risk it. He reached out and grasp her forearm. She didn't jerk or pull back; she just continued to look straight through him. Adrianna's look was very unsettling. Of course, the reason she did it had to be more unsettling to her, and what her past was like.

Adrianna focused on Rand's face, her eyes serious, "I can adapt. You'll have to help me though." She looked almost pleading.

He didn't understand what she meant by help. He stood up and took the stool that Murphy had vacated so he could look into her eyes and try to get a read on her.

"Adrianna, I'm sure you can do anything you want. I know you can adapt. But I don't know what you mean by help."

Adrianna studied his face, then her look glazed over again to the void-of-all-voids. She heaved a ragged sigh. The look on her face was so neutral all that was present were the words coming out of her mouth. It was disconcerting. Rand fought to control his anxiety about it, about her.

"You'll have to let me practice how I should look when I play the part I need to play, Rand. I have one protection setting when I'm faced with danger; you've seen it now many times. I embrace it to defend. It's been a part of me ever since I was very young and all the bad things started happening to me."

The little Rand knew about Adrianna's slaver background had to be the reason for this. That much he understood. It seemed like she could talk about it, about how to correct it so they could be successful. He didn't know, however, if he should take it slow or jump straight in. In fairness to himself, he was scared of Adrianna. Whatever was behind her face, buried in her mind, was not something he could relate to on any level. He decided to ask permission. Yes, that was going to be the best thing here.

"Do I have permission to help you learn how to play the role you need to play, Adrianna?"

She looked down. "I'm sorry you're afraid of me, Rand."

He blinked, not sure what to say. A young woman like her, a normal young woman, like many women he knew, might need a hug just now. Rand wasn't so sure if he extended his arms to try hugging her that he might pull back empty stumps. Adrianna was wired so tight the agony of her past was teetering on a minuscule precipice. He just wasn't sure what to do or say, so he said nothing, controlling his impulse to comfort her.

She looked up at him. Her eyes were hopeful this time.

"I want to get this right and I want to do this well. I have to, Rand. Jennifer gave me this chance to help her. I can't let her down. Please help me. I won't hurt you. I promise."

"I want to touch your face. Will you let me do that, Adrianna?"

She nodded.

He reached both hands out cupping a cheek in each one.

"Okay, this is how I'm going to help you. When I ask you a question, I'll manipulate you're facial expression to how I think you should respond to play the role of a freebooter. I may even touch your forehead and eye brows. Okay?"

She dipped her head once.

"And by the way, I'm no longer scared of you, Adrianna. I'm concerned for you, that's all. I know you aren't going to hurt me."

Rand inserted his thumb tips on either side of her mouth and pushed up her lips into a small smile. Her lips quivered and resisted at first then she understood he was already starting to help her show the correct emotion—to practice it.

"We're just going to have a conversation, okay?" He continued. "I'll talk with you, ask some questions that a freebooter would normally be asked, and we'll practice your emotional responses. Just relax and try to remember what your face feels like when you react. Sound good?"

Adrianna raised the corners of her lips confirming the best she could.

They practiced for over four hours.

ELEVEN

Bonisabella Brigham was her own gatekeeper. She stationed herself on the staging pleasure base, not her resort. This had to be the case given who met Adrianna in the docking bay. The woman took what could only be termed as a HUGE interest in her cargo. Brigham was thrilled to see it arrive.

"You came from Bonita's didn't you?" The big black woman asked.

Adrianna and Rand had made good progress and discussed how Adrianna needed to play the role of a freebooter. She was a confident person by nature, and she needed to emphasize that part of her persona. She was conscious of not going back into her facial shell as Rand had termed it. Adrianna had to think hard to prevent her body and face from going into defense mode, but being aware of it made it easier as did her commitment to helping Jennifer. It was a driving guidepost bracketing her performance.

"Yes I did, listen…" She scanned the heavyset woman's face, "What's your name again?"

"Iz."

"Okay, look, Iz, I need food and a change of clothes. You understand? I'll let you and whoever you want climb all over the cargo in my hold after I eat. It wasn't easy getting here. Bonita Boss was a real bitch. But you know that. She keeps everyone starving on her shit hole of a base. I finally had to just take the cargo and her ship." Adrianna shrugged like she didn't care what the woman did or did not think of that.

"Hey, I'm not complaining. I just don't know you. How the hell did you know that coming here with that cargo would help you move it?" Suspicious, sure, that wasn't a surprise.

"My techie scanned her net and found out Bonita had been sitting on the Voltaics for a while. I came to the closest place to get SOME EFFIN' FOOD!" Adrianna's voice grew to a scream. Her face was flushed and she placed her hand over her holstered laser pistol. It was clear she was in no mood for 25 questions.

Bonisabella Brigham gave a smug look. She could. She wasn't hungry. She weighed just south of 300 pounds. Her look turned resigned, as though she expected something like this. Dealing with freebooters was commonplace for her. How could it not be? The dredges of space frequented this pleasure base. She had seen it all.

"Relax—what did you say your name was?"

Adrianna's face turned dark, not blank, just dark and dangerous.

"I didn't, and I may never unless you stop with the questions."

She pulled the LP out of the holster now, letting it rest at her side. Without waiting she turned toward the blast hatch off to her right. At the same time Murphy and the two IAs came out of the pilot hatch of the *Payman* behind her. The *Payman* had a rounded snub nose where the cockpit was located. Just behind the front view port was the hatch. Murphy jumped down to the deck followed by the two insect aliens. Stopping quickly, they flanked Murphy still both with their little vests on and LP holsters.

Murphy yelled. "Don't take too long all right! We need grub too!" She glanced sideways at both the IAs in turn. "They don't need clothes, but I sure do!"

Adrianna hesitated, turned and nodded, then swept past Bonisabella Brigham without a second glance. She hurried through the blast hatch leaving Brigham staring at Murphy and her two crew mates.

There wasn't even a hint of surprise or curiosity in Brigham's face. She carried herself like an old-fashioned woman. She was in her mid thirties, walked around with, of all things, a clip board, and didn't even have a hand comp. She used a pencil to scribble notes. When people met her, they were disarmed by her looks. She weighed 280 pounds. Her dark ebony skin was hidden under a plus size cut-and-sew poly long sleeve Tee and black leggings. The multi-color black, brown and tan rib-knit V-neck top was presentable enough to look professional. Her chubby smile was genuine, and her black teeny weeny afro haircut parted to one side. It was her dark brown eyes that revealed what her appearance did not. They were authentic and clever. Brigham was, behind her modest trappings, brilliant.

"So, you gonna just stand there or you gonna tell me who you are?" Murphy spat. Not disrespectful, more playful than that, but impatient as was her nature.

The large woman dipped her head. "Iz, and you?"

"Daw."

"Okay, Daw. I've not had success speaking with crew like yours," she said referring to the two IAs. "Mind if I ask how you do it?"

Murphy put her hands on her hips like this was plain stupid. She threw a nice dose of impatience in her spirited response. Every word she spoke grew in volume until she was yelling so loud her neck veins looked like curvy ropes on a table under her tats.

"It all has To Do WITH BEING FED!" The two IAs did their little circle dance thing around each other out in front of Murphy then returned to either side of her.

Bonisabella smirked. She knew she was dealing with a player, someone that could think fast just like her. She shook her head.

"Point taken."

She turned and left through the blast hatch. On the other side of the hatch someone was waiting for her. Bonisabella looked over at her assistant, Snide Jannigan, coming to a halt next to the taller man. "What'd you think?"

Snide's appearance was more refined. He was tailored in a sheen grey suit and pants. The white button down shirt collar pinching his thin neck looked like a razor blade. No tie was appropriate, so he didn't wear one. He was lean to the point of being hollow cheeked. Eating was not his past time. He often thought if he could find a way not to eat he could save countless hours. Almost 50-years-old, most of this his hair was a thing of the past with just a little small patch of greying black peach fuzz above each ear. His blue eyes were honest. He respected Bonisabella and knew how intelligent she was. He never painted a rosy picture when there was bad news to tell. He believed it was better to communicate bad news as fast as possible rather than delaying. Snide was right about that. It had served him well working with such a formidable lady like Bonisabella.

That's why his look was serious when Snide let Bonisabella know what he thought.

"The pilot has a standard background. I'm not surprised she took matters into her own hands. There's a part of her past that I can't figure out though. But, from the looks of her, it may be a slaver past. She seems high strung enough. The pilot probably would've used her LP if you had pissed her off any more. But food overrode her impulse. Besides, you're a buyer, and she wants to get paid. Now, as for the techy and her creatures, I don't have any info on them yet." He didn't tell Bonisabella something he didn't know, never a good idea; he left it to her to figure out what she wanted next.

Bonisabella shot him an approving nod. She knew there had been little time since the cargo ship docked to get an accurate picture of the crew, but that was okay. The *Payman* had the optimized battery packs she had badly needed for weeks now. She couldn't care less that Bonita Boss wasn't in the picture anymore. The bitch had been trying to blackmail her for almost a month to up the price. Now the equipment she needed to keep her resort up and running was right on the other side of the blast hatch. She had no intention of letting it get away.

She came to a decision.

"Snide, make sure that pilot gets a cred line on base, okay?" She waited.

Snide carried a slate, one that was piped into the base's net. He keyed it out of sleep mode, pecking a few dozen commands into it, the soft glow of the light blue vid screen reflecting off his thin face.

"Done." He pulled his gaze up from the small screen looking at Bonisabella.

She tilted her head. After about two minutes, Snide's slate pinged. He looked down at it.

"The pilot got her first purchase gratis, food rations," he confirmed.

"All right," Bonisabella's look turned thoughtful. "The women and the insects seem to be working together." She jerked her head at the blast hatch referring to Murphy and the IAs. "What do you think of that?" She relied on Snide as her sounding board. He was always deliberate and forthcoming with his opinions, whether good or bad.

"On the surface it doesn't bother me. But the woman in there has to be pretty intelligent if she's able to work with them as equals. I mean, from what we've already seen, they're part of her crew. This is new territory for us. Up until now all we've done is capture and enslave their kind. It bothers me that the one ship that brings in the equipment we need the most has someone on their team that smart. It doesn't add up."

Bonisabella smiled to herself remembering why Snide was so valuable. He complemented her strengths by covering her weaknesses. She was distracted by the chance to keep her resort running by upgrading its power sources. Snide wasn't distracted by that at all.

"Why don't I just ask the techie how she got the insect aliens to join her team? If I don't like what she tells me, we can get one of our friends on base to just kill them. The one problem I see with that is that I don't know how to install and calibrate the Voltaic equipment. It'd take time to find someone to help us do that. That's the biggest downside to eliminating them that I see."

"Maybe we can force them to do the work we want. Keep the pilot on ice and force—what was her name?"

"Daw," Bonisabella answered.

"Force Daw to install the stuff." Bonisabella was shaking her head as Snide said it.

"What?" He asked.

"A few things, first we have to keep the thoughts of whoever travels to the resort free from mind mensuration. If we threaten her pilot, Daw will be thinking about that the whole trip out to the resort. If someone is scanning Daw's mind telepathically, like we already know is possible, then that gives them the opportunity to pull her thoughts for inspection. If a telepathy team reads her thoughts, they'll know that I'm holding Daw's pilot hostage. In turn, that betrays the reason for Daw's trip. We've gone to too much trouble staging visitors on this pleasure base and enclosing clients in deadening booths to slip up now. The deadening booths prevent telepaths from reading minds—period."

"I see your point. Maybe it's just best not to tell Daw anything at all. Just purchase their cargo and ask them to deliver it where it's needed. If they ask about the destination, we tell them what we're telling everyone that delivers cargo to the resort for us—pleasure base for the wealthy."

Bonisabella nodded in agreement. "We don't need to get creative at this point. We have supply ships coming and going to the hunting resort and we don't tell them anything. All they know is that the cargo they deliver is needed. It's been working. The freebooters get paid and they don't think about anything else that would betray their thoughts to anyone scanning their minds. The dedicated docking bay on the resort is nondescript. Their cargo is unloaded and the freebooters never see the other side of the blast hatch. Compartmentalization has been working its magic since day one with no security breach." She nibbled her lower lip.

"But?" Snide saw her apprehension.

"But, *this* cargo is different. It can't be left in the docking bay. It has to be installed, calibrated, and the old equipment removed. When we installed the initial startup Voltaic equipment nine months ago, I knew the battery packs wouldn't last indefinitely. It was easy to avoid anyone knowing what that equipment would be used for. You helped me solve that problem. You suggested we just enslave the installation crew and make them the first test prey— the hunting prey group for Gather 1. Your plan worked well, and it helped us get the kinks out of the Pullback. Now charging 2.2 million creds per client is easy."

Snide saw where Bonisabella was heading with this, status quo, doing nothing different, nothing that they had not already had success with. Not broke, don't fix and all that nonsense.

But this wasn't nonsense. The power to keep the time device—called the *Pullback*, and the device that shielded the resort from telepathy—called the *Absorber*, operational was massive. Both devices had to work flawlessly if they wanted to keep charging 2.2 million creds buy-in for a hunt. If Bonisabella couldn't pullback the day, reset it, then the *Guarantee* for her clients was useless. If just one client died and failed to resurrect as a result of the Pullback malfunctioning due to lack of power, the resort would collapse. By the same token, if the shield absorber that surrounded the resort failed, then scans could find its location, and telepathy teams could read the minds of anyone on it—again a disaster. The Pullback and Absorber were interconnected and inseparable, both reliant on nothing more simple than power, power that had to be periodically upgraded—power that could be upgraded with the cargo that was on the other side of the blast hatch they were standing next to now.

The decision was clear.

"Bonnie, let's allow the pilot and her crew to eat and clean up. They're not going anywhere in the condition they're in. We don't have to look anxious. We can just treat them well then negotiate terms. Once they eat and clean up, they'll be ready to do what they always do— look out for themselves and get paid. They'll work with you. You have a good disposition when it comes to dealing with freebooters like this. You give them room to move. You leaving the cargo bay and not seeming too excited was smart. You're good at thinking on your feet; just keep doing it."

Bonisabella nodded. "This Daw seems smart." She twitched her head sideways, a decision clear in her mind. "If she and the IAs can install the Voltaics, I'm going to let them. I can always decide how to dispose of them after I get what I want." The ease with which she was used to throwing away human life was habit forming. She was doing it unconsciously now. And she was doing it a lot, making huge profits off it. The lack of emotion in her decision indisputable proof of the monster that had formed within her—not just a monster, an evil blight of a human being, a hideous pestilence of sin.

Murphy was smart. Bonisabella was right about that. Even more so than smart, she was practical. The instant Brigham left through the blast hatch, she darted back into the cargo ship to grab what she needed, something very obvious, not high tech. She ran over to the hatch, placed a synth glass cup against the hatch, and pressed her ear to it. Murphy had just heard every word Bonisabella Brigham and Snide Jannigan said. Even for her, the blasé manner in which they discussed snuffing out life made her breath catch. Brigham didn't even know she had already met her match in a cunning lady by the name of Murphy Alyse.

When Murphy sensed she needed to stop listening, she jogged back over to the ship popping back into the cockpit. She fingered the release on the tailgate cargo ramp on the *Payman*. The ramp was at the rear between the two small jet nozzles used for propulsion by the bulky cargo craft. The ramp lowered contacting the deck with a loud scrape. The IAs sensed what was coming next and scurried around the back of the ship.

Payman cargo ships were shaped like a rounded, blunt-nosed arrowhead. The cockpit and crew space was crammed into the front of the nose. Then the large cargo hold fanned out behind the flight deck on either side. The ramp was between the two small engines that were synchronized to perform as one. The engine and life support components were tucked in the back of the cargo hold on either side of the cargo ramp. The components and engines were minimal, only large enough to give the craft enough power to build up speed, carry a few people, generate gravity, and not much more.

Just then Murphy got a ping on her hand comp. Adrianna was bringing food and clothes. She confirmed the message, then hopped back out the open cockpit hatch down onto the deck. She turned and jogged down the length of the ship rounding the back corner in front of one of the engine nozzles. She cut the hard left up the ramp not paying attention to the two IAs waiting behind the ship.

Overhead bins lined each ceiling corner at the rear of the hold. There were two five-foot wide, two-feet high storage bins, one on each side. The left one was refrigerated and could be used for perishable food. The right one was for dry provisions and storage. This bin was empty except for a cramped space for Rand to hide in. Murphy shot a glance back out the open ramp hatch, saw the two IAs waiting, then thumbed the release button opening the bin door swinging it upward a few inches on hinges. She didn't open it all the way, no need. Rand would be able to hear her talk just fine. Before she spoke, she again looked out the ramp hatch. She was becoming familiar with how the IAs be-haved. If they were calm, and not doing little movements or their circle dance around each other, then she perceived they weren't stressed; therefore, no one was in the cargo bay yet.

Murphy remained facing the open hatch, her outstretched arm on the bin door up high to her left, ready to shut it closed at any second.

"Brigham's the gatekeeper, Rand; she's not on the hunting resort." She continued summarizing what she heard Brigham and Jannigan discuss. When she was done, she noticed the IAs stir. They were agitated. Her hand slapped the bin lid shut before Rand could reply. The motion of closing it propelled her out through the hatch and down the ramp. She turned to see Adri-anna coming toward the rear of the ship guiding a small anti grav cart. Murphy was famished; there was no acting in that at all. She almost dove at the open cart pulling out an armful of food. Adrianna was chomping on something of her own and let it happen.

Adrianna reached in after Murphy was done and threw two ration packs, one after another, in the direction of the IAs. One IA caught them both. The speed at which it snagged the food out of mid air looked effortless. The two creatures had to be as hungry as the humans, probably more so, given their frenetic pace of inbred movement. They started in on the rations in their own way. The IA that caught the rations used a protruding digit from an upper leg to slice open the two plasti bags it was holding lengthwise, opening them like a clam shell. The movement was so fast it wasn't visible. It held one in each upper leg, pitched its thorax forward, its head dipping into the sliced opening. It used its mandibles to masticate the food in a chewing-like motion. In the other upper leg, it held the other pre-opened ration bag while the second IA dipped its thorax pushing its mouthparts into the opening, eating the contents of that one. The one that held both bags let them drop to the deck the instant they were finished.

Murphy jogged past the creatures up the ramp, stopped in front of Rand's bin, opened it, and shoved a ration pack in, closing it. Almost before she got the lid shut, she was tearing the perforated top of the plasti seal bag of her food. She plopped down beside a pallet on the cargo deck and greedily began shoveling food into her mouth. She glanced up between swallows to see Adrianna hand two more rations to the IAs; they grabbed one each this time.

Adrianna turned wiping the back of her mouth with her dirty shirt, and strode up the ramp coming up short in front of Murphy who was still munching feverishly seated on the deck next to a Voltaic pallet. Adrianna cleared her throat, then lifted a plasti bottle of water to her lips gulping noisily. She burped, not covering her mouth, at the same time tossing the other bottle of water she was holding to Murphy. Murphy outstretched an open hand letting the bottle smack into her grasp. She dropped the ration bag into her lap, unscrewed the bottle top, and gulped down half the water almost choking.

Murphy looked up at Adrianna.

"Thanks. I'm weak I'm so damn hungry, and from hearing that psycho Brigham and her Demon Boy talk about killing us at their earliest convenience."

Adrianna had been around Murphy long enough now to know how she was. She waited.

Murphy took a few more gulps of water and burped herself. Her look was one that Adrianna had not seen before. Was there fear in her face? Couldn't be, not from this woman, but it sure looked like it. For the first time since almost being raped back at Bonita's, Adrianna was worried. If Murphy was afraid, something was wrong. Very wrong.

"What Murphy? What is it?"

Just then Rand's bin hatch opened a few inches and a lone hand extruded from the four-inch crack bin lid opening, signaling he needed water too. Adrianna turned out through the ramp hatch and returned in no time with another plasti bottle of water handing it to him. It disappeared through the gap. Several gulps could be heard muffled by the partially closed lid.

Adrianna focused back on Murphy. Murphy looked out the ramp hatch verifying the IAs were calm before she spoke.

"Brigham's going to let us take the cargo to the resort, but she hasn't decided if she wants to let us live after we help her." Her face was serious when she said it. "Not only that, she has this business-like assistant guy who is so analytical and calculating he's treating all the killing he and Brigham are doing as commonplace, like figures on an accounting ledger, snuff out

X number of people, get X number of creds. The psychos are charging 2.2 million creds buy-in, Adrianna. I don't even want to tell you what happened to the team that installed the initial Voltaics nine months ago when the resort first opened..." She trailed off.

"Bet they were test subjects." Adrianna and Murphy looked up to find Rand's face peering out through opened bin above them.

Adrianna shifted her gaze back to Murphy finding nothing but confirmation painted across her face. Murphy nodded.

"Spot on, he is. Spot on." She confirmed. "Mr. Fullrider knows his space scum. It was her demented assistant's idea to use the installation team as beta test subjects to test the first use of the Pullback." She shot a look up at Rand then up at Adrianna standing in front of her.

"That's right, resetting the day is called a Pullback. They DO have a time device on that resort." She looked down in her lap; the food was disgusting to smell and see all of a sudden. She caught a gag in her throat, then turned her head and spit the phlegm that she'd gathered in her mouth off into the corner of the hold. When she looked back at them both again, the conviction etching her young, strong face was a physical energy of its own. She stood up. Another first was that Murphy started to leave the cargo hold without another word, like she was done talking, and was going to take the rest of this perverse state of affairs into her own hands and end the misery once and for all—by herself.

Rand and Adrianna both reached for her. Murphy jerked her leer up at Rand then at his grip on her shoulder. He was leaning way out of the bin where he'd lunged to grab her. Murphy turned her robotic stare on Adrianna who had outstretched a hand into Murphy's chest. Her hand just happened to land on Murphy's right breast. She didn't seem to care.

"There's something I found out, Murphy. Please wait, listen to me! Let me tell you what I saw on base. It's got me puzzled. I've never seen something like this on a pleasure base before." She removed her grip on her breast staring into Murphy's eyes.

"Please wait until we talk about this. I promise, I'll let you end this. I trust you. I trust your opinion, and I need it now. Please, Murphy…"

Murphy had started breathing hard. It was so unlike her to lose her bearings, to come unraveled. It scared both Rand and Adrianna to see her unhinged like this. They both already knew she was dangerous, but this focus on destruction was something more.

Rand gently squeezed her shoulder before pulling back his hand.

"Please, Murphy, listen to what she has to say." He was not sure she was hearing him.

She did.

"All right." Her body deflated with a long, ragged breath. Her shoulders sagged back to normalcy, and she crossed her arms waiting.

Adrianna too looked back out the open ramp hatch. The IAs were motionless. Could they be hanging on the next words Adrianna and Murphy were going to say? It was impossible to tell, but it sure seemed like it.

"There's a huge Medico presence on the PB, Murphy, an infirmary. It takes up at least a third of the base. Pleasure bases never waste that kind of space on something that doesn't bring in hard creds. I can't figure it out. I want you to help me."

Murphy thinned her lips considering what Adrianna had said for about two seconds before coming to a conclusion—a fast one. She looked matter-of-factly into Adrianna's eyes.

"The supply of hunting prey is not limitless. They patch some of the injured prey up when they're short on bodies then send them back to the resort to be hunted again." How she knew and understood the meaning of what Adrianna had told her made her the unparalleled person she was.

"And the infirmary itself doesn't take up a third of the space on the PB. No way—there's a private Medico landing bay that takes up most of the space. I'll bet there aren't but six or eight beds in the infirmary, maybe less. This cunning bitch and her demon seed of an assistant doesn't want anyone seeing who comes and goes from their little field hospital…or why, or when the hunting prey die, they don't want to explain it to anyone."

Adrianna knew not to ask Murphy, *How can you know all that?* It was fact. And it meant something very important. *Do we cut our losses and run? Or do we do the right thing, the hard thing, the necessary thing, and shut down this pleasure base and the hunting resort too?*

Rand understood it. He knew that the bigger decision would come next, but for now he said what all three of them were thinking.

"Krachy could very well be in the infirmary. He's a skilled warrior and probably's been injured and patched up more than once." He didn't say it with a smile because he knew that getting him back was only step one. It was step two that was going to be the massive decision, even a more colossal undertaking— shutting down the hunting resort. And for now the three of them were going to have to make that decision alone.

Adrianna was staring at Rand when he said it. Then she shifted her scrutiny back on Murphy. Murphy uncrossed her arms, relaxing noticeably.

"Addy, you may have just saved Jennifer's short man hunk." She crinkled her lower jaw not smiling, but glad that at least one good thing might come from all this horror today. She hadn't forgotten about killing two people on Bonita's pirate base. The gravity of her actions hadn't caught up with her yet.

Again, Adrianna didn't ask the obvious. Murphy had been right about everything she surmised so far. *How could Krachy not be here? And, how could he not be alive?* It was nice to consider, but only framed in the larger backdrop of all the death and suffering, and the death and suffering that may be yet to come.

"How do we rescue Krachy and shut down that foul bitch's resort at the same time?"

Murphy had an idea about that. "We don't have to rescue Krachy. We distance ourselves from his rescue altogether."

Adrianna looked up at Rand who was grinning. "Solid AND bold bitch, you are that Murphy. You are, you are."

Adrianna's forehead puckered. She didn't understand. "What? We can't leave Krachy, I won't leave hi—!"

Murphy shot out a hand cupping Adrianna's left tit. It didn't startle her; it just made her wheel her look back at Murphy.

"That's a job for Jennifer, right?" She removed her hand. "All we have to do is confirm Krachy's here on the PB. You trust Jennifer too, don't you?" Murphy smiled.

Adrianna nibbled the corner of her lower lip then matched Murphy's reassuring smile.

"Fuckin' A I do!"

Scratching noises came from behind Adrianna. In haste, Murphy jumped up and shut the bin lid as Rand pulled himself back inside. The two women exited the ship down the ramp looking around the small landing bay. The star twinkling depths of deep space beyond the bay's magnetic containment field were clear of incoming ships and no one else had come through the blast hatch—they were alone. They shifted their attention back to the IAs. The two of them were not doing their little circle dance now; they both stood on their hind four legs upright, shifting from leg-to-leg-to-leg so fast the scratching noises seemed like a constant sound.

Murphy was standing beside Adrianna. She swung her right arm into Adrianna's stomach getting her attention. Adrianna turned to her.

"They want to help," Murphy explained.

Again, Adrianna fought the urge to question it, question the logic, question how the heck Murphy knew all these things before they happened! She just did.

"Let's let them." Adrianna looked over at her nodding.

Murphy reached into her grungy blue fight suit pocket pulling out her hand comp. She tapped at the screen for a few seconds then turned the screen toward the two IAs. It was blinding fast the reaction it had on one of the creatures. It pitched forward, dodged past the two women, scaled the back of the cargo ship, then leapt the short distance to the landing bay ceiling, simultaneously pivoting in mid-air grabbing the ceiling and turning upside down. It moved lightening fast toward the only thing up on the ceiling, the O2 recycling vent. It scurried over to the vent in a blink and did something with its six legs that caused the dura steel grate to drop from its moorings and fall down onto the deck in front of the cargo ship. It was in through the opening and gone in a mere split instant.

The two women looked at one another then back at the remaining IA who wasn't where it had been not three seconds earlier. They both searched the landing bay spotting it already next to the vent the other IA had just left through. It remained there in what looked like vigilance, like a sentry at its post, or a friend waiting to greet another friend returning from a mission.

This time Adrianna understood.

"It's waiting for its partner to come back through the vent. I guess all we have to do is wait ourselves—"

Almost before she finished her sentence, the IA that had left darted through the vent so fast they would have both missed it if they weren't looking at the opening. Its partner didn't follow; instead it leapt from the ceiling down onto the front of the ship out of sight. It reappeared again, scurrying fast up the far wall of the landing bay holding the fallen grate in two legs. It had the grate back in place and secured before Adrianna and Murphy could turn to face the IA that had just returned. The IA was back in front of them, not agitated, standing on its four back legs.

"You showed the IA a picture of Krachy didn't you, Murphy?" Adrianna asked not turning to face her, just staring at the short tan creature in front of her with admiration.

"Uh huh," Murphy replied.

The second IA made its way back to a halt beside its partner and instead of doing their circle dance around each other they did something neither woman had seen them do before. They pitched forward on all six legs. The left IA scurried back a few feet like it was giving its partner more room. The IA that had just returned turned its abdomen toward the two women and waited.

Murphy didn't have to ask, so she didn't. What she showed the IA earlier on her hand comp was question enough.

The back end of the IA's abdomen bobbed up-and-down. It stopped. Then bobbed up-and-down again twice. It did that several more times.

Adrianna grinned, "That's a yes isn't is, Murphy?"

Murphy turned to her. "They have been watching us. Our body language, and yes, an up-and-down is a yes, damn right it is!"

Adrianna could finally give the one person in her life that meant the most to her good news—Jennifer. She had fulfilled part of her debt she wanted to pay forward to Jennifer for saving her from the hideous life she was destined never to escape at the hand of the slavers. She sighed.

"I want to give Krachy hope."

"Hope Adrianna, we're almost halfway there." Murphy turned to the IAs which were standing side-by-side, their compound eyes affixed on the two women. "Thank you, you gave us great back up this time!"

No movement was forthcoming from the IAs; emotion was not an instinctual part of their race, as it were, but that was okay. They were quick, decisive, and determined teammates, and that was good enough. Murphy sensed the rest of it, what was driving them.

"We're going to get your friends off the hunting resort too. We haven't forgotten."

The two IAs didn't react. Murphy sensed they expected as much and realized that she, Adrianna, and Rand had only good intentions in mind for them. This was certainly an inimitable team, matchless in its crest.

Adrianna persisted. "Krachy needs to know we're going to help him."

Murphy studied her for a moment and nodded. "You should go tell Rand. He can help us think of a way to get you into the infirmary."

Adrianna brushed past Murphy climbing the ramp excited to share what they'd found with Rand.

TWELVE

"It's never that simple. It just never is."

Rand jerked his head back-and-forth looking at the two women standing in the cramped confines of the cargo hold. They had closed the ramp and were taking a few minutes to discuss their next steps. The IAs were in the landing bay to head off any visit from Brigham or her Skinny Demon Boy Jannigan.

"You can't think Brigham would fall for that, Adrianna. Brigham has too much to protect! She's not going to let you in the infirmary unless you're bleeding out, and maybe even not then. She's an evil bitch, remember?" He took a swig of water then bent back at the waist stretching his back after being in the overhead bin for so long.

Adrianna considered what he said. "You're right, faking an injury won't work. I could go pick a fight with someone bigger than me and let them pound on me some; that'd get me enough damage, but yeah, Brigham may just toss me out an airlock instead of treating me though. Then how do we verify if Krachy's in the infirmary? The other question is do we trust the IAs recon that he is?"

Murphy spoke up. "Whatever we do we need to do it fast. When I listened to them talk earlier, they wanted to give us time to eat and clean up. Brigham will be back soon; count on it."

Rand was staring down at the deck. He looked worried.

"What is it, Rand?" Adrianna asked.

He looked up, his forehead crinkled with indecision.

"Just what I said. This is not that simple. An infirmary, here, on a PB, maybe with it's own landing bay. What else does that mean? It's never just one thing with people like Brigham. It's always layers, tiers of deceit and profit. I've been around people like her before."

Adrianna wasn't following him; Murphy thought she might be. "There's another reason, maybe several reasons why they have an infirmary here. We don't have to figure out what those reasons are."

Adrianna jabbed her a questioning look but Rand just nodded, his lips thinning, urging Murphy towards it. Murphy considered it more.

"We only have to figure out what Brigham's reasons are. What would she do with an infirmary?" She hesitated, then wondered aloud, "What do you do with bodies, live ones that are damaged or almost expired?"

"That part is easy," Rand replied. "You do just like we were going to let Bonita Boss do. You carve up the pieces and sell them off. The parts are worth more than the whole, basic rule of thumb. If the bodies are reparable, you send them back to the resort so you can make more profit from them being hunted; that's two tiers of treachery right there."

"But you think there's even more don't you, Rand?" Adrianna asked.

"Most certainly," he took in a long breath. "Body parts and hunting prey are a start. What's inside of us is valuable too."

"Huh?"

"Blood, Adrianna, blood," he scanned both women in turn. "Brigham kidnaps pinatens, humans, and insect aliens as hunting prey. She can sell off body parts, hunt them, and use their blood for experiments, experiments that she'd get paid for—paid to supply the raw materials. So look at this now, three species times three tiers. Now we're getting closer to what I'd expect from someone like her. Nine cost centers, profit centers, whatever."

"This is getting complicated," Murphy scratched the top of her head nervously, "And time sensitive. Look, the way I see it, it doesn't matter whether Krachy is here or not. I mean it matters, but either way this den of death on the pleasure base has to be shut down too. Jennifer can't be expected to rescue just Krachy. There may be many people, or creatures, that need liberated from this hell hole. We're gonna have to leave that up to Jennifer. Right?" She turned to Adrianna.

"Jennifer wouldn't be able to leave a group of injured people without helping. That's not how she's wired. You're right; she wouldn't leave them, so there's not really a decision for her to make there. I know her; she's going to be upset—no, that's not the right word. Jennifer's going to be *furious* when she sees what has been going on here. I wouldn't be surprised if she took out her frustrations on the people that run this PB."

"So the question still stands—We should let Jennifer do what she has to do, right, Rand?" Murphy asked.

"All right, we can do that. But we're going to be in the same situation when we get to the resort. There may be many, or dozens, of prey that will need to be rescued. In the end, it doesn't matter if the IAs are right or not about Krachy being here. We're going to check out the only other place he could be anyway—the hunting resort. We just go to the resort and shut it down because we have a way to get there, to be led to it, to find it. If Krachy is there, we get him back along with all the other prey. This will be big, more complex; we'll need a bigger ship with better life support. This cargo ship has lots of room, but can't make enough O2 and scrub it loaded with people."

Murphy was considering what he said. "Well, she has to have a ship, why not use hers?"

Rand's brows drew down. "You mean Brigham's ship?"

"Of course I do."

"I'm not gong to ask you how that might be possible. You already know that we have to get the coordinates for her resort before we make a move on her. We can't damage Brigham until she tells us where her resort is actually located."

Adrianna was shaking her head.

"You disagree, Adrianna?"

"I do," Adrianna confirmed.

"Care to share?"

"We make a move on Brigham first, once and for all. We have all the tools we need right here to do it. This end of her op needs to be shut down just like the resort. There are ways to get the information we need; I can explain those ways in detail. They were done to me."

Adrianna's face went back into its facial shell, her unreadable past doubtless on her mind now. Then her look changed dangerous, no longer blank and unreadable.

"I'm tired of going in the side door on this thing. Jennifer needs her man, and I'm going to deliver that to her along with the coordinates to the hunting resort. Brigham and her Skinny Demon Boy are the keys to all this. They're here and time is running out. I can give them all the incentive they need to spill it!"

Rand had no doubt she could coerce and incentivize Brigham and her Demon Boy to spill whatever secrets they had. It seemed all the emotion lessons they'd worked on were lost on Adrianna now; a dark determination was behind her defensive look. It overrode everything, and every emotion, because it was her default mindset. She had kept it together long enough to get them on the pleasure base. He agreed; now was the time to act. They did have the tools to do it. The insect aliens were going to be a part of it, no doubt.

Just then a pounding came from the ramp hatch behind them. A dull bang, bang, bang, more like a strong fist pounding on the door asking to come in. The startled look on all three of their faces said the same thing: *How did whoever it was get past the IAs without them being warned?*

Rand drew his laser pistol not willing to climb back up into the overhead bin. Adrianna turned and did the same, both of them aiming at the closed hatch. Murphy shrugged one arm accepting that the decision to act was pretty much being made for them by whoever was pounding on the hatch. She shuffled over to the scan pad to the right of the ramp hatch then turned sideways to look at both Adrianna and Rand in turn. Rand went down on one knee in a shooting stance aiming at the hatch. Adrianna inched back around the corner of the pallet behind her shielding herself as she peered around the corner taking careful aim. She nodded once. Murphy passed her hand over the scan pad and the ramp started to open. She darted back behind Adrianna realizing that if a fire fight was to ensue she was no help without a weapon.

When the ramp made contact with the deck, Adrianna and Rand relaxed. Murphy was behind Adrianna and could see the tension in her shoulders ebb. She peeked around Adrianna's shoulder to see the tall, determined, and very welcome frame of Jeffrey Jansen standing at the bottom of the ramp. Jennifer and Dimitri were just behind him as was Channing Altimer.

"Don't shoot—I give up." Jennifer raised her hands in mock submission as she brushed past Jeffrey then took a few steps up the ramp coming to a stop and studying the three of them.

"You lot look a mess," she observed, then turned to her left. Rand, Adrianna, and Murphy stepped over to the open hatch and, following Jennifer's gaze, looked right bending their necks around the corner past the engine nozzle to see what Jennifer was looking at.

The two insect aliens had Bonisabella Brigham and Snide Jannigan wrapped in duct tape around the legs, knees, wrists, and mouth looking quite helpless just inside the closed blast hatch. The two prisoners were sitting against the bulkhead.

The three fake freebooters looked at each other in confusion, then Murphy let it register that the IAs had taken matters into their own *legs*. Feeling safe now, Murphy pushed past Adrianna, almost knocking her down, sprinted down the ramp as Jennifer jumped out of her way, then leapt into the arms of a smiling Channing Altimer. She jumped up wrapping both legs around him, hugging his neck, at the same time latching onto his mouth with her lips. She sucked on him and ground into his waist as though Channing had been deployed for two years on a mission and had just came home to his newlywed wife.

Jennifer looked at Rand and Adrianna.

"She's fine," she said referring to Murphy, "What about you two?" She asked looking at the both of them in turn.

Adrianna smiled, "We think Krachy's here, on the pleasure base." Rand nodded.

Jennifer's eyes shot open not expecting that. Her knees buckled, but as could be expected, Jeffrey Jansen cradled her shoulders pulling her back into his broad chest. Jennifer was speechless. She looked dumbfounded more than anything else.

Adrianna stepped down the ramp coming right up to her, looking into her eyes.

"We have all the backup we need; let's go get him."

The gleam in her eyes when she said it made Jennifer's chin quiver. Jennifer couldn't use her mouth. She couldn't believe that it might be so simple as to walk out of the landing bay and find Krachy alive, here, and now. Adrianna reached out touching her shoulder.

"The IAs identified Krachy from a picture. We think he is in the infirmary. We haven't seen him and don't know what condition he's in."

While Adrianna was talking, Dimitri walked over to a scared looking Bonisabella Brigham. He pulled out a laser blade from his pocket turning it on. The high hum of the deadly weapon registered on Bonisabella's face as a BIG problem coming her way. Dimitri went down on one knee, but instead of cutting the gag off her mouth, he sliced the tape from her knees and ankles. In a fast act of support, the two IAs that had been standing motionless off to either side of Brigham and Jannigan took one ankle each in their front two legs, gripping the heavyset woman. They pulled hard opening her legs far apart. Fear gripped Brigham; she gasped as best she could through the duct tape around her mouth then looked into Dimitri's dangerous eyes.

"I'll only ask you once. Is my Lord's fiancé Krachalavito Bantor in the infirmary?" The laser blade was humming loudly positioned not two inches from Brigham's vagina.

Brigham didn't have to look down at it. She could hear it, and she was terrified what might happen next. Her neck fat was jiggling with fear, but she managed to nod up-and-down several times and say a muffled word, "Yef."

Dimitri didn't take the weapon away. Instead he inched it closer burning the crotch fibers on her leggings. A small puff of smoke drifted up to Brigham's nostrils. When she smelt it she closed her eyes, waiting for the pain that had to be coming next. It didn't. Instead, after what must have been 20 seconds of holding her breath, she opened her eyes.

Dimitri was robot still, unflinching, holding his position. The hole in her leggings revealed her privates. The legging material was bowed a good inch out away from her groin because her obese thighs were spread pulling the material.

Dimitri kept his eyes on her. "We're going to verify that."

The IAs continued holding her short legs open. Jennifer had come up behind Dimitri with Jeffrey at her side. She looked down at Snide Jannigan who had a front row seat to the coercion. The threatening look on Jennifer's face made Jannigan gulp, but it was fast because she stepped over his bound legs and was out through the blast hatch followed by Jeffrey and Adrianna.

Through the blast hatch Adrianna reached out pulling at Jennifer's arm. She knew where they were going. Jennifer seemed to be moving forward in a half daze.

"This way," Jennifer realized what Adrianna was trying to do and stutter stepped a few times holding up just long enough for Adrianna to get by her and lead the way. Jeffrey had his laser pistol out at his side pointed down.

Adrianna led them into the heart of the pleasure base. She had been there earlier when she bought food and clothes. She'd only had time to feed herself and the others. Her grimy brown shirt, courtesy of Rifle Man, was still on complete with blood stains around the collar. The lighting changed, as did the sound. Zen mystic vibes played in hushed tones as the trio made a right down a faint purple-colored hallway. As with all PBs, privacy was the number one rule. The three of them were not challenged; that was not how these bases operated. Security was always light, the owners knowing that if someone paid the outrageous docking fees, they didn't do so to cause trouble. They did it to enjoy the amenities.

A sturdy middle-aged man in a dark long sleeve tunic and trousers rounded the corner almost bumping in to Adrianna. The man was Adrianna's assigned Fixer. All clients that landed on the PB were assigned one.

The Fixer took in the three people looking familiarly at Adrianna. He saw the purpose in Adrianna's face and, instead of challenging her, he looked back seeing the tall duo coming up behind her, Jennifer and Jeffrey, and decided to do just that—give them their privacy. He planted a foot then spun back out of the way against the hallway bulkhead letting all three of them pass. As Jeffrey approached the Fixer, he reached out and grabbed the man hard by the bicep digging in his fingers making his point clear.

Jeffrey pulled the man out away from the wall, hesitating a few seconds to let Adrianna and Jennifer get ahead of them. He looked down at the shorter man, his words evolving into a rumble.

"You're coming with us. Don't touch your slate or you forfeit the hand that touches it."

The Fixer believed what he had just heard, swallowed, and nodded, stumbling a bit being pushed hard down the hall following the two women. One right turn and the next hatch was the infirmary. Adrianna and Jennifer rushed past it and turned waiting for Jeffrey to deliver the key in the way of the Fixer. The lighting was low and other than a passing servo droid no one could be seen close by. That didn't mean no one was close; it was just hard to tell with nothing to focus on in the dark, purple, blueish light.

The Fixer was jerked to a halt in front of the scan pad then yanked hard so he would look over his shoulder at Jeffrey.

"Open it, and only it! You set off a silent alarm and you forfeit both hands."

During their quick journey to the hatch, Jeffrey had pulled out a laser blade knife, holstering his pistol in turn. The red-orange color of the laser shank contrasted sharply with the dark surroundings. The high hum of the lethal weapon was not audible over the Zen vibes music, but that didn't matter. The intention to use it was plenty motivating for the Fixer.

"I have to touch my slate to open the hatch. I don't even know what's inside; I just collect the rent. Please don't slice my hand off, I—"

The speed at which the laser blade nicked the Fixer's upper cheek was expertly delivered. It said: *I know how to use this, I know well, and I just missed your eyeball on purpose.*

"No dissertation, just follow instructions!" Jeffrey ordered.

The Fixer shut his eyes from the shock of the pain, shooting a hand to the injury, but it was snagged in mid air by the large, strong hand of Jeffrey Jansen. The man opened his eyes focusing on Jeffrey's sinister leer.

"Open it NOW." Jeffery ordered, but didn't shout. No sense in bringing unwanted attention.

The Fixer, Ser Laris, nodded trying to pull his hand from Jeffrey's grip. Jeffrey let go watching Ser Laris reach down to his belt to unclip his slate. Laris opened and shut, and squinted and blinked the eye above the small cut. Blood started to drip down his cheek onto his shirt. Finally focusing on his slate, he poked several commands in, the hatch moving aside. Jeffrey shoved him through the hatch ahead of him, Jennifer next, then Adrianna.

Once inside, Adrianna swung a hand over the scan pad closing the hatch. The first thing that hit them was the smell. The odor wasn't antiseptic like you'd expect a Medico to be. It was moist, almost like there was dirt in the room. *But that couldn't be?*

Jeffrey still had ahold of Ser Laris' bicep, then, without warning, twisted at his waist generating breakneck speed with Laris' surprised body, slamming him back into the bulkhead just beside the closed hatch. The man grunted, exhaling all the air in his chest, then crumpled to the deck motionless.

The three of them tried to focus, their eyes fighting to adjust to the very low cream, tan light in the room. The problem was what they were seeing wasn't registering in their minds. Their minds said this was supposed to be an infirmary for healing, but what they were seeing was unorganized and misleading. Murphy had been right about the number of beds, but the six beds were not full size. They were shorter, maybe four feet long, and much more narrow than a usual bed. The six beds were very close together under other things against the far wall.

The room was wide but narrow, wide enough for the six thin beds side-by-side, with at least 10 feet on either side, under many unrecognizable things suspended from the ceiling. The ceiling was high, maybe 20 feet.

Jennifer took two steps before something bumped her forehead that started to sway and yaw in a figure-eight-like motion. She reached out to grab what felt like someone's foot. As soon as she touched the foot, it raised, and the now recognizable torso of a human man tilted down. The ankles, waist, wrists, shoulders and head were suspended by thin wires. This one human still swayed with its legs now higher than its head, but the swaying and yawing started to slow. Jennifer noticed a tube snaking down one of the suspension wires down into the person's mouth.

Jennifer stepped back, her eyes focused now, to see at least a dozen similarly hung bodies suspended in two levels, six lower, then six higher, above the narrow small beds. The bodies hung staggered. By reflex she tried to scan the shapes of each body to see if she could pick out Krachy. She couldn't and was sure that none of the suspended humans were him. It was clear several of them were women by the shape of their hips and shoulders. She scanned the beds now starting to lose hope.

The swaying body stopped moving with the feet still above its head. It was clear the wires suspending it were programmed.

The touch of Jennifer's head against the toe of the man caused a computer to raise its legs.

The feet of the man were high enough that she could step closer to the six beds. There was movement in every bed. What was in them was covered by a thin tan sheet; she started to feel hope again, but the size was all wrong. Jennifer's next step felt squishy. She looked down; it was dirt. *Dirt?*

By reflex she darted her gaze to the left wall. She saw at least fifteen closely packed small tunnels. No, they weren't tunnels. They were small round chambers. For a few seconds it didn't register; then she felt Adrianna's hand on her shoulder.

Adrianna was looking at the chambers too, as was Jeffrey. They both knew what they were. Unlike Jennifer, who had refused to know the whole truth about the atrocities that had taken place on planet 0875 last year, the both of them knew what this meant. Jennifer did not.

Jennifer could feel the revelation in Adrianna's entire body through the connection of her resting hand on her left shoulder. For Jennifer, this was now going to be the time for her past to catch up with her, and for her to make the most horrific statement of fact that would change her life forever. She was more than mortified by the revelation. She had always known it would only be a matter of time—a matter of time before the abhorrent acts of the insect aliens that had backed the previous Protectorate of Markem Tanner Kory on planet 0875 would make their grim payment due on her soul. Today was that day.

The suspended man's body dipped, its feet level with its torso again. By then Jennifer had shrugged off Adrianna's hand and lunged at the first sheet she could get ahold of in front of her. She ripped it off flinging the thin blanket behind her to the deck. Under the cover was the body of an insect alien with the head of a human being.

Jennifer's lungs expelled an involuntary howl of bitter agony.

"Nooooo!" She gasped trying to breathe, "No, no,….Oh, NOOO, please, please, NO!"

With each subsequent lunge she pulled the cover off another, then another, *Hybrid Insect Human*. Krachy's face was not among the first four she uncovered; then the fifth sheet flung aside and his face *was*. Jennifer froze.

The neck was skeletal like, wiry, with tan insect alien appendages disappearing into the bottom of his head. Krachy's face was gaunt, hollow cheeked, but clearly recognizable. His hair was long, ghoulish like, stringy and matted. But the eyes, it was the eyes that almost caused her to pass out. They had no eye lids; they were small, like a human, but they were compound eyes—unblinking, emotionless, loveless, and soulless. Jennifer's vision retreated into darkness. It was the only place to hide to escape the hopeless misery of her severed heart.

***

When she came to, Sami was looking down at her. Jennifer didn't care where she was. All she wanted Sami to do was to hand her something that she could point at her head and end her life. But that wasn't going to happen. Not now, not today, and not with Sami looking hopefully into her eyes. Hopefully? It was an emotion Jennifer would not let invade her pain. It was not going to be allowed to touch her crippled heart; all she wanted was to be with the only man she ever loved, dead, in heaven, not in pain, and free. How dare Sami give her a look of hope. Jennifer's friends must have known how she would react because when she tried to lift her arm to punch that hopeful look off Sami's face, her arm wouldn't move. It was tied to the bed frame. She wasn't in the Medico Bay in the Damage Control section on Rand Fullrider's light cruiser *Brandish*. Jennifer was in her small cabin on Rand's ship.

Sami smiled gently. "It wasn't Krachy. Hear me? It wasn't him. It wasn't, Jennifer. No. It. Was. Not. Him."

Jennifer tried to swing at her again for being so cruel as to try to trick her with more misplaced hope. The left arm was bound too. *Damn it*, she thought to herself. Instead, she just turned her head away pressing her eyes hard shut. Jennifer now considered just starving herself to death since these so-called friends wouldn't give her the tool she needed to end things.

Sami wouldn't relent. "I would never lie to you, Jennifer. Get used to it."

The sound in Sami's voice gave Jennifer pause, gave her heart a chance to beat without pain, but she still didn't open her eyes or turn to face Sami.

"Brigham, or her Skinny Demon Boy, Jannigan, used Krachy's DNA to create a Hybrid Insect Human. Krachy's still on the hunting resort."

Sami stopped and reached down untying Jennifer's right wrist. The buckle of the restraint snapped off in Sami's grasp; then she waited.

Jennifer jerked her wrist free and flinched like she was going to strike Sami. But she stopped herself. She billowed a frustrated sigh, opened her eyes, and looked up at her. Sami was motionless waiting to let Jennifer club her in the face, or temple, or any other part of her body if she wanted to. The trust in Sami's face stopped Jennifer's rage letting it retreat a safe distance so she could speak.

"You wouldn't lie to me would you, Sami?"

As proof, Sami leaned over her body unbuckling the other wrist restraint. She sat back up and shook her head.

"I owe you everything I am, Jennifer. I would never, ever, let you go on hurting by lying to you."

Jennifer eased herself up on her elbows. "He might be alive then?"

A thin thread of hope was mirrored on Sami's face. It was not urgent, it was not convincing, it was just truthful to the point of being cautiously optimistic, but not overly so.

"Krachy was alive right before the two IAs with Rand, Murphy, and Adrianna captured Brigham. Dimitri interrogated Brigham while you were out. I believe what Brigham told him. We all do. I won't tell you we know with certainty, but for the first time in all this, we do know Krachy was alive not two hours ago."

"I wanted to kill myself. I'm so ashamed I felt like that in front of you."

"You don't have to ever apologize to me for who you are, Jennifer. You accept me with all my faults. I've wanted to kill myself more times in my life than is believable for a person so young. To even remember all the instances that made me want to stop living, it's just not right. I know how awful you felt when you saw what you thought was your man. But this isn't over yet," Sami glimmered with optimism. "We have all the team back together now, Jennifer. And Brigham gave us the location of her resort. We're heading there now."

By way of confirmation, Jennifer could feel the swift light cruiser changing course under her back. She had to lean in the bed to compensate for it.

"What about, you know, all the..?" Jennifer trailed off snapping her mouth shut, fighting back the pain of seeing all those helpless, genetically modified, and innocent creatures back in the infirmary.

"We made the decision for you. Like we should. We did the right thing."

"You mean..?"

"Oh yes, we brought them all with us. Rand's Medico staff is first rate. The humans and genetic creatures that were alive are on board now being looked after and treated. But there were several humans and pinatens that were not so fortunate..." It was Sami's turn to feel ashamed.

Jennifer waited.

"Brigham was harvesting body parts from the humans and pinatens auctioning them off. Once her prey from the resort were beyond repair, she dissected the bodies and sold their organs. The suspended people in the infirmary were in different stages of being dissected. There were three humans and two pinatens still alive, not dissected yet. They're being treated and should survive. As for the Hybrid Insect Humans, that's just another dilemma of decision making we always run into. But for now, they are on board too, quarantined in a makeshift med bay set up in the cargo hold. Those people weren't responsible for what happened to them. Brigham told us why they were being bred."

Jennifer was there again, there at the point where she just didn't want to know to save her sanity. *Damn it all, if it wasn't happening again!* Repeating itself, like a bad nightmare that wakes you up soaked in the terror of your own scared fluids— that feeling of total helplessness and despair at what others are capable to doing to another life. But this was different. Jennifer was different. She had just lived through the horror of finally understanding what had taken place on planet 0875 last year. She now knew what Krachy had kept buried in his soul the past year, the harsh burden of not speaking about it, or sharing his despair because of it.

"Tell me, Sami."

"The IAs, the head of their Collective, have been paying Brigham to breed humans and pinatens with insect aliens.

Brigham uses the larvae chambers you saw on the wall of the infirmary to grow the pupa. When the pupa emerged, they were kept in the small beds sedated.

"The IAs are not capable of space flight. They want to be, so they are trying to breed that knowledge and skill into Hybrid Insect Humans. The Collective also figure once they become space faring they'll need to protect and defend themselves, so they're also breeding warriors. Krachy is a skilled soldier, so they used his DNA to breed one of their warriors. Brigham had this side enterprise running, multiplying the benefits of the hunting prey she kidnapped by using their blood, their DNA, to keep the breeding going as a side business and sell organs too. Brigham takes blood from all the kidnapped prey, even the IAs she kidnapped. It's a mess of horrors, Jennifer. But, that's all stopped now. The other hatch in the infirmary led to a dedicated landing bay. Jeffrey placed an explosive charge on that hatch, and another explosive charge on the infirmary landing bay containment field. He blew them both once we left the pleasure base. Everything in that infirmary was sucked out into space."

Jennifer welcomed the news. The truth of it was terrible, but the designers of it, the people who thought it up, were now captured. Then she thought about something that tugged once again at her heart. It showed on her face.

"What Jennifer, what is it?"

"Adrianna," she searched Sami's eyes, "she didn't know that Krachy was an experiment. I mean his DNA was. She thought he was in the infirmary. She has to be devastated. To think she hurt me like that when she didn't even know."

"The two IAs with her didn't know either. One IA did identify Krachy from a picture. The IA saw his face on one of the hybrid insects in the infirmary. It was a mistake; the rest of his body was covered. Adrianna's gonna be okay. You'll want to speak with her." Sami stopped, not sure what to add.

"I will."

"Thanks for not slugging me," Sami said.

"Who's idea was it to tie me down?" Jennifer wasn't seeking revenge; she may just want to thank the person.

"Ian's."

"WHAT!?"

"Jennifer, Ian's been checking in behind your back every so often. For some reason you don't think he should, but he doesn't care. Rand's ship does have a tight beam vid comm that works, ya know."

"Damn," Jennifer shook her head, "Ian always knows what's best for me. I'm beginning to hate it."

"Yeah sure, you love him and you know it."

The loud sigh of submission came out her nostrils this time.

"Yes, I do."

Jennifer was pretty sure she could face what was next now. Her head injury was still there, still close to the surface and at times painful, but she was ready. She needed to be. She was up against a Collective that could read her mind. That had to be considered and dealt with. The Collective knew she was coming to stop them, to stop their pipeline of raw genetic materials. They were not going to get what they wanted if Jennifer was alive to prevent it.

THIRTEEN

"I don't trust myself. You'd better do it, not me." Jennifer said, back in her black slacks and light green long sleeve blouse. She was referring to any contact with the two prisoners to get more information from them, or anything else for that matter.

Dimitri nodded, not disagreeing with her logic. It was more like a warning he could tell. The look of fire in her eyes spoke volumes to what she would do if left in the same room with Brigham and her Skinny Demon Boy Jannigan. Dimitri was sitting across from her at one of the tables in the small mess hall on *Brandish*. By default, the mess hall had become the team's meeting room.

Dimitri sat between Murphy and Sami. Jennifer was flanked by Channing and Jeffrey. Adrianna was at the head of the narrow table. The two insect aliens, ever present, were on top of the table off to the right. They were small enough to perch there without issue.

Adrianna and Murphy look refreshed. More hot food had done wonders for their morale as did a coerced private session of close personal contact Murphy had compelled Channing to partake in the second they were back on the ship.

Channing found that his concentration worked best if he seated himself across the table from Murphy instead of next to her. She submitted to the inconvenience without objection for some reason which surprised him; she seemed to have changed since she went out on her own with Rand and Adrianna.

271

Channing sensed something bad had happened while she was away. The look in her eyes was urgent—desperate was more accurate. He hadn't known Murphy long, but the urgency of their love making had to mean something had happened, something that in time she may be willing to share with him.

Fresh clothes helped too. Adrianna was back in her grey leggings and black quarter zip pullover, sleeves rolled up. Her hair was in its usual single ponytail.

Jennifer approached Adrianna as soon as Sami left her cabin. Jennifer would not have any of Adrianna blaming herself for things that she didn't know, or couldn't know, or decisions she had to make under pressure. The relief Adrianna felt knowing Jennifer was not hurt by her mistake was overwhelming. It was over, and it was in the past.

Jennifer looked at Murphy across the table to her left. As she did, all of them had to grab the table and lean compensating for the course change in Rand's fast attack ship. They were getting close to the resort; it would all be over, one way or another, very soon.

"I'd feel better if you convinced me again our minds cannot be read by telepaths, Murphy," Jennifer reasoned.

Murphy had on the new clothes Adrianna had picked up on the pleasure base, a simple blue knit long sleeve shirt and flat front stretch twill tan pants.

"It all has to do with attenuation, the measurement of absorbed and deflected energy as it passes through material. Think about picking out a pair of sunglasses. When you get a pair of sunglasses, you want them to protect your eyes from sun damage; the main focus is the tint of the lens, not the thickness. The device Brigham and Jannigan were using to mask their presence on the pleasure base has everything to do with attenuation. Like how the attenuation of light varies because of how sunglass lens are tinted. This same basic concept applies to telepathy protection. Similar to different lens tints attenuating light rays, different materials attenuate telepathic energy. The device Brigham was using to prevent telepaths from reading her mind mimics the molecular structure of tin and lead."

Jennifer scrunched her face. "So hunters like John Paul Sark and Lev Babinot were given one of these devices when they traveled to the resort? They were given one to shield them from having their thoughts read?"

Murphy was patient with Jennifer's misunderstanding. Channing watched her body language and couldn't help but notice it. Patience had not been a part of her personality repertoire before.

"No, Brigham's a stingy bitch, remember? The device she and Jannigan used on the PB was very advanced. The device sent out a large enough absorber to mask their presence on the pleasure base. They have, correction *had*, lots of customers going to the resort after staging on the PB. It was cheaper to have the shuttles Trask provided through his company Fleet-Up installed with little rooms, cages, whatever. Dimitri told me Brigham called them deadening booths. The booths were made from cheap lead or tin. Anyway, these booths had the same effect as the Absorber she had someone design and install for her on the PB."

"Expensive…" Channing offered.

"Yeah very," Murphy confirmed, "but at over two mil creds per hunter, Brigham could afford it." She looked back at Jennifer. "Rand's engineering guys hard wired the Absorber device into *Brandish's* defense grid, the electronic counter measure sys on the ship. After that, all Rand has to do is pump out a steady stream of ECM and the Absorber device does the rest. *Brandish* is a lot smaller than the pleasure base. The mock lead-tin

ECM Absorber wave corrals the ship. The Insect Alien Collective can't probe through it. *Brandish* is nothing but a big hole in space now, enveloped by the ECM Absorber…we can't be mind monitored, no one on board can."

"All right, I think I get it now." Jennifer hesitated, the picture of Krachy's ghoulish face on the body of the hybrid insect human still fresh. She feared that only seeing Krachy alive would erase the horrific image imprinted on her mind. At least she hoped it would. Sami sensed it.

"So we arrive and what, the IA Collective are going to be at the hunting resort too?" She tried to keep things moving forward, always forward, with the aim of getting Krachy and all the kidnapped prey back in one piece.

Jennifer was staring at the table top. She looked up emptily.

"The IA Collective are not going to be at the hunting resort—at least not in force," Jeffrey determined. "They still live on planet 0875, Sami. The Collective was the end customer, Brigham's backer, nothing more than a revenue center for her in all this. The Absorber that she has installed on the resort prevents the IA Collective from knowing that she's been kidnapping insect aliens to be prey too."

"What?" Sami was confused.

"Don't you get it? If the leaders of the Collective knew that Brigham was kidnapping their kind, other IAs, do you really think that she would be allowed to breed hybrids for them? They don't know Brigham's using IAs as prey on her hunting resort. There's no way they do. If they did, they wouldn't work with her."

"Then what's all the breeding of hybrid insect humans on the PB all about then?" Channing questioned.

"Brigham breeds a crop of hybrids then stuffs them in one of the deadening booths on a FleetUp shuttle and ships them off to planet 0875. Once the genetically created hybrids arrive on planet 0875, the Collective determines if the genetics are acceptable. At that point, the Collective has a decision to make: assimilate or destroy. Can the creatures Brigham creates in her death lab on the PB be assimilated into the existing Collective colony with the desired traits? Or if they don't measure up, they're just destroyed, exterminated.

"You have to remember that the Collective is trying to obtain space flight and all the intelligence that goes with it, up to and including a warrior caste to defend it when they achieve it. If the hybrid insect humans, or HI pinatens, can be incorporated into their Collective and get them closer to these goals, they're assimilated. This has got to take time, time for the newly bred creatures to fit themselves into their culture.

"Also, consider this, Channing: Unassimilated creatures remain a threat to the Collective until they are absorbed and produce positive contributions that benefit the entire colony. There has to be a chance that the creatures Brigham is breeding will attempt to revolt because of their new intelligence and skills."

"What are you saying, Jeff?" Sami's eyes grew; she inched closer.

"I'm saying that just like humans, splinter groups of like-minded creatures can band together to overthrow and revolt. The Collective has never seen this problem because ALL of their members ALL think alike. But not now, now with the introduction of a new breed or several new breeds trying to be assimilated into their population. The more unassimilated creatures, the larger the chance for revolt."

"Jeffrey, you didn't answer my question."

Jeffrey looked around the table. The two IAs one table over were very still. Again, it seemed they were hanging on the words they were going to hear next.

"I'm saying that the small scale of Brigham's breeding operation that we just shut down would make no appreciable impact on getting the Collective to their goals. I'm saying Brigham's breeding operation is just one of many. Maybe hundreds, maybe more…"

Jennifer stood up; she looked white, like she was going to get sick.

"I, I, can't—" Then a wave of determination fought to gain purchase on her face. She sat back down. The truth, this was the truth that she promised herself she wouldn't run away from. There was no turning back because Krachy's life depended on her moving forward, always forward. She couldn't deny, however, that her head was hurting. Her previous injury was still with her. She was clear headed enough to know that the truth and the injury were two different things. She did need to take a break. Yes, the truth was a lot to take, to understand, but so was the pain she was feeling. She was still not over her concussion. She was going to face this truth, but she needed to back away from it. Only problem was, there was not much time to do it.

That wasn't the case for Channing beside her. He had already gotten sick after he saw the breeding room on the PB. Now what Jeffrey was talking about was a network of breeding centers that could not be known with certainty, that could not be shut down by stopping what they had just stopped. He was getting sick. The conversation that he and Jennifer had back on the planet Basley kept running over and over in Channing's mind: *I've started out on missions like this before. It may have been different circumstances, but the end game always seems to play itself out the same way. I hate that it will, but it just does. There is something bad waiting for us, Channing. The last mission I was a part of I had to tell Krachy not to tell me the truth about the end game to protect my health. You're probably not going to understand this unless you've been on my side of the table.*

What was even more ironic, and sickening, was that Channing *was* on Jennifer's side of the table right now. Oh, how he wished he'd never gotten himself into this mess—

The thought froze as the bile in his stomach lurched. He jumped up, dodged around Adrianna and through the galley's open hatch. His retching in the galley sink was loud.

Jennifer hung her head knowing all too well how Channing felt. When she looked back up she turned to Jeffrey wrapping an arm around him.

"You're right, Jeff." She pulled back, "This mission is playing out that way, just like you said." She sighed fighting fatigue. "I understand it, I'm just tired. How long until we get to the resort?"

"Less than two hours," Dimitri answered.

"I'm not going to be much good unless I get a few minutes rest. You know when to come get me."

With that Jennifer stood up, wobbling a bit, catching herself on the tabletop with a hand. Jeffrey stood up to help her. She pushed his arm away, righted herself, then turned and left through the hatch behind her.

The water was running in the galley sink; Channing could be heard slurping gulps down, belching several times as he did. He came out through the hatch still looking unsteady. He swallowed hard and found his way back to his chair, the empty seat beside him like a huge glaring void. Channing felt much more sorry for Jennifer than he did for himself. She was trying so hard, had tried so hard, to do what was right, what was just, in the past and even now. He felt small and ineffective in the shadow of Jennifer's absence in the room.

Murphy got up coming around the table to lean over and wrap her arms around Channing's neck from behind, nuzzling her face into his ear. She was comforting him, like a normal person. *Boy*, he thought to himself, *that feels nice*.

One of his hands went to her arm around his neck and squeezed it affectionately.

"Thanks," he pushed the side of his head into hers.

"Anything for you, Chazzy," Murphy pulled back turning to look into his eyes.

When he turned back to look at her, she bobbed her eyebrows up and down several times. He smiled, just then noticing that she didn't have a ring on any of her fingers.

Murphy had changed; there seemed to be no doubt about that, but so had Channing. He was not the naïve person he was when he first got involved with these people. Seeing their struggle firsthand and watching them risk so much, with so little in the way of defense, was sobering. He had been thinking about that a lot: It was true. The intent of these people grew as the layers of evil wove itself into an ever-growing path. The wider the path, the more these people blanketed it, not just with their determination, but with their character.

This was not just about getting one man back anymore. This was about putting an end to cruelty that had been created by beings that had no regard for morals. That were using living things as targets for sport and to create more living things that they had no right to create.

"Who's going to be the one to tell Jennifer? And who's going to convince her she can't go AND try to stop her from going?"

Rand scanned Jennifer's team. He had come into the mess hall after Jennifer left. Jennifer was not going to be allowed to go in, to be a part of the team that went to the resort. That was Rand's call; he knew about her health, or lack thereof.

Channing stood up. He cleared his throat.

"I will. Jeff or Dimitri can't very well try to tell Jennifer what to do." He glanced at Adrianna then Sami returning his eyes to Rand.

"If I need backup, I'll get Adrianna and Sami to help, but let me speak to her alone first."

Rand nodded. The approach to the resort had hit a snag, a big one.

"All right," Rand accepted Channing's offer as if it would work. He didn't have time to debate it.

"Jennifer has time to rest, then you can tell her. We're still about an hour's flight time from the resort. I had to stop the ship here because the Absorber field Brigham has installed on the resort is much more powerful that I thought it was going to be. If I bring the ship too close, I fear *Brandish* will get enveloped by it. The readings we're getting are weak, but they're there. I'm afraid if I take the ship too close we'll be affected by the time device."

Channing stared at him seeing the stress on Rand's face. "What do you mean?"

"Channing, I don't know what time, when, the damn day will reset. You get it? I have no way of knowing what resort time is."

"We can find that out, Rand." Dimitri spoke up from his seat on the far side of the table.

"Yeah, I know, just ask Brigham right? It's not that easy, Dimitri." Rand shook his head.

"What if she lies to you? I mean, that may be her way out of this. If she tells you that her resort is working on a 20-hour clock for instance, and her Pullback resets the day once every 20 hours, what happens if she's lying? What I'm saying is that if the Pullback happens when you're not ready for it, you start back where you began. Brigham may tell you that the start of resort time is at a certain time, but if it's not at that time, the strike team goes back in time losing all the progress they've made. It's hard to explain, but I have to know with absolute certainty when the day is going to reset. Whatever window resort time is, 10 hours, 20 hours, whatever, that is the full amount of time we have to infiltrate and shut it down."

Murphy was fidgeting, wanting to say something.

"What, Murphy, what?" Rand shot both hands to his hips staring at her. "You got something to say, say it."

"It's automated," she said.

"How's that?" Rand asked.

"The Pullback is automated. It might be on a predetermined clock, but that's not a problem. I've been thinking about it. I may have been wrong about worrying about the reset."

"Tell me all of it, Murphy, I've got a lot at risk here. Convince me."

Channing sat back down next to Murphy as Rand angled to the right side of the table sitting down next to Jeffrey. Murphy swiveled looking past Jeff at Rand.

"We don't have to take Brigham's word for anything. No matter when the reset happens, whoever is enveloped by the Pullback will remember the previous day, just their progress will be reset. Their physical location will move to where it was at the moment it was the previous day. All this time Brigham hasn't even had to be on the resort. The time device has to be automated to work that way.

"Think about all that Sami, Channing, and Dimitri discovered before we left Basley. Brigham has been traveling a lot, meeting new clients, qualifying leads, identifying prey, paying Trask for FleetUp shuttles, paying other companies for services, etcetera. She doesn't even have to be on the resort or doesn't even want to be. Her day would reset every so many hours; it would be maddening and inconvenient for her. Brigham has a group of workers on the resort keeping things running, the specialized equipment, meals, weapons, greeting clients and providing lodging."

"I see what you mean," Rand agreed.

"But, you're right about not getting too close with the ship," Murphy continued. "It's a risk of too many people, too many lives, if I'm not right about everything. That's why you should send just one shuttle."

"Just one, that's not many people or fire power."

"I know, but a small group has to infiltrate and fight their way past the damn hunters, remember? Remember the hunters have a say in all this. Whoever they see they're going to try to kill. The group you send will have to fight alongside the prey team and kill the damn hunters before the resort can be shut down."

Rand held up a hand.

"Wait a minute, just wait a minute here. That can't be right, Murphy. The group I send only has to take out the equipment that powers the time device, the Pullback. Once that, and only that, is shut down, I can dock *Brandish* as I see fit."

Murphy was shaking her head.

"You just don't get it."

"What damn it?! What don't I get?"

"We don't know how many hunters there are, Rand. You hear me? We don't even know how big this place is. What if there are hundreds of hunters? Are you going to try to kill or capture all of them?"

It was Rand's turn to shake his head.

"You're wrong, Murphy. There can't be hundreds of hunters. The pipeline of clients can't be that large. It costs 2.2

million for each hunter! Besides, there can't be that many prey to make it sporting if hundreds of hunters were trying to kill so few prey."

"I wasn't making myself clear, Rand. What if there are hundreds of *beings* making sure the hunting takes place. I'm saying that just like our friends behind you that helped us get this far, there may be hundreds of insect aliens maintaining and running the resort."

"What the hell, Murphy?" Rand looked baffled, like everyone else at the table.

"Just because the resort became operational seven months ago doesn't mean Brigham hasn't been breeding hybrid insect humans and pinatens long before that, breeding them to run the thing."

"For shit's sake..." Rand was dumbfounded. He'd never even thought of that, but that could be the case.

Murphy nodded. "Yeah, until I saw the breeding room on the PB, and until I heard Jeffrey lay it all out, that there could be hundreds of breeding centers just like the one we just shut down. I didn't think the scale was that big either, but now we have to assume it is...don't we?"

"Then we're back to where we started. Why don't I just take *Brandish* in and use the fire power we have to end this?"

"Because the hybrid insect pinatens that have been bred may have been bred to prevent just such a thing from happening. They may have been bred to do one thing and one thing only— protect the workings of the resort—period."

"She's got a point, Rand," Jeffrey chimed in. "The IAs want space flight and defenders to keep it, but who's to say that Brigham, or hundreds of other evil a-holes just like her, haven't been paid to breed hybrid insect resort workers too. If the IA Collective can pay the breeding centers to breed the intelligence for space flight and defense, what's to say that the Collective is not paying for all this with something other than creds?"

Channing was looking pale again. He swallowed seeing where Jeff was headed with this.

"You're saying that Brigham, and others like her, are being paid with hybrid insect resort workers instead of creds? That's what you're saying?"

"Yes. I'm also saying that this might not be the only hunting resort, too."

"Oh my god, no," Channing was dizzy. *How could it be this large in scale?*

Before he asked, Murphy answered, "He has to be right, Channing. How could two pieces of equipment as sophisticated at the Pullback and the Absorber be invented and used on just one resort? It would never have been cost effective for Brigham and Jannigan, uh uh, no way. We may have been looking at this from the wrong angle all along. The resorts *are* the reason for the breeding centers. But since the Absorber is masking everything taking place on it, humans are being opportunistic and making a profit from the buy-in fees, and running organ sales as a side enterprise—humans like Brigham."

Murphy continued, "The Insect Alien Collective does not know what the newly bred hybrid insect resort workers are being used for because their telepathy can't penetrate the Absorber on the resort to find out. They only know that they are getting newly bred space flight and defense hybrid IAs to help them reach their own goals. When I said all of the workings of the resort have to be automated, that means that the newly bred hybrid insect resort workers ARE the automation behind the autonomous functioning of each resort."

"So what, delivery of supplies, people, weapons, and clients don't even know this is going on? They don't see the hybrid insect resort workers when they land on the resort?" Adrianna asked.

Dimitri looked at her, "Brigham told me deliveries are compartmentalized. I didn't understand what she meant until just now. The deliveries are dropped off inside an isolated landing bay. The transfer of payment is by computer, so no interaction of any kind is needed with humans or IAs. Once the delivery ship or client shuttle leaves the resort, the hybrid resort workers can enter the landing bay to retrieve what was delivered or direct the clients to their accommodations, whatever."

Adrianna leaned forward elbows on the table. "So the clients see the hybrid resort workers then, right?"

"Sure, why not?" Murphy said. "That may be an integral part of the marketing: Come and interact with new life forms, and kill them, too. Don't forget what kind of person Brigham is, Addy."

Rand turned to look at the two IAs behind him. He wheeled back around.

"Our two friends, just like us, have someone they care about on the resort being hunted."

"Maybe not, Rand," Sami reasoned.

All heads turned to Sami.

Sami took in a long breath and let it out.

"Our two friends may not have someone they care about being used as prey. Maybe they have someone they care about that has been genetically altered and shipped to the resort to be used as a hybrid insect resort worker. It could be that, right?"

"It could," Rand agreed. "All this time we've been thinking about prey. But existing IAs could have been taken from their general population and genetically modified to be workers. The currency for paying breeding centers like Brigham's is insect aliens that can be morphed into resort workers by breeding centers, given by the IA Collective to the resorts to be modified. It's hard to know with certainty, and we don't have to know it all. What we do need to know is that this resort is going to be shut down. That much is for certain."

Rand considered all the complexity, and came to the decision that he had heard all he needed to hear. He stood up.

"I'm going back to the bridge to explain this to my team. I'll let you know what I decide, how I intend to approach this." With that he pushed back from the table, turned, and left through the hatch.

***

Rand had come and gone back to the mess hall in less than a hour to tell Jennifer's team the plan to infiltrate the resort. In that time, Jennifer had a power blackout in her cabin. All the hurt, despair, then resurrection of hope caused her to pass out the instant her head hit the pillow.

When Channing rapped on her hatch, she yelled, "It's open," from inside. He passed a hand in front of the scan pad stepping in. She was dressed in a dark blue flight suit and had already clipped her laser pistol on the belt. She was reaching down to pick up her black bum bag off the bed when she saw it was Channing standing just inside the closed hatch.

"You can't go," he said without preamble. "Rand won't allow it, not in your condition, Jennifer. I'm sorry."

While he knew how tough a person Jennifer was, he could also see the scars of her weakened body etched across her tired face. He began to think he could take her in a stand up fight. She looked drained and effete.

"I see." Looking at him for a few moments, she dropped the bum bag back onto the bed. Jennifer's face didn't transform into a raging force of determination; instead, she shuffled a few paces easing herself down onto the side of the bed. She set both hands in her lap and nodded at the chair in front of the comp desk. Channing stepped over and sat down.

"I was afraid of that, but not surprised." The admission looked to be more relief than anything else. Channing understood.

"You don't want to be an obstacle instead of an asset do you?"

"Yes, very much so, Channing. I'd go if I was needed, but I know that my impact would have been limited at best. I would just be a liability. I don't want to be that, not for Krachy."

Channing leaned forward perching his elbows on his knees rubbing his hands together then clinching them.

"You have never been a liability, Jennifer. Not since the first day I met you."

Jennifer smiled, "I'm glad I met you too, Channing—"

Channing rapped on Jennifer's hatch; she yelled, "It's open," from inside.

He had just done that; it was not a mistake! He passed his hand over the scan pad hurrying inside to find Jennifer already sitting on the side of her bed looking up at him.

"It just happened," he observed as he again stood in front of her, not certain he was right.

She nodded. "It did, Channing; our day has just been reset."

Channing sat back down remembering what she and Jennifer had just talked about right before the Pullback.

"Rand decided to send in a commando strike team first."

"I guessed as much."

Jennifer pulled her LP holster off her belt setting it on the bed beside her bum bag.

"There's going to be much more waiting for him than a few hunters."

Channing wasn't clear how she could know that.

"Channing, I saw it all over your face in the mess hall earlier. The only part you're forgetting is that *the end game always seems to play itself out the same way*. Since we aren't at the end game yet, there'll be plenty more things that'll still shock us. It always finishes that way, unfortunately."

Jennifer held up a hand before he could begin filling in some of the pieces that her team had deduced. It was as though she didn't need to know, not because it wasn't important, but because it would add noise to what really was. Instead she asked a simple question.

"Will Rand let me be an observer on the bridge?"

"Yes, he thought it might make up for not being allowed to go."

She stood up looking resolute and steadfast.

"Then let's go."

Jennifer and Channing slid in through the bridge hatch. Rand's voice could be heard through the hatch even before it was opened. They stood just past the threshold trying to make themselves small. Rand was pacing around from station to station pointing, talking, and sometimes yelling orders to one of the three officers on the bridge. This was a side of Captain Fullrider Jennifer and Channing had not seen. It wasn't unexpected, all things considered.

Rand's command chair looked new. The arm rests weren't frayed or shiny where you'd expect his elbows to be perched for long periods of time. Even the comfortable looking seat lacked the distinctive half-rounded imprint of his backside that Jennifer remembered from her chair on her ship *Viper II*. In fact, the damn thing didn't even look used.

Seeing the two of them, Rand turned and paused in mid-sentence. His facial features softened. He strode over to Jennifer grabbing her bicep.

"You can sit in my chair; I don't use it anyway."

He pulled her toward it, helping her ease herself down. She thought she must look pretty bad if he thought he had to help her walk and sit. *Forgot to look in the mirror,* crossed her mind...*my bad, I guess*. Channing stayed where he was. He was in a dark blue flight suit like her. So was everyone else on the bridge.

"Thanks," she said, but Rand had already turned stepping up behind the Nav Officer manning his console.

"Enhance it. Give me a better look," Rand ordered.

The black haired Nav Officer punched at his keypad looking up once at the large vid screen on the wall at the front of the small bridge, back at his panel, then back at the vid screen again. The vid screen started to focus.

Rand urged him along.

"Yeah, that's better. Almost there...got it, enhance that, right there."

Jennifer shifted her gaze at the vid screen taking in a breath as she saw the hunting resort for the first time. It wasn't what she expected. She kept her thoughts to herself. She was a guest and didn't want to be left out by dribbling on with her mouth ruining her chance to see how Rand would infiltrate the target.

The hunting resort was cylindrical, and it was rotating gently on its long axis. The light reflecting off it from Basley's class B yellow star was bright on one side. That's why it was obvious it was rotating. The brown textured skin of the resort was ribbed; the ribs ran the full length of the cylinder except at both ends. The ribs stopped just short of the ends. The view was longways at an angle down its length, so Jennifer could only see one end.

Rand turned taking a step closer.

"I haven't found an electronic frontier, no hard defenses. The output of the Absorber is strong, though. I don't know how the optimized battery packs, the Voltaics, and solar sails are providing that much power making it as strong as it is. I was expecting an equipment station or maybe an abandoned asteroid mine, not something like this."

He waved a hand at the vid screen.

"We can't even find the solar sails; they're not close by or we would have identified them on our scans. The Voltaics must be integrated into the cylinder, but I don't know how that could be possible. The battery packs have to draw current from the solar panels somehow. All the ones I've seen are integrated into the panels and hard wired. It's freakin' bugging me that I can't find the power source, the solar panels I mean."

"May I?" Jennifer asked Rand, taking her eyes off the vid screen.

He nodded.

"The solar panels aren't panels like we know them. The ribbed skin of the entire resort absorbs solar energy. The ribs multiply its surface area exponentially, every peak and valley adding to its efficiency," she reasoned, shifting her eyes back to the vid screen, then back to Rand's face.

Rand turned and studied the vid screen for what seemed like a minute. He turned back around.

"How do you know?"

"It's what I'd do. I mean, it's the only way I can think of to keep the huge thing maintained and operating. Channing gave me a quick update on how the resort is automated in the lift tube on the way up here. He was right; that is important. It explains why everything is self-contained."

"How so?"

"Rand, we know the IAs haven't obtained space flight. How could the…" Jennifer looked back at Channing who took a few steps closer stopping just behind her chair. "What did you call them—?"

"The hybrid insect resort workers," Channing answered.

"How could the hybrid workers maintain the power gener-ating systems if they had to fly from the resort to each orbiting solar station? They aren't capable of that. So they constructed the resort so that everything can be accessed from the inside of the cylinder. Has to be, don't you think?"

"I do." Rand studied her. "You're a crafty space wench ar-en't you, Bane?" He smirked.

She couldn't help it; despite everything that was at stake, his confidence was infectious. She smiled back at him.

"I am, Captain Fullrider. I've seen a thing or two."

"I like you without makeup on, but next time comb your do, okay?"

He was still pleased with her answer when he turned back to his Nav Officer. He bent down talking to him in a much more relaxed tone this time. It was clear that Rand didn't like unknowns, like not knowing why his scans didn't identify the source of all the power that was needed to run the resort.

Despite the familiarity he was showing her, Jennifer fought to keep her tongue in check. She fell back on what she'd picked up in Temper Control Therapy: *I'm responsible for controlling my own actions and reactions.* That phrase was repeating itself over and over in her mind. She liked that she was able to ex-ercise those learned skills now, especially since both Dimitri and Jeffrey were not around. It felt like an empty cavity in her chest not knowing where they were. She wanted so bad to ask Rand if they were a part of the commando strike team that it was hurting her head, but she kept it to herself, had to. This was not her show. Rand was allowing her to be a spectator, and she didn't want to blow it now that they were so close. Her head would just have to hurt. *Woman up,* she commanded herself. *You can do it.*

Rand must have sensed what Jennifer was thinking; he was a very intelligent leader. He turned looking at her.

"Adrianna, Sami, Dimitri and Jeffrey are part of the strike team. I'm not going to risk the entire ship on a recon until I know I can bring it back in one piece. I've seen first hand what Adrianna can do under fire. I trust her judgement. She asked that the other three be allowed to go, so I let them."

Jennifer sagged in her chair. Dimitri and Jeffrey going were one thing, but both Adrianna and Sami too? This she didn't expect. Besides Ian, those four people constituted what she considered her entire family. She gulped several times, her legs starting to shake. Her eyes blurred, fighting back tears. She was, she could: *I'm responsible for my reactions*. She "womaned up" even harder, not saying anything, falling back on the promise to herself to stay steadfast for Krachy.

Adrianna and Sami were on their own quest; Jennifer had to respect that, respect that fortitude in them, for her. It's just she loved them all so much; it hurt to think they had to risk their life for what she wanted. The picture of Ian speaking to her on Adrianna's hand comp back at the hospital on Basley haunted her thoughts: *Will you please let Adrianna, Jeff, Dimitri, Sami, and Channing get Krachy back for you, Jennifer?*

Well, she had stupidly agreed to it. Now it was happening. She righted herself in her chair determined to leave everything that was next up to Rand.

Rand saw what she was doing, the admiration of her effort to do it a bright twinkle in his eyes.

"They didn't go unprepared," he assured her.

She waited, afraid her voice would crack if she spoke.

"Trust me." He turned back to his Nav Officer leaning closer to his panel.

"How much longer?" His officer looked up at him, "About five minutes."

Rand turned back to Jennifer hitting her and Channing with a decisive look each.

"So my interrogation team worked on Brigham, and of course she lied. She told us that the Pullback would happen in three hours from now. Well, as you felt, it happened less than fifteen minutes ago. The Pullback can be adjusted to any time frame they pick. The time reset can be changed to activate anytime they want. It's not on a scheduled clock—no way. I know that now. So to impress upon her that she'd better not lie again, I had Jannigan's thumb removed in front of her. The guy's a bean counter and didn't react well to the pain. Brigham saw and heard it all, more than anxious to spill the rest of what we needed." Rand didn't seem upset by what he had ordered his team to do.

Brigham and Jannigan were in the business of misery. Rand had decided it was time they experienced some of that misery themselves. Jannigan had already received a healthy dose. For Brigham, the threat of pain always worked best if it was delayed as long as possible. As soon as a prisoner was injured, the fear of further torture diminished. It was always that way; the threat of the pain is much more powerful than the act itself. Once the actual act took place, it was easy for the prisoner to fall back into despair and not care any longer what happened to them. Jannigan was an easy target to demonstrate on.

"Brigham told us the that the Pullback window is variable; the time reset can be changed at will. I don't know what she thought she was gaining by not telling us all this in the first place. She's been under constant guard since the second we captured her. Maybe she was just desperate," Rand shrugged.

"Turns out there are two compartmentalized landing bays, one on either end of the resort. One is for incoming hunters and the other for incoming prey. From what Brigham told us, the prey are dropped off in the empty bay with the blast hatch leading to the resort unlocked. None of the hybrid insect resort workers have any interaction with them at all, none. After the group of prey get hungry and thirsty enough, they venture through the blast hatch out of necessity at which point there is food waiting on the other side. The blast hatch locks after they find their way through it. At that point, they are the hunting prey—no instructions, no rules, just the use of their own intelligence and skills, which from what we know is formidable. They have to adapt fast and are forced to do it or die."

"What about the clients, Rand?" Channing asked.

"They land in the client bay on the opposite side of the resort, and are greeted by specialized hybrid resort workers. The workers don't speak or otherwise communicate with the clients, but this is all explained in a welcome packet Brigham has given the clients in advance. Each genetically trained group of hybrids perform a different task for the clients. It all runs like clockwork with no intervention from Brigham whatsoever. Murphy concluded that the automation on the resort was hybrid insect resort workers themselves. She seems to have nailed that one."

Jennifer knew there was a punch line. It was coming. This was all good background information, but the real purpose of what he had in mind was coming. She could feel it.

Rand glanced back at the chrono on the panel next to his Nav Officer, then turned back to face them.

"Murphy reminded me that I didn't need to wait for the Pullback, that we would remember the previous day, or time, before it happened. She was right. She's also my on site intel for the strike team. She's running comms on the attack shuttle."

"You're going in through the prey landing bay aren't you, Rand?" Jennifer couldn't wait any longer to know.

"Yes, the strike team should be landing there any minute. Brigham is on the strike team shuttle as insurance. Her reaction when we land and push her through the airlock first will guarantee we got the right landing bay, not to mention if we're met by hybrid workers or not. Brigham's going to be prey. A very disadvantaged part of the prey. Her shackles aren't going to be removed, which will limit her movement and not give her a chance to get out of our sight."

Rand said it with disgust, but there was satisfaction behind it too—satisfaction that she was going to feel the fear of death biting at her heels just like so many others she had sentenced to the same repulsive fate. Jennifer and Rand also knew Brigham was heavyset which would be a significant drawback of its own.

"We can't risk going in through the client landing bay," Rand continued. "If Murphy is right, there may be hundreds of workers genetically trained to defend the resort, so the strike team intends to fight alongside of the prey teams and retreat through the prey landing blast hatch rescuing as many of them as we can, as fast as we can. That way we only have to fight through hunting teams that have to be limited in number. It's the best strategy we have. I just can't see waiting any longer. People and IAs are dying, and I have to stop it."

Rand saw the question on Jennifer's face before she asked it.

"Yes, the two IAs that helped us were allowed to go in with the strike team. They deserve a chance to help rescue their friends after everything good they did to get us this far."

FOURTEEN

"You're going first. You either waddle out the airlock or I throw you. Decide!"

Sergeant Lance Albrecker was the head of the strike team. There were his orders, then there was God. Rand Fullrider had always given his strike teams complete autonomy on Ops. This was no different. Albrecker stood just behind a very scared Bonisabella Brigham. She hesitated when the airlock hatch swooshed aside. That was a mistake.

The servos in Albrecker's powered dura body armor whined as he lifted his leg, placed his boot on Brigham's large behind, then kicked her out through the open hatch. She shrieked with pain crashing to the landing bay deck.

Three more dura armor-clad commandos followed Albrecker out into the landing bay fanning out for cover. The last one through the hatch accidentally, or on purpose it wasn't clear, nipped the soft flesh on the back of Brigham's calf with his boot strike when he landed on the deck. Another shriek of pain erupted from Brigham's throat, but she wasn't able to grab at the tender wound. Her hands were shackled in front of her and she was too heavy to reach down around with both hands to squeeze the calf.

Brigham had led the strike team to the correct landing bay. This was where prey teams disembarked. This is where prey teams started to wonder what lie ahead of them on the other side of the innocent-looking blast hatch, and this was where

Bonisabella Brigham was grabbed, picked up, and frog marched straight out through the blast hatch, pain or no pain.

Brigham hobbled, not only because her calf was bleeding from the gash that ripped a slicing hole in the back of her leg, but also because both ankles were chained together with a mere foot of slack. One of Albrecker's commandos passed his flechette rifle over the scan pad as Albrecker and another commando tossed her through. She struggled to move after she landed, but was smart enough to scoot sideways out of the way of the threshold to avoid another injury. Brigham shimmied on her stomach, then stopped, gulping in air from the effort.

Albrecker and two commandos entered the resort. The last commando positioned himself far back from the open blast hatch near the attack shuttle as backup.

It was snowing on the resort.

The snow was only visible 40 or 50 yards just inside the open blast hatch, but it was coming down way past that, maybe two or three-hundred yards away. It was a fine mist, but it was snow-like, and it started covering Brigham's body fast. She curled up in a fetal position trying to make herself small. When she did, the hole that Dimitri had previously burned through her crotch leggings was visible. It was a humiliating sight if people that had sympathy for her had been present to see it. There weren't any, but neither were any of Jennifer's team. They were all still on the attack shuttle, the two insect aliens included, waiting for Albrecker's command to proceed or not.

Albrecker looked for cover ignoring the visually confusing long, round, immense environs of the resort. Once he was inside, there was only up and down, side to side. The spinning rotation of the enormous cylinder created gravity, so it seemed like you were standing in one place instead of circling around and around. Albrecker felt heavy, and it wasn't because of the powered dura armor he was wearing. The resort was not 1 G. It was more than that. More like 1.2 G, and the increased gravity was very noticeable. The servos in his suit whined just that much louder with each step. He could tell. But a quick glance at the mini HUD above his right eye signaled that his suit was making the necessary adjustment. After his sixth or seventh step, the power output of the suit increased matching his weight with 1 G once again. That was very noticeable too.

None too soon, the first of two rocket boomers whizzed by his head. The first one was way high, and the small missile impacted above and to the left of the open blast hatch behind him, exploding into the wall, but not doing any damage. The second one was lower and off the mark missing Albrecker, but it didn't miss Bonisabella Brigham. When he finally found some cover behind an outcrop of faux rock, he looked back. The explosion was settling, but Brigham's body, or parts of it, were just returning to earth, or simulated earth, or whatever the floor in the resort was called. None of that made a difference to Brigham. She was dead. Large chucks of her splattered against the wall near the blast hatch, the biggest piece visible out through the open blast hatch in the landing bay. It had just come to rest, sticking to the deck of the bay.

The projectile came from Albrecker's right and then up. Before he could shift his attention to the direction it came from, the other two commandos opened fire. Their flechette rifles unleashed a wicked, air piercing *thift-thift-thift-thift-thift*—Albrecker's enhanced mic registered a yelp of pain. He looked right and up the curved side of the resort. It was a gradual curve, but he was already getting used to it. There was a man sprawled across a ledge over a hundred yards away. He was in white snow gear but visible now with blood soaking the spot where his head and part of one his shoulders had been. Albrecker reminded himself that if the Pullback happened the dead man would resurrect, being that much more experienced with the boomer having remembered his mistake from the previous moments.

Then Albrecker shivered involuntarily. Another terrible, much more disturbing thought invaded his focus. He didn't want to let it take purchase, gain footing, because if it was true...*Well it couldn't be. It just couldn't.* He said that to himself, but didn't believe it.

Inside Abrecker's helmet he heard the crackle of his commo.

"All clear I think, Boss. He was set up waiting for someone to enter through the blast hatch. We must have caught him by surprise tossing Brigham in first. He didn't set up the tripod on the boomer accurately. No other thermal images in sight. Still scanning..."

"Thanks, Mark," Albrecker breathed. His heart was racing; he'd almost bought it. No doubt, if the man that was using the weapon was more skilled, Albrecker would just be a memory now.

"Are you seeing what I'm seeing past the snow line, Mark? Copy?"

"I am, Boss. Looks like there's another *season* laid out over there. You copy?"

"Copy that—"

"—Hold on. I'm tracking moving targets, two, no four, past the tree line, left, about 80 degrees up the slope. Looks like they're in *fall*. Copy?"

Albrecker inched his head over the faux rock and wiped at the front of his visor pulling wet snow away from his line of sight. He growled a subvocal command into his suit comp. The visor dimmed bringing up the infrared scanner. Sure enough, four beings were moving among the rocks just above the simulated tree line. The escarpment they were on mimicked the slope of a mountain; 80 degrees up the slope was almost half way up the side wall of the cylinder. Above that, a full 180 degrees above, was the mountain top. It jutted down into the cylinder ominously as if suspended there by magic. But it wasn't magic. It was gravity in perpetual motion, turning round, letting everything in the tube hug the ground it was anchored to.

The targets were in interminable fall. Albrecker wasn't surprised Mark had seen it. The resort was set up with four seasons. Where they entered was winter. About a quarter of a mile past that, fall started. It was hard to see beyond that with the peak of the mountain above dipping hard into the center of the cylinder, but Alberecker was certain he would find summer and spring beyond that. Then it hit him, and the logic of it seemed so simple.

"Mark, prey enters into the worst season putting them at an immediate disadvantage. The resort accommodations, where clients stay, are in the most pleasant part of the resort. Spring is where the customers stay, fronted by a sweltering hot, desert-like summer section that is barren enough to see prey coming across the parched, flat, sandy surface. You copy?"

Mark hesitated, but Albrecker knew it was for a reason. After a minute or so, he replied.

"Copy that, Boss. You're right as usual."

The smile could be heard in Mark's voice.

"I pulled up Hi Res, and the ping I got off the far wall of the resort measures just over one mile. I see the different seasons. They do go in order just like you said: winter, fall, summer, spring."

"Copy that," Albrecker coughed.

Mark noticed. "What, Boss? What else do you see? Copy?"

It was framing itself sickeningly in Albrecker's thoughts, the briefing Rand Fullrider conducted before they deployed, and a talk with Murphy. What Albrecker learned during that briefing had to be the answer, and it was going to change everything. He was hesitant to even say it, but he'd never keep the truth from his team.

"Boss, comeback. You copy?"

"Mark, I think we have a big problem. I think I know how the automated hybrid insect resort workers are going to defend the resort. Copy?"

"Copy, Boss. What, you see them forming up for an assault? I'm not registering anything on scans, over."

"There won't be a formation, Mark. If it happens before I finish explaining, remember that the rocket boomer assault will be more accurate next tim—"

The servos in Albrecker's powered dura body armor whined as he lifted his leg, placed his boot on her large behind, then kicked her out through the open hatch. She shrieked with pain crashing to the landing bay deck.

Albrecker knew he was right! The thought was fresh in his mind even though the time on the resort had reset. He wheeled around to the other three commandos behind him ready to deploy out the airlock hatch of the attack shuttle into the landing bay. He yelled as loud as he could.

"Mark, Adonis, Kimberly! Guard the blast hatch, move, move, move, move!"

Without hesitation, the three armored commandos leapt past Albrecker, dodged Brigham's large body, their servos working overtime trying to sprint the short distance to the blast hatch. The hatch was opening!

Kimberly was first out and first to the widening gap. She shoved her flechette rifle through the growing slit and fired off a full clip of projectiles yawing the barrel nose of her weapon in a tight figure eight to cover as much of her field of fire as she could.

Adonis was next to her trying to close the blast hatch, but the scan pad didn't work— once, twice, a third time. Albrecker could hear him curse over the commo.

"Fuck it!"

Then Adonis smashed the butt of his rifle on the scan pad destroying it. He shuffled to one side giving Mark room to stride up to it while he was pulling wire clips from the hip bladder on his belt. Two, then three wires connected with the internal components of the smashed scan pad. Marked thumbed a few buttons on his hand comp connected to them. The hatch closed, but just barely in time.

The blast concussion against the other side of the hatch sent a deafening shock wave through the dura steel door flipping the three armored figures like pretty playthings hurdling them through the air, arching over 10 feet backward before impact. Their sliding bodies scrapped the landing bay deck loudly, the three of them coming to rest in staggered succession.

Albrecker hated that he was right. Two thoughts entered his mind: *stay or retreat*. He was going to do one or the other, but not before he got his three commandos out of harm's way. His visor flipped up, his face red with urgency.

"You, Jansen! You, Volodya! You two, IAs! Now! Get my people back in the shuttle! Move it, move it, move it!"

He exited first sprinting off a few steps to one side to cover them while they jumped down to the landing bay deck doing what they were told. It was taking too long, but he knew his commandos were much more heavy in their armor. He had to be patient; he was trying. But never, not for an instant, did Albrecker take his aim off the still closed blast hatch.

After what seemed like 10 minutes, but was really only one, his commo crackled.

"We're good, we're in, Boss," Kimberly reported shakily.

"The suits short circuited but are back on line. Come back in, retreat."

Albrecker took a split second to glance back at the shuttle, his rifle still fixed on the blast hatch. His three commandos were not in sight; neither was Brigham. A silly thought darted through his mind: *Leave no one behind*, even if it was a piece of filth like Brigham. Still, he was proud of Jennifer's team. *They did good, and worked fast.*

Albrecker did board the attack shuttle, and he did have his pilot leave, but not to retreat, only to stay a safe distance from the resort to regroup. If another Pullback happened now, he'd deal with it, but just being out of the range of the rocket boomer let him think clearly and consider his options. The boomer wouldn't be effective in zero G. His pilot could avoid it.

Albrecker's helmet came off landing noisily on the deck. His first impulse was to blow a hole in Brigham's face. But he didn't. The sneer he planted on her as she watched him was a thing of hate though. He controlled his urge, looking over at Murphy who was swiveled around facing him. She was seated next to the pilot in one of two chairs in the small cockpit.

"The Pullback IS their defense!" He barked. His dark brown eyes looked sinister, his jaw rippling as he grated his teeth. He radiated pissed off in waves, but Murphy understood.

Murphy didn't shrink under his glare. "I'm sorry I didn't think of that."

Albrecker rotated toward Brigham. He absently handed his rifle to Kimberly who was standing beside him, not trusting it in his grasp when he asked her, "Where's the power source for the Pullback, the time machine?"

Was Brigham smirking? Did she actually have the gonads to be enjoying what was happening? It sure looked like it. Albrecker sure must have thought so. *Okay, no more Mister Wait*

And Kill You Later, he thought. He snatched his rifle back out of Kimberly's grasp, squeezing off a round. The grabbing and blunt *thift* like one fluid motion. Brigham's head exploded backwards painting the bulkhead with brain and skull.

"Guess we do it ourselves," Albrecker said so nonchalantly that it even surprised Murphy. And she had done something very similar back at Bonita's to Rifle Man and Gleam Boy.

"I guess you're right," Murphy said.

Brigham was so heavy she merely sagged in the shock seat she was in. What was left of her head lulled back tilting to one side.

Albrecker shot a look at Murphy expecting an answer. She was okay with that. She was also okay with a dead Bonisabella Brigham. The issue was: Would she stay dead? Her damn time device had to be the reason she smirked.

"Large, the power source for the Pullback has to be large," Murphy reasoned. "That much power isn't in the skin of the cylinder. I saw the Voltaics. They're bulky as shit, un-wieldy. There has to be a place on the resort where there's enough room for them, and enough space so they can be wired in parallel, all together. You see anything like that when you were inside?"

Everyone in the small attack shuttle swiveled to look at Albrecker.

"I sure did."

Albrecker hesitated like he was picturing it again or maybe working up a strategy. His hesitant response was a bit maddening to everyone else after what he just did with such unadulterated urgency and ruthlessness—Not a judgement by anyone, mind you. If there was a person that deserved a dart through the brain case, it was Brigham. It was just that Albreck-er wasn't sharing.

Kimberly wasn't afraid of her commander. She wheeled her rifle around her waist, slamming it into his stomach. The loud clang off his armor was more attention-getting than impactful.

"You gonna tell us or what? I have a date later."

Mark snickered. The date was with him. Kimberly looked at him and winked. Through it all, this was just another deployment for the commandos. Priorities were priorities, after all. Mark cleared his throat because Albrecker looked over at him with an expectant gaze.

Mark answered, "The mountain, the power source is inside the mountain that's in the fall section of the resort."

Dimitri looked up at Mark from his shock seat. "Explain."

Albrecker pursed his lips letting Mark handle it.

Mark took off his helmet holding it by his side. He had a nervous habit of tapping it against his thigh. Click, click, click, click, his helmet was like a security blanket or maybe it was the expectation that a fight was forthcoming and he had to stay sharp, always alert, always moving in some way, to be ready for it.

Mark was fairly young, about 40, sandy blonde hair, greying temples, and more than one scar on his forehead and chin. His grey eyes landed on Dimitri. Click, click, click...

"There are four seasons, four zones in the resort. We entered into winter, snow and everything. Beyond that, fall, complete with a one peak mini mountain range and leafless trees and evergreens. A desert next, summer, then the guest accommodations are situated in spring. A mile long, maybe half mile in diameter."

"The *Guarantee* works huh, Mark?" Murphy asked.

"Sure does! The guy we killed when we first entered the resort was probably the same fucker that tried to shoot a boomer through the blast hatch after he resurrected." He shook his head. "Fucker!"

Adonis already had his helmet off. He was a black man, wiry, thin faced, with a close 'fro cropped against his dark skin. His almost black eyes were casual.

"We find the access hatch to the power source on the cylinder skin, blow it, drop in, and blow the Voltaics inside the mountain." He shrugged. "How hard can it be?"

Click, click, click, click…

"Not very hard by definition there, A-Don, but a tad predictable don't you think? These damn hybrid insect resort workers know we're here, right? We might never make it to the access hatch on the cylinder skin in a hundred lifetimes. Ya know what I mean? They'll just flip the Pullback switch and we end up back here, pounding our puds."

"As we go down slowly, as we go down slowly, as we go down slowlyeeee…"

Murphy had stood up and was nothing short of back to her old self. She was singing a tune she liked and swaying her shoulders to a groove only she could hear. It was like a light switch had been flipped. Adrianna looked at Murphy from her seat and wasn't that shocked. With Chazzy not around to curb her ingrained emo tendencies, Murphy's real personality had to come to the surface eventually.

The three commandos squinted a bit, then saw Murphy's vibes, felt them, and joined in. It was a weird scene, three dura armor figures, swaying in unison to a tune only Murphy could hear inside her head. But the commandos seemed to hear it too. Whatever it was, it relaxed them.

Adrianna turned looking back into the small compartment behind her. The two IAs were bobbing their abdomens in little jerking movements joining in.

Albrecker took all this in for a minute or so resigned to let his team blow off the adrenaline dump without interruption. He was just glad they were alive. Besides, it seemed as long as the attack shuttle was not on the resort the Pullback wouldn't be used. What was the point? They'd all just go back in time still on the shuttle. The hybrid insect resort workers had to be controlling the Pullback themselves—had to be!

Murphy twerked her thin hips, a little strange considering she was in dura leg wraps and a dura vest, dark flight suit under it all. She stopped, smiling.

"Nice moves." Murphy directed the compliment at the others that had joined in.

"Now for something completely different—Get this."

The switch had flipped yet again; she had more than one personality setting. Adrianna had seen The Emo Skank, Grapple Woman, The Wart, The Hacker, The Assassin, and now The Beatnik. Murphy was a collage, and Adrianna enjoyed seeing it because, despite everything, she liked her very much.

"Do tell, Oh Keeper Of Our Next Move, Alyse," Sami spat. She was seated between Jeffrey and Dimitri.

Murphy straightened like she was surprised to hear her last name, but enjoyed that it was coming from Sami nonetheless. "Sure."

The rest of the humans and IAs stopped what they were doing and looked toward her. Murphy sighed.

"Where do you keep the Pullback switch? I mean…Is there even a switch to activate the Pullback?"

It was increasingly common for the rest of Jennifer's team not to follow Murphy and her line of thinking. She didn't mean to speak in riddles, but she couldn't help it. No harm, no real foul that, but this time one of Albrecker's team did follow. They had a different point of view on the Op than Jennifer's team. Beyond that, they were not as close to all of it, as familiar with it, as Jennifer's team, a fresh perspective, so to speak.

Adonis sucked his lower lip crinkling his chin.

"There isn't one. There isn't a switch."

"You. Da. Man. Adonis," Murphy beamed.

Albrecker was already following Murphy's line of thinking, and it looked like in the few seconds that had just elapsed, he had formulated a plan to solve all their problems.

"How do we get them to run interference?" He asked Murphy.

"Should be easy enough."

Adrianna, Jeffrey, Dimitri and Sami's head pivoted in turn from Adonis, to Murphy, to Albrecker, trying to follow their conversation. No luck.

"Stop!" Jeffrey grunted. "Share, damn it!"

Albrecker looked at him.

"The two IAs with us can read minds just like the head of their Collective. The telepathy the IAs have is the only way to explain their targeted help. They were just moving body parts to be polite, to attempt to communicate with us. Rand told me what they've done. Murphy did too. There's just one catch…"

"…Ahhh, sooo, Strong Leader of the Strike Team, you are as wise as you are gifted in the ways of war."

Murphy had a crooked smirk locked onto Albrecker, and for the first time anyone had been around the guy, he smiled too. Murphy covered the rest of the team with her gaze.

"The insect aliens have not been able to communicate to us using telepathy because their kind speak a language our minds can't understand.…There's no button, no switch, on the resort to activate the Pullback. The genetic hybrid insect resort workers activate it telepathically."

"But…but…?" Dimitri prodded.

"But the two IAs with us CAN communicate to their own kind using telepathy. Their own kind are on the resort—the hybrid insect resort workers." Murphy brushed past Albrecker down the narrow shuttle confines coming to a stop in front of the two IAs.

"We need you to run interference on the resort. Stop the genetic resort workers from MIND activating the Pullback until we rescue your friends and all the others, humans and pinatens. Oh, and by the way, make sure to tell your friends that are on the resort being hunted—We're coming to get them."

The two IAs started doing their circle dance around each other, their little vests nowhere to be seen. They were small enough, it was easy room-wise, but once again, when they started their dance as close as they were to each other, something happened that no one had seen before. The carapaces of the tan little creatures rubbed against each other noisily. The scratching sound grew in volume to a fever-high shrieking pitch causing everyone to throw their hands over their ears trying to deaden the squeal. Then it stopped, not audible any longer. But the two IAs didn't stop. In fact, they moved even faster, blindingly fast, their tan colors almost meshing into one.

Murphy turned back around. "We can land on the resort now, Sergeant."

Albrecker nodded as he and the others removed their hands from their ears.

"The catch, what's the catch?" Sami was staring at the IAs mesmerized by their performance. She didn't look at Murphy when she asked.

Murphy reached over snapping her fingers next to Sami's ear several times. Sami blinked looking up at her.

"The interference the two IAs are doing is not audible to our ears or mind, Sami. Trust them; we can land now." She nodded once, then looked over at Albrecker.

Albrecker barked the order to land at the pilot who turned back to his flight console and began guiding the ship back to the resort.

Murphy shot a hand up to the ceiling steading herself as the shuttle turned.

"Oh, and the catch is we still have to fight the hunters on the resort. Our IA friends are pumping out a steady stream of their own brand of electronic counter measures preventing any of the resort workers from mind activating the Pullback, but we still have the distinct pleasure of killing the bastards that paid for all of this to happen if they get in our way. You good now, Sami?"

Sami sneered, extending a fist for Murphy to bump. With her other hand she flashed a bobbing Hook 'Em Horns.

"I'm good. Just give me a weapon," she grated her teeth.

Murphy smiled taking it on herself to arm Jennifer's team with Adonis' help. Jen's team wore the same dark blue flight suits under dura leg and vest wraps. Fair protection, but the plan had never been for Jennifer's team to lead, only follow.

Albrecker watched Murphy and Adonis pass out the weapons. He sighed running a hand through this black hair then scratched at his beard-stubbled face. He was about same age as the others on his team. The four of them had a lot of miles behind them working together. He hated thinking how close they'd all come to dying at the hands of some idiot amateur safari-seekers.

His decision made, Albrecker stepped over to instruct the pilot on what he wanted *this time*, and how he wanted it. The small attack shuttle banked on a new course picking up speed.

What he wanted this time was to shake things up, no more of this Come Through The Blast Hatch They're Expecting crap. Besides, Albrecker had a choice now thanks to the two insect aliens swirling their ECM dance in the back of the shuttle. The hybrid insect resort workers were never going to attack in force. He knew that now. They only used the Pullback to defend the resort.

Click, click, click… Albrecker looked down at Mark's helmet tapping out a soothing rhythm against his dura clad thigh. It always relaxed him to hear it. Mark's unconscious habit meant that he was ready.

Albrecker glanced at Kimberly's face; it was passive and calm. Her blue eyes contrasted sharply with her dark black hair. Her fishbone braids were done up in a protective style close to her scalp. She had several thin cornrows which supported two large braids that ran down the sides of her head. She chose to wear the two pigtails the rows created down when on an Op. That made it easier for the pigtails to slide down into the back of her dura armor suit collar, not to mention put on her helmet.

When Murphy and Adonis were done handing out the weapons to Jennifer's team, Albrecker looked at everyone gaining their attention with the sound of his voice.

"We're going in through the client landing bay this time. My commandos go in first. We secure the landing bay and meet any of the resort workers that come to greet us. Remember what you're going to see; don't get distracted." He shot a look at Adrianna.

"The resort workers are going to have insect alien bodies with human heads, just like the ones we rescued from the pleasure base," Adrianna cautioned, then added, "Don't get caught up staring at their eyes."

She felt she needed to say that even though every person on the shuttle had: A) either seen the original breeding center on the pleasure base, or B) had visited the makeshift quarantine Medico set up in *Brandish's* cargo hold.

"It shouldn't be necessary to kill the resort workers," Albrecker continued, directing that reminder at his team.

"I'm good," Kimberly confirmed. She turned, "A-Don, Mark, you good?" She flashed a look at each man in turn. They both dipped their heads then put on their helmets. Kimberly did the same.

Albrecker braced himself on an overhead grab feeling the shuttle land.

"Wait for an order before you exit. We're going to clear the hotel, or whatever they call it, where all the clients stay. If we run into clients that aren't out hunting, we warn them once, then drop them if they don't surrender, no negotiations!"

The conviction with which he said it made it clear he wasn't happy about nearly being blown up earlier, even more so that his three commandos barely escaped.

"The hotel where the clients stay can't be that big. We're going to clear it room-by-room. If we take prisoners, I'll have one of my team bring them back to the landing bay. That's where all of you come in." He swept Jennifer's team looking at each person.

"Touchdown," the pilot called out. He had just guided the shuttle through the magnetic containment field that protected man and equipment from the vacuum of space inside the client landing bay, easing the craft down on its landing gear.

The commandos checked the action on their loaded flechette rifles thumbing the auto slides. Jennifer's team had laser rifles, no auto slides to check, just a power stick housed in the butt. Murphy was staying on the shuttle, intel only.

"One last thing," Albrecker still had his helmet off addressing Jennifer's team. He couldn't have looked more serious.

"You people have a friend on the resort. Krachy may not be the same person you remember. There's only time to say this once: I'll try to rescue every being that's being hunted. But, hear me folks, I'm not going to sacrifice our lives or put *Brandish* in danger to do it. If we need backup, we're leaving until it comes. We're clear on that, right? I want a 'yessir' outta all of you!"

"Yessir!" Echoed back at him from Adrianna, Sami, Jeff and Dimitri.

Albrecker hit Murphy with a hard look.

"I want to hear it from you too, Murphy. Say it!"

Murphy gulped. She knew she was a loose cannon at times, but not today, not with what she'd been allowed to be a part of. She'd never been such an integral part of something this important in her whole life.

"Yessir!" She yelled.

The airlock hatch started to open giving Albrecker time to shove on his helmet. Kimberly led the three commandos out through the open hatch. Murphy stepped up behind Albrecker grabbing his arm. He looked back at her.

"Hurry, Lance." She looked pale.

"I'm afraid the two IAs are going to die if they do that much longer."

Albrecker looked over at the spinning tan cluster and nodded.

FIFTEEN

What Sergeant Lance Albrecker's strike team saw inside the client landing bay on the hunting resort wasn't much of a surprise. They were so focused on staying alive, the sight of eight capsules on the bulkhead wall didn't faze them. The pods were empty, and they didn't aim anything dangerous or shoot back.

Kimberly could live with that. Considering her last landing through the prey landing bay, this was a welcome change.

"Looks like we already found the hotel, Boss."

"Copy that." Albrecker kept his eyes on the blast hatch in the center of the bulkhead wall. There were four pods uniformly spaced on either side of it about seven feet off the deck. Recessed foot holes served as ladders so the person could climb up and into the sleeping pods. Next to each pod was a blue LED name tag.

Mark and Adonis stood well back from the blast hatch like Albrecker, the boomer shock wave fresh in their minds too. They covered Kimberly as she made a close, but not too close, inspection of the illuminated name plates. They were easy to read.

"No names on the first two," she commented walking quickly from right to left, stepping past the third pod.

"John Paul Sark, 0875 #12," she strode past the blast hatch, "0875 #13, Lev Babinot, no name, Boratinsky Alvosky." She backed up to stand next to Albrecker looking at him.

"My guess: two humans, one pinaten, and two insect aliens. Boss, there are fuckin' IAs on the resort hunting for sport just like the humans and pinatens."

"How's that possible?" Mark asked. "The IAs are supposed to be part of this big Collective and all think alike. Why would they hunt for sport? Better still, how are they paying for it?"

Murphy's voice crackled on the group channel.

"They pay with bodies. I mean insect aliens they donate to be bred into hybrid insect resort workers. The IAs have VIPs just like the humans and pinatens do on the resort that paid to hunt. I don't believe the two IAs on the name plates are the two IAs our ECM dancing friends are looking for, can't be. The two IAs we are looking for are acting as hunting prey just like Krachy." The disgust in her voice was strong. The underlying implication even more disturbing: There were splinter factions of the Insect Alien Collective that had independent thought and dark motives.

"Holy shit," Adonis muttered.

"Focus people," Albrecker growled trying to hide how sick the discovery made him feel too. "We've got a job to do. The only way to do it is to breach that hatch—"

—It was opening.

All four commandos tensed. Four hybrid insect resort workers proceeded in through the blast hatch, two-by-two, in a very non-threatening way. It certainly was the eyes; it was very hard not to stare at them. All four of them had the heads of a woman with compound eyes, their six legs carrying them fast into the client landing bay. Two went right, two went left.

Albrecker and his team tracked them with their rifles, the tiny chrono in Albrecker's head ticking realizing that he couldn't just stand here and watch, but he also knew he'd better make sure they weren't a threat.

The decision was made for him.

"They're not a problem, Lance. Please, just go, move into the resort. Our team can watch them. Go!" It was Murphy.

Albrecker heard the pleading in her voice; she needed him to finish this. Murphy was worried the two IAs were dancing themselves to death. Not only was that a terrible fate for them, but when their swirling ECM wave stopped, it would end his chances to rescue anyone at all.

"Copy that. Proceed inside," Albrecker ordered, Kimberly taking point. The four of them were in through the open blast hatch fast.

Back in the client landing bay, the women hybrid insect resort workers weren't a threat. They were setting up the landing bay for new guests. It was clear they were on auto pilot, genetically programmed to do their setup tasks when a shuttle landed. Retractable tables popped out from the bulkheads on either side of the attack shuttle, complete with chairs bolted to the hinged panels. The first two workers activated the auto table-chairs. The second two were carrying refreshments in their front two legs, their thoraxes raised, walking smoothly but quickly, one to each table. They placed the carafes on the table tops, leaving the tray with mugs and something that looked like finger food. Steam was rising from the just baked food.

Not only was the client landing bay the capsule hotel, it was the ward room and lounge. That fact became more obvious when the first two women hybrid resort workers moved past the auto tables and activated auto couches on both bulkheads. The couches clicked into position on their hinged panels. The tables and couches gave a fine view through the open magnetic containment field out into deep space behind the attack shuttle.

The second two workers were already gone, the first two quick on their heels, their genetically programmed greeting tasks complete.

Albrecker didn't have to say it. Mark did.

"It's not 1.2 G now, Boss...the hell?"

Albrecker was with the program now, all of the insanity of this death trap making total sense to him now.

"The higher G is only in winter putting the hunting prey in a defensive hole the moment they step foot on the resort. Clients get the 1 G we feel, with the help of a grav gen in this part of the resort I'd guess, to make it easier on them."

There were hatches on either side of the wide corridor the four commandos walked down. Albrecker felt the time pressure and acted.

"Jansen, Volodya, you two clear the rooms through the blast hatch in the corridor. The workers don't seem a threat. If you run into one that is, you know what to do. Move now! Adrianna, Sami cover the landing bay. Don't go room-to-room with Jansen and Volodya. Move it!" A chorus of acknowledgments came back through his helmet.

Kimberly stopped up ahead, already at the end of the corridor. Albrecker stared past her. The hatch at the end of the corridor was open to the entire resort. Unlike the prey landing bay, this bay was not on the perimeter of the cylinder. It was in the center of it, which meant the hatch opening in front of them had about a quarter mile distance in all directions from the opening to the ground of the circling resort. Albrecker knew why, and he knew how the outer structure of the corridor they were standing on would be shaped. The shape was simple and effective; he just knew it would be. Just like everything else.

"Kimberly hold up," she shuffled to one side letting Albrecker brush, more like clank, past her. Looking out the open hatch, Albrecker told his commandos the way it was going to be.

"I go in alone. You three cover me from here, at least until I give you the okay to join me—"

"—Boss, now wait just a damn minut—!"

"Can it, Mark! I mean it! No time to argue. Do as I say!"

Before more dissent came, Albrecker stepped off the ledge at the same time flipping the anti grav harness on in his suit. Instead of gliding down, he shot up fast, pushing the tiny joypad in his glove hard in that direction. Seconds before Albrecker hit the ground in a grassy forest of trees, he righted himself landing on his feet. He landed at a run, pumping his knees hard, the suit servos whining rhythmically with every step. Small saplings weren't a problem; he just ran over them. He dodged bigger trees, varied his route, and expected to be fired upon at any second. He wasn't. He thought he knew why: The prey targets Mark had originally spotted on their first landing attempt were located in fall, clear on the other end of the resort. That meant the hunters would probably be in winter, fall, or summer trying to close in on them, he hoped...

About two minutes later, Albrecker reached the edge of spring taking shelter behind a closely grouped stand of trees just this side of the flat, sandy expanse of summer out in front of him. He looked back, breathing hard, catching his breath.

The opening to the client bay was visible jutting out from the center of the resort wall, and like he guessed, it was shaped like a funnel. The tip of the funnel was the open hatch he'd just come through. The sides of the structure receded just like a funnel, expanding uniformly outward at a steep pitch until they contacted the far resort bulkhead.

The resort wall was a baffle, just like one you could use on a birdhouse perched on the top of a pole in the middle of a lake. The steep slopes of the baffle prevented creatures from climbing up the sides to enter the birdhouse. This was no different. Simple but effective—Prey couldn't scale the steep slopes to get into the client bay. The shape looked so effective that Albrecker doubted anyone even tried it, just another part of the hopeless odds prey were up against in this evil trap of horrors.

"We've got eyes on you, Boss," Adonis confirmed. "No targets visible on scans. You're clear."

"Copy that."

Albrecker took a breath, stood up, and eased out of his hide around the stand of trees pushing off hard. He felt the sand below his boots offering more resistance; after eight or nine steps, the servos increased power. On step ten, he was tripped flat, crashing to his chest, the air heaving out of his lungs with the impact.

The next set of things happened so fast Albrecker didn't even have time to catch his breath. He caught a glimpse of an arm rise up out of the sand next to his head. A fleeting thought scared him: *There's life underground!*

The arm was powerful and grappled around the back of his neck forcing his face into the sand. On the other side of him he felt pressure on the outside of his suit.

The pressure grew heavier and heavier.

Sand was pushed over Albrecker's helmet, blocking out all light.

The pressure was severe and constant.

It was quiet.

The arm around the back of Alberecker's neck jerked him so he would look to his right.

His helmet increased the light shining out the front of his visor to compensate for the darkness.

Staring back at him was a man's face, his two eyes looking directly into Albrecker's.

"You're not very smart, are you?" The man said.

Albrecker was still catching his breath, and really confused. His eyes adjusted to the small space in front of his visor. The man was lying under the sand beside him. It was clear now that the weight on his body was more sand. They were both buried in it. What wasn't clear was how it happened so fast.

The man didn't seem in any big hurry, just mildly curious.

"Please tell me you aren't the leader of the rescue team."

Albrecker could finally see the chamber in front of his visor that was clear of sand. The soft orange light from his helmet reflected off the sandy sides of the six-inch-hollow. He looked up recognizing a curved piece of tree bark the man had used to shield their faces from the sand that had been pushed atop them both. Their noses were four inches apart.

"I am," Albrecker cleared his throat. "Nice to see you alive, Bantor." For the second time that day, Lance smiled.

"—Boss, we don't have you on scans, come in! Copy that, report!?" Mark shouted.

Krachy was so close he heard it. His looked turned annoyed.

"Tell 'em to cool their jets."

Albrecker did.

"So what's the plan then, Sergeant? Please tell me you are *at least* a Sergeant."

No use answering that. Time was wasting.

"The ECM stopping the workers from resetting the day is going to stop any minute. We gotta move!"

"The question still stands, Sergeant: What's your plan? The hunt for today, if you didn't know, is that a locker full of rocket boomers were opened by the hunters, and they're playing with their new toys until we get blown up."

Albrecker realized Bantor didn't understand.

"We have a plan, damn it! I said my team stopped the resort's ability to reset the day. But I don't know how long it will last. We have to go, NOW!"

Realization started forming first in Krachy's eyes, then reached the corners of his lips as he turned them up crookedly. As quick as it happened, his look of hope was gone.

"Only three of my team are here. The other one is injured and hiding. We can't leave her behind."

It was going to be a tough sell, but Albrecker had to try.

"Let me get you three out, then we'll come back for her."

Sand was starting to slide in from around the curved bark from Krachy shaking his head as Albrecker said it. *Oh well, it was worth a try.*

"Try again." Krachy's voice was immovable.

"I have three commandos as backup."

"Better."

"Jansen, Volodya, Sami, and Adrianna, too."

"I didn't hear the magic word, Sergeant."

"*Jennifer* is back on the ship. Does that finally convince you, you hard-headed bastard!?"

It was hard to tell if Bantor was convinced. It was clear he'd been through a lot. Hiding in the sand was a savvy move. Krachy and his small team couldn't be scanned under the sand, and the desert area they were in was not very inviting to search. If the hunters couldn't see anyone on the barren surface of the sand, they would look in the other sections of the resort that had more cover, Basic Camouflage 101, as it were.

Bantor closed his eyes. It was as though he was trying to catch a nap! Albrecker's blood pressure shot through his eyes. *What the hell was this idiot doing!?*

"Bantor, Bantor!" Krachy didn't flinch, his eyes still shut. "Wake up for Crissake!"

Bantor didn't. Not for another 15 seconds. Then his eyes parted.

"My team is ready."

Albrecker sensed what he'd just done. The fact that other insect aliens were being hunted on the resort couldn't be ignored. The IAs Bantor had just communicated with telepathically had to be the friends of the two IAs spinning their ECM dance back on the attack shuttle. Bantor must have been communicating with them. What was certain, however, was that Albrecker didn't know the resort like Bantor did, and Albrecker knew Bantor's background, all of it. Still, he did have an idea.

"Try this: I send down my commandos, they hump your team back to the client bay while I go get the injured woman."

Krachy coughed a billow of fine sand from around his mouth.

"You have to give me your word you won't leave her, Sergeant. Look at me and tell me you won't."

Despite himself, Albrecker gulped. Dangerous, exhausted, at wits end, desperate, nothing to lose, all these things could be seen in the chiseled dura steel behind Krachy's request. Albrecker understood, and had no intention of lying to him.

"If it means my life, she comes with me out of here."

"Almost good enough," but due to exhaustion, false hope, or being able to survive as long as he had on the resort without dying, Krachy was not finished. He gave Albrecker nothing short of a look of death to ram home his point.

"You fail me, Sergeant, and I'll kill you. No one is left behind. NO ONE!"

"Understood. Where is she?"

"Atop mini Mount Hope; we dug our way, I mean the two insect aliens on my team dug a way, into the top of the hill. The batteries and time displacement equipment only extend so far up into the cavity of the mount. My team sometimes hides there, but mainly move around a lot, never staying too long in one place."

"Tell me about the gravity in the middle of the cylinder." It had been bothering Albrecker since the moment he stepped foot on the rotating behemoth. He had to know.

"Weapons fire from the ground into the air curves," Krachy explained. "The gravity fades the higher you go, then the sphere of influence returning to the ground on the other side of the cylinder takes hold again. It's the single most effective way we've had of staying alive all this time. We try to stay directly across the cylinder from hunters. They can't hit us at a half mile, especially since the gravity bottoms out in the *Mid Zone,* as we call it."

"I know how to get her now. The top of the Mount is in the Mid Zone, isn't it?"

"Yes, but..."

"But what, Bantor?"

"There's gravity on the slopes of the mountain. Whoever built this place made sure there was strong gravity on the slopes to make it hard to climb and get away. The pull of it gets stronger the closer you get."

"Where are your other two team members?"

"They're the ones that covered us with sand. The IA's back seven legs, all moving in unison, can cover a person is two-seconds flat, Sergeant. They're two feet from your back right now, buried in the sand beside you."

Albrecker didn't understand why Bantor said seven instead of eight legs, but let it go.

"Mark, Adonis, Kimberly, come in? Copy?"

"Copy, Boss." It was Mark.

"I have three for pickup. I'm just in front of the stand of trees that was my spring hide, 20 feet in from the edge of summer. Bantor and two IAs covered us with sand. You three get here and extract them. Move it!" He yelled.

"Copy that!"

Krachy explained, "The place where she's hiding is a little billet with a makeshift access hatch facing winter. She won't be expecting you; I don't have any way to tell her you're coming to rescue her. She can't read my mind like the two IAs on my team."

Albrecker was preoccupied with another problem, but he heard Krachy and said, "I'll deal with it, Bantor. What's her name?"

"Lori."

"Bantor, why haven't any rocket boomers gone off since I arrived? They have to be tracking me. What the hell is going on? The hunters can't be that blind. They tried twice in rapid succession when we came in through the prey landing bay in winter?"

"All I can say is that with the effin' time reset they get smarter every day. If the hunters haven't shot at you, they have a damn good reason. I've killed so many of the a-holes only to see them resurrect the next day that much smarter." For the first time, a hint of despair crossed Krachy's face. He was running on reserves and his nerves were shot.

"10 seconds, Boss. All clear for pick up."

Albrecker grunted an acknowledgment to Mark.

"10 seconds, Bantor. We got this, you understand? We ALL leave together. Say it, say it to me…"

Krachy had closed his eyes. It looked like he was nodding off, maybe even passing out. The anticipation that he might live through all this had to be draining, physically and mentally. Albrecker nudged him. No, it wasn't that—arms were digging the both of them out of the sand.

Krachy opened his eyes when he felt it. He was yanked free from the sand by servo driven arms and heaved up over Kimberly's shoulder in a fireman's carry. He let it happen, too exhausted with hope, with faith, that it was all ending now.

Krachy's naked body was dirty. It was hard to tell what were bruises or dirt. The sand cascaded off him leaving a trail of tan mist behind. Kimberly had him up over her shoulder turning toward the client bay hatch in a blink. She slammed the joypad in her glove as hard as she could urging the AGH in her suit straight for the hatch.

Mark, then Adonis, did about the same with the two IAs that had scurried out of the sand next to Albrecker. They were so small they were scooped right up. The injuries on them were different: no bruises, but indentations, divots in the carapaces of either one in varying sizes and spots. One of the IAs was missing a mid leg on its right side. Before Albrecker stood fully erect, they were gone too, held tight in the commando's arms b-lining it straight toward the hatch following Kimberly.

The 185,466 pound elephant in the resort felt like a ticking bomb ready to end all the unexpected good luck Albrecker had up until this point. The omen was ominous, and it was completely absurd. There was no answer for it, and that was most frightening of all: The hunters had not tried to kill him.

Albrecker had made a promise: He'd promised his life that Lori would live. He lifted up off the sand in a flash, using the power limits of his AGH, surging in front of a dusty cloud of sand cascading off his suit behind him.

Mount Hope was directly in front of him just past summer. Albrecker was on the curve of the resort where, instead of the mountain being upside down in relation to him, it was right-side-up. He moved fast over the featureless sand below, gaining altitude, feeling the weight of not being fired upon like a physical thing, an entity of doom, that was tricking him into believing that he was going to save Lori—to save her, and get a hug around his neck for being so gallant. *What a crock!* If there was ever a more preposterous name to give a mountain in this hellish asylum, Mount Hope was it.

Albrecker's speed blew the remains of sand off his suit. Over two-thirds of the way up the steep slope of the mountain, he subvocalized a command flipping on his infrared scanner. What was he looking for? Anything, any sign of heat, of life, of a crack near the fast approaching peak of the mountain revealing where Lori was. He started to slow and circle. He was at the top. The bile in his throat started to make him nauseous. Albrecker was a slow moving target, feebly searching for something that he didn't even know was there. Then he saw it, or did he? *Maybe, it could be.*

Albrecker killed the infrared and did the only thing he could think of to confirm it. He pulled a plasti squirt bottle of water from the bladder on his thigh having to fight to grip it with packed sand all around. Once free, he edged himself closer to the slope with his AGH pointing the bottle at the rock face. The servo assisted fingers squeezed the bottle harder than he expected. Water squirted at a slight depression, no joy. Again, at another gap in the rock. *Nothing, or was it? It could be.* Albrecker squirted again; the water a foot below where he aimed the stream disappeared into a crack. He squeezed a line of liquid left to right watching the water leak into a crack that shouldn't be there.

Albrecker didn't hesitate. Reaching in the bladder on his other thigh, he extracted a palm-sized vibra-mine. He shook it to get the sand off. The device was a little wedge, four inches wide. He wound up like a pitcher and slammed the wedge point first into the crack. Talking into his suit, he vocalized the command.

"Secure!"

A small, silver metal spike darted from the back of the wedge striking the rock behind it, anchoring the mine with a puff of white smoke where the piston gained purchase.

"Activate!" He yelled.

The little wedge pushed forward on the piston inching the slit in the rock open a few inches, then more, then he growled, "Spread!"

The two sides of the wedge expanded outward vibrating the opening wider until it was almost a foot wide. On went Albrecker's headlamp searching for life in the billet.

"Krachy sent me to rescue you!" His voice boomed over the suit mic. "Lori?! Lori?!"

Nothing.

"Lori?! Show yourself. I'm here to help. If this helps, listen," he dialed back the volume. "Only I'd know this, Krachy was rock climbing and asked Jennifer to marry him."

Albrecker tried to wait—he did. Knowing he'd painted himself as an immovable target hovering at the top of this stupid mountain caused bullets of sweat to start dripping down his forehead into his eyes. *This isn't workin—*

"—Romantic little shit isn't he?" A strained voice came from the opening. Lori's dirty face appeared. It was her!

"Open this thing, climb on, and we're outta here. Hurry!"

Lori disappeared out of sight, then the awkwardly shaped door on the billet popped out of its frame and fell rolling down the mountainside. A cord of what looked like braided tree bark attached to the underside.

Grabbing the opening on either side, Lori tried to lift herself up, but couldn't. No worries, Albrecker reached down into the hole, but she yelled at him.

"I can't, my leg! My leg below the knee is gone. I can't stand up!" She was shaking so bad her skin was quivering over her whole body.

Albrecker popped his visor up inching the AGH joypad in his glove to move his face closer to the hole. He looked into her bloodshot eyes.

"The woman who thinks she can and the woman who thinks she can't are both right. Which one are you, Lori?"

She blinked.

Albrecker smiled as Lori extended her arms over her head letting him do the rest. As he pulled her from the hole, he couldn't help but notice that the nipple on her left breast had been sheered off leaving a mess of puss that wasn't healing. He shrugged her easily over his shoulder careful not to touch the exposed, ragged bloody stump under her left knee. He could feel what now seemed like Lori's rapid convulsions, not just quivering, through the metal skin of his armor now that her weight was anchored over him. He thumbed the joypad, just having turned, when IT happened.

The billet coughed a blaring shockwave from the blast. Lori fell off his shoulder yelping a pathetic squeal of fear. Albrecker's arm shot out instinctively, himself tumbling out away, feet over head, slammed sideways by the powerful explosion shooting out from inside the mountain. His powered hand snatched her wrist in a desperate grab—crushing bone. Lori didn't scream; she passed out.

Just as well, he reasoned, looking back at the last few seconds in slow motion. The elephant had finally appeared; it had thrown it's trunk sideways swatting them like rag dolls, end-over-end, as they fell to their fate. Albrecker's vision cleared. Lori was still in his grasp speeding down the side of *Mount Misery* with him toward the rocks below.

*AGH, AGH…*He pushed his fear aside, *That could help!* It did, but not at first.

Albrecker's suit had scrambled into emergency mode to protect its circuitry. *Well, that's inconvenient,* he thought calmly. *Maybe I'll bounce when I hit.* Then, realizing Lori wouldn't bounce made him try again. He jammed the joypad in his glove, the circuits coming back online, allowing him to direct the grav wave of his harness out and up at the last second. Leveling off, he pulled Lori, yanking her limp body into his arms with ease assisted by the powered suit.

Albrecker slid out his boot toe contacting the deck of the open client hatch easing back on the AGH's joypad, planting both boots firmly past the ledge. His visor flipped up. Lori was breathing, still unconscious in his arms. The servos whined powering his quick steps down the corridor out into the client landing bay. He froze, his boots scraping loudly to a halt.

Jennifer's team was huddled on the left side of the bay around the auto table against the bulkhead. They weren't armed. Albrecker panned right. Kimberly, Adonis, and Mark had their helmets off huddled near the other table. They weren't armed either. Krachy and his two IA teammates were laying on the deck just in front of the attack shuttle, the three of them barely moving, looking filthy, injured, but still alive.

The armed beings in EVA suits flanked the attack shuttle. Their helmets were off. One insect alien and a man Albrecker didn't recognize held laser rifles pointed at his commandos. On the other side of the shuttle, which essentially sectioned off the landing bay in two, were two men Albrecker did recognize along with another IA, all three pointing laser rifles at Jennifer's team.

Lev Babinot's head jutted out of the top of his EVA suit, the black of space beyond the bay's containment field behind him a stark contrast. His weapon tracked toward Albrecker.

"Drop the bitch!" He snarled.

Albrecker looked down at the helpless woman then back at him.

"No."

Babinot's eyes shot open.

"I'll fire!"

"Haven't you killed enough things that can't fight back, you smelly piece of rat shit?"

"I won't ask you again—" The words caught in his throat. At that exact same moment an EVA suited person drifted fast into the landing bay from the top of the bay's containment field opening behind him. With surgical precision, the person slammed the butt of his flechette rifle into the side of John Paul Sark's head standing to Babinot's right, then lunged left cracking the carapace head of the IA to Babinot's left.

Babinot's head swiveled in stunned confusion right, left, then the person in the EVA suit jammed the rifle barrel into the back of his head. Babinot tensed, swiveling his head cautiously. The person in the EVA suit flipped up his visor raising a gloved finger to his lips.

Channing Altimer pooched out his mouth as he breathed, "Shhhh," ordering Babinot to stay quiet. The IA and Sark were out cold on either side of Babinot.

Channing projected his voice for the benefit of Boratinsky Alvosky and the other insect alien on the far side of the shuttle. The shuttle blocked their view; they couldn't see him.

"Last time I ask!" Channing shouted in a voice that somewhat resembled Babinot's voice.

It didn't matter. The other EVA suited person that had been hiding out in space drifted quickly down from the top of the containment field behind Alvosky and the IA, but this person was not a forgiving soul. Two rapid fire *thift-thift* darts erupted through the front of Alvosky, then the IA beside him, blowing gushing holes of colored fluids unique to each being. They crumpled to the deck dead.

Jennifer Bane threw off her helmet. She dropped the smoking rifle, running over to the front of the shuttle bending down over Krachy cradling his head.

His eyes opened seeing her.

"You need to do something about your breath, honey," Jennifer smiled, remembering a fond time not too long ago when Krachy showed up at her side when she needed it most.

"C'mon, gimme some sugar, baby." Krachy could barely muster the strength to grin crookedly, but it was there, no doubt about it.

Jennifer leaned down kissing him gently, holding both cheeks in her gloved hands.

EPILOGE

"I couldn't share, Lance. Maybe Krachy was right when he said it to you back on the resort: You are dumb!" Murphy was once again back to her old self, as annoying as that could be at times.

Lance Albrecker let it go. Every conversation with her was a futile attempt to stamp her ego back down. Murphy was so pleased with herself for coming up with the idea to save every-one's life that there was no reasoning with her.

Brandish was breaking orbit over Basley. Everyone that had taken part in the rescue was in the mess hall except Rand.

The two IAs that danced the ECM swirl survived, barely, and were still in Medico along with their rescued insect alien prey friends that had been a part of Krachy's small team. All four of the IAs were being treated. It turned out that the two IAs that were part of Krachy's team were the two friends that needed to be rescued. They weren't a part of the hybrid insect resort work-ers or a part of the hunting party.

The IA dancers wouldn't have lived if Murphy hadn't act-ed. They were near collapse when they were able to stop, but not before Murphy had Rand drop Channing and Jennifer off at the Voltaic hatch on the skin of the hunting resort. They blew the hatch, then blew a nice chunk of the Voltaics preventing the time device from functioning. That was when the IAs were able to stop their dance.

Jennifer and Channing had made their way down the skin of the resort well clear when the charge exploded.

Unfortunately, they didn't know Albrecker was saving Lori atop mini Mount Hope at the exact same moment. The blast wave shooting out of Lori's billet was not a hunter's rocket boomer that just about killed Lori and Albrecker. It was the explosion inside Mount Hope that Jennifer and Channing created that almost did.

The hunters were not in the resort at all. They had gone EVA and hid themselves on the outside of the client landing bay waiting until Jennifer's and Albrecker's teams were most vulnerable, ambushing them all.

Channing and Jennifer did pretty much the same thing. After the explosion, they used the anti grav harnesses in their EVA suits to sneak up behind Alvosky, Babinot, Sark, and IAs 12 and 13. The two of them had hid out in space just beyond the client bay containment field before drifting down behind the villains to ambush them.

"If I had told you, one of the hybrid insect resort workers may have read my mind," Murphy reasoned, looking at Albrecker who was leaning against the bulkhead near the galley.

"Why didn't they?" Adonis asked standing next to Albrecker. "I mean, how'd you make your comm to Rand to tell him to send in Jennifer and Channing without the workers knowing, reading your mind?"

Murphy was standing next to Channing. She turned to face him and whispered.

"Should I tell 'em, Chazzy? You know, reveal my superior intellect. And, if I do, will you reward me in the manner I have become so happily accustomed to?"

Channing's hand shot over his crotch before she could beat him to it. He was getting to know her well.

"Sure, sweetie, enlighten the masses," he said airily.

Still standing in front of Channing, Murphy turned pressing her behind into him for a cushy little grind. Still grinding, in full view of everyone, she looked over at Adonis.

"I put my head next to our two IA friends as they were dancing in the back of the attack shuttle. The ECM wave they created to stop the workers from mind-activating the Pullback enveloped me too. I commed Rand and explained what to do. After the commo, I stayed right next to the dancing IAs so my thoughts would stay wrapped in their ECM wave." She smirked, "Worked good didn't it?" She pirouetted away from Channing ending up beside him leaning against the bulkhead wall. He made no attempt to hide his chub: none, nada, nunca, nil.

Rand entered through the hatch.

"I found a pretty good spot to put down. The patient ready?" He asked referring to Krachy who was sitting in one of the chairs at a table. Krachy was skinny; almost as much as that, he was buff, really buff. The increased G he was exposed to, along with the running, the hiding, the killing, the foraging, and looking out for his small team every waking minute had defined his short, stocky, muscled body. Krachy was downright ripped.

All that was true, but he was still so weak he could barely sit in his chair without shaking.

"My parents haven't seen a shuttle land on their street before. But I trust you, Rand. Set it down wherever you can," Krachy said.

Rand turned saying, "Five minutes then..." loud enough for everyone to hear as he left through the hatch.

Jeffrey and Adrianna sat on the other side of the table from Jennifer and Krachy.

Sami and Dimitri were one table over taking everything in plenty happy to be next to each other in calmer circumstances for the first time since they had fallen in love. Kimberly and

Mark shared the table with them. Mark turned to look at his boss standing behind him near the galley.

"Lori doing okay?"

A strained voice, not Albrecker's, turned Mark toward Krachy. Krachy eased himself straighter in his chair with Jennifer's help.

"Doing pretty good," he answered in Albrecker's place, staring at Lance while he said it. "As good a time as any, I guess…"

It took Krachy what seemed like 10 seconds to stand up, but he finally did. The underside of his left eye was black, a part of the eyeball dark red where the blood vessels had been smashed. He limped coming around the table approaching Lance and extended a hand.

"Thank you, Lance. You're a man of your word. I owe you her life. I had nothing left to give Lori." He had to look up at the taller man. It looked like Lance was a bit surprised, from the strength in Krachy's grip, or the gesture, it wasn't clear.

Lance smiled at him trying not to grip Krachy's hand too hard. The guy looked like he might keel over at any second.

"How'd you know where I'd break from my hide at the tree line to cross summer, Krachy? You and your team were waiting for me at that spot, weren't you?" His look was playful, but you could tell Lance wanted Krachy to share the professional secret just the same.

Krachy winced accepting Lance's arm around his waist to steady him without comment.

"I killed nine of those assholes breaking cover from hides I manufactured just like that one."

"But how—?"

"—Lance," Krachy grinned crookedly, "Every night while the bastards were partying, I would reshape the woods on the edge of spring making the hides as attractive as possible for the hunters to use. That was about the only thing Lori and I joked about for weeks. They were amateurs, remember?"

Lance actually blushed.

Everyone braced where they were; the light cruiser was banking, making its approach to the Bantor residence on the outskirts of Minos City on the edge of the Shavertooth Wilderness Area.

Lance pulled out a chair for Krachy, guiding him down in it.

Jennifer sat upright feeling the ship slowing under her feet. She looked over at Channing. Before she could ask him about what he intended to do with his prisoners from the resort, Lev Babinot, John Paul Sark, and IA #13, Channing strode over to her pulling her up by the arm. Jennifer trusted the guy, and let him do it. Jennifer's hair looked great. Krachy was her de facto stylist having learned how to do up her hair in a tousled lob cut back on Biltmire Space Station. Doing her hair on the return flight was Krachy's own brand of physical therapy, seated the whole time, of course. With a little eye and check highlights, Jennifer was attractive. But Jennifer's real glow came from having her short man hunk back. She radiated from it, about it, with it, and because of it!

Channing addressed Jennifer rather formally. He always had a tendency to be a bit stuffy since the first time they met.

"Before you get off the boat, I have something to say to you, Jennifer."

He cleared his throat, then turned and extended his hand out in Murphy's direction. He wanted her by his side when he did it. Murphy raced over, not opening her mouth, or making a move for his junk. She *had* grown a great deal, even learning how to control herself when it counted, like now. She nuzzled up to his side gripping his hand with both of hers.

Channing continued, "Any man would be proud to have you as his friend. All these people admire you for a reason. I had to make you drag me along from the very beginning. Not once did you hold it against me or give up on me. Thank you for that. Thank you very much."

Jennifer smiled, never good with being the center of attention, speeches, or the like.

Murphy pulled at his hand, shrugging up and down against him.

Channing glanced at her remembering.

"And I would have never met this woman if it wasn't for you, Sami, Jeffrey, Adrianna, and Dimitri."

He swept his gaze over all of them appreciatively. He was still a bit of a tight-ass, but being around Murphy much longer would cure him of that.

Sami stood up, looking at Adrianna a table over. Adrianna stood up too.

Jennifer saw the look in the two lady's eyes, but couldn't place it. She knew they loved her, but the emotions etching their young faces were driven, maybe even critical.

Channing and Murphy turned dropping their grip, shuffling to one side. Murphy took the lead this time.

"Go ahead guys. This is it, right?" She was watching Adrianna and Sami come around the tables as they stopped next to Jennifer flanking her.

"I get to go first, Jennifer." As Sami said it, she smiled at Krachy sitting over near Lance. She raised her voice, taking a step back, pulling Jennifer by the arm so Krachy could see them both. Her eyes locked on Jennifer's.

"I don't have a last name. I want to take Bane as my given name: Sami Bane." Her head swirled to Adrianna.

Adrianna smiled at Jennifer. Not looking at Krachy, she said, "Me too, soon-to-be Jennifer Bantor. I want to be part of your family for real." Her eyes darted to Sami.

They both hugged Jennifer between them. Not audible to anyone but Jennifer, they each whispered up into her ears. "Please."

Krachy stood up and limped around the table bracing himself on Jeffrey's shoulder for a moment when the ship started decelerating. Steadied, he made it around the table stopping in front of the three women. Out of the corner of his ear, he heard slurping sounds, like someone was eating a peach. He looked over at the table where Mark and Kimberly were seated. They were lip-locked going at it. It got quiet in the room. Mark extracted his face from Kimberly's noisy vacuum. He noticed everyone staring at him. His eyes widened, head turning to get a confirmation from Lance.

"What?" Mark asked innocently. "Rand blew the resort out of space when we left, right, Boss? We're done with the mission, yes?"

Lance smiled nodding, "Carry on."

Krachy smiled broadly turning back to Jennifer and her two *nieces* was the best way to describe them now.

"You knew about this, love?" Jennifer asked him, her face flush from the joy of it all.

Krachy shook his head.

"Nope, but I like the shit out of it anyway."

By way of proof, he stepped up to all three of them wrapping his arms around them trying to squeeze the best he could. He was rail thin, lithe, short, and warm—very warm. He pulled back.

"Take a seat ladies. You get to see where I grew up."

Jaymon and Vana Bantor heard and felt Rand's light cruiser approach way before it landed. They had about seven acres, give or take, of partially wooded land with a modest one-level ranch house on it. What was rather spectacular about the house was not the land it was on: It was the land it was in front of. The Shavertooth Mountain Range and Wilderness Area was behind the property. Stunning and magnificent, the view from the Bantors' couldn't be matched, at least on Basley that is.

The couple came cautiously out their front door. Rand landed his sleek-looking attack light cruiser well clear of the front yard in a field just the other side of the air car road fronting the Bantors' property. The cruiser pivoted, landing with its ass-end pointed toward the road and their home. The cargo ramp winded down impacting the soft grass just off the shoulder.

Jaymon and Vana didn't walk down the long driveway. They waited, not sure what was going on.

Krachy limped down the ramp. He was so thin at first his parents didn't recognize him. He hobbled across the road pushing as best his very sore body would allow. The couple started walking slow at first, then, their recognition registering, they picked up speed. Mom and Dad started smiling.

The others from the mess hall began meandering down the ramp not wanting to ruin the moment when Krachy was reunited with his parents. Jennifer let it happen too hanging back, just on the other side of the road.

By way of moral support, Jeff, Dimitri, Sami, Adrianna, Channing, and Murphy stayed close to Jennifer. All of them knew what Krachy's parents thought of her.

Rand, however, made a hard charge down the ramp, dodging the others, then overtaking Krachy with ease, pulling up short in front of Jaymon and Vana. Breathing hard, he tried to address them, but the two of them were looking past him, wanting to get to their feeble looking son still inching his way up the long drive.

Rand would have none of it, his command voice a model of undivided attention and strength.

"Mr. and Mrs. Bantor, I am Basley Space Ops Commander Rand Fullrider."

The Bantors hesitated, looking at him.

"I have taken it upon myself to be a courier or sorts today, a messenger dropping off something very important to you." He stepped aside, the Bantors looking from him, to Krachy, to him.

"I have a *Fragile Delivery* just for you! Your son, and all the fine people that saved him from a resort that has been hunting beings for sport."

Krachy smiled coming up the drive.

Vana Bantor ran the short distance slowing when she got next to her son seeing his condition. Starting to cry, she eased her arms around him.

Dad Bantor glanced at Rand extending a hand, shaking it before sandwiching his son between he and his wife.

Jennifer smiled, Sami and Adrianna stepping up beside her. The look on Jennifer's face changed; she looked crestfallen, but in a good way. Adrianna and Sami shot a look at the three Bantors. Mr. and Mrs. had their short arms open motioning with their arms for Jennifer to join them. Was that it? Was that what they were seeing?

Before she doubted it was happening, Jennifer's long, fast, strides started covering the distance.

Jeffrey and Dimitri looked delighted watching their liege lord run up the drive.

"No need to tell Jennifer there was a breeding center inside the client bay funnel we searched, huh?" Jeffrey said to Dimitri not taking his eyes off Jennifer.

Dimitri didn't turn to look at him.

"Nope, no need to do that, Jeff. Plenty of time when we shut down the next one…if then."

"Yeah, if then," Jeff agreed.

Jennifer came to an anxious halt, Krachy's back still to her. Jaymon Bantor looked in her eyes.

"C'mon honey, come get some. You've earned it."

His smile ripped the pain of Krachy being lost in her life right out of her heart. She could breathe again.

Vana turned then, seeing the look on Jennifer's face.

"You're family now, Jennifer. Come get in on this."

Her smile pulled Jennifer into the huddle. The two women cried happy tears. The two men enjoyed the moment.

Jennifer had to lean over to hug the three short people.

References:

Image Metadata:
FileSize: 182 KiB
FileModifyDate: 2024-05-22T10:44:22.000+00:00
FileAccessDate: 2024-05-22T10:44:22.000+00:00
FileInodeChangeDate: 2024-05-22T10:44:22.000+00:00
FileType: JPEG
FileTypeExtension: jpg
MIMEType: image/jpeg
JFIFVersion: 1.01
ResolutionUnit: inches
XResolution: 96
YResolution: 96
ImageWidth: 1024
ImageHeight: 1024
EncodingProcess: Baseline DCT, Huffman coding
BitsPerSample: 8
ColorComponents: 3
YCbCrSubSampling: YCbCr4:2:0 (2 2)
ImageSize: 1024x1024
Megapixels: 1
SEED ID: _8c664148-4453-49d3-97cc-1541a507064b

Prompts used:

The scenario is science fiction. A full body shot of a worried expression of an American athletic woman with light green eyes and a bob cut hairstyle and light brown hair, wearing a sci-fi suit holding her husband on the floor who has short brown hair, wearing army uniform, covered in dirt. They are looking at each other. The background is inside of an empty spaceship. Photorealistic, cinematic.